the Realm of Persephone

CAROLYN KELLEY WILLIAMS

For my beautiful mother in her garden.

INTRODUCTION

This story is fiction. Like any myth or fairy tale, it didn't really happen, and yet it is true.

No person has experienced this story exactly as it is told here.

This Zoe Thomas did not exist, yet her experiences can be heard in any twelve-step meeting. No Percy Thomas or Elizabeth Thomas Templeton lived these lives or did the things described in this modern retelling of an ancient myth.

No Chief or Mrs. Chief has lived as an actual person, nor has there been a Suzanne Thomas, Zoe's long-lost cousin; or Anna, Zoe's friend; or Christine, David Wolf's fiercely Evangelical wife.

Gudrun Skjerne, MD, PhD, though not an actual person, can be recognized in many a psychotherapist's consulting room where, day after day, she evokes and regulates the powerful psychic energies needed to heal the effects of trauma.

And David Wolf and his enchanting little daughter, Kathy? Though they are also imaginary creatures, their spirits have, in a sense, existed in the world and are a true gift for anyone fortunate to have encountered them.

Paradoxically, the creatures dwelling in the Realm of Persephone, the vast, boundless deep of the human unconscious—Cat, the Dark

Mother (the Crone aspect of the Triple Goddess), and her erotic, troublesome consort, the Spider King—are real, in the sense that they represent factual, dynamic entities in the psyche that profoundly affect a person's response to the woundings that are the human condition.

C.G. Jung and his colleagues and adherents, among them scholar and mythologist Joseph Campbell and social historian and psychotherapist Dr. Ira Progoff, have provided evidence of their existence with studies and insights into the human psyche.

Dr. Progoff has written that there are processes taking place beneath the surface of awareness that are as real, as subject to law and to scientific principles of understanding, as are the processes of the body.[1]

The role and purpose of depth psychology, says Dr. Progoff, is to describe these processes in the depths of persons, to ascertain the ways by which they unfold, and to devise practical procedures with which to undertake the task of healing psychic wounds in the midst of the perpetual crises in which we modern persons find ourselves, and to expedite and enlarge the natural growth of persons.

A further role of depth psychology, Dr. Progoff continues, is its unique ability to evoke the creative energies of the deep psyche and, in doing so, to allow persons to have an experience of meaning, and a profound awareness of the transpersonal realm, opening our awareness of the sacred, so that we know, in an immediate and personal way, both the depths and the heights of our existence—in other words, we are able to realize the magnitude of our human personality.

The reality and influence of our inner, imaginal life has been

1. Ira Progoff: *Depth Psychology and Modern Man*. New York, McGraw Hill Book Company, 1959, p 10

confirmed more recently in scientific laboratories by neurophysiologists, and the impact of psychic phenomena has also been given serious consideration by epigeneticists and other scientists who investigate the cross-generational effects of trauma on our cells and nervous systems and, therefore, on our behavior as individuals and as members of families and larger social groups and, ultimately, of whole cultures.

The depth psychologists and other scientists and students of myth, psyche, body, and spirit tell us that the deep psyche expresses profound human truths by way of images and symbols, which become our personal dreams and universal myths.

Rarely do we *choose* to encounter these powerful energies and mysterious symbols arising in our depths, yet our ability to plumb our depths and decode their mysteries seems somehow to heal the inevitable woundings of life.

It also opens our eyes to beauty and our hearts to compassion.

It is with these considerations that this tale of wounding and healing is told.

Carolyn Kelley Williams

Phoenix, Arizona, 2024

PART I.
The Call To Adventure

... Furthermore, we have not even to risk the adventure alone, for the heroes of all time have gone before us. The labyrinth is thoroughly known. We have only to follow the thread of the hero path, and where we had thought to find an abomination, we shall find a god. And where we had thought to slay another, we shall slay ourselves. Where we had thought to travel outward, we will come to the center of our own existence. And where we had thought to be alone, we will be with all the world.

Joseph Campbell
The Power of Myth
New York, Doubleday, 1998, p. 123

CHAPTER 1.
Thunder in Winter

On an early February morning in 1972, Zoe Thomas stood on the front porch of the Ohio home of her childhood. Her father had died the evening before.

A storm was brewing, and the winter sky was purple. Flickers of lightning and sudden thunder stirred feelings of dread. It wasn't right, thunder in winter.

Zoe noted that the front porch steps were treacherous, with an icy path down the center, just the width of her mother's small foot. Her father would have cleared the steps if he had not been dying.

Zoe had not put on a coat before stepping out of the house into the bitter morning air, and now she was chilled.

She turned and paused, her hand on the door handle, about to enter a world forever changed.

Inside, everything was silent. Zoe's mother was resting in a darkened room upstairs. Encounters were to be avoided, especially as her mother came up from sleep, not wearing her hearing aids, achingly vulnerable, so Zoe went toward the basement. To take inventory. If the house must now be sold, she would need to clear it out.

Zoe had rarely been in the basement during the past twenty years. It was her father's realm. It was poorly lit, and it smelled of him, an organic smell, somewhat unpleasant.

She slid the bolt back and pulled the door open, feeling for the light switch among the fly swatters at the head of the stairs. The light didn't help much. It was high up, like a pale moon above a canyon carved by a river over millennia.

The canyon walls were ancient cans of paint, vacuum sweeper attachments, coffee cans filled with rusty nails. Detritus of half a century.

At the bottom of the steps, a second bulb was suspended from the overhead shadows on a frayed cord, and in its faint light, she drew back, appalled: old storm windows blackened with grime, antique lawnmowers, broken lamps with torn, water-stained shades, window fans, orange crates filled with twisted shoes and rotting galoshes.

She brushed past trousers and wash dresses suspended from the ceiling on hangers and made her way to her father's office, a tiny room where he had done his writing. There was evidence he had used the room recently. A small typewriter was still on the desk, and part of an article dated a few months earlier lay beside it.

She sat at the desk and thought about her father, sitting in this same chair. Percy Thomas had been a gentle man. Serious. Studious. Exacting. A man of thought. As a young man, he had planned to be a minister. But his true calling had been to teach. He became a professor of music.

Zoe felt a sudden sting. Reaching inside her blouse, she discovered a swelling on her right breast. A wave of panic swept through her.

I've been bitten, she thought, horrified. Pushing the chair back and leaping up, she tore her blouse open, turning toward the light to find the spider—she knew it had been a spider. But there was nothing except a burning red wound on the upper outside curve of her breast.

Since childhood, Zoe had been terrified of spiders. When she was six, a girl at summer camp had chased her, taunting, "This is a black widow spi-i-der. If it bites you, you'll di-i-e."

Zoe tried to hold on to her reason, but an inner voice kept saying, *I've been poisoned,* and her lips and forehead grew numb, as they always did when she confronted spiders.

Then came nausea, the metallic taste, the buzzing in her ears. She was going to faint.

She sat again and slumped forward until her head was between her knees, hoping the spell would pass, but the nausea and buzzing grew overwhelming.

She seemed to be falling into swirling mists and darkness that grew ever more impenetrable, down, down, down into boundless chill, until she lost all sense of time and orientation.

And then, nothing.

Zoe opened her eyes. The world was crimson radiance filled with a ravishing fragrance she could not quite name. Then she remembered: strawberries. She was eye-level with a strawberry, fat and vivid, studded with tiny dark seeds. And then another, and another, a profusion of strawberries, not more than an inch from her eyes. She was lying in a field. It was daytime. Sunshine warmed her body. She was clothed in a soft, nubby garment.

Except for these sensations, her mind was blank. She closed her eyes again and let the sun and the fragrance of strawberries fill her.

Then, a new awareness. Lips on her cheek, barely noticeable. She did not open her eyes, accepting the kiss as if from a dragonfly that had come to rest for a fraction of a second and then darted away. It was a fleeting moment, except for a lingering odor, like overripe fruit, slightly disturbing.

She opened her eyes to discover a man's face, and great arms lifting her, oh, so gently. Now, she was being carried across the field and she did not question this. She closed her eyes again, aware only of the man's breathing and the humming of insects.

She must have slept, for when she came again to awareness, she was in a room, alone, lying on a coarse wool blanket. She felt feverish and wasted, as if she had been ill. It was twilight in the room. She raised up onto her elbow, but her head felt so heavy she pulled herself back and leaned against the headboard, looking around. The room was plain. Beneath a window was a table with an elaborate brass candelabra holding six unlighted candles. On the wall was a small, round mirror in a gilded frame. Under a door, light shone.

Zoe swung her legs over the edge of the bed. It was high, and she had to drop to the floor. She nearly collapsed; her legs were weak. Carefully, she took a few steps, but she suddenly felt dizzy, so she turned toward the table to steady herself.

Looking up, she was startled by her dim reflection in the mirror. A pale young girl of no more than twelve looked back at her. The girl's eyes were green, with fair red-gold eyelashes and, though indistinct in the shadowed twilight, golden hair falling in wispy curls around a fragile face.

"So, this is who I am," she murmured.

There was a sound outside the door. A cough.

The light became sepia, and the brightness under the door flickered into the darkening room. Zoe went to the door and stood listening for a long time.

Someone was building a fire. She heard snapping sounds of wet wood and smelled smoke.

Anxiety finally drove her to open the door.

The man looked up from the hearth where he knelt, carefully placing a large log onto a fiercely blazing fire. He was an older man, with greying, thin hair, a large head with narrow-set eyes, a great beak of a nose, and deep creases around his eyes and mouth. He had huge shoulders and a great barrel chest.

"Oh, Zoe," the man said, as if he was not surprised to see her. "I've made you a fire. Did you rest? Here, have some juice. See? A glass of orange juice on the table, waiting for you."

"Thank you." Zoe couldn't think of anything else to say.

She went unsteadily to the table and sat. She took a tentative sip of the warm juice. It had a thick topping of pulp. The pulp was unpleasant, and the sweet juice made her slightly ill.

"I've been working while you slept," the man said. "I'll fix you some food in a little while."

Zoe looked around. They seemed to be in a country cottage, very old. The fireplace was in a part of the room that appeared to be a study, with shelves laden with books rising to the low ceiling, and, along one wall, file cabinets.

The man whistled softly to himself, an insistent little tune. When he became aware that Zoe was watching him, he went to his desk and sat, patting his knees. "Come here, darling, and give me a kiss. Do you love me?"

Zoe amazed herself by going immediately to him and sitting on his lap. He offered his lips, and she kissed him. It was a lover's kiss he gave back to her. She surrendered with dispassionate calm.

"Do you love me?" he said again, smiling. It was not a question.

He held her against his chest, murmuring, "Oh, darling, darling."

Then he stood her up, as if she weighed nothing. He sighed a rasping, shuddering sigh and also stood. "Are you hungry? I'll make us food."

He moved with a strange, lurching walk into the kitchen, where there was a sink, an ancient stove against the wall, and wooden cupboards with colored glass panels. He motioned for her to sit at the kitchen table as he began noisily assembling cooking utensils.

She watched him work, not certain if she was dreaming, accepting what was happening without question. The bright fire lit the room and made Zoe uncomfortably warm. Outside, night enveloped the cottage.

"You don't eat well enough," the man said. "If I didn't feed you occasionally, you'd die of malnutrition. I don't know what you eat when I'm not feeding you, but it's obvious it isn't nourishing. Well, I'm going to give you a decent meal."

He filled a huge pot with water and lit the stove; while he waited for the water to boil, he opened a brown bag and from waxed paper unfolded a slab of strong-smelling fish. "Smoked eel. You like smoked eel, don't you? And steak tartar."

He ripped apart another package, this one containing raw ground beef, and with great speed and skill, diced an onion. He added spices to the beef and dark liquids from bottles and cracked an egg and mixed them all together with his hands, shaping two mounded portions and carefully placing them on plates, with a shower of onion pieces over and around them.

"And good black bread. And summer sausage. And ripe, rich avocado to make your lovely skin even more beautiful. And of course, May wine. We can't have a feast without May wine."

Zoe watched him from the table and listened silently as he chattered on in a deep, resonant voice. "And look, my darling. Lobsters."

He tore open another package and, from a pile of seaweed, lifted two small brown lobsters for her to see. Their legs grasped at the air as he dropped them into the boiling water.

"Now, go and wash your face and hands, and when you come back, we'll have our feast."

She found the bathroom and ran water into the bowl and splashed it over her face and throat. It was all so strange. She seemed to be a part of his world. But how? The situation was a mystery to her. She was a mystery to herself.

Suddenly, music flooded the cottage.

"Mahler," he said as Zoe came back to the kitchen. The music was like a broad, deep river flowing around Zoe and the table and the man. He had brought the candelabra from the bedroom and lit the candles.

He lifted the lobsters out of the boiling water, their shells now coral-colored, and cracked one open with his fingers, pulling out the steaming white flesh. "Ah, a female. Eggs. A great delicacy. For you, my darling."

He placed before her a plate laden with lobster, eel, steak tartar, sausage, black bread, and avocado. He poured golden liquid into two melon-shaped wineglasses on tall stems.

"*A votre santé.*" He touched her glass with his own and drank long and deeply, watching her. When Zoe didn't pick up her glass, he handed it to her, and she drank, too. The wine tasted like the music.

The only light in the room came from the fireplace and the candles. The flames exaggerated the man's huge head and beak, the deep creases around his mouth, his sorrowful eyes.

"Eat, child," he said. The wine made her dizzy. The sight of the lobster eggs in thick green paste repulsed her, but she dipped a bit of lobster into butter. She gagged on the lobster, hoping he wouldn't notice, forcing herself to swallow.

"Don't neglect the sausage, my sweet." He kept urging food on her, cracking open the lobsters, their claws, their tails, their bodies, until all the white and coral meat had been pulled out and the broken shells were heaped in a smelly mound. When he finished eating, he cleared the dishes.

Zoe had hardly touched her food.

He said, "Too much talking." He was growing drunk.

"Come into the bedroom. Let me love you." He picked up the candelabra and took her hand.

In the bedroom, the warm candlelight flooded over the bed, as he stripped away the heavy cover and let it drop onto the floor. He stripped off his clothes, and Zoe's, and lifted her up onto his body as he lay back heavily. There was a long pale scar down the center of his chest.

"Death has wiped his hand across my chest," he said.

Zoe rested against his body like a small silver fish thrown up from the ocean onto rocks. The music was the ocean, now, swelling, sweeping in waves over them. A woman sang,

> *Komm! Hebe dich zu höhern Sphären!*
> *Wenn er dich ahnet, folgt er nach.*

The man asked, "Do you know what she's singing, dearest? 'Come! To the higher spheres ascending. Then drawn by love he'll follow thee.'"

His hands flowed like the ocean over her and the music flowed over them both. A great swelling chorus sang, the voices going higher and higher:

> *Alles Vergängliche*
> *Ist nur ein Gleichnis;*
> *Das Unzulängliche,*
> *Hier wird's Ereignis;*
> *Das Unbeschreibliche,*
> *Hier ist's getan;*

Das Ewig-Weibliche
Zieht uns hinan.

He whispered, more to himself than to Zoe, "All these transitory things are only symbols. These passing earthly things are only symbols. The transcendent shines through them. Whatever is unfulfilled on earth is attained here. The eternal feminine leads us on, the eternal feminine carries us upward. *Das Ewig-Weibliche. Das Ewig-Weibliche. Das Ewig-Weibliche.*"

"Zoe? Zoe?" A woman's voice. "Zoe? Are you down there?" Her mother's voice. "Zoe? Is that you? Are you in the basement?"

Zoe came suddenly to consciousness, sitting at her father's desk. Her mother was calling from the head of the stairs. Before Zoe had a chance to respond, she heard the basement door close. She was plunged into darkness as the bolt slid into place. The footsteps went away.

"Mother!" Zoe shouted. "I'm down here. Turn on the light. Turn on the light! *Mother!*"

She stood, unsure of where or how to move. Her eyes were open, but she saw nothing. She turned around and around in the tiny room, trying to find a light switch. She heard her mother's footsteps moving about in the kitchen—coming closer, going away, coming closer, going away. Her mother must not be wearing her hearing aids.

"Mother! Mother!" Zoe bellowed, having trouble getting her breath. She found the door of the office and scraped her hand on something sharp on the frame. She stumbled over the threshold, catapulting into hanging clothes. *Spiders in these clothes.* A sticky web clung to her fingers, and she clutched at one of the dresses to wipe it off. There were little hard, round objects in the web.

She reeled forward. Somehow, she found the stairs and crept upward. Then she was at the top of the stairs, clutching the doorknob, pounding on the door. She sank down on the top step and huddled among the paint cans and brooms, sobbing. Finally, her sobbing subsided, and she sat numbly, with fevered cheeks and bruised hands.

After a long while, her mother opened the basement door and turned on the light. Reaching for a broom, she jumped back, startled. "Why, Zoe. I thought you'd gone out. Did I shut you in the basement? Oh, I'm so sorry. Please forgive me, dear."

In the darkness, a kind of numb detachment had come over Zoe.

"It's all right, Mother. I'm fine." She stood slowly and stepped into the hallway. She briefly hugged her mother, who seemed very small, and went upstairs to wash her wounds.

Zoe was choosing a casket. Her mother had asked her to choose "something nice." The showroom was filled with burial containers, gleaming wood and brass and satin, expensive as automobiles. The salesman enumerated the virtues of each. Did she want a watertight casket? Zoe thought about it. A watertight casket would be useful for crossing the River Styx.

Music started in her head. A great, resonant chorus. *Den alles Fleisch es ist wie Gras,* sang ethereal sopranos within her. *All flesh is as grass… and all the goodliness of man is as the flower of grass. For lo, the grass with'reth, and the flower thereof decayeth.*

Brahms made death seem so voluptuous, so splendid, so sensual.

Blessed are the dead; blessed are they that mourn, the inner voices continued. Is Daddy blessed? Am I blessed? *…for they shall have comfort.* Shall I have comfort?

Herr, lehre doch mich. She could hear the baritone's voice, out of an expectant silence. She knew this music so well. She had grown up with it. *Herr. Herr, lehre doch mich. Make me to know the measure of my days on earth. Man passeth away like a shadow. He heapeth up riches and cannot tell who shall gather them.*

Her father surely had not heaped up riches.

"Have you decided about the casket?" the salesman said at last, waiting beside her expectantly. His loud voice startled her, interrupting her inner music.

She acknowledged him with a sad smile, but she was thinking of her father's body decaying in the dampness of a pine box. She had grown up on Dracula lore and knew the fate of bodies in pine boxes.

Equally terrible, however, was the thought of her father forever lying in watertight, airless, changeless neutrality. The salesman's confidence seemed to promise that the casket would remain watertight until the last trumpet.

A bass voice sang, *The trum-pet shall sound.* Now, the *Messiah* started in her head. And an inner trumpet played with the clean, precise phrasing her father, a trumpeter, had used. She always heard it the way her father played it. She stood in deep concentration, dutifully playing the inner music all the way through the trumpet's final trills and completing the orchestral resolution before turning to the salesman, who was trying not to show impatience.

"I don't think the watertight casket will be necessary," Zoe said. She selected an oak casket, neither expensive nor inexpensive. She hoped her mother would consider it "nice."

Protestants, at least the Congregationalists and other decorous Midwesterners gathered for Zoe's father's funeral in the plain New England-style church with its austere white interior, were not given to displays of emotion. Everything was subdued, dignified, restrained, in the manner so dear to Zoe's Puritan forebears.

The minister spoke about her father's goodness. Percy Thomas was the kind of person a minister appreciated when called upon to speak in such circumstances. He could say without irony that Percy Thomas had been a good man; a temperate man; a devoted husband and father; a good citizen of his community and the greater world; an active member of his church; a dedicated teacher. He had lived a life of service, filled with acts of kindness performed without fanfare. He had not set the world on fire with large achievements. Rather, he had lit it steadily with a series of small illuminations.

Hymns were sung, scriptures quoted. Afterward, hands were shaken, embraces given. At the back of the church, people spoke quietly with Zoe and her mother. Kind friends, smiling sadly, murmuring sympathetic words, their eyes suggesting tears.

Then the mourners proceeded slowly to the cemetery and

gathered at the snowy graveside. Zoe and her mother stood dry-eyed, each absorbed in her own inner process, as more words were said and the shovelful of earth—*dust unto dust*—was tossed onto the lowered casket.

Then, as if performing a solemn dance, the crowd dispersed, and Zoe took her mother home.

On this visit home, Zoe slept in the front bedroom. Years before, after Zoe left for college, her mother had moved Zoe's things here from her childhood bedroom so her father could use that bedroom for his upstairs office, and, when he became ill, as his own bedroom.

It was to this front bedroom that Zoe had brought her new husband after their Chicago wedding, for her parents gave a reception to introduce him to their hometown friends.

That night, Zoe and her new husband got drunk and made love noisily, and as their drunkenness increased, he drew their erotic romp out of the bedroom and downstairs to the living room, where they made no effort to stifle their cries as they rolled naked on the velvet sofa among her mother's needlepoint pillows and then slid onto the carpet, knocking over the heirloom rosewood chair before they stumbled, laughing and breathless, back upstairs.

They left two empty wine bottles on the coffee table for her father to clear away before her mother woke at nine the next morning, groggy from her sleeping medicine.

At the time, though Zoe did not acknowledge it to herself in so many words, she sensed a dark struggle happening between her husband and her father. It seemed, even then, as if her husband had staged the lovemaking as a public event, a spectacle of the young man triumphing over the old.

The King is dead. Long live the King.

Of course, none of that had been said. She doubted her husband was even aware of what he'd done. He was not an insightful or psychologically astute person.

Her father had known, though. Zoe was sure of that. And now, all these years later, she was shamed by the memory. It must have hurt him. In retrospect, it seemed cruel. Her husband flaunting his privilege. Her own complicity.

The next morning, Professor Thomas had brought coffee to the bedroom, standing in the hallway with the tray in his hands, asking permission to enter. Zoe's husband opened the door, hastily buttoning his shirt over his nakedness, and Zoe sat up, hungover and disheveled, drawing the sheet up to cover her breasts.

Everyone was polite.

It now seemed significant that her sex life with her husband had never again been so intense. They were ill-suited to one another. She wanted slow, intimate lovemaking. He liked X-rated movies and sex in drive-ins. When, after two years, he abruptly left her for another woman, she suffered only a single week of murderous rage while he moved out, taking his garlic press, his coffeemaker, his backgammon set, and his expensive clothes.

Zoe was surprised to find herself relieved when he was gone.

Now, lying restlessly in that same bed, in the aftermath of the funeral, she felt she had betrayed her father at some deep level, and she burned with shame at the memory. As the night waned, she must have slept, but she woke to a silent house at seven in the morning racked with exhaustion.

Zoe's mother sat across the table from her at breakfast. They drank the strong coffee her mother favored and ate toast. Her mother was not wearing her hearing aids; she said she needed to ease into the morning before the day began pounding on her eardrums.

They communicated with sad smiles and sign language. They didn't need to talk. They knew each other very well after thirty-five years.

But not really. They had never been together without the moderating influence of their husband-father. He had always been between them, carrying messages. He'd interpreted Zoe's mother to her, not allowing her mother to speak for herself.

That realization was new. Zoe could hear her father's voice:

Zoe, your mother needs to hear from you. Please try to write once a week. It's little enough to ask.

Zoe, your mother would prefer that you not marry right away. She's not ready to go through the strain of a wedding.

As a young child, when Zoe awakened in the night feeling afraid, she'd call her mother. But her father came instead, saying, *Zoe, you mustn't wake your mother. She's not well. She needs her rest.*

Then he'd get into bed with her.

Now, sitting with her mother at breakfast, Zoe wanted to ask, "Did you love Daddy?" But conversation was futile when her mother was not wearing her hearing aids. And Zoe doubted her mother would speak her heart about such a matter, anyway.

Then Mrs. Thomas surprised her by saying, "I shall miss your father. But I'm glad his suffering is over." That was all. A statement to the silence.

Zoe reached across the table and patted her mother's hand.

Over the next days, a curious thing happened. Zoe's mother, who had always seemed so emotionally fragile, assumed a kind of calm. She mourned, of course, as was seemly for a widow after forty years of marriage. But she did not weep in Zoe's presence.

Meanwhile, Zoe opened a checking account for her mother and taught her to write checks. She conferred with the resource people her mother would need—the doctors, the pharmacist, the Medicare representative, the hospital social worker, the hearing aid people, and the friends who would give her rides to church and concerts and the grocery store.

By the time Zoe said goodbye two weeks later and returned to her own life in Chicago, her mother seemed to be on an even keel.

CHAPTER 2.
The Undiscovered Country

Zoe had been back in Chicago for about a week, getting caught up with everything at the office.

As her mother grew stronger back home, Zoe felt herself fragmenting, and she had no time for that. She was the administrative director of the International Association of Depth Psychologists, or IADP, which, despite its grandiose name, was a small, elite group of mostly male psychiatrists who from time to time met at interesting locations around the world to read scholarly papers to one another.

She worked closely with the IADP's founder and president, Walther Lehrer, MD, PhD, "the Chief," as he was called by associates, sometimes with admiration, sometimes with resentment. The Chief was a psychiatrist of wide renown. He traveled frequently and had a small private practice with mainly socialite women who suffered more from neglect by their CEO husbands than from diagnosable symptoms.

Zoe's office was next to his in a sumptuous suite in the John Hancock Center, on North Michigan Avenue.

The Chief entrusted the running of his entire operation to Zoe. At age thirty-five, Zoe had developed a reputation as the one who made things run smoothly. Her warmth, charm, and persuasive flattery with the men worked miracles.

Only one officer was a woman: Gudrun Skjerne, MD, PhD, the scientific director of the International Congress, the IADP's main activity, which was held every other September. This year, it would be in Amsterdam. Plans were already well underway.

Zoe had worked with Walther Lehrer since graduating from college. It was her first real job. As the IADP grew in importance, so did Zoe's responsibilities. She and the Chief were a good team. She absolutely understood him and his needs. He was brilliant, complicated, and more successful at running the world than intimate relationships, to which his wife and children could attest. Zoe understood that, too, and compensated for it, moving gracefully through the personal minefield of his family life and the political minefield of the IADP.

Walther Lehrer and Zoe both knew he couldn't get along without her.

But the two weeks in Ohio dealing with her father's death and funeral and then getting her mother settled into well-organized widowhood had put Zoe behind. The Chief had called her daily the entire time she was in Ohio. Now that she was back in the office, his attitude about Zoe's loss was clear, though unspoken. *Be done with your father. He's dead. I need you now.*

This left Zoe no time for grieving. She went from demand to demand. She spoke daily with her mother, shouting reassurances—her mother's hearing aids didn't work well with the phone—doing her best not to show exasperation.

One morning, Zoe woke before dawn. Though she was exhausted, she planned to go early to the office. In her bathroom, she discovered a huge black spider on the gleaming porcelain of the washbasin. The spider was so large Zoe couldn't imagine how it could have gotten up through the drain. The spider's legs spread out, vivid against the white bowl; it was almost two inches across, with a great, bulbous, motionless body.

She would have to kill it, but she feared it would sense her presence and try to escape. Moving slowly, she pulled off a handful of toilet paper. As the spider darted up the side of the bowl, she slammed the toilet paper down and leaned her whole weight into the task. She turned the paper over and pulled it apart to be sure the spider was dead. The legs were broken and crumpled, and the body's contents spread grotesquely yellow on the paper. She dropped the wadded paper into the toilet and flushed it away. With a shudder, she put down the lid of the toilet and the nausea began. Her head buzzed, and for the second time in her adult life, she fainted.

Zoe woke, naked and alone, in the bedroom of the cottage. It was morning. Birds were making music. The light was golden, gentle, warm; the candles had burned completely down. The room smelled smoky and sweet.

Zoe touched her body, moving her hands over her small breasts, the hollow cup of her abdomen. She raised up onto her elbows, looking down at the slopes of her thighs sweeping to her knees, her shins, her feet vulnerable and far away. A tear swelled from the corner of one eye and rolled down her temple into her ear.

Her clothes were neatly piled on the wooden chest.

There were sounds outside the room and she quickly dressed and opened the door, moving hesitantly toward them. A young girl was in the kitchen. She was perhaps twelve, like Zoe.

"Here's coffee," the girl said, pouring steaming, dark liquid into a blue mug and handing it to Zoe. "I've just made it."

The girl was golden, like the light. Her thick, short, sun-streaked hair fell over her ears and forehead. She had tan cheeks, deep-set hazel eyes, and a wide mouth, with full, laughing lips and perfect teeth. She wore a sleeveless shirt and khaki shorts that showed muscular arms and long, tan legs.

"You're here with him, aren't you?" the girl asked, in a voice that sounded like a cello. "You're lucky to be alive. He eats young girls. Catches them in his web and wraps them in silk." With her hands, she described a web and then a spider, moving toward its victim. "When he's ready, he eats 'em."

She looked appraisingly at Zoe. "You're quite a morsel. I think I'll eat you myself." She licked her lips and made a growling sound, followed by a husky, cynical laugh.

"Who are you?" Zoe said, sipping the coffee. It was delicious. She'd never liked coffee before.

"Cat."

"Cat?"

"Catherine. But no one calls me Catherine. I'm Cat."

"And who is he?"

"Who is *he?*" Cat exploded with laughter. "Who is *he?*" Her teeth gleamed as she laughed. "You don't know?" She danced gleefully around the kitchen. "Oh, I love it. I love it. She doesn't know who he is. She spends the night with him, and she doesn't know who he is. Oh, I love it."

Cat slapped her thigh again and again.

Zoe was annoyed. "Who is he?" she asked again.

"Oh, now she's annoyed," Cat taunted, still gleeful, still springing about. "This is one feisty miss." Cat's eyes sparkled. "I like 'em feisty."

She made faces at Zoe, wiggling her eyebrows up and down and cackling. "Dumb, but feisty."

Cat circled Zoe, poking at her with sharp taps of her fists, barely touching her. Zoe's annoyance made the blows seem more painful than they really were.

"Cat. Stop. Stop it."

"What a dummy," Cat crowed. "Beautiful, but dumb. 'Who is he?' she wants to know. Oh, I love it. I love it."

All the while, she pelted Zoe with quick little blows.

"Cat. *Stop* it." Zoe burst into tears.

Cat stopped dancing and looked intently at Zoe. "Tears. Now she's crying. They always resort to tears, the beautiful, dumb ones."

She sighed with mock exasperation, swaggering to the other side of the kitchen. She leaned against the sink, crossing her legs.

"He's the Spider King, dummy. You've spent the night with the Spider King. You're even dumber than I thought. Lucky you've got me to look out for you."

"Cat, you're talking in riddles."

"I'm not talking in riddles. You're just not too bright. That's your problem. Lucky you're beautiful. Makes me feel protective."

Cat sprang across the room and put her arm around Zoe's shoulders, guiding her into another part of the room and sitting her down on a sofa, as she balanced on the arm, one foot on the floor.

Both were quiet for a moment. Then, with a sudden, graceful movement, Cat leaned over Zoe and kissed her on the mouth, no longer mocking. They looked deeply into one another, as if into a mirror. Zoe felt herself plunging deep into a pool.

Suddenly, she broke the surface. "Cat. What if he comes back?" Zoe pushed Cat away and sat up, expecting the man to come angrily into the room.

"What if he does? So what?"

"Cat. We can't stay here. We can't stay. He'll find us."

Zoe struggled to her feet and ran out of the cottage, onto a lawn and down a grassy hillside toward trees. Cat sprang behind her, catching hold of her as they reached the forest. They fell among ferns onto soft layers of pine needles.

With a hiss, Cat caught Zoe's wrists and held them together over her head with one hand, while with her teeth she pulled up Zoe's shirt. Then she pulled up her own shirt and lay her small breasts against Zoe's breasts and her belly against Zoe's belly and they rolled over and over, Cat biting her neck with sharp, burning little bites.

Suddenly, Zoe's whole being burst apart into myriad shooting stars, and she fell back, wide open as the sky.

Cat snarled and reared up, a bobcat, and sprang away among the trees.

Then everything disappeared.

Zoe returned to consciousness, lying on the carpet of the hallway outside the bathroom. She had the distinct feeling she'd had an orgasm, stirring inexplicably out of the inner darkness.

She felt a sinking despair. *I'm going crazy!* And then, *I don't have time to go crazy. Too much to do.*

She got up unsteadily and stumbled into the bedroom. Little post-orgasmic tingles and spasms shot through her lower body as she walked, but there was no pleasure in the sensations. When they died down, they left a painful, cramping ache. She fell onto the bed and wept for a long time.

When she arrived at the office around ten, pale and distracted, she told the Chief she thought she had the flu. She finished some paperwork and went home again.

Zoe realized she was facing an ordeal. She had never lived in the world without her father. Since childhood, she'd feared he would die and leave her alone with her mother. Her mother, the junkie.

Well, *junkie* was too strong a word. Her mother didn't use heroin or cocaine. She had the middle-class WASP-woman addiction. Sleeping pills. And uppers and downers.

For as long as Zoe could remember, her mother had ingested a dazzling array of mood-altering chemicals. In her mother's defense, they were prescribed by her doctors. The internist prescribed sleeping pills, checked her blood pressure, patted her hand, and wished she would change doctors. The psychiatrists gave her the hard stuff.

Zoe, despite her professional connection with psychiatrists, stayed out of her mother's medical matters. Her father doled out the medicine. *He* was willing to assume responsibility in that way. *He* married her. *He* chose her. Zoe had not. Given the option, she would have chosen a different mother. Or better still, she would have avoided the matter of a mother entirely, springing full-grown from the head of her father, like Athena from the head of Zeus.

Zoe liked to imagine her mother was as much a disappointment to her father as she was to Zoe. He never actually said that, but there was an implied complicity between Zoe and her father.

As a child, Zoe went with her parents on many car trips. The time Zoe particularly remembered was when she was perhaps eight, and her mother was going through a period of depression and sat in the back seat, weeping. Her mother always sat in the back seat on these trips.

What made this incident memorable was that Zoe had just thought to herself, *Daddy and I don't need her. We'd be better off without her.* And her mother, from the back seat, said, with a weepy voice, "You two don't need me. You'd be better off without me."

Somehow, her mother's tears were Zoe's fault. Everyone agreed that if only Zoe would be more considerate of her mother's needs, and less selfish and self-centered, all would be set right. But how?

Needs. Her mother had them. The Chief had them. Curiously, in her entire lifetime, Zoe could not recall a single time when anyone, even a therapist— and there were plenty of therapists over the years— had inquired about *Zoe's* needs. Well, they did sometimes, but she brushed their questions aside. When she really thought about it, she doubted she had any needs.

Needs, like God, were for other people.

These thoughts came to Zoe as she lay in bed, feeling feverish. After leaving the office, she'd slept all afternoon and evening, and now it was almost midnight, and she was wide awake. Too late for dinner. She was very tired.

And, she realized, she was angry. Yes. Angry. She was angry with her father. That was a surprise. She was accustomed to anger toward her mother. Why, exactly, was she angry with her father?

As she considered this question, there seemed to be two aspects to her anger: She was angry that her father had married Elizabeth Sheldon, the woman who became her mother. But though emotionally fragile, her mother was also talented and charming. At least, others seemed to find her so.

There was more, however. Zoe was *furious* with her father for having died, leaving Zoe holding the bag. A bit of gallows humor there.

Zoe got her penchant for gallows humor from her mother. As far as Zoe could tell, there was no humor at all on her father's side of the family. Wit was one of the few things she appreciated about her mother. And about herself. It was one of her charms.

Zoe had other charms, too. For all her self-loathing, she liked that she was bright and gifted and had a cultured (if crazy) upbringing. She gave her parents grudging credit for bequeathing to her Cultural Privileges. Not that Cultural Privileges helped her deal with the Real World. But they *did* add a certain zest to her personality.

And some people considered Zoe beautiful, but *that* she couldn't see. Zoe would have preferred to do away with her physical existence, living entirely in her mind. Not that she was spiritual, although a New Age guru had once told her she had "a clear channel to the cosmos and great spiritual gifts."

The guru was off base regarding her spiritual gifts. "Dead are all the gods"—*thus sprach Zoe.* And she meant it. Not just the local deity of the Congregationalists and Methodists. *All* the gods. Zoe was an atheist. And now that her father was dead, she felt herself to be completely alone in the universe.

Of course, she still had the Chief. But that wasn't much consolation.

The guru had also said, "Your task this time around is to learn to look at the world through the eyes of a woman. You *must* come to accept that you've been born into the body of a *woman.* You must do that to move on."

Easy for you to say, Zoe thought. But he was right that she resisted looking at the world through the eyes of a woman. She *had* always been disappointed with herself for being born into a female body. The victories of the decade's "women's lib" movement were tentative and few, and she was still a second-class citizen. Especially among psychiatrists. At the heart of it, Zoe, despite brilliance, education, and competence, was still a handmaiden.

Zoe was wide awake now. She turned on the emerald and purple stained-glass Tiffany lamp, a gift from the neurosurgeon she'd known in Boston. Wild nights at the Ritz. He always leapt onto her as she entered the hotel room and ravished her on the floor, without so much as a hello. But what excellent taste in lamps.

A voice in Zoe's head mocked her. *The Tiffany lamp? You sold your soul for a Tiffany lamp? Surely you don't consider such a bauble recompense for your soul. Surely you realize that such things are not gifts. You worked for that lamp and threw your soul into the bargain. That's a pattern in your life, in your career. And for what? A paltry thirty grand a year. The neurosurgeon and the Chief make twenty times that and get to keep their souls and the glory. Worst of all, you sleep with them without passion.*

That was true. Her relationship with the Chief was more like what once was called "a marriage of convenience." From time to time, Zoe spent a night with him when they were at a conference. Not regularly. It depended upon whether Mrs. Chief was with him or not.

And there was a darker, more complicated aspect. *You know the Chief uses sex for power,* the voice in her head said. *You know he uses sex to manipulate you. And you're no better. You use sex to manipulate him. But he doesn't make a pretense of sincerity the way you do. You're worse than he is. He is a mere opportunist. You are a liar.*

In the sensual glow of the Tiffany lamp, her life looked ugly to her. This self-excoriation continued until it became unbearable. She switched off the lamp and lay restlessly in the darkness. She turned onto her side and curled into the fetal position. She touched her breast, and her fingers found the spider bite, which, even after three weeks, was still swollen, still sensitive. She shuddered, thinking of her ordeal in the basement.

Too terrible. Time to shut down.

Zoe came to awareness in the cottage, sitting at the kitchen table. It was mid-morning. The light made the small, beveled windowpanes sparkle and throw rainbows across the ceiling, the table, and Zoe's hands, which lay cupped, opened upward, and ready to receive—what?

She was her twelve-year-old self, in her white shorts and terrycloth shirt, her elfin, barefooted self, fragile and vulnerable. A delicate child of life, filled with sorrows and unanswerable questions.

The screen door creaked and slammed. The Spider King came suddenly in, lurching and looming. He filled the cottage to overflowing with his clumsy hugeness.

Zoe looked up at him, as he bent over and took her face in his big hands and kissed her.

"Today, I introduce you to the great poet Rainer Maria Rilke," he said. "You must not go another day without knowing Rilke. '*Sein Blick ist vom Vorübergehn der Stäbe.*' Today, darling, it is time for our Rilke."

He took a chair from the kitchen and led her into the office area. He sat at his desk chair, the kitchen chair facing him. He gestured to her to sit. Clumsily, he paged through a ragged, worn book of poems.

"Listen only to the music of the language, my darling," he said. "Rilke's heart will speak directly to your heart. You will understand." He frowned and squinted his small, pale eyes as he read.

Sein Blick ist vom Vorübergehn der Stäbe
so müd geworden, dass er nichts mehr hält.
Ihm ist, als ob es tausend Stäbe gäbe
und hinter tausend Stäben keine Welt.

He shifted heavily in his chair, so he and Zoe were almost knee to knee. His chair rolled and tilted and squeaked under his weight. Zoe leaned forward, fully attentive.

"Do you get the sense of it, my treasure? Are you able to take it into your heart? Let me give it to you again."

He read the lines again, slowly, with great feeling, and then read further.

> *Der weiche Gang geschmeidig starker Schritte,*
> *der sich im allerkleinsten Kreise dreht,*
> *ist wie ein Tanz von Kraft um eine Mitte,*
> *in der betäubt ein grosser Wille steht.*

He repeated the last line with greater intensity. "Do you sense the meaning, Zoe?" She nodded, silently. His voice was resonant; the rich sounds were sensual on his tongue.

He continued.

> *Nur manchmal schiebt der Vorhang der Pupille*
> *sich lautlos auf—. Dann geht ein Bild hinein,*
> *geht durch der Glieder angespannte Stille—*
> *und hört im Herzen auf zu sein.*

His voice and expression indicated that the poem had ended. He sat back in the chair. "Ah," he said. He seemed to look inward for a long time. Zoe sat patiently, watching him.

Then he stirred himself and sat forward again. "Come, sit on my lap, darling, so you can read the German along with me."

He opened his arms, holding the little book up and away in one hand as Zoe moved from her chair onto his lap. He closed his arms around her and held the book in front of them both, pulling her close. His breath was mildly unpleasant, like rotting apples.

"Try to say it with me, Zoe. Look at the title. *Der Panther.* You know what it says, don't you, darling? It's the same in English."

"Panther," Zoe said softly.

"Yes. Now, let's read it together, in German, so you can feel its majesty, its music. Then, together, we'll discover its meaning. I want you to know greatness, Zoe. Read the poem with me, dearest."

Zoe's voice was a soft, light echo of his deep, resonant one, as together they slowly made their way through the German. Sometimes, he would stop to let her go ahead of him, correcting her pronunciation, encouraging her, urging her on.

"Good, good. You have a gift for this. Ah, you are so intelligent, so intelligent."

Zoe did not smile at his praise; she looked down at the page with complete concentration.

"Do you have a sense of what Rilke is saying, my darling?"

"A little," she said, shyly.

"Can you tell me? Has his heart spoken to your heart?"

"He is very sad . . ."

"And is only Rilke sad?"

"Is the panther sad, too?"

"Perhaps Rilke *is* the panther. Perhaps we *all* are."

He sighed a tremulous sigh and let the book rest on Zoe's knees as he reached his big hands up and placed them gently, protectively on her cheeks, rubbing his face against her hair.

She placed her hands on his. Zoe and the Spider King sat that way, silently, for several minutes.

"Yes," he said at last. "Yes. And where does our sad friend, Rilke, discover this panther? Where are panthers, these grievous days?"

"In the zoo?"

"Yes, darling. In the zoo. *Im Jardin des Plantes, Paris.* Rilke has gone to the botanical garden in Paris where there is a zoo, and he is standing before a cage in which a panther paces, around and around, turning in cramped circles, 'im allerkleinsten Kreise dreht.'

"Can you see it, darling? A magnificent panther, with his powerful, velvety shoulders tensing and releasing as he turns in his cage, his great paws softly striking the dirty cement of the cage floor—not earth, for he has been taken from his rightful place in the wild, where he would have been free to live as he was intended to live. And why? Because he is so beautiful. People want to keep him locked up for themselves because he is so beautiful."

The Spider King's voice grew more intense. "We have done this to him because we love his beauty. We have fallen in love with him because he is so beautiful. And in our love for him, we have taken him from the wild and made him our prisoner. We have imprisoned him so that every day we can see him and experience his beauty. Yes. We have wanted to love him and to know his beauty, and in loving him, we have imprisoned him.

"Oh, Zoe. Zoe. We do terrible things, sometimes, in the name of love."

The Spider King sighed again, a great, rasping sigh. His voice caught in a sob, and he held Zoe more closely against himself.

"But let us look again at the poem, dearest." He stroked her hair with a quick, heavy hand. "What do we know about this panther? We know he is a strong and mighty creature, because Rilke speaks of his powerful, soft strides, his *'starker Schritte.'*"

He continued to stroke Zoe's hair absently as he waited for her to absorb this thought.

"And what do we know of the spirit of the panther? Rilke tells us much about the spirit of this great creature, dearest, with only a few words. We come to know this panther very well. That is Rilke's greatness.

"Look, Zoe. Look at how Rilke lets us see into the inner world of the panther. Rilke tells us that the panther sees only the bars of his prison. Rilke lets us know the panther has seen them for so long that he no longer sees anything else. The whole world has become nothing but bars. There is no other world. Listen. He says, *'... und hinter tausend Stäben keine Welt.'*"

Tears flooded Zoe's cheeks—her own, and, mixed with them, the Spider King's. "Ah, my darling, we know his sadness, don't we?" he murmured into her hair.

"The poor panther," Zoe whispered. "What happens to him? Does he die?"

"No. The panther doesn't die. But his spirit does. Rilke tells us about the panther's spirit, his mighty will—*'ein grosser Wille.'*

"To Rilke, the panther's pacing is like a powerful, ritual dance around a central point where the creature's mighty will stands numb. Ah, Zoe, Rilke was a wise and knowing person. He has told us the truth."

Zoe needed to move. Her legs tingled. The Spider King sensed her discomfort and opened his arms so she could stand. Immediately, she turned and sat down again in her chair, facing him.

She looked expectantly at the Spider King. Her face was flushed. "Does the panther ever get free?"

"No. 'Only, at times, the curtain of his pupils quietly lifts,' Rilke says. An image has entered. '*Dann geht ein Bild hinein . . . geht durch der Glieder angespannte Stille.*'"

The Spider King looked up quickly at Zoe with tears in his eyes. He lifted his hand, and, with a simple movement arcing from his eye to his chest, revealed to Zoe exactly what happened.

"An image enters, moves through the tensed stillness of his shoulders, plunges into his heart, and is gone. The image is gone, my darling child. The hope of freedom dies." His voice was a sob.

"Oh!" Zoe caught her hands to her mouth. Her eyes glistened with tears. "Oh!"

Zoe came to consciousness in a clutch of fear, with a line of poetry ringing in the darkness. *Sein Blick ist vom Vorübergehn der Stäbe.*

She had fainted again. It terrified her that she was losing control. It terrified her that her spider phobia was again so strong. It seemed that things happened during her fainting spells and somehow carried over into her waking life in inexplicable ways, but she had no idea what they were.

It wasn't like dreaming. If she paid attention soon enough after waking from a dream, she could retrieve and "work with the dream," as the Jungians called it.

But all that was left after these fainting spells was the tag-end of an orgasm, or, just now, words from a poem. What poem? She repeated the words to herself. *Sein Blick ist vom Vorübergehn der Stäbe.* A poem by the great German poet, Rainer Maria Rilke. The first line of his beautiful poem, *Der Panther,* which she had learned when she was in college, a poem she loved so much she had committed it to memory.

But why had a line from *that* poem come to her now? What did Rilke have to do with anything?

The Chief was in an anxious state when Zoe arrived at the office, late again. "Oh, Zoe. Call Amsterdam right away. We need rooms for the Italians. Four doubles."

The Chief did not welcome Zoe back, apparently forgetting that she had left early the day before. He did not ask if she was feeling better. But never mind. This lack of concern for her was nothing new, though somehow today she felt more vulnerable to it.

The phone call to Amsterdam lifted her spirits temporarily. As she waited to be connected to the young woman with the impeccable English and radiant skin who was working on the Congress at the beautiful little Dutch hotel where it would be held, Zoe imagined the manager's office just off the lobby, the cobblestone street in front of the hotel, the funny little cars parked at odd angles. A few feet beyond the tiny parking area were the canal; the trees that at night sparkled with white lights; the tall, narrow row houses; the ubiquitous bicycles; the arched bridges—all intensely picturesque.

She had first stayed at this hotel with the Chief two years ago when they were making site visits. It offered the appropriate elegance and rich ambiance for the Congress.

The phone call and arrangements complete, Zoe felt her annoyance with the Chief return. She considered pointing out his callousness about not mentioning her having felt ill yesterday and leaving the office early. For fourteen years, she had been trying to embarrass the Chief into treating her as something other than an indentured servant. He was still as demanding and inconsiderate as he'd been when she walked into his office at twenty-one, reeling from the blows of college.

In those days, she was so accustomed to suffering that it didn't seem odd that the Chief expected her to work seven days a week, or that he acted as if she were shirking her duty if she wanted to take the weekend off. Gradually, Zoe had weaned the Chief off her weekend work sessions, but she could not persuade him to become a considerate human being.

But his clients adored him. The women fit a pattern: bright, educated, attractive. They almost always had drug- or alcohol-addicted teenage children. Zoe liked the Chief's clients, though she looked down on them (she was not proud of this) because their husbands' money paid their bills, and they did not have jobs. Instead, they had migraines and gave elegant, catered parties and were always renovating their condominiums and waiting for custom-made furniture to arrive from Portugal.

"Mrs. Lehrer will not be coming to Amsterdam," the Chief announced, mid-afternoon. His wife's absence meant Zoe would sleep with him, at least on a night when there was no 7:00 a.m. administrative meeting the next day.

Zoe thought it odd that he always referred to his wife as Mrs. Lehrer. She wondered if he called her Mrs. Lehrer when talking with her at home. *Mrs. Lehrer, I should like to schedule sexual intercourse for Thursday night.*

The Lehrers had a magnificent mansion on Astor Street with five bedrooms, and a ballroom on the top floor with a harp in the front window that could be seen from the street. Behind was a three-bedroom coach house, which they rented to PhD candidates and medical students, who helped manage the mansion and their frequent social events.

Mrs. Lehrer was a former opera singer. She was aristocratic, breezy, irreverent. Lately, she raced Lotus sports cars for fun. Zoe imagined she found the Chief unbearably stuffy.

Zoe and Mrs. Lehrer were not exactly friends. They gave one another a polite, if somewhat cool, embrace when professional occasions brought them together. Mrs. Lehrer sometimes confided in Zoe, but never anything personal, and generally at her husband's expense.

At a recent cocktail party, her topic was his type-A personality. She and Zoe and several others were standing, glasses in hand, in the private club high above the glittering city and the dark mystery of the lake.

"Walther and I were in the UK several years ago," she said, "staying with friends in Oxford. Our hostess, with great fanfare, served afternoon tea. It was an impressive ceremony, and Walther was, indeed, impressed."

Her voice grew conspiratorial. "When we returned home, Walther ordained that we, too, should have afternoon tea. He requested that

I prepare it in the traditional English manner, with sterling silver and Wedgewood cups and plates. He arranged his schedule so he could be home at four in the afternoon on the agreed-upon day." Her diamonds sparkled. She sighed.

"When the day came, he *blew* into the house at five minutes to four—he's always punctual, of course—and stormed into the sunroom where we had set up operations. He perched on the edge of his chair while Ellen served. Ellen's one of the graduate students who live in the coach house. Somewhere, she'd found one of those little black maid's uniforms, with the white doily for an apron and the starched, perky white cap; it was her own idea, a stroke of genius."

Mrs. Lehrer took a sip of wine.

"So, Ellen carried in the huge antique silver tray with the tea service, the Wedgewood, the scones, the George the Third tea-strainer, the mound of perfect red and green seedless grapes with those ridiculous grape scissors, the tiny cucumber, salmon, and chicken salad sandwiches, a variety of English cheeses and cute little cakes, the whole production."

She paused to get her breath. "And Walther *gulped* down half a cup of the Earl Grey tea, carefully brewed, of course; nothing so banal as a tea bag would do for this occasion. He slapped some breathtakingly expensive Scottish marmalade onto a scone, stuffed it into his mouth without tasting it, glanced at his watch, brushed a crumb off his sleeve, and said, 'Well, I've got to get back to the office.' Then he *rushed* out again."

She and her co-conspirators looked across the room to the object of their derision, in his three-piece suit, working his own crowd, a puff of smoke curling up from his pipe.

"Later, Walther said he didn't know what the English see in afternoon tea. He thought it was a waste of time." She sighed, and they all laughed.

"Well, that's Walther."

What the Chief thought about having such a wife, Zoe could only imagine. He never discussed Mrs. Lehrer, except in the most general terms, complaining about the cost of her racing car obsession and her other extravagances.

What the Chief thought about Zoe, she knew very well. Despite her competence and her many skills, the Chief would say, "You've made a stupid mistake. What's the matter with you? You must be getting senile." He probably thought he was being funny.

Zoe worked until 8:00 p.m., two hours after the Chief left for home in his Mercedes. Then she went home herself. She was still feeling exhausted after yesterday's emotional ordeal, and she intended to eat the cold lamb chop left over from dinner earlier in the week. Instead, as she took the lamb chop out of the refrigerator, she fainted.

Later, she awoke on the kitchen floor, sobbing. Blinking away her tears, she stood up and looked at the clock. 4:00 a.m. Why was she sobbing? Perhaps this was just grief at the death of her father. The funeral had been just a few weeks ago. It was normal for a child to grieve the death of a parent.

But was this normal grief?

Zoe was knowledgeable about psychology. In addition to her work with the Chief, she had spent years in therapy and other healing practices. Her adult life had been populated by therapists, gurus, and support groups. She knew she had a "father thing," and had worked on her hostile feelings toward her mother. She had done dream work and Transactional Analysis. She'd been Rolfed. She had done creative visualization, chanting, affirmations, positive self-talk, meditation, yoga.

When all else failed, she stopped drinking and went to AA.

All these experiences had improved her. She was highly functional. She had a brilliant career; she managed better than most to handle a difficult boss; she had come through her divorce relatively unscathed.

Well, there *had* been a week of obsessing about killing him and the Other Woman, but once the shock of discovery wore off, acceptance and relief set in. For all his charms, her husband had been a big responsibility: a practicing alcoholic. She had been one, too, though she didn't realize it at the time.

Until her marriage, she'd had an assortment of interesting, accomplished men in her life. Mostly other people's husbands. That *could* have been construed as dysfunctional and was certainly politically incorrect.

But she was, she thought, realistic about what a man could do for a woman (not much). To her, men were something like polo ponies: entertaining, if you could afford them. She considered herself independently wealthy, emotionally speaking and, although she enjoyed riding them at the polo grounds, when she was done, she was content to hand the bridle back to their trainer to brush them down, water them, and put them away.

She went to the bathroom to take an aspirin. She had a throbbing headache. She peered into the red eyes looking back at her from the mirror. So, if she was such a marvel of mental health, why was she having these fainting spells, and why had the spider phobia become so intense?

These things were apparently connected to the death of her father. But how?

CHAPTER 3.
Elizabeth Thomas: Emergent, Unexpected

It was two months since Zoe had made the trip home to be present as her father transited the earthly plane, from the realm of polarities and paradoxes, time and change, beauty and pain.

Zoe had been summoned to his bedside with an early phone call that Monday morning, and had made the long drive from Chicago, through the bleak, perfectly flat fields of northern Indiana and Ohio, with their stark trees, drifted snow, and dark, angled fence posts.

She arrived around 4:00 in the afternoon and went directly to the hospital. Her father was resting quietly, eyes closed. Those eyes had often filled with tears in recent months.

Pale as death on the neat pillow, the bedclothes undisturbed by movement, he breathed shallowly, irregularly. Occasionally, he uttered a rasping sigh, his yellowish hands motionless, the IV needle taped into a bruised vein.

Zoe stood for a long time, watching him.

At some point, he stirred, and his eyelids fluttered open. "Take care of your mother."

"I will, Daddy."

He did not open his eyes again.

Someone suggested that Zoe go out and have dinner. The nurse promised to call her at the restaurant if something happened. Zoe went alone, because her mother had also been hospitalized, her own health broken. She was sick with exhaustion from the long ordeal of nursing her husband through the final months of cancer. She cared for him while there was something she could do. Then, when she could no longer manage at home, they both went to the hospital to be cared for by others.

It was over suddenly. Despite the time she'd had to prepare for this moment, it was not at all the way Zoe had imagined it.

Just as she ordered dinner, the call came. By the time she returned to the hospital, her father's bed was empty. Whether her mother was at his bedside when he died, Zoe didn't know. The nurses and doctors were engaged in caring for the body elsewhere, performing their secret rituals, changing the bed, cleaning the room, preparing the death certificate.

Now, the first week of April, Zoe was visiting her mother again. The snow had melted, and everywhere, there was a feeling of warm, sweet awakening.

As Zoe stood on the back porch while her mother made breakfast, she smelled the earthy odor of freshly turned soil. Mother Nature seemed to be digging in the garden below the porch, pushing a small trowel into the soil to loosen it, bringing up the dark underlayers, startling earthworms and water bugs from their sleep, breaking up clumps of winter-hardened dirt.

The forsythia bush at the back corner of the house was dancing an extravagant fandango wearing a fluffy yellow dress, making a scandalous display of passion above the modest crocuses in their simple lavender frocks.

Zoe needed to take care of things. She needed to meet with the lawyer, order a tombstone, check on her mother's finances, and see firsthand how her mother was managing.

Zoe also was curious about her mother. She'd been thinking a lot about their relationship. Her father was no longer a buffer between them. And he was no longer there to dole out her medicine, pay the bills, plan the activities, run the errands, and make the decisions. Now, these responsibilities fell to Zoe.

What made it difficult was that Zoe had disliked, sometimes even hated, her mother since she was six years old.

As Zoe had described it to myriad therapists, she was six when her mother abandoned her for a career in the Theatre of the Trials of Daily Living. The stage was right there at home, and Elizabeth Thomas had treated her audience of two to an ever-changing series of characters.

There was her Scarlett O'Hara, manipulative and selfish ("Ah'll think about that tomorrah"); her Blanche Dubois, the helpless victim ("Ah depend on the kahndness of strangahs"); her Chekhov heroine, who paced and wrung her hands in the boredom and quiet desperation of the provinces; her Eleanor Roosevelt, giving inspirational speeches in a high-pitched, clearly articulated, somewhat annoying voice; her Eleanor of Aquitaine, vindictive, embittered, eloquent. And her signature role, the *Mater Dolorosa, in tableau,* motionless and silently weeping, eyes cast downward.

But never, as Zoe told it, had Elizabeth Thomas simply been a *mother.*

But on this April morning, as Zoe stepped into the warm kitchen for breakfast, a thought struck her: Maybe the problem hadn't been her mother at all. Zoe had been a peculiar child. Secretive, odd, phobic, grim, judgmental. A resentful, difficult little person.

Zoe pulled out the chair and sat across from her mother at the table. "Would you care for some coffee, dear?" Mrs. Thomas said, smiling sadly.

"Yes, thank you." Zoe looked at her mother's gentle blue eyes and her small, trembling hand as she poured the pitch-black coffee into a delicate porcelain cup, graciously offering Zoe a toasted English muffin.

Suddenly, Zoe regretted all those years of complaining about her mother in therapy. This gentle little person sitting across from her could not be Eleanor of Aquitaine or a Chekhov heroine. As she had, so many times during the past weeks, Zoe once again felt the ground sinking under her, felt herself slipping into an opening in the earth, along with her life, her assumptions, and everything else she thought she knew.

And now, something occurred to her that she had not thought of for years, certainly not in her adult life.

She saw herself as a little girl, being dried with a big, fluffy white towel by her father after her bath. She could not have been very old, for he had stood her up on the toilet seat. She remembered turning around so he could dry her back and her legs. She remembered turning around again to face him and reaching toward the ceiling so he could dry under her arms, and then extending her fingers as he methodically dried each one. Then she remembered holding her breath and squeezing her eyes closed as he toweled her hair dry with an almost rough, overpowering movement that engulfed her whole head, blinding and deafening her, nearly causing her to lose her balance.

She saw herself standing there afterward, her pale, silver-blond hair falling in damp strands, a fresh, dry towel wrapped around her body and tucked into itself under her arms. And she remembered her father lifting her off the toilet seat and standing her gently on the floor so that he could sit and comb her hair.

It was so real to Zoe that she felt it in her body even now. This memory stirred memories of other evening baths, always given to her by her father.

"Mother," she said, "could we talk about my childhood a little? There are some things I've been wondering about."

"Of course, dear."

"Mother, I have a memory that Daddy gave me baths when I was a child. Did that really happen, or am I making it up?"

Her mother, surprised by the question, hesitated as she took a sip of coffee, delicately holding the cup.

Zoe looked appraisingly at her. She was a small woman, an older version of Zoe, still attractive at seventy-one. She had been thirty-six when Zoe was born. A series of realizations flashed through Zoe's mind in rapid succession:

I was born when she was just a year older than I am now.

She had already lived longer than I've lived before she became my mother.

She had a life that didn't include me, of not being my mother, a life longer than my whole life.

It seemed strange to Zoe, considering the thousands of hours she had spent in therapy, sifting through the minutest details of her childhood, that she had apparently missed so much, some of it so obvious.

It had never occurred to her to think about who her mother was as a *person*. A woman with an identity other than Elizabeth Thomas, Collapsible Mother of Zoe Thomas, the High-Strung, Neurotic but Charming Wife of Percy Thomas.

Zoe felt a surge of anger toward her therapists. Weren't they supposed to notice those things and confront the client? Weren't they supposed to help the client get to the truth and dispel the fantasy?

What were her therapists *doing* all those years, besides taking her money, and listening to her drone on about her apparently distorted version of her childhood? Not one of them ever confronted her with anything.

And why was she feeling so disoriented now? Why was she still getting psychic surprises, after fifteen years of the best therapy money could buy?

Just a few months ago, she'd thought she understood everything. But somehow, when her father died, the intricate pattern of the world as she knew it began to fragment.

The evening baths, for example. It struck her as odd that a father should have been bathing a young child. Wasn't that the mother's job?

Zoe came back to the present moment and rephrased her question. "Wasn't it unusual for Daddy to be bathing me?"

After a moment, her mother said, "It was a difficult time."

"Why?"

"Things were not what I expected." Zoe waited for more.

Elizabeth Thomas shook her head as if to clear away painful thoughts.

Then she said, with an enigmatic smile, "Your father was very devoted to you. He was completely absorbed in you from the very beginning. I considered myself fortunate. The husbands of my friends took much less interest in their children than your father did in you."

Again, she shook her head, and closed her eyes briefly, as if seeing it in her mind. "When you were first born, he decided you should have a music box; he wanted to introduce you to music right away, but he didn't want the first music you heard to be out of tune. Music boxes aren't always well made, from a professional musician's point of view. So, he searched and searched, listening to dozens of them until he found one that played the opening bars of *Eine kleine Nachtmusik* perfectly on pitch. He bought that one for you, to soothe you and quiet you if you cried. Although you rarely cried. You were a good baby. I considered myself fortunate. A devoted husband and the most perfect baby in the world."

There was a slight flicker of a frown and another pause. "I thought I was fortunate that he wanted to give you your feedings, wanted to bathe you. He wanted to do all the things mothers usually do for a child. It was obvious he adored you. You were the center of his world."

She sighed again.

"What about you, Mother?"

"Me? What do you mean?"

"Did you feel shut out? Because of all his focus on me?"

Before Mrs. Thomas could answer, the phone rang. The caller wanted to make plans for a bridge club gathering. By the time the call was over, the opportunity to continue the conversation had passed.

Zoe spent the rest of the week with her mother, then returned to Chicago with much to think about. Her mother, the emergent, the unexpected!

Zoe was stunned by her mother's equanimity these days. Apparently, Percy Thomas's death had resolved some inner conflict for her.

But Zoe Thomas's world was coming apart.

CHAPTER 4.
Wolves and Humans

Back in Chicago, everything seemed askew. The buildings in the part of Chicago known as the Magnificent Mile, where Zoe spent her work life, seemed off-balance. The faces of strangers looked ominous.

Twenty blocks farther north, Zoe entered her townhouse with great anxiety. She'd developed the habit of leaving a light on by the front door—she rarely got home before dark—and sleeping with a light on in her bedroom.

At the office, Zoe felt herself pulling away from the Chief. She realized she was dreading the sexual encounter in Amsterdam. She couldn't imagine saying no to him, but when she thought about being with him, she felt revulsion.

Her other affairs with married men over the years Zoe had managed with a perfect balance of engagement and detachment, in the great French courtesan tradition. She had an air of sensual amusement, ennui, and superiority, and a recognition of the absurd so characteristic of her favorite French author, Sidonie-Gabrielle Colette.

Like Colette, Zoe prided herself on not suffering over affairs. She was not one of those women who cried herself to sleep on

Christmas Eve or her birthday, waiting for a *sotto voce* phone call from the man she hoped would leave his wife and family to marry her, a call made from the library of his elegant suburban home, or the laundry room of his expensive condominium. She did not need assurances that he was miserable and missed the only woman he truly loved. No, no, no. She did not expect or want these men to leave their wives for her.

Zoe's liaisons were not about love, although they involved mutual affection and appreciation. Even the neurosurgeon, arrogant as he was—Zoe did not take his arrogance personally, assuming it was simply one of his professional credentials— had thought enough of her intellect to offer to put her through medical school. (She declined.) Zoe had relationships with sophisticated men of achievement, with busy schedules and the wealth to afford the best restaurants and hotels for trysts.

Zoe considered herself a superb lover, generous, patient, and skilled, with a body that was both slender and voluptuous. She had satiny, luminous skin and hair, and the world's softest mouth (they all agreed). These qualities were combined with a marvelous sense of humor and a keen intellect. She dressed beautifully, had fine jewelry (thanks to these same men); she could order in flawless French and charm the most snobbish *maître d'* by selecting exactly the right wine for any entrée. A delightful companion, marvelous conversation, no strings. What more could any man want?

But that was before. When she decided to marry, she had lunch with each of her paramours—there were half a dozen of them—and said goodbye, thanking each for a wonderful time, assuring him she would never forget him. Each took the news as was suitable for a sophisticated man, telling her he loved her, now that it was safe to do so. And, with a gentlemanly hint of a tear, each wished her happiness in her marriage.

These days, it was only the Chief. Despite her efficiency, Zoe was simply too busy for affairs. More importantly, at thirty-five, she found them less enthralling than she had at twenty-five. She'd wearied of adjusting to the men's peculiarities and quirky needs. Having to remember which side they liked to sleep on, for example. This was a matter of no small consequence; the man awoke cranky and fatigued if Zoe did not discover and assume his wife's sleeping position.

She'd also wearied of remembering the men's preferred liquors, the names of their pets, the schools and special talents of their children, their smoking habits. The Chief favored a nauseatingly pungent pipe tobacco. Worst of all, he liked a pipe *before* sex, which made his mouth taste terrible. Zoe found she just didn't have the chops for these affairs anymore. The Chief was all she could manage. And now, even he was becoming burdensome.

One of the things Zoe appreciated about being thirty-five and sober was that at last she had gained a sense of mastery over her circumstances. As a child, she hated being ruled by circumstances. She detested not knowing what was going on. That's why she read so much, why she always tried to figure things out. She didn't care if the news was bad. She just wanted to know what the news *was*.

She liked it that she was settled in her life; she savored being comfortable and having a routine. Now, a pattern of regular AA meetings replaced the therapy sessions and the complicated relationships. She "worked a good program," adhering with dedication to AA requirements: Don't drink. Go to meetings. Work the steps.

Keep it simple. AA was the only other thing she did these days, besides her job and attending to her mother's needs.

On a gentle, warm Sunday morning in late April, Zoe was preparing the soil of her small garden for its annual planting. Although she was rarely home, she made a single concession to domesticity: On one weekend each spring, she planted a garden, and on subsequent weekends throughout the summer and autumn, until the first frost, she watered her garden and savored its beauty.

She had removed several pavers from her patio and created a plot of soil a few feet square. Four narrow flower boxes lined the wrought-iron fence that protected the patio and kept burglars away from her sliding glass door. A terra cotta head of Demeter looked down on the garden from the brick wall.

As Zoe loosened the soil and pulled out the broken remnants of last year's garden, the rich, sensual harmonies of a Brahms symphony floated down around her in the warm air. The music was not loud, but it was very clearly Brahms. The Second Symphony.

Who would be playing Brahms? The neighbors she knew did not favor classical music. The music seemed to be coming through the open upper window across the passageway from her, from the townhouse that had been vacant since Ted, her only friend in the complex, had been transferred to California several months earlier. Had he sold his townhouse?

Someone was in there. Someone who listened to Brahms.

By mid-afternoon, her little garden was beautiful. She'd planted a low, delicious-smelling juniper among the flowers, planning the combination of fragrances and colors carefully, sprinkling some spunky orange and yellow marigolds among the magentas of the impatiens, the brick reds and pinks of the geraniums, the purples of the petunias, the blues of the pansies. Now, she was full of admiration and savored the results of her efforts.

"The May Day Carol," a song her mother had taught her years ago, played in her mind. *'Tis nothing but a sprout, but well budded out, by the work of our Lord's hand.* Well, not our Lord's hand. More likely, Demeter's hand. Demeter was, after all, the goddess of grain and the fields, and perhaps extended her concern to city gardens and townhouse plots.

Zoe was intensely non-Christian, but she was under orders from AA to get a spiritual life, to develop a relationship with a power greater than herself, so she wouldn't mistake herself for the one running the universe.

"You can have as your higher power whatever your soul longs for," they told her, so she was gingerly exploring *what her soul longed for.* She thought it might be the concept of a Great Mother who would love her unconditionally and not abandon her.

She had certainly never felt these things from her human mother.

So far, planting her garden, with the Mother Goddess Demeter supervising from the wall, was the closest Zoe had come to experiencing the sacred, and on this April day, with the sunshine spilling over her and the beautiful budding plants at her feet, it comforted her to feel part of the great cycle of seasons.

She hoped this would qualify as a spiritual life.

Suddenly, a man emerged from Ted's house. He pushed the storm door open and wheeled a bicycle out, resting it against the wall as he turned back to close and lock the door.

He wore cut-off jeans, a T-shirt, and a faded red cap. He had fine, muscular legs.

Why is that? Zoe thought. *Men get the gorgeous legs.* His whole body was muscular and trim.

After locking the door, he turned his bicycle around in the passageway, and something in his movement told Zoe he treated whatever was in his care with infinite respect. In that instant, she felt she knew everything about him. Not consciously, but later, she remembered that moment as a kind of epiphany.

Then he noticed Zoe in her garden and turned to meet her gaze with the most intense blue eyes Zoe had ever encountered. Dazzled, she lowered her own eyes to read his T-shirt. *Wolves and Humans. An Exhibit Sponsored by Defenders of Wildlife. Yellowstone National Park. Boise, Idaho.* There was a picture of a beautiful timber wolf with a gentle, noble expression.

"Wolves and humans," Zoe said. "Are you an appreciator of wolves?"

"I *am* a wolf."

He flashed a smile. She had never seen anyone do this so winningly. He was beautiful. Sensual lips.

"David Wolf."

Zoe considered whether he was teasing her, then realized that he had introduced himself.

"Oh, David Wolf. What a wonderful name. I'm Zoe Thomas."

They looked appraisingly at one another.

"You must be a friend of Ted's," Zoe said.

"Yes, he's an old friend. He was kind enough to let me take shelter in his house. My wife has fired me."

"Fired you?"

"She wants a divorce. She's found Jesus and seems to prefer Him to me."

"Oh."

"Very difficult to understand. She changes the requirements from day to day, and I have trouble keeping up with her spiritual transformations, or whatever they are. But I worry the most about our daughter. She's just four, and it's much harder for her. She's right in the middle of it."

A sorrowful look came over his face. "But I hope we can straighten things out. It's only just happened, so everything is very volatile. Meanwhile, I've gratefully taken shelter here. Things were intolerable at home, for all of us."

Zoe looked into his eyes, which had a suggestion of tears. She was impressed with his openness.

"That's a special kind of pain," she ventured, "having someone you love going through a spiritual crisis. And being separated from your daughter."

Zoe had heard myriad sorrowful stories of marriages in various stages of disrepair. And she knew how fierce and baffling people could be when they were burning with religious zeal. That was one of her objections to organized religion. It could be so destructive.

She considered saying something about refried Christians but decided against it. Too much pain here.

"I want Kathy to grow up in a happy family," he said. "I thought we *were* a happy family, but obviously I'd missed something. But I hope we can work it out." The finality in his voice told Zoe he'd said as much as he cared to.

"I hope you can, too."

She smiled kindly, wanting to give him a small offering to ease the pain. "I heard your Brahms this morning. It added to the pleasure of my gardening. Thank you for that."

"Oh." He flashed another smile. "Do you like Brahms? I was hoping I wouldn't disturb anyone. I'm not used to living this close to neighbors. In my house in Highland Park, I can play music as loudly as I want in my study downstairs, and if Kathy and Christine stay upstairs, even they don't hear it. We have an old house with high ceilings and good, thick walls, the kind that aren't built anymore. That's why I prefer to restore old houses. I believe people should be able to play music as loudly as they want without someone on the other side of the cardboard demanding they turn down the Brahms."

It was obviously a sore point with him. "Here, with my wolf ears, I can hear people two houses away blowing their noses and punching numbers into their microwaves. I hear their toilets flush, and their answering machines take messages. I know a lot more about the people in this neighborhood than I care to."

He sighed and smiled ruefully. "Except for you. This is the first I've seen you. You don't seem to be home much."

"No, I'm a workaholic. I live at my office." A pause.

Then, not wanting the conversation to end, she said, "You mentioned restoring old houses. Do you do that as a vocation or an avocation?"

"It's my business. The most honorable thing I could think of to do, given my peculiarities. To take the past and, with the proper skill and materials and creativity, shape it into something beautiful and habitable for the present."

"I've never heard anyone speak so poetically about rehabbing buildings."

"I'm fortunate that I love my work. And it gives me a chance to be outdoors a lot. I can't stand being closed in. I went to law school and tried to practice law for a few years, but I found it too confining. I took to howling. I'd be sitting at my desk on an upper floor of the IBM building and tension would build up in my shoulders and my ulcer would start eating at me, and then suddenly, I'd feel the urge to howl. I'd close my eyes and tip my head back and cup my hands around my mouth and I'd howl. I discovered why wolves do it. It relieves tension. After howling for a few minutes, I'd feel much better. But it had a certain disruptive effect in the office."

He laughed. "All those corporate lawyers, in their three-piece suits, with the gold watch fobs across their bellies, sitting in their corner offices with the Oriental rugs and the investment artwork and the photographs of their children and their wives who are, to a woman, on the boards of the symphony and the Art Institute and Michael Reese Hospital . . . well, they found it upsetting.

"It soon became apparent to everyone that I didn't belong there. So, I walked away from it. I haven't had a moment's regret. My wife, unfortunately, has. In fact, she felt betrayed. She had married a promising lawyer at a fancy law firm and got, instead, something that was becoming more like a critter and less like a senior partner every day. I can't really blame her. It hasn't been easy for her."

Zoe was charmed. "I'm sure the howling was an enormous improvement in the corporate environment."

"The secretaries loved it. But for some reason, the partners found it annoying."

He smiled and turned his bicycle. "Well, I should let you finish your gardening. I'm going to ride my bike around the neighborhood for a while and look for houses to rescue. Perhaps I'll see you again. I've enjoyed talking with you."

He wheeled his bicycle along the passageway toward the front gate, then stopped and turned back. "I'm a little embarrassed. I seem to have monopolized the conversation. I've been alone so much lately that when I find someone willing to listen as graciously as you have, the words just come pouring out. I apologize. Next time, I'll give you a chance to talk. I promise."

"Oh, the story about your corporate howling is much more interesting than anything I could have offered. We workaholics lose our juice. Perhaps I should take up howling."

Zoe picked up the hose and prepared to give her flowers a soaking.

With a wave and one last, luminous smile, David Wolf pedaled away, his bicycle spokes clicking softly.

CHAPTER 5.
Ritual Sacrifice

It was spider season. There seemed to be spiders everywhere. Scarcely a day went by that one didn't go darting across the white tile of Zoe's first floor or wait darkly in a complicated nest in the corner of her garden.

Monstrous black ones with fat, round bellies made webs in the huge windows outside her office at the Hancock Center. Every time she looked up from her work, she saw them there, clumsily busy with the doomed insects that had been blown into their webs. She watched with horrified fascination the death throes of many an innocent. Where did the spiders come from? More importantly, where did they go when they abandoned their webs?

One night, Zoe awoke to find a small spider on her pillow. She crushed it with the sheet, but waking out of the vulnerability of sleep and seeing the spider so close to her face overwhelmed her with terror and precipitated another fainting spell.

Darkness enveloped the cottage, and the night-sounds of summer began. The Spider King was ceremoniously laying a fire, apparently indifferent to the night's warmth.

"This is the night of nights, my treasure," he murmured. "We must prepare for it properly, each element of the ritual in its time."

He kneeled at the hearth, placing logs carefully, one after another, onto the cradle of the grate, making a little fortress of logs with the science and artistry of da Vinci.

"There must be a fire on the hearth. Fire is essential to ritual, you know. Prometheus's gift. You remember, don't you, Zoe, what Prometheus suffered that we might have a lovely fire? Chained to the cliff, the vultures tearing at his liver?"

This did not require an answer. He was absorbed in building the fire. As it flared up, he struck his hands together, satisfied, and stood, a little breathlessly.

"You must rest. Close your eyes for a few minutes while I work. Many things await us, and you must not be sleepy, my joy. Come, close your eyes. I'll awaken you."

Young Zoe went to the sofa and lay on her side, curling her legs up and wrapping her arms around herself. The Spider King pulled a soft cover over her, and she closed her eyes. She was uncomfortably warm as she listened to him moving heavily around the cottage, coughing sharp, dry coughs; clearing his throat; gasping for air, sighing, whistling repetitive tunes.

She pretended to sleep.

After a while, she heard him go into the bathroom. Bath water began. Then she felt the floor jar with his heavy steps as he came and stood beside the couch and said, softly, "Zoe, it's time to wake up. It's time for you to bathe yourself. You must come cleansed, purified, to our ritual. You are to be the priestess."

He sat down beside her on the couch, caught both her hands in one of his, and with his other hand, cupped her chin so she looked directly into his face. "Zoe, I want you to do something special for me on this special night. After you have finished your bath, I want you to come to me naked, my treasure, my dove, my priestess. Will you do that for me?"

Zoe nodded.

She spent a long time in the bathroom. After she finished her bath, she dried herself and combed her hair. The steam had cleared from the mirror, and she could see her pale, shining skin and her green eyes looking solemnly back at her. It was long past time for her to go, but she sat, naked, on the edge of the tub.

The Spider King did not call Zoe, but she could feel his summons. At last, taking a deep breath, she opened the door of the bathroom and went into the office area, where he sat with eyes closed before the fire. The room was dark now, except for the firelight and the dancing light of dozens of candles, in brass and crystal holders on the mantle, on tables, on the windowsills.

"Ah. Come, priestess."

As Zoe went hesitantly toward the Spider King, he pulled a stool so he could sit. Gasping and coughing at the effort of shifting his weight, he opened a small box filled with rouges, eye shadows, brushes, eyeliners, lipsticks, and creams. He had her kneel between his knees and, in the flickering firelight, made up her face, spreading rouge lightly across her cheeks and touching her eyelashes with mascara. With his large fingers, he brushed color over her lips.

Then, he lifted Zoe to her feet, and standing awkwardly, he placed a large, round mirror in her hand.

"Look, darling. See how splendid you are."

Zoe did not recognize the exotic creature looking back at her from the mirror.

The Spider King left her for a moment, then returned with two long-stemmed glasses filled with a golden liquid.

"Wine, my priestess. Gift of Dionysus. Let us thank Dionysus for his vine, his grape." He placed the wineglass in her hand and touched his glass to hers. He drank heavily. She hesitated.

"You must drink, priestess," the Spider King said. "You must drink."

She took a tiny sip. She shuddered. It was too sweet. He held the glass gently to her lips so she would drink more. The wine filled her mouth. She swallowed it, almost choking.

"This is the night of nights, Zoe. This is the night we were born for, my darling."

Then the Spider King left Zoe alone. She sat staring into the fire, tense and upright. Perspiration beaded and glistened on her temples and upper lip. Her mind flew up, like a sparrow, and clung with little gray claws to the top of the window frame.

Suddenly, the Spider King stood before her. He was naked, except for a heavy, dark cape that fell from his shoulders to the floor, held around his neck by a copper and leather thong. The cape was made of the hide of a bull.

He wore a headdress with two curving horns and cheek pieces of animal hide that swept down and clasped under his chin. It transformed him completely, making him into a bull, huge and terrible. Zoe saw his little eyes looking out through the dark, rounded eye sockets of the mask. Only his nose and mouth were free.

In his right hand was a long oak staff, with ivy vines and leaves carved around the shaft. The head of the staff was shaped like an erect penis, of ivory or polished bone, honey-colored and gleaming. He thumped the staff on the floor.

"Come! Let us celebrate the sacred marriage."

He reached for Zoe, summoning her to the bedroom. She went silently with him, trembling and stumbling.

The small bed had been pulled to the center of the room. It was spread with animal hides—fox, bobcat, deer, and smaller wild animals, the flickering firelight playing over their ears and whiskers and teeth, making them seem alive, their glass eyes watching.

Surrounding the bed was a forest of candles on tall, elaborate wrought-iron and carved wooden stands, their flickering light filling the room with moving shadows that turned and swelled and dipped like spirit dancers.

He went out again to retrieve a wine goblet and fell to his knees before Zoe, who stood trembling by the bed.

"We are no longer who we were," the Spider King murmured. Holding the goblet up, he saluted her, drinking heavily. Then he put the goblet to her lips. She, too, drank heavily.

"You are Life," he whispered, his voice full of reverence. "I kneel before you.

"Now, you must understand what will happen. You must realize that you are the female principle. You are the sacred field."

He stood awkwardly and put the goblet aside. "You receive the male principle. The field must be plowed on behalf of Life."

He lifted her to the bed and made her lie back. She closed her eyes.

"The sacred field is not plowed by any mortal man. This is the field of the Goddess. It must be plowed by the God. By no other."

With the staff, he lifted her knees slightly and spread her legs. Then, in one sharp movement, he thrust the head of the staff into her vagina.

"With this, you become the Goddess." He grunted with the effort of his thrusting, and she screamed.

He swept her up into his arms, sobbing, and pulled the head of the staff out of her. Blood flooded onto the animal skins and down her legs, which jerked and trembled. She convulsed. Her eyelids fluttered, and she saw flames everywhere, moving up the sides of the bed and into her body.

Cat sprang into the doorway with a bow and arrow. With a swift movement, she placed the arrow and drew the bow taut, as the Spider King turned in amazement.

Dropping Zoe, he raised his hands as if to shield himself, as Cat shot the arrow into his heart, crying, "Kill him, Justice-Bringer!"

The Spider King shrieked, grasping wildly at the arrow, trying to pull it out. He staggered back, crashing to the floor and knocking over the candles. They blazed, splashing burning wax across the floor.

The room erupted into flames.

Cat flung away her weapon, seized Zoe's body in her arms, and carried her out of the bedroom and cottage and into the darkness.

Behind them, the thatched roof ignited, sending up blossoms of sparks and then long stalks of flame into the sky, making the sound of a thousand dying animals screaming in anguish.

Running from the swirling firestorm, carrying Zoe until she could run no more, Cat fell, gasping and sobbing, frantically laying her own body over Zoe's, trying to protect her from the heat that swept in waves over them, even at the forest's edge.

After a long time, rain fell. It was a gentle rain that washed away the blood and caressed with cool fingers the tear-swollen faces of Cat and Zoe as they lay, their arms around each other, lost in pain.

CHAPTER 6.
Gudrun

At the office Monday morning, after the intensities of the weekend—planting her garden, encountering David Wolf, and suffering another fainting spell, which left her emotionally ragged and exhausted—Zoe said, "Chief, I need some time off. I'm not feeling well. I think I'm having a nervous breakdown."

As she said this, she swallowed a sob.

"Well, don't," came the reply. "You can't have time off. Not until after the Congress. There's no time for you to fall apart, Zoe. If you still need some time after the Congress, you can have a week. Rent a car. Drive into the Dutch countryside. Very pretty. But now, I can't spare you."

She felt defeated. He didn't even look up from his work, and Zoe suspected he didn't notice the desperation in her voice, the sob.

Therefore, she did what she always did. She kept on keeping on, and the moment passed.

Several days later, Zoe received a phone call from Gudrun Skjerne, the Danish psychiatrist she'd never met but had spoken with many times. Zoe worked regularly with her by phone because Gudrun was the scientific director for the Congress.

Zoe often wondered what Gudrun looked like. Her voice was musical and warm, and to Zoe, she sounded beautiful. She also sounded like a wonderful therapist: kind, competent, compassionate.

"I'm coming to America next month," Gudrun said. "I hope to spend some time with you and Walther to finalize plans for the Congress; September isn't that far away.

"I'll be in Chicago for seven weeks. Would you be so kind as to let me know if Walther will be in town in June, and when I could come to your office?"

She was always polite. Her English was perfectly grammatical, although she pronounced certain words quaintly. She frequently drew in her breath at the end of a sentence, a charming little reverse sigh.

"Of course, we'll gladly meet with you, and yes, Walther will be in town in June."

"It will be a busy time. What's especially exciting to me is an opening at a gallery where my paintings will be shown. Also, I have another project, rather more complicated, involving a conference at DePaul, so I'll need to plan my time carefully."

"Your *paintings*? You're an artist as well as a psychiatrist?"

Gudrun laughed warmly. "Oh, yes. And I'll tell you a secret, Zoe. The paintings are my *real work*. In fact, many of my clients eventually become artists." She laughed again. "I don't intend it that way. It just seems to happen. Yes." The little in-drawing of breath.

"How wonderful that you're an artist. Will it be possible for me to see your work? Will the show be open to the public?"

"Yes. I'd be honored. The owner of the gallery has graciously offered to give a reception for my opening, on Saturday, June third, with lots of champagne, dainty morsels of food, big bowls of flowers, bright candlelight, a string quartet playing Mozart, and everyone dressed elegantly. I've bought a beautiful outfit especially for the occasion."

She laughed again. "It will be very festive. I'd love for you to be there. I'll have the owner of the gallery invite you, along with Walther and his wife. You could bring a friend."

"Thank you. It sounds delightful, Gudrun. I'm so impressed that you're an artist, in addition to your scientific achievements. I'm especially looking forward to meeting you, though I feel as if I know you already."

"I'm looking forward to meeting you, too, Zoe. I'll be busy at the gallery until the opening, trying to be certain the paintings are hung in the proper order and right side up. But perhaps I'll be able to meet with you and Walther on the Monday or Tuesday following the opening."

Zoe arranged for the Chief to meet with Gudrun on Monday, but he could not attend the opening. He and his wife had other plans. He didn't seem impressed that Gudrun was an artist.

Zoe wondered if David Wolf would be interested in being her date.

The following Saturday morning, Zoe was again in her garden, watering her flowers, breathing in the delicious fragrance as the dark soil grew wet in the spray.

Working in her garden produced intense, positive feelings: pleasure at the sensuous earthiness of digging in the soil, the perfume of the flowers and pungent spice of the juniper bush, and, yes, even an unexpected sense of connection with her mother, who had seemed to receive such pleasure from her own small garden as Zoe was growing up.

Zoe left the office early on Friday, determined that she wouldn't think about the Chief until Monday.

Everything was quiet. No comforting Brahms from across the passageway. The only sound was the water whispering from her hose. She turned off the water and sat on the low stone step, leaning her head against the patio door. Despite the loveliness of her garden, she had to admit that she was unhappy.

At that moment, the door across the passageway opened, and David Wolf stepped out. Zoe felt her heart give a little leap.

"Good morning," he said. "Your garden is thriving, I see."

Zoe stood and moved closer to the fence, placing her hands on the wrought-iron bars—*as if I'm looking out from a cage.* The thought intensified her dark mood.

"Without much help from me, I'm afraid. I'm not a good plant mom. I'm neglectful. Fortunately, the impatiens are not impatient. They're rather forgiving. I need that."

David flashed one of his million-watt smiles. "So do I. At least, that's what Christine tells me. She's not forgiving, however. *She's impatient.*"

"No bicycle today?"

"No. I'm going to spend the afternoon with Kathy. She wants to have lunch at Bucky's Circus and go to the beach. She hasn't reached the age where her demands are complicated, such as cars and summers in Paris. I can handle Bucky's Circus and a trip to the beach."

"I'm not doing too well with complicated demands."

"You? You seem the soul of competence. Look at your flowers."

"They're just putting on a show to impress you. Nothing to do with me."

"Zoe," he said, looking at her intently. "Are you always so hard on yourself?"

She was embarrassed. She was so unaccustomed to having anyone pay attention to her that she almost cried. "I guess I do sound rather negative."

"I do too, these days. A divorce can do that."

"I know."

"Well, I've got to head north. I don't want to keep Kathy waiting. She's the only one who seems happy to see me these days."

"David . . ." Zoe wanted to tell him *she* was happy to see him, but she decided against it.

"Have a good time with Kathy. It's a beautiful day for the beach. Probably for Bucky's Circus, too, although I couldn't say for sure."

"Well, if you ever get the urge to fling yourself headfirst into a tub full of colorful Styrofoam balls, or ride up and down in a little helicopter, or run around for an hour screaming at the top of your lungs with a lot of four- and five-year-olds, let me know."

"I'll give it some thought."

She offered a farewell smile and a wave.

Late the next afternoon, she met him again in the passageway. This time, she was outside her door and her arms were full of groceries.

David was wheeling his bicycle. "Well," she said, "you look more like yourself with your bicycle."

"I've had a great ride, all the way to Morton Grove and back. Riding is the best therapy."

Zoe put the bags of groceries down and turned to him. "How did it go yesterday?"

"Oh, Kathy and I had a good time. We always do. But when I took her home, Christine greeted us at the door and reminded me that my soul is in the thrall of Satan. That's her favorite theme, these days."

Satan was a favorite topic for Zoe, too, though not the way Christine meant it. During the dark night of the soul that comprised her college years, Zoe dropped out of theatre school in junior year for complicated reasons and changed her major to English literature.

As an English major, she fell in love with Milton, and she saw in the Lucifer of *Paradise Lost* the perfect image of how she felt herself to be. For, like Lucifer-turned-Satan, she had fallen from grace into negativity, darkness, and shame. She found strange comfort seeing herself in that tragic, but satisfyingly literary, way.

And though that was a lifetime ago, she seemed to be slipping again into her old negativity and self-loathing. But now, on this gentle April afternoon, her habit of gallows humor took over as she chatted with David.

"I've always had a fondness for Satan," she said with a cynical laugh. "He used to be God's favorite, you know. In those days, Satan was named Lucifer, light bearer, and he was the most beautiful angel in heaven until he had the nerve to think for himself. God, the self-righteous old coot, cast him out, and poor Lucifer fell and fell, and finally landed in a lake of eternal fire, which burned and never consumed, and Lucifer found that everything hurt. Especially his feet, which somehow, during the fall, had turned into cloven hooves; and his head, which had grown horns. He was a mess. Poor Lucifer! He paid dearly for his defiance."

She laughed again, aware of the bitterness in her voice. "Unfortunately, I know how he felt."

"Oh, I'm so sorry to hear that! But you know your Milton, I see."

"David, you're the first person I've met, besides the professor who taught the course at Northwestern, who has heard of Milton."

"Well, it's been years. Doesn't generally come up in conversation. But Satan does, at least in my conversations with Christine. She sees Satan everywhere. She's convinced that he's running me. And who knows? Maybe he is."

His voice also became bitter. "She's scary, with her Evangelical fanaticism. We can't seem to have a rational conversation anymore. She didn't used to be like that. She used to be delightful. And funny. And beautiful. She's still beautiful, but there's nothing else left of the lovable Christine. She's a holy terror."

"Poor David . . ."

"Poor Kathy. I can take it. I don't like it, but I can take it. But I worry about what all that punishing God stuff is doing to Kathy. I feel so frustrated."

He shook his head and frowned. "I don't want to put Kathy in the middle of a theological argument. She's only four. What does she know or care about any of that? She just wants to play with her Barbies.

"I don't want to tell her that her mother is full of shit. But she is. Christine's using a fearsome, wrathful, punishing God to control a four-year-old child.

"Kathy's such a good little girl. So eager to please. And her mother rages at her, threatens her for the least thing these days. I don't know what to do.

"Kathy's complaining of headaches. She never had headaches before." He pressed his hands to his own temples.

"Perhaps a family counselor could help."

"Christine absolutely refuses any kind of counseling. Her church fathers won't allow her to seek help outside their tight little circle. They claim the Bible has all the answers. They've cut her off from the rational world. They think they know everything and that all the rest of us are lost in Satan's darkness. It's frightening and insulting."

Zoe had her own strong opinions about this dark aspect of religion but thought it better to be affirming. "David, Kathy still has you. I'm sure that's a great comfort for her. Alas, childhood isn't the idyllic time it's imagined to be in popular thinking."

"Kathy's childhood *was* happy until Christine went crazy. Kathy's still a happy little girl when she's with me."

David frowned and shifted his weight, then turned his bicycle toward his front door. "Oh, Zoe, forgive me. I've done it again; I've poured my troubles out to you. But it's your own fault. If you didn't listen so well, I wouldn't tell you these things. I don't go around telling my troubles to anyone who can't run faster than I can."

Zoe smiled ruefully. "To tell you the truth, David, it's a relief to hear about someone else's troubles for a change. I'm bored to tears with my own."

She paused and took a breath.

"David,"—this was a moment she had let herself imagine—"why don't you come in and I'll make us both some iced tea and you can tell me more. I'm the world's finest iced tea maker. Sun tea. A bit of heaven. *Real* heaven, the kind that brings happiness to the troubled soul. In fact, come to dinner. Stir-fried chicken. Delicious."

"I appreciate your invitation, but I don't want to disrupt your day. You probably have better things to do than taking in a wounded wolf." He started to turn away.

She reached through the bars and lightly touched his hand, which gently opened to hers. Their spontaneous movement and the warmth of his hand briefly enclosing hers stunned her with its intimacy. Then, quickly, they moved their hands apart.

After a moment, she said, "I was just going to have dinner and wallow in self-pity. Builds character to feel sorry for someone else. Please come. Besides, I love animals."

"Well, I'll give you an hour to rethink your invitation. I need to put my bicycle away and take care of some other things. If, after that, you still feel up to a visit, I'll come."

"Wonderful. And if you bore me with your troubles, I'll get even with you by telling you mine."

"How can I pass up an offer like that?"

David came to dinner. Not right away. It was clear he'd taken time to shower and dress; he smelled wonderful. Aramis. Zoe knew men's colognes. Zoe also showered and dressed and redid her makeup. She, too, smelled wonderful. Rive Gauche.

Zoe knew the seduction of fragrances—not that she had any thought of seduction. She no longer involved herself intimately with men going through divorces. They were emotionally tattered and torn. They usually were impotent and penniless and drank too much. In fact, Zoe was completely uninterested in any kind of intimate relationship with a man now. Fortunately, David wasn't a man. He was a wolf.

An hour later, David arrived with a bouquet of red and white carnations and a bottle of wine. He took her hand in his own warm hand and smiled irresistibly. No bravado; simply grace and a trace of shyness. *A gentle man*, Zoe thought.

Zoe noticed everything about people: how they moved, how they spoke, how they smelled, how they entered a room. She had the sensibilities of an artist. Or a co-dependent.

Never mind. David was here now, looking around with interest. Her townhouse was filled with treasures, objects collected from artist friends and her travels to distant places. Hundreds of books and records, the latter mostly of classical music. Photographs.

"You have a remarkable library," David said. "I recognize some old friends in your collection. Rilke, Dylan Thomas, Rumi. I'm always interested in people's books. I learn a lot about them that way. I think we're going to be chums."

"Chums? Oh, yes. Let's be chums."

They went slowly through the three floors, as David discovered and commented. They sat, finally, on the sofa on the middle level, where the living and dining room and kitchen were.

"Would you like some of your wine?" Zoe said. "It looks like a special one."

"Not unless you'll share it with me."

"Well, I promised you sun tea." She paused. "And I don't

drink alcohol."

"Sun tea sounds good. I don't drink much anymore, either. I'm in such a volatile state these days that alcohol makes me snaky. I find myself curled in the corner of the kitchen, darting my tongue out and rattling my tail. It's better not to start at all."

"Clever of you to notice that about yourself. I needed a team of experts. Therapists, blunt friends, AA."

"Well, they've done wonders with you."

"Thank you." Zoe considered saying something disparaging about herself and decided not to, given his comments yesterday. This nice man, his eyes filled with admiration, had just paid her a compliment, and she felt as if she had somehow misled him. Suddenly, tears flooded her cheeks.

"Zoe." David took her hand. "I didn't mean to upset you." He smiled kindly and gazed into her eyes. "Are you all right?"

Zoe shook her head and hurried upstairs to the bathroom to get control of herself.

After some time, she came sheepishly back to the sofa and flopped down, sighing. "Oh, David. How embarrassing." She laughed without mirth. "It's just that I can't handle kindness. Say one kind thing to me, and as you saw, I come apart at the seams. I should have warned you."

She looked down at the floor. "Oh dear. Now, that sounds like self-pity. Shit. I've stepped into quicksand. This is humiliating."

"Zoe, Zoe. It's all right." He put his arm gently around her shoulders. "You know, you remind me a lot of Kathy. She beats herself up, too. And then she cries. And then she gets mad at herself for crying.

"What helps is for me to find her owl for her. She has a little stuffed owl called Memory. I give her Memory and a hug and take her to Bucky's Circus so she can dive into the colored balls. Maybe I should take you to Bucky's Circus for supper. Do you want to?"

Zoe brushed away her tears. "No, thank you. I'm all right now. I've got the veggies and the chicken all cut up. This was just a sudden summer storm. Sun's coming out, now." She smiled to prove it. "Oh! I forgot about the sun tea. Let me get some for you."

She went to the kitchen. He followed, leaning gracefully against the counter, watching her appreciatively as she poured the tea over ice cubes into two Waterford crystal goblets.

"Ah, Zoe; you do the simplest things with elegance. Oh, I'm sorry. I shouldn't have said something nice. I don't want to set you off again. Although you *are* rather adorable when you cry."

She sighed but said nothing as they went back to the sofa. Her emotions were complicated. He carried the two glasses, and she brought the pitcher of tea.

"David, you're perfect the way you are. I'm just frayed around the edges these days. My father had the nerve to die and abandon me to my mother, the former actress, and Adolph Eichmann, my boss."

She was startled at how angry she felt as she spoke.

"Oh. The death of a father. That's a hard one."

"Yes, I was very close to him. We were always allies. I expected him to live forever. The rational part of me knows no one lives forever, but the other ninety-nine percent is appalled at his death. I'm trying to come to terms with that."

"Well, don't be surprised if it takes a couple of years. The death of a parent is one of life's great losses. Robert Bly says the quality of our life is the quality of the grieving we do. I'm trying to do that with my marriage. Grieve it fully and let it go. Of course, because we have Kathy, we can never let the relationship go completely. But I'm afraid the marriage is over. Irreparable damage has been done. That's a kind of death, too, so I know something of how you feel."

"What sort of woman would want to divorce someone who understands these things?"

"A foolish one."

He laughed, and then said, seriously, "I think we create our own heaven or hell. Christine, seeking heaven, has created hell. She sees only what is wrong with the world.

"Not that life with me was heaven, by any means. I've been very dumb about a lot of things. I neglected her badly before Kathy was born. Not from lack of love. I was trying so hard to build for our future that I forgot about our present. I don't blame Christine; she's looking for answers. Unfortunately, the answers she's found leave no room for me. I can't go on her spiritual journey with her. She thinks I've failed her, and I probably have. She hates me for it, but I don't know how to do it any better."

"Oh, David. Such sadness in the world."

He nodded, but then added, "And such joy. Plenty of both."

"So I've heard. I seem to be especially attuned to the sadness lately." Her cheeks felt feverish. She took a sip of the cooling tea.

"I work in psychiatry," she said. "My boss is a psychiatrist; he's president of an association of psychiatrists. I read all the important articles and books in the field. I've been through years of psychotherapy. I'm not anesthetizing my feelings with alcohol these days. As they say in AA, reality is for people who can't handle drugs."

With a smile at her own humor, she took a deep breath and

continued. "I was unprepared for my response to the death of my father. I don't seem to have the right tools. I find the loss overwhelming. Sometimes I worry about my sanity. It's very hard, David."

"Zoe, I've only just met you, but I get the sense that you'll find your way through this ordeal. I see your intelligence and courage. Anyone who has the courage to quit drinking has already shown great daring."

Zoe started to cry again. "Oh, David, I'm hopeless. You've just got to stop saying kind things to me. You're going to ruin me for dealing with the rest of my life."

His voice was gentle. "Zoe, kindness never ruined anything, except what the world didn't need."

He found a paper napkin on the kitchen counter and handed it to her. She blew her nose noisily.

He said, "I don't know anything about your boss, but hearing you call him Adolph Eichmann didn't exactly conjure up a compassionate human being. Have you ever considered getting another job?"

"Out of the question. I'm an indentured servant."

David adopted a mock-gangster voice. "Listen, lady, do you want me to have dis guy put to sleep? Dis is Chicago, you know. Home of da cement overshoes."

Zoe laughed. "I appreciate your offer. But he's not really a monster. Just inconsiderate. In his heart of hearts, I think he appreciates me."

"Don't be too sure. We men can be unconscionable users, I'm ashamed to say. Especially when we latch on to a giver like you. You *are* a giver, aren't you?"

"Dammit, David. Do you have to see right into my soul?"

"I have x-ray vision. I see everything."

"I believe you do."

David stayed for the stir-fried chicken, and they talked until ten when he noted she was tired and said it was time for him to go home.

Before he left, she invited him to go with her to Gudrun's gallery opening.

He graciously accepted, shook her hand, thanked her for the wonderful evening, and left.

CHAPTER 7.
Ancient Murmurs

For several weeks, Zoe saw nothing of David. At last, it was Saturday, June third, the day of Gudrun's opening at the Ancient Murmurs Gallery, a few blocks west of the Magnificent Mile.

Zoe greeted David at the door of her townhouse and stepped toward him into the warm summer evening.

She wore a flowing silk chiffon dress. David was elegant in a dark suit, a touch of silver at his temples, though Zoe imagined he wasn't older than perhaps forty.

His blue eyes smiled as he murmured, "You look beautiful."

"You do too, David," she said, as she slipped her arm through his. "I'm glad you've joined me for this adventure. I've never seen Gudrun Skjerne, though we've talked many times on the phone. I've formed an image to go with the voice."

"How old is she?"

"Fifties, maybe. But there's a girlishness about her. She's not the least bit formidable, despite her scientific credentials. My boss isn't impressed that she's also a recognized painter. But I find that the most intriguing thing about her."

They took a cab to the gallery, which was up a short flight of steps, on the first floor of a loft building. The large rooms were filled with elegant people, all obviously having a marvelous time. Somewhere nearby, a string quartet was playing Mozart. The rooms smelled delicious, a combination of freshly brewed coffee, perfume, and oil paint.

A smiling young woman looked up at them expectantly from a table near the door and gestured to a guest register. Zoe wrote in the book and handed the pen to David. She was eager for a glimpse of the paintings.

"Let's look around a little first," she said. "I'd like to see her work before we meet her."

They squeezed past prosperous-looking men and sparkling, richly dressed women, all with their backs to the artwork, artworks themselves.

"This is quite an occasion," David murmured. "Gudrun Skjerne must be something special."

They stopped before the first painting. It was a small, square canvas showing a woman's face, partly turned, as if she were kissing her dark reflection in a mirror, lips meeting lips. The pale face was framed with golden hair, and its blue eyes gazed tenderly into the green eyes and dusky face of the reflected shadow-self.

Zoe stood before the painting for a long time, her feelings flowing like seaweed stirred by deep currents. David walked on, standing with quiet intensity before the next painting.

Zoe did not move. *That's me*, she thought.

It wasn't that the woman in the painting looked like Zoe. It was as if Gudrun Skjerne had painted Zoe's inner self.

For a while, the room, with its golden hoard, its laughter, its music, went away.

After a long time, Zoe moved on, stopping before a large, torn-paper collage with handwriting in a voluptuous script that ran like a border around the outer edge.

> Isn't that just like you! You've got all the selfishness
> of the Fuñels and the Colettes combined! Oh, why
> did I ever marry you?

In the center were layers and layers of pale pastel papers in subtle tones of mauve, pink, peach, purple, yellow, and violet. The colors of sunsets. Or bruises.

The handwriting continued,

> Because, my beloved, I threatened to blow out your
> brains if you didn't.

The writing formed a kind of opening into the bruised, suggestively sexual center.

Zoe recognized the quotation. It was from Colette. Colette's first husband, Willy, whom she had married when she was nineteen, had been almost twice her age. He abused and exploited her physically, mentally, emotionally, and sexually.

Zoe had never forgotten what Colette wrote, somewhere, about him: "In a few hours an unscrupulous man will transform an ignorant girl into a prodigy of licentiousness. Disgust will not deter her; disgust has never been a hindrance. Like morality, it comes later."

Moving from picture to picture, Zoe lost track of time. The paintings whispered secrets. Many had the mythic quality of dreamscapes. Often, a woman moved through the shadow-world, pale and sad. Or she sat, pensive and distracted. Or she stood, facing away from the viewer, looking into the distance, her back conveying vulnerability and profound suffering.

Often, Zoe's eyes filled with tears.

David's hand, softly taking hers, drew her into the present.

"You were so absorbed I hesitated to break your concentration, but I've found Gudrun, and she's eager to meet you." He guided Zoe through the crowd toward a small, smiling woman, who reached both hands toward her.

"Zoe! Zoe, Zoe. How good of you to come. Your David tells me you've been here for a while. Have you had any champagne or a raspberry tart?"

Gudrun's hands were warm and soft; she smelled of jasmine. She embraced Zoe.

"Hello, Gudrun. I'm delighted to meet you. From our conversations, I imagined you to be tall."

"Tall? Why did you think that?"

"Because you're so accomplished."

Gudrun laughed. "Oh, pooh. I'm just a workaholic. I can't bear to be idle. Not a good sign, I assure you. Very neurotic."

"Your work is amazing," Zoe said. "I find it very moving."

Gudrun held Zoe away from her and looked keenly into her face.

"I'm so glad. Sometimes I feel a little guilty because I simply report what I see inside of me. It seems it should be more difficult, this business of creating an artwork. Of course, I spent years in life-drawing classes, so I ought to have learned something."

A smiling man stood expectantly at Gudrun's elbow. Seeing him, Zoe said, "Gudrun, I'd love to take you away somewhere so we can have a long talk, but you should be collecting everyone's admiring comments, so I won't monopolize you. Perhaps when you come to the office, or sometime before you go back to Denmark, when we're not on the Chief's agenda, I'd love it if you could find time to have lunch or dinner with me."

"I'd love to; and we have that meeting with Walther on Monday morning. I'm sure he'll have very many important things to do and will rush off somewhere, so perhaps we can find some time then. But now, please stay and enjoy our bribes."

Zoe and David moved slowly through the crowd.

"A remarkable artist," David said. "A remarkable person."

They made their way into another room, where there were only a few people talking quietly, drinks in hand. The room was peaceful. There were a dozen small, matted watercolors and charcoal drawings.

The focal point of the room, clearly placed for impact, was a single, huge canvas, perhaps five by seven feet, alone on a center room divider. There was a long, polished wooden bench before it.

The painting showed a pale girl standing larger than life, looking not at Zoe but beyond her, with an expression of—not fear, exactly, or grief, or loss, or surrender. And yet all of those were suggested. The girl's feet were bare. In one hand, she held a hyacinth blossom. In the other, a pomegranate.

Around her shoulders, like a shawl, was the body of an egret or a swan. Its wings and splendid feathers made a regal cloak. Its long neck and head fell like a pendant between her breasts.

Beyond the girl was an arched doorway. The air was full of mysterious, archaic symbols. Beyond those, a pale sliver of moon hung in the night sky.

At the girl's feet, sitting with its back turned to the viewer, and looking up at the moon, was a wolf.

Encompassing the girl was the figure of a looming man. Not a frightening man, exactly, but a shadowy one. Like the girl, he had an enigmatic expression on his partly hidden face. He was large, and his arms came around her body. His dusky hands rested intimately on her lower pelvis, across her hips. His naked feet were a dark echo of her smaller, pale ones.

Zoe's first response was physical—a powerful contraction in her lower abdomen that pulsed upward through her body, leaving an aching pain that did not subside for several minutes. She reeled back from the painting and, almost falling, sat down heavily on the bench. A series of trembling spasms shook her entire body. She felt faint.

Seeing Zoe fall back, David sprang toward her, taking her hands. "Zoe, what is it? Are you ill?"

"I don't know," she gasped, shaken by another spasm. "I have to get out of here."

She stood and ran from the room, struggling to control her panic and slow her pace. She didn't want to attract attention as she made her way through the crowd and down the front steps, out onto the sidewalk. In the warm night air, the panic subsided.

David came up beside her and put his arm around her shoulders.

"I'm all right now, David. It's passing. I'm all right."

He looked at her intently and then took her into his arms, saying nothing. Zoe felt his emotion.

"It was a panic attack," she said. "I'm all right now." She let herself be held. One last spasm shook her, and then she took a deep breath.

He released her and she started walking rapidly away from the gallery, with David beside her. After a moment, she slowed her pace.

"Oh, David. You must think I'm certifiable. Every time we're together, I seem to come unhinged."

"I'm just glad you're all right. You frightened me."

"I frightened myself. Something about that painting—"

"It's an amazing painting," David said, "but it obviously has some special meaning for you. Imagine the chaos if everyone who saw it had the same reaction you did."

Zoe laughed, but her voice had an edge of hysteria as she said, "All those elegant people with champagne glasses and plates of canapés casually strolling into the back room and suddenly rushing out again, trembling and weeping.

"The gallery would have to post a warning sign: 'Pregnant women and people with a heart condition, asthma, or high blood pressure should not view this painting without permission from their physician.'

"Or, in my case," she added, "their psychiatrist."

They stood at the corner and laughed and laughed, and then Zoe wept. And they walked again.

"Do you want to stop someplace and talk?" David asked. His voice was kind.

"You mean you're not afraid to be seen with me in public? You aren't afraid I'll run amuck at any moment?"

"Nah. You're a piece of cake."

She laughed again, this time with genuine amusement.

"Fruit cake," he added affectionately, and gave her a brief hug.

But he saw that Zoe, despite her laughter, was still devastated, so he hailed a cab and took her home.

The following Monday morning, Zoe and Gudrun met with the Chief. He spent a couple of hours questioning and challenging them about the Congress. By the end of the meeting, they had agreed upon the plans.

He asked Zoe to take Gudrun to lunch at the restaurant in his private club. The Chief had a spare apartment in the building, so he enjoyed special privileges, such as access to that gorgeous restaurant. He offered his apologies for not joining them.

The two women sat at a window table, where they could look down on the penthouses and swimming pools and rooftop gardens of the fabulously wealthy. In the background, Lake Michigan glittered in the sun.

Despite the view, however, Zoe was completely absorbed in her conversation with Gudrun. Everything about Gudrun was beautiful. Her compassionate eyes; her musical, slightly husky voice. She had small hands with fingernails that were unadorned and bluntly cut, hardworking hands that spoke as expressively as her words. She had a soft, womanly body, with unabashed breasts and hips and a small waist. Loveliest of all, her face. Gudrun had laugh lines around her mouth and eyes, lines of character, of intelligence, and of fifty-some years of living in the world with intensity and good will.

"Were you pleased with the opening of your exhibit?" Zoe asked, after they had ordered iced tea and salads.

"Oh, yes, yes, yes. The gallery people were most gracious and fussed over me outrageously.

"And I was happy to see many of my Chicago friends. I lived for fourteen years in the States, attending college and medical school and doing my residency at the University of Illinois, and then more graduate work at the University of Chicago."

She paused, then added, warmly, "I was particularly pleased that you and David could come. That was kind of you."

"It was unforgettable, Gudrun."

They finished their salads, which were followed by coffee and mints.

Hearing about Gudrun's time in the States, Zoe offered a bit about herself, her Ohio childhood, her journey to Chicago to study theatre at Northwestern, her stumbling into her present career, her brief marriage and divorce.

Gudrun listened intently. Sipping the rich, fragrant coffee, she was quiet for a few moments.

Then she said, "Zoe, I have a project you might find interesting. May I tell you about it?"

"Of course."

"You said you trained as an actress, but your life took you in another direction. Perhaps you'd be willing to return briefly to acting to participate in a little play I've created for a conference of psychologists at DePaul.

"I'm hardly a playwright, Zoe, and my play is hardly a play. It's just three short acts, rather symbolic, without scenery or costumes, and lasting not even an hour. It's the centerpiece of the conference, which has the fancy title, *Incest, Feminism, and the Sacred Feminine.*

"Since I'm organizing the conference, I thought this play could spark some interesting comments. I must confess that my real reason is that I'm writing a book on incest. The conference and the play are subtle ways to pick the brains of my colleagues and maybe get some interesting perspectives for my book."

Gudrun's suggestion stirred Zoe's remembrances of her Northwestern years, that anguished time when she had decided, in junior year, to change her major from theatre to English literature. Her life until that decision had been completely focused on a career in the theatre. She'd gone to Northwestern because of its famous theatre department, after performing in summer stock and community theatre since childhood.

But at Northwestern she realized she did not love the theatre enough to give her life to it, and this realization had left her without a plan for the rest of her life, but with painful experiences and a wounded sense of self.

Later, in therapy, she came to the realization that her *mother* was the truly gifted actress. Her mother had acted in a theatre troupe for several years after college and later had performed on the Chautauqua Circuit. Her mother had always spoken of that time as the happiest time of her life.

Considering this in therapy, Zoe realized how truly screwed up she was. Despite the disdain she felt for her mother, she still had planned to give her life to the fulfillment of her *mother's* unrealized ambition and potential.

But all that was too complicated and painful to mention to

Gudrun. She said, simply, "I haven't acted for years. I've closed the door on that chapter of my life."

"It was just an impromptu thought when I heard about your background in the theatre, especially that you attended the School of Speech at Northwestern. Several of my actor friends are Northwestern graduates, and they very much value the training they received there.

"Again, Zoe, we won't *stage* the play; it's just a table-reading, with my good buddies from the theatre company *l'Air du Temps*."

Gudrun paused to take a sip of coffee and give Zoe time to reconsider the invitation. She added, her voice warm, encouraging, "It could be fun, Zoe. Something you and I could do together besides carrying out Walther's big plans."

Another pause. "But no pressure, dear. Either way, perhaps you'd like to see the script? I'd love to have your thoughts on it. I have an extra copy with me. Would you be willing to read it?"

"Of course, Gudrun. I'd be honored."

Gudrun handed her the script.

Zoe put the lunch check on the Chief's account, said goodbye to Gudrun with an embrace, and took her time going back to the office, still enveloped in Gudrun's warmth and charisma.

CHAPTER 8.
Encounter with the Sacred

Encounter with the Sacred:
A Mythic Journey of Healing
by Gudrun Skjerne, MD, PhD

*Prologue. The scene opens in darkness. Over the sound
system comes a woman's rich, contralto voice.*

CONTRALTO VOICE
Land birds grow silent.
The sea smells dark and bitter.
The Boatman comes
to cast the child adrift.
Face hooded, looming
on the shadowed shore,
he draws the anchor up
and tosses the tether onto
the bed--its flowered quilt
a garden from her mother's hands.

It happens nightly.

CHILD'S VOICE
(*calling*)
Mother, Mother!

CONTRALTO VOICE
She always calls.

BOATMAN'S VOICE
(*menacing*)
Your mother cannot hear you.

CONTRALTO VOICE
The child knows what comes next.
The sea erupts in flames.

CHILD'S VOICE
(*desperate, yearning*)
Mother! Mother!

CONTRALTO VOICE
The water roils and hisses.

BOATMAN'S VOICE
(*cruel*)
Foolish child, when will you learn?
Your mother sleeps.

CONTRALTO VOICE
All night,

the bed-boat drifts
in the burning sea.

ACT I.

(Mythic time. Lights come up on a gray landscape, with a chorus of six old women pacing back and forth aimlessly. The only object on stage, other than a stark, simple arch upstage, is a single, skeletal tree with six empty seed pods, which gape open and dangle from its jagged branches, suggesting devastation and despair.)

OLD WOMEN
(wringing their hands, pulling at the dusty, gray rags covering their hunched frames)
Cold. Cold.
Never did we imagine our lives would come to this.
Our wombs are empty,
our breasts hang dry and flat, bereft of nurturance.
Cattle give birth to monsters.
The fields, once fertile, begrudge us even thorns.
We eat thistles and sand.
Birds are silent.
Clouds of dust roll down from the mountains,
blinding us, filling our lungs with grit.
Our hearts are broken.
We would be fevered
were we not so cold, so cold.

(Hecate enters slowly through the dark arch as

the chorus women finish speaking. She is fearsome,
gaunt, regal. She walks slowly, supporting herself
with a jagged cane. As she reaches center stage, she
strikes the floor once with the cane and addresses
the audience, her fierce voice harsh with outrage.)

HECATE
Only I saw what happened.
Only I know how she was taken,
torn from her mother's golden world,
her innocence ruined in darkness,
her childhood shattered,
her youth made old without wisdom,
the bud of her body forced to open too
soon, too soon,
her petals, fragile as insect wings,
ripped away
and flung to the winds of hell.

(strikes the floor with her cane and looks around,
rageful)

She was happy, laughing with her friends
in the sunlit field,
and she noticed a blossom more beautiful
than any she had seen before.
And she left her friends, for the blossom
enthralled her, called her to her doom.
As she stretched her fingers to touch its beauty
the earth beneath her opened, gaping wide
and he came forth--he and his chariot
and thundering horses black as pitch.

(*strikes the floor with her cane*)

He seized her, carried her,
terrified and struggling, down.
The earth closed mutely behind them--
closed, as if nothing had happened.
But he, Hades, King of Darkness,
claimed her as his queen,
to rule over shadows.

(*Hecate strikes the floor four times to end her speech.*)

CHORUS
So terrible an act, to take a child before her
    time.
Her inconsolable mother, Golden Demeter,
knows not her daughter's fate.
The grieving mother wanders an empty world,
    bereft.
And everything is wrong.
Yes. Everything is wrong.
And all of us, once beautiful and young ourselves,
    must suffer.

(*Lights down.*)

ACT II. SCENE I.

(*The present. Margaret, a psychiatrist, and Kay,*

her client. Lights come up on Margaret's consulting room, filled with artwork, books, and light filtering through leaves from trees visible outside the many windows. On a table, stage left, is a huge vase of freshly cut golden mums. The atmosphere of the room is comforting, richly calm, peaceful, an expression of Margaret herself. Margaret and Kay are seated stage right in large leather armchairs, facing one another. Next to Kay's chair is a small table with a box of tissues.)

KAY

(twenty pounds overweight, about thirty-five, attractive and voluptuous as an overripe peach, large breasts stretching the buttons of her blouse, sits, tense, on the verge of tears long unshed) I'm sick and tired of being sick and tired, Margaret, as we say in AA. I've been sober for five years, and I should feel better than I do. My life is still a mess. You are my hundredth therapist. I'm having an affair with my thousandth married man.

MARGARET

(slim, all seriousness and professional efficiency, about fifty years old, long, dark hair contained in a twist and held at the back of her head by a tortoise-shell clasp; streaks of silver-gray frame her face; she wears horn-rimmed glasses; her voice is a rich contralto) That's a lot of therapists. A lot of married men.

KAY

You're my first woman therapist, by the way. Not my idea, but the psychiatrist who referred me to you turned me down. Said he wouldn't touch me with a ten-foot pole. Well, he didn't exactly say that, but that was the impression I got. It probably concerned him that I'd had an affair with my former therapist. I finally realized that I was helping the therapist more than he was helping me. We terminated when I suggested he should be paying me.

MARGARET
(*doing her best not to show shock and outrage*) An affair with your therapist?

KAY
Not his fault. My MO. And . . . forgive me for saying this, but I should let you know up front I'm not sure I want to do therapy with a woman.

MARGARET
(*voice still neutral, nonjudgmental*) Why not?

KAY
(*wipes frantically at herself, as if trying to brush bugs off her blouse*) Girl-cooties! Yuck.

MARGARET
(*loses her professional neutrality and bursts into laughter*) "Girl-cooties"? What does that mean?

KAY

I don't much care for women. Oh, I love 'em. But Margaret, they make such a mess of things. When they write books, there are typos, bad editing, amateurish illustrations . . . you know. Everything has to be agreed upon by committee. It takes a million years to "reach consensus," so no one can get anything done. I love 'em, but I wouldn't want to be one.

MARGARET
(*wry*) I don't want to alarm you, Kay, but you *are* a woman.

KAY
(also wry) Oh. Say it isn't so!

(Lights down.)

ACT II. SCENE II.

(*The Underworld. Hades, King of the Underworld, and Persephone, the abducted daughter of Demeter, Goddess of Grain. Persephone is now Queen of the Underworld. As the lights come up, Hades looms large as he stands behind the pale Persephone, who is fragile and very young. Hades has one hand on her belly, the other cups her small breast. He wears purple velvet robes and a golden crown. She also is dressed in deep purple, but her gown is diaphanous, her nakedness barely hidden by the folds of the fabric. She, too, wears a golden crown, much smaller than his. At stage left is a table set for a banquet, piled high with fruit, other food, flowers, and goblets of wine.*)

HADES

(*his voice velvety, seductive, cajoling*) Come, my queen. Share the feast. You have rejected all my offerings--my jewels, my love. You have taken nothing into your sweet body since our wedding. Except, of course . . . (*he smiles lasciviously*)

PERSEPHONE

Am I your queen? Was that a wedding? Have you offered me love?

(*Hades removes his hands from her body and steps beside her. He picks up a pomegranate from the banquet table, and, with a slash of a jeweled dagger, cuts it open. With another slash, he cuts a small piece and offers it to Persephone. His formerly seductive voice is insistent, has an edge of threat.*)

HADES

Here, my queen. Taste this, at least. Take the ruby flesh into your mouth; allow the savory juice to moisten your lips and tongue. Let the sweet juice course down your lovely throat. Crush the flesh, the dark seeds between your teeth. Partake, my love.

PERSEPHONE

(*drawing back*) No. (*turns her head away, then murmurs dreamily, as if to herself*) I am so hungry. I promised myself I would not succumb. I was not willing. And yet--

HADES
(*lifting the fruit closer to her mouth, his voice commanding*) Eat.

PERSEPHONE
(*pleading, to the empty air*) Mother . . . Mother. (*a pause, then urgent*) Mother! I am so hungry. Is it wrong to taste this one small thing? Perhaps it will give me strength, or please him, or help me avoid his vengeance, or even save my life? (*a long pause*) Mother! (*again, a pause*) You do not answer me.

HADES
(*his voice more intense, insistent*) Persephone. Taste this pomegranate. Eat.

PERSEPHONE
(*yielding at last*) But six seeds, only. Six seeds. (*she eats, then cries out in fear*) Oh! What have I done?

(*Lights down.*)

ACT II. SCENE III.

(Margaret's consulting room, nine years later. The lights come up on Margaret and Kay, seated in the same brown leather chairs facing one another, the box of tissues on the table beside Kay's chair. Margaret appears much the same; her hair is a bit grayer and

still contained in a twist at the back of her head;
she wears the same horn-rimmed glasses. Kay, however,
is much changed. No longer overweight, she is slim
and dressed tastefully in a tan pantsuit with a
jacket and pale lavender sweater. Her golden hair
is a cap of curls around her face, which is serene
and smiling, though a little flushed.)

MARGARET

So, Kay. How do you feel now that our work together
has been completed?

KAY

(*handing her an envelope*) I've written a poem for
you, a kind of summary of our nine years together.
Margaret, I'm so grateful. I thought, when I came to
see you that first day, that I was getting second-
best, working with a woman therapist. But now, I see
that you, with your special skills and intuitions,
your embodiment of what is wise and beautiful and
strong about a woman--I see that working with you
was exactly what I needed. You've helped me know and
accept myself as a woman.

MARGARET

(*opening the envelope and drawing out a folded paper,
briefly reading, smiling; she looks up*) Kay, on your
perilous and challenging nine-year journey of healing,
you did what was essential: you encountered the
Goddess. And by the Goddess, I mean what symbolizes
and personifies the sacred feminine, the valuing of

your feminine self, which was lost in the relationship with your father. In the situation of incest, the father separates his daughter from herself by way of their dark shared secret, and he separates her from her mother and from her family and friends. Yes, even from society at large. He carries her down into his dark world.

(*Margaret, still holding the letter, stands and walks behind her chair, as if it were a podium from which she is giving a lecture. She leans toward Kay for emphasis.*)

MARGARET
The abducted one must be retrieved from the father's dark world. She must be reunited with her mother. And because in incest, too often her own mother cannot retrieve her, the rescuer must be another woman. A woman of power. Oftentimes it is a woman therapist, who becomes charged, in the containment of the consulting room, with sacred energy--that is, with the necessary life-energy to make the profound and essential change in the client's sense of self. I think that has happened here, Kay, with us.

(*Having delivered this important message, Margaret returns to her chair and sits. Kay says nothing, but listens intently, realizing that what Margaret is saying is the truth of her experience in their work together.*)

MARGARET

In our relationship, Kay, it wasn't me as a human being you encountered as the Goddess, but what I represented to you--what I symbolized. Through our relationship, over time, in the closed, protected, and sacred container of the consulting room, you've been able to take in and integrate into yourself my love and valuing of you. You experienced my witnessing of your story and my protectiveness, as Persephone experienced her own mother goddess, the great goddess Demeter, who moved heaven and earth to win her daughter's freedom and at last was able to bring her back from the Realm of Shadows, into the light.

(*Kay smiles and nods but still says nothing, realizing that Margaret has more to say.*)

MARGARET

And, dear Kay, in the consulting room, in my own way, I moved heaven and earth to bring you back from that dark realm into which your life circumstances had abducted you. And you have shown great courage and have done years of difficult work with much dedication. You've always soldiered on, even when the going was rough. And now you're ready to have your life, to live it fully.

KAY

(*her voice intense*) Thank you, Margaret. You've been a magnificent Goddess. Of course, I know you're human,

but when I needed the Goddess, you became the Goddess.
I experienced the sacred feminine through you.

MARGARET
(*with a rueful chuckle and a shake of her head*) But
Kay, you weren't easy. I worked hard to gain your
trust.

KAY
(*amused, teasing*) What do you mean, I wasn't easy?
It took me only five years to begin to trust you, to
not sit with my arms crossed over my chest to protect
myself from "girl-cooties." (*They both laugh.*)

MARGARET
(*leans forward and hands the poem to Kay*) Thank you
for this poem, Kay. Will you read it to me?

KAY
(*takes the folded page and opens it. As Margaret did
earlier, she stands, to give the poem proper emphasis*)
There's one stanza for each year . . . (*she reads,
a little self-consciously at first*)

> *One.*
> The blossoming field is bereft,
> like the mother and the budding playmates.
> The girl--she was so young--

(*Kay's voice becomes unsteady, and tears come to
her eyes*)

The girl--she was so young--
gone. Carried down into darkness.

(*repeats the last line and interrupts herself with
intensity*)

That young girl was me, Margaret. She was me!

(*takes a deep breath before continuing, her voice
becoming stronger and steadier, as she is drawn into
the feeling of the poem*)

> *Two.*
> How dreadful his act.
> The dark face of love
> is shame. Soft violence.
> *Three.*
> One throne is empty.
> Where is the Queen?
> Weeping,
> dreaming uneasy dreams.
> What has become of her child?
> *Four.*
> Someone has seen!
> The Watcher at the Crossroads,
> Ancient Wise One, Crone,
> who knows the hidden cause of suffering,
> sees into the depths.

(*again interrupts herself*)

That's you, Margaret, the Watcher at the Crossroads.
Not an ancient crone, but surely wise with ancient
wisdom.

(*Kay takes a deep breath before continuing. With each
stanza, she becomes more sure of herself, more engaged
in offering Margaret the poem.*)

KAY

> *Five.*
> "Look to Hades, that
> thief of delicate beauty
> who cannot bear the light,"
> the Watcher says.
> *Six.*
> Aiee. The Queen, distraught,
> falls into darkness of her own.
> But another aspect of herself,
> called Mother Goddess,
> now awakens, powerful and wise.
> *Seven.*

(*fully engaged in the poem by now, her voice intense
and dramatic*)

> A clash of powers, a struggle.
> The girl, a maiden, now,
> grown wise beyond her years
> while imprisoned in darkness
> must at last be freed.

The triumphant Goddess wills it.
Eight.
The maiden, pale as death,
steps into a blaze of light,
into the field from which,
as a girl, she once was carried down.
Nine.

(*chokes back tears as she reads the last stanza*)

"Welcome, my daughter," the Mother Goddess
     cries.
"Savor the sunshine. But darkness is within
     you now.
You are forever changed. Take your dark
     knowledge,
darling, your travel between the worlds,
to become a guide to those who are
fallen into darkness of their own. Lead them,
as I have led you, back again into the
     light."

(*hands the page back to Margaret*)

Oh, Margaret, I wanted to say something to honor our
time together, which has been so amazing, so healing.

MARGARET
(*also standing, embracing Kay*) Thank you, Kay. It's
been a privilege to work with you. And the hopeful thing
about coming through dark times is that sometimes,

often, I think, we do, indeed, become Wounded Healers. In the dark places to which we are carried, our hearts are somehow opened to compassion, and what we learn there can indeed become a boon, a gift, to others. Knowing you as I have come to know you during our time together, I feel certain that will be true for you.

(*After another quick embrace, Kay exits Stage Left. Lights down.*)

ACT III.

(Mythic time. The Underworld. Upstage, center, is the arch with darkness behind it. The six chorus women of Act I now wear colored scarves around their shoulders. The women are divided into three pairs. The first pair, with spring green scarves, represents the Maiden aspect of the Celtic Triple Goddess; the second pair, with gold scarves, represents the Mother aspect; and the third pair, with purple scarves, represents the Crone aspect. The tree, which was desiccated and skeletal before, is full of bright flowers and jeweled fruit. The women dance a graceful but solemn dance, spiraling two by two into a center, where Hecate stands with arms raised. Then they spiral outward again.)

THE TWO MAIDENS
(chant in soprano voices while the others are silent but all the while moving in the spiral dance)

Call me the Maiden; I am the springtime, I am life
blossoming.
(they repeat the chant three times then stop
chanting but continue dancing)

THE TWO MOTHERS
(chant in alto voices while the others are silent,
but as all dance the spiral dance; after repeating
the chant three times, they stop chanting but
continue dancing)
Call me the Mother; I am the nurturer; I am the
cherisher.

THE TWO CRONES
(their voices are deep as they repeat their chant
while the others are silent, but all three pairs
dance the spiral dance)
Call me the Crone, I see things hidden; I govern
endings, eternal beginnings.

(After three repetitions, they stop chanting. Then
all three groups chant their own words together in
harmony, again and again. After a few minutes, the
dance and chanting end. From the archway, upstage,
Persephone steps through in her diaphanous lavender
gown. Hecate, who has been waiting center stage,
turns and places a gold scarf around Persephone's
shoulders.)

HECATE
(arms upraised)

Rejoice. Life has returned to our blighted land.
Lambs are born. Gardens are lavish with greens.
Worms press upward; chicks burst shells. Fish,
awakening in murky depths, swim free. Water
sparkles. Our daughter, Dark Maiden, steps once
again into the light.

CHORUS
(together, slowly, clearly)
We can scarcely believe our eyes!
We thought she was lost forever to shame.
But look! She is shining.

HECATE
(lowers her arms, and gestures toward Persephone)
Alas, there is darkness behind her eyes,
and a tear trembling in her smile. No one returns
from the Realm of Shadows unchanged. She can never
be the same. But now, do you see? She is even more
beautiful, and sadly wise, for she knows
the journey into darkness. Also, she knows the
return to blessed light.

(All turn to face the audience. The Chorus and
Hecate raise their arms in triumph and rejoicing.
They chant together, their voices growing ever
stronger, as Persephone stands center stage, silent
but smiling.)

CHORUS AND HECATE
No one returns from the Realm of Shadows unchanged.

She, Beloved of Life, returns with wisdom for
us all: deep knowing, compassion, healing love.
She knows the terrible cost of suffering, knows
the awful descent into darkness. She guides us--
ourselves once wounded, wandering, lost--now healed
and joyous,
again, into the light.

CHORUS AND HECATE
(together, they raise their arms in rejoicing)
Now healed and joyous, again into the light.
(Persephone raises her arms and joins the others.)

ALL
(chant)
Again, into the light! Yes!
Again, again, again, again,
Again, into the light! Yes!
Again, again, again, again,
Again, into the light!

(Lights down.)

CHAPTER 9.
Invitations and Revelations

Having finished reading Gudrun's play, Zoe wept for a long time, for reasons she didn't fully understand. Of course, Gudrun's writing was beautiful and moving, but Zoe's strong response was surely because of something more.

It all felt terribly familiar: Kay calling women "them" as if she were, somehow, not a woman.

And especially the opening, with the frightened child calling for her mother, and the Boatman saying, *Your mother cannot hear you. Foolish child, your mother sleeps.*

How did Gudrun know? *How did she know?*

These thoughts haunted Zoe for days.

The following Sunday morning, after so much intensity, Zoe felt emotionally ragged. She needed the quiet comfort of her garden.

Also, she needed to stop thinking about the office. Instead, she needed to reflect on all that had been stirred by reading the play. In the play—it was uncanny. She couldn't believe how, in that first scene between Margaret and Kay, Kay talked about her affair with the therapist and the "thousand" married men. Zoe, somewhere in her earlier life, had had an affair with one of her many therapists and with an assortment of married men.

And at some point she had no doubt tried to brush "girl cooties" off her blouse, or at least had considered it.

And she'd voiced the same complaints about the time-consuming and annoying need, in women's groups, to achieve consensus. She'd participated in several over the years. Lately, she avoided them, begging off because of the demands of her career, but really because she found them tiresome.

And she had never even considered therapy with a woman. Like Kay, she'd felt she would be getting second best. Of course, she had not known Gudrun then.

The play also had clarified that incest separated the daughter from herself, and from her mother, her friends, and society at large. It caused years of shame and dysfunction in the daughter's life.

This sounded terribly familiar and seemed to call into question her whole life—or explain it.

Suddenly, the vibrant bells of St. Michael's interrupted Zoe's ponderings. The bells continued for a long time, and Zoe sat on the low stone step to simply rest in the beauty of their music. Then, the bells stopped, and everything seemed to catch its breath.

Zoe forgot Gudrun's play and her own troubling thoughts. She opened her eyes and looked around. The begonias and impatiens, the geraniums and marigolds and pansies, were blooming their little hearts out. *Demeter's jewels*, Zoe thought. Demeter seemed like a loving mother, smiling down, cherishing and blessing them all.

And Zoe had the briefest flash of a memory of her mother standing in the backyard garden so long ago also smiling, and seeming, Zoe thought, like Demeter, to bless the miracle of the seeded earth and growing things.

And in that breathless moment on this Sunday morning, to her astonishment, Zoe felt herself to be included in that blessing.

Moments later, in a flurry of quick, light footsteps, a little girl appeared out of the shadows of the passageway, all breathless and rosy, like a windblown blossom. She had a pinafore with dainty flowers of pink and lavender and yellow, a fluffy skirt, lavender anklets with lace, and lavender bows in her golden hair. She wore shiny patent leather shoes.

The child stopped suddenly outside the fence and looked intently at Zoe.

"Hello," she said. "I'm Kathy. I'm four years and eleven months and three weeks old." With a sense of great importance, she added, "I'm going to be five next Sunday. On Father's Day." She had David's vivid blue eyes and earnestness.

"Hello, Kathy. I'm glad to meet you. I'm Zoe. Happy birthday, next Sunday. Are you excited about becoming five?"

"Oh, yes. My daddy and I are going to have a party at Bucky's Circus. Will you come?"

Zoe laughed. "That's very generous of you. Especially since we've only just met."

"Oh, I know who you are," Kathy said with authority. "Daddy told me. He said we should take you to Bucky's Circus. I could show you how to jump into the colored balls."

"That sounds like fun."

"One of your plants is broken," Kathy said with concern. Zoe turned toward where the little girl was looking. A stalk of the big coleus plant lay on the sidewalk, wilting. Zoe reached through the fence and picked it up.

"Oh, the poor coleus!" She spread the limp stem with its drooping leaves across her palm and held it so Kathy could see. The leaves had a center of bright magenta, an intricate border of purple the color of midnight, and a ruffled edging of pale green.

"Maybe an animal broke it off," Zoe said. "But do you know what, Kathy? There's something special about the coleus plant. If we take this broken stem and put it into a vase with some water, it will grow roots in a few weeks. Then we can plant it again, and it will grow and thrive and be more beautiful than ever. Isn't that wonderful?"

"Yes. May I have it? I'll put it in water at my daddy's house and we'll grow it and make it well. Then we'll put it back into your garden."

"What a good idea. Of course, you may have it."

Kathy thanked her as David came up to the fence, carrying a pink and purple Barbie suitcase. He set it gently down.

"I see you two have met," he said. "I told Kathy you might be in your garden."

"Hello, David. Yes, we've met. Kathy has already shown me she's a very kind person. She's offered to nurse the broken coleus back to health."

Kathy held the wilted stalk up for him to see, gently petting the leaves with a small finger. "Daddy, if we put it in water, it will grow roots, and we can plant it again in Zoe's garden." Kathy looked earnestly into David's face.

"That's great, Kathy." He stroked her hair.

"Zoe is going to come to Bucky's Circus with us for my birthday party."

Zoe looked hesitantly at David. "Well, maybe we should be sure, first, that my coming won't disrupt any other plans."

"It would add to the festivities," David said. "Christine is giving a kiddie party for Kathy on Saturday afternoon, so Kathy and I decided to have our own party next Sunday, after church. It would be especially nice to have you come too. Can you?"

"Oh, please do!" Kathy said, jumping up and down. "Bucky's Circus is *so* much fun."

"Since you've made me feel so welcome, I'll be happy to. I love to celebrate birthdays. I think it's wonderful to have your own special day when everyone tells you how glad they are that you're here in the world. I'm sure everyone feels that way about you, Kathy." Zoe smiled at Kathy.

"My daddy does." David knelt and gave her a hug. "I sure do, Kathy." His voice was soft and suggested the depth of his feeling.

"Your daddy told me about the fun things to do at Bucky's Circus," Zoe said. "But I'm afraid that I'm probably too big for the helicopter that goes up and down."

"But not for the colored balls. You can jump into the colored balls."

David said, "They usually want people to be eight or younger, but maybe we can get special dispensation for Zoe."

He smiled at Zoe and then turned toward his front door. "Well, we'd better let you tend to your garden. Come on, Kathy, let's get you out of your fancy church clothes and into some play duds so we can go to the zoo and visit our family."

"Oh, goody." Kathy ran to the door of David's house.

"Your family?" Zoe asked.

"The wolves." He called after his daughter, "We're wolves, aren't we, Kathy?" Kathy let out a little howl.

Zoe laughed, delighted. "That's a wonderful howl, Kathy. You must teach me how to do that."

"I will. Come *on*, Daddy. Let's go see the wolves." She danced around, howling, in front of the door.

"I'm coming." He picked up the Barbie suitcase, which looked very small in his big hand.

Then, speaking softly to Zoe, he confided, "Christine gets *furious* when we howl. She accuses me of encouraging Kathy's animal nature, which, according to her reading of the sacred texts, must be controlled and, if possible, stamped out. What you heard just now was a small expression of defiance. But Kathy understands that we must be discerning about when and where we howl. She's very canny."

He reached through the fence and briefly touched Zoe's hand. Warming to this touch, she said, "Have a good time. And say hello to the wolves for me."

On Monday, after another meeting with Zoe and the Chief, Gudrun invited Zoe to lunch. She chose a small restaurant that specialized in crepes, fabulous coffee, and flaky French pastries.

She wore an elegant dress. She'd swept her pale blond hair back to show fiery opal earrings. On her wrist, bracelets gleamed warm gold. When the waiter had seated them at a quiet corner table and they had ordered, Gudrun asked Zoe her thoughts about the play.

"Beautiful, Gudrun. You spoke volumes in a few short scenes. And what's most amazing to me, and a little embarrassing, is that somehow, you captured my spirit in Kay, though I never did therapy with a woman. All those male therapists I spent time with, trying to get uncomplicated, would not have made possible a transformation such as Kay experienced. They would not even have thought in terms of the sacred feminine . . . or the sacred anything else."

"Alas, it's not likely to happen with a male therapist."

"Anyway, it's a wonderful play, Gudrun. Congratulations."

Zoe wasn't ready to mention her powerful emotional response to the Boatman, and the child futilely calling for her mother, and the other troubling parts. That was too raw for this lovely restaurant on a social occasion.

"Thank you, Zoe. And what do you think? Will you play my Kay? I think you'd be perfect for the part."

"Oh—that I don't know. I'm no actress, these days."

"I was hoping you'd consider it, Zoe. Northwestern gives you excellent acting creds. I can see you as a wonderful Kay. And, as I said, I've also enlisted the help of some delightful theatre friends from my years in Chicago. They're now members of *l'Air du Temps*. You no doubt know of that respected acting company."

Zoe did.

The waiter brought coffee cups and filled them with dark,

steaming coffee. Gudrun thanked him with a radiant smile, then turned her attention back to Zoe.

"Years ago, when I was going to school in Chicago, I was struggling with whether I wanted to become a doctor or a painter. Later, I decided to be both, but back then I had to steal time from my medical studies for painting classes at the School of the Art Institute.

"I also spent a lot of time with my many actor friends, designing sets for their plays. We had such fabulous times, and they're still dear friends after all these years."

She sighed happily.

"And several musician friends from those years are generous enough to enrich the script with their music. There's a gorgeous score by my composer friend, Charlie Stark."

The waiter was back with their crepes, setting the plates before them, winning another beautiful smile from Gudrun, who, Zoe noted, was gracious even in the briefest of encounters.

For a few moments, they gave their attention to the crepes and the raspberries in *crème fraiche* on delicate lettuce leaves.

"Delicious," Gudrun murmured. "Are you loving it, Zoe?"

"Yes, Gudrun. I'm loving it."

After talking briefly about other things, Gudrun returned to her play.

"The whole thing won't take a lot of time, Zoe. Two weeks of rehearsals and then the performance on Sunday, July 16. These are professionals, and everyone is busy, so we'll work fast. Then I must go back to Denmark.

"Please say yes, Zoe. I think you'll enjoy my friends, and I know they'll enjoy you. And most important, I'd love to work with you on something other than Walther's big projects. Something for the creative and more interesting parts of us."

"I don't think I'd be up to it emotionally, Gudrun. I was in tears by the time I finished reading your script.

"But I'm in tears a lot these days, in the aftermath of my father's death a few months ago. Oh, the death was not unexpected. He had cancer, and he'd lived a good life. I'm doing my best to deal with it. But I'm rather fragile, emotionally, and also, Gudrun, considering that I had quite a strong response to some of your paintings at the gallery, I'd probably need to be carried away from rehearsals in a straitjacket."

"I'm sorry to hear of your father's death, Zoe. Of course, you are grieving. It's to be expected. And I *am* a psychiatrist, you know. Tears are my stock-in-trade; I'll know how to handle you, if you need handling. But I doubt that will be the case. Doing the play may even be therapeutic. As for my paintings, I'm not surprised you had a strong response. I intend that. I consider it a compliment. Yes."

She sighed again, with her characteristic in-drawing of breath.

"I'm not a professional actress, Gudrun. I'd be out of my element with your *l'Air du Temps* friends."

"Zoe, you'd be an amazing Kay. It will make me so happy for you to say yes."

While Gudrun beckoned to the waiter to bring cups of fresh coffee, a tremendous struggle went on within Zoe. Along with the anxiety stirred by the thought of being in a play was an equally strong desire to please Gudrun.

Also, Zoe felt flattered that Gudrun seemed genuinely to want her to *be* in the play, and she realized, to her astonishment, that she had a sudden powerful yearning to return to the experience of working with other actors to bring a script alive. She was surprised to discover she missed that experience.

And she *had* shown promise, despite her savage self-criticism. She would not have given so many years to the theatre without at least a few successes. So, after a long pause, Zoe amazed herself by saying, "How could I say no, Gudrun? I love to make you happy."

"Oh, Zoe!" Gudrun clapped her hands, and her golden bracelets danced and jingled. "Yes, yes. I am happy."

Zoe's heart was racing. "I can't believe I've said yes, Gudrun. I'm terrified."

Gudrun laughed. "Oh, Zoe. Pooh! You face more terrifying things every day with Walther. We'll have a wonderful time doing this together. You'll see. And what's especially wonderful about the play is that Charlie's music is truly gorgeous, reminiscent of Mahler's *Kindertotenlieder.* That will add to the emotional impact, and to the enjoyment."

"Gudrun, how wonderful. I know that music. It means very much to me. And now that I've actually said yes, and now that I know about the music and, of course, with your wonderful script, I'm even excited."

"So it's official, Zoe," Gudrun said with delight. "And since you've said yes, I'd also like to have you play the part of Persephone. A little wicked trickery on my part. I'm rather shameless."

She laughed happily. "But just three small scenes for Persephone. My friends will play the other parts and will be the chorus. They're delightful people and I love them very much. You will too, and they'll make you feel like one of them. No need to memorize anything. We'll work from scripts."

"Gudrun, you're the only person in the universe who could have gotten me to say yes. You're irresistible."

Gudrun laughed again. "Yes, I am. Everyone says so. And now that it's settled, I must send you back to Walther, so he won't think I've stolen you away from him. He wouldn't like that. But oh, Zoe, this is a worthy cause. The conference is important, and the ideas we will present can heal lives."

Gudrun called for the check. She paid the waiter and thanked him for his attentive service, adding a tip as generous as her smile.

Then, with a warm, jasmine-scented embrace, she led Zoe out of the restaurant and hailed a taxi for her.

Getting in, Zoe watched as Gudrun turned to walk back through the neighborhoods she had so loved during her student years, to the loft apartment where she was staying with a friend.

Several days later, Zoe sat across from her friend Anna, having lunch in the Solstice Room at an elegant department store, sipping broth from a delicate demitasse cup with a gold rim.

Zoe had invited Anna to meet her here, because a year before, in this same restaurant, Anna had revealed to Zoe that she was dealing with a traumatic issue that was tearing her own life apart, the recent realization of childhood incest with her Baptist minister father.

Anna had shared Zoe's angst-filled college years and had suffered her own dark night of the soul at Northwestern. And though their lives had taken them in different directions—Anna now had a PhD degree in chemistry and worked at Northwestern University Medical

School—they still met from time to time for soul talk.

"Anna," Zoe began, after they had savored the broth and the popovers with strawberry butter and the scoop of chicken salad on a croissant and were drinking coffee before returning to their offices, "This is hard for me to say, and even harder for me to believe. But I think—" She took a deep breath. "I think I might have been abused by my father. Sexually."

Just saying the words shamed her.

Anna impulsively leaned toward Zoe with a look of compassionate concern. "Zoe, I'm so sorry." She didn't ask for evidence or proof. She simply waited for Zoe to go on. Behind thick lenses, her kind eyes never left Zoe's face.

"Anna, last year, when you told me about your own experience, it was the furthest thing from my mind that I'd ever be saying this to you. But some weird things have been happening to me, and I'm thinking they might be related to sexual abuse."

She leaned back in her chair and closed her eyes, as doubt flooded through her.

"I don't know," she continued, hesitantly. "My father died this past February. Ever since, I've been having fainting spells, strange physical symptoms, crying jags. Since this is the first time I've experienced the death of a parent, I didn't know what to expect. I hoped for a while these things would pass.

"But it's been four months, now, and it's getting steadily worse. And it's frightening me, Anna. Sometimes I feel as if I'm going crazy. I'm beginning to think my strange experiences might be about sexual abuse. Nothing obvious or violent, like rape. I don't even know what, exactly."

Anna nodded thoughtfully. "Sometimes it takes a while before the memories come . . ."

"And the nightmares," Zoe said. "I wake at four in the morning, after nightmares I don't remember, and I'm crying, or overwhelmed with fear, or even sexually aroused, but not pleasantly. It's terrible. And work is a disaster."

"When I started sessions with a therapist who specializes in incest issues, if I'd been working in a regular office, I would have been fired. But I was working alone in my laboratory, doing research that involves only computers and percentages. The only reactions were between the chemicals. I cried for months, alone in my lab, and I couldn't think about anything but incest."

She sat back for a moment. Then, as if realizing how grim this sounded, she said, "But it has gotten better, Zoe. It gets better with time and the right kind of work."

"With time and the right kind of work, Anna? I don't *have* time for this. I have so much *real* work to do for my career!" Zoe's voice was a sob. "I don't even want to think about it. I feel so horrible, even mentioning it to you. And I feel as if I'm betraying my father by saying anything."

She felt short of breath and lightheaded. Her hand trembled as she picked up the coffee cup. The coffee by now was cold. She quickly put the cup down. The waitress had already left their checks on the table and had finished waiting on them. Not wanting to encourage them to linger, she no longer refreshed their coffee.

Then Zoe added, "If my *mother* knew I was having this conversation, she'd kill me. And oh, Anna, what if I'm wrong?"

Anna was silent for a moment. Then she said, in a voice

unfailingly calm and kind, "One of the hardest and most important things, Zoe, is coming out of hiding. Carrying the secret of incest is a terrible, isolating, lonely burden. The healing begins when you tell it for the first time. So today, you've taken a courageous and very important first step." She smiled reassuringly.

"Thank you, Anna." Zoe's eyes filled with tears. "Oh, dear. And I seem to cry all the time."

"I know. That's part of the healing process, too. You need to cry and to grieve the death of illusion, the betrayal of innocence, and the shattering of that most sacred bond, the bond between parent and child. You need to mourn the loss of the parents you wanted to have and should have had and didn't.

"And then you need to bring the wounded child out of the darkness where she's been hiding all these years, frightened and alone, unable to tell her terrible secret. You need to comfort her and promise her that no one will ever harm her again, because now you'll be taking care of her and protecting her."

Anna smiled and picked up both their checks. "And in time," she continued, "you'll experience a freedom such as you've never known before, and there will be no more dark secrets. You'll be free to live your life fully and joyfully."

"Thank you for your encouragement, for your friendship, and for lunch, Anna. But I don't even know for sure that I *was* sexually abused. Maybe I'm making it up. My mother tells me I've always been overly dramatic."

"People don't make this sort of thing up, Zoe. All of us go through self-doubt. It's too painful to think parents we loved and trusted could betray us so profoundly. We don't want to think it could be true. And when you live in the world of incest, you learn to doubt your own senses."

"But Anna, I don't have any memories. I don't even know *why* I'm thinking something so terrible about my father. We *loved* each other. I adored him. And I was the most important person in his life. He told me that. And I know he meant it."

Zoe shook her head and looked away, distractedly. "I'm sorry I even mentioned this. I'm probably just being paranoid." She laughed grimly.

The restaurant was now almost empty. Someone had turned on a vacuum cleaner and was moving among the empty tables.

Gathering the two checks and her purse, pushing her chair back from the table, Anna stood. "Zoe, it's all right. You're not crazy. But go slowly with this. It's difficult work. Painful work. Don't push yourself."

Zoe also stood, and they both paused. Anna touched Zoe's arm and, speaking in a low, gentle voice, almost as an afterthought, she said, "Zoe, I go to an incest survivors' support group on Saturday mornings. Looking across the table into the faces of people who understand what you're going through because they've been through something similar, and who don't shame you for telling the truth, or try to minimize its importance, is very helpful. Essential, in fact. It helps to validate your experience. If you think you'd like to come some Saturday, let me know."

They stopped at the hostess's desk while Anna paid the checks, then they went down the escalator, past the glittering jewelry counters and expensive purses and out the front door onto Michigan Avenue.

Zoe hugged Anna. "Thank you again for lunch, Anna, and for hearing my story. But another support group?" She shook her head and shuddered, though the bright summer day was very warm. "I don't think I could stand it. Especially about something so yucky. Incest doesn't have the glamour and pizzaz of alcoholism."

Anna smiled and cocked her head, appreciating the irony. "I know, Zoe. I know. No pressure, my friend. No one chooses this. Or does the recovery work willingly. But it *does* help. The support group is just an option."

"I'll think about it," Zoe said.

The following Saturday morning, to her astonishment, Zoe found herself seated in the incest survivors' meeting. The day after her lunch with Anna, and after a restless night of arguments with herself, she phoned her friend and asked about the meeting. Anna was encouraging, and they met for breakfast beforehand and chatted casually until meeting time.

The meeting room, on the first floor of the hospital a few blocks from Zoe's office, had a conference table, around which a dozen middle-class men and women sat quietly, absorbed in their thoughts, and seeming to Zoe quite normal, considering their reason for being together.

Yet, almost to a person, both the men and the women held in their arms stuffed toys—teddy bears, or Raggedy Ann or Raggedy Andy dolls, or zebras, or unicorns. One woman rested her chin on the soft head of a large pink pig with a blue bow around its neck.

Even Anna. She pulled out of her purse a cloth doll in a gingham pinafore with braids and dimples and a little pocketbook. Anna leaned toward Zoe and whispered, "The child in us was betrayed and hurt; that child must be comforted and reassured. That's why many of us bring stuffed animals, dolls, and toys to these rooms."

Waiting anxiously in the silence, Zoe thought to herself that she had never had a stuffed animal. The thought struck her hard. "Why didn't I have a stuffed animal when I was a child?" She puzzled about this for a few minutes. Then she answered herself. *Because I never had a childhood.*

As everyone waited in meditative silence for the meeting to begin, Zoe tried to remember something about that childhood. Grade school, for example. Again, the thought struck her, as it had several times recently, that she had no memory of her early school years.

Who was my second-grade teacher? She didn't know.

What did my second-grade classroom look like?

What was third grade like? What did I learn?

What were the names of my friends? Did I even have friends?

All she remembered was being lonely and confused and afraid of the other children.

Then a searing, long-forgotten memory came to her. It was first grade. She was hiding on the playground long after school had adjourned, afraid to go home, trying to avoid an older girl who'd been following her home every day. The girl taunted her, stepping on the backs of her shoes, pulling her hair, and sometimes hitting her.

Today, that would be called bullying, she said to herself. But she had accepted that abuse as her due, bearing it with silent surrender, and telling no one, especially her parents.

With second grade, all memories stopped. She discovered, as she waited, that the memories did not resume until sixth grade, when her breasts started developing. With great persistence, she'd sewed tucks in the brassieres her mother bought her, hoping to flatten her breasts and make them go away.

When she menstruated the first time, the first sight of blood made her think she was dying. When her mother explained that this was a normal part of being a woman and she would bleed each month during her childbearing years, Zoe wept with outrage and humiliation at what she felt to be the ugly betrayal of her body. She shouted at her mother, "I don't want to be a woman!" and she closed herself in her bedroom in despair.

Childhood, for Zoe, meant suffering, humiliation, and loneliness, with no hope of anything better ahead. Realizing this now, as memories flashed through her mind, Zoe quietly wept for herself. A woman across from Zoe wept, too, with deep, abdominal sobs.

"Welcome to each of you, and especially to the newcomers."

It was the young woman chairing the meeting, who had come at last into the room and joined them at the table. As she sat down, she nodded warmly at Zoe. "Our program is based on the twelve steps of Alcoholics Anonymous, which have been adapted to help those of us who are victims of incest become *survivors* of incest."

There were readings, but Zoe had trouble listening. Her head was a cacophony. What she remembered of the meeting later was the comforting atmosphere of the room. The feeling of safety. And the tears, as people spoke of their struggles with daily living, with brutal employers, with fearsome nightmares, with abusive intimate partners or therapists, or with devastating visits home to their families of origin.

These were all expressions of the terrible price of their betrayal as children, still being exacted decades later.

Zoe especially remembered their faces looking back at her with acceptance and understanding as she told them, briefly, that this was her first meeting, and that she was wondering if perhaps the missing piece of her life's puzzle might have fallen into place for the first time.

They smiled and nodded.

At the end of the meeting, they told her they hoped she'd come back.

CHAPTER 10.
Into the Forest Where It Is Darkest

Something profound was happening to Zoe. Somehow, an inner life was stirring in her depths, beneath her conscious mind. This inner life seemed to have its own agenda, to be intentional and dynamic.

Zoe did not realize consciously that this was happening. Still, there was subtle evidence of it, in physical symptoms, in flashes of awareness that were gone as soon as they happened, or inexplicable surges of feeling, as if stirred by ancient tales told around a campfire at midnight, fading to nothingness in the morning light.

And now, near dawn one June morning, when so much in her outer life was challenging her, when the life she knew and understood was turning to ashes, when her sanity seemed to be fragmenting, and when Gudrun was offering hopeful and challenging possibilities, Zoe was taken down again.

No encounter with a spider or fainting spell carried her to her inner world this time. It happened in a half-remembered dream.

This time, she came to inner awareness as her younger self on the lawn of an estate crowning a bluff overlooking the sea. A long road lined with trees and formal gardens swept up to a great manor house. Regal stone steps and a wide terrace framed a huge carved oak door with a crest above it.

The great house drew her because she heard music. Someone inside was playing the piano.

As she touched the heavy front door, it swung open on its own, and she stepped into a grand entrance hall. Except for the music, there was no sign of anyone.

Zoe went cautiously through several rooms, each of which had a great fireplace; oak-paneled walls; and enormous, gleaming crystal chandeliers suspended from elaborately sculptured ceilings. High above the floor, lit from above by shaded brass lamps, hung huge portraits of tall, aristocratic men and women with sensitive-looking horses and dogs.

Zoe discovered the music room at last, in a part of the house that looked out toward the sea.

Cat, whom she recognized, somehow, as the young archer, her friend and rescuer from fading encounters in the Dark Realm, sat at a grand piano, her eyes closed as her hands moved over the keys.

Zoe recognized the music: the Moonlight Sonata. Cat leaned into the keyboard, her face expressing the music's moods: sometimes brooding, sometimes rapturous, sometimes demonic. Zoe was astonished that Cat could draw such power and intensity from the keys.

Cat finished and opened her eyes. "Well, hello. Would you like to sing?"

She opened a small score and played the melancholy first notes of a Mahler song and softly sang, "*Nun will die Sonn' so hell aufgeh'n.*"

Zoe moved behind Cat where she could see the music and sang,

…als sei kein Unglück, kein Unglück die Nacht gescheh'n!

She paused as Cat played an aching interlude. Then the song continued,

Das Unglück geschah nur mir allein! Die Sonne, die Sonne,
sie scheinet allgemein.

Once again, Zoe translated to herself, *the sun shines brightly, as though night's darkness had brought no misfortune. The sun shines for everyone else; I alone suffer misfortune and loss.*

The song stirred great sadness in Zoe. *You must not surrender your heart to the darkness,* it said. *You must bathe your heart in eternal light.*

After another sorrowful piano interlude, Zoe sang,

Ein Lämplein verlosch in meinem Zelt!

A little lamp went out in my world…

Such sorrow. Sorrow and loss.

Zoe sang with Cat's accompaniment for a while. Then Cat suddenly stood and said, "Zoe! How could I forget something so important! The old woman has summoned you. I must take you to her."

"What old woman?"

"Oh, Zoe, you're always asking foolish questions. The Dark Mother. This house is *hers,* little fool. All this is *hers.* She's an unholy terror. Very powerful. Your friend, the Spider King, is her consort. Even he is terrified of her."

"Do you mean the Spider King didn't die when you shot him? But everything went up in flames."

Cat laughed bitterly. "He's like a cockroach. There's no getting rid of the weirdo pervert creep."

"Cat, how could he have survived that fire?"

"Zoe, you little numbskull, the Spider King can't be killed. He's eternal. I shot him to get his attention. I thought he should know what he was doing to you was wrong. Don't you understand?"

"No!" Tears flooded Zoe's cheeks.

"Oh, little one, little one." Cat held Zoe, stroking her hair. "My poor little one. You seem so small, so innocent, so helpless. And now, the Dark Mother has summoned you. Oh, my poor darling. I must take you to her."

"Child, you must go on a journey. Something must be set right. Only you can do it."

Cat had left Zoe alone with the old woman, who was fierce and very angular. Her gray hair was bound into a tight braid and twisted like a crown of snakes around her head. She sat before a fire on a huge, carved oak throne.

To Zoe, it seemed the flames emanated from her.

The old woman was dressed in black. Across her bony chest was a breast-piece of gleaming dark copper. In her right hand, she held a heavy oak cane. At each end was the head of a dragon, and the shaft was formed of their long dragon bodies, with legs and tails entwined around one another. The dragons seemed to breathe and undulate in the firelight.

"Why am I here?" Zoe whispered.

The old woman thumped her cane on the marble floor. A hollow echo pulsed through the vaulted room.

"You do not ask," she said, not unkindly. "You listen. Something of great value has been stolen. You must retrieve it."

The old woman's voice was sharp and clear. She was hawk-like; her yellowed skin was taut over the arch of her nose. The knuckles of her hands were swollen, her fingers twisted.

"It will be a dangerous journey," she said. "Perhaps you will fail. Perhaps you will not have the cleverness to figure out what is required of you; perhaps you will not have the courage to endure the sufferings; perhaps you will not have the willingness to keep going when you are bone-tired and have lost your way."

"Must I go?" Zoe asked. Her voice was tremulous.

"You must."

Zoe fell to her knees, weeping with fear.

"If you stay behind," the old woman continued, "you will die a slow death, more agonizing than the worst ordeals you will endure on the journey, and more fearful than the most dangerous monster you will confront on the path. That I promise you."

"What must I do?" Zoe was weeping with anguish now.

"You must travel the Road of Trials until you have reached your destination. Then you must retrieve what has been stolen and bring it back."

"What is my destination?"

"You will know that when you come to it."

"What has been stolen?"

"You will know that when you find it."

"Do *you* know?"

"That is neither here nor there."

"I can't do this."

"Nonsense." The old woman thumped the cane. "It will be very interesting. You'll learn many valuable lessons. It won't be all ordeals and monsters. And if you do what you're asked to do, the reward will be very great."

She thumped the cane again. "Come, come. Don't be such a crybaby. Let's drink together. A toast to you and your journey."

She lifted a heavy crystal goblet from the table beside her. The moment the old woman's fingers touched the goblet, it filled with a golden liquid. She handed it to Zoe. "Drink, child."

Zoe drank. She had never tasted anything so delicately sweet.

The old woman took the goblet from her and drank the rest herself. She closed her eyes for a few moments, as if in deep meditation. "You have tasted hope."

She placed the empty goblet back on the table and slowly stood up.

"Now, you are to go out the front door and cross the lawn and enter the forest where it is darkest."

She opened her arms to Zoe, who went to her and allowed herself to be enfolded in a hard, uncomfortable embrace. The breastplate pressed painfully into Zoe's cheek. The old woman kissed Zoe on her forehead and patted her face roughly with her twisted hands. Then she murmured, "You have my blessing, child. Now, go."

Zoe made her way to the mighty entrance hall and heavy front door, which swung slowly open and thudded closed behind her.

Outside, it was dusk. Nighthawks screeched and darted; bats flew in erratic, jagged patterns against the darkening sky. There were twinkling spots of light where fireflies rose and hovered in the mist over the lawn, and the bushes and trees hunched and seemed to move back and forth like large, lumbering animals.

Zoe sat on the top step of the marble stairs that led down from the terrace to the crushed stone walkway. Beyond the lawn, the forest loomed, dense and unknown.

"I'm to go into the forest where it's darkest," Zoe said aloud to herself. "I can't."

"Sure, you can, kiddo." It was Cat. She sat down beside Zoe on the step and put her arm around Zoe's shoulders.

"Cat! Oh, Cat! I've got to go on a journey. I'm so afraid! I must go into the forest. I must bring back something that was stolen. I don't even know what it is, or where I'm supposed to go. The old woman said if I don't go, I'll suffer. I'm terrified to go, and I'm terrified to stay."

"If the old woman says you must go, you must go. But don't worry. I'll help you when you need me."

"You mean, you'll come with me?" Zoe sat up and looked eagerly into Cat's face.

"No. I can't come with you. But I promise to help you when you need me. Haven't I always been there when you needed me most?"

"Yes. You have. Oh, Cat. Yes."

"Come on, kiddo. We have little time. Let's not be glum. Let's walk around the garden together for a few minutes."

Zoe went with Cat down the steps onto the path. Their feet made soft crunching sounds as they walked. Cat draped her arm protectively over Zoe's shoulders, and gradually they moved toward the forest. The darkness became intense.

Cat turned one last time to face Zoe. Suddenly, she drew back, letting go of Zoe's hand. As Zoe watched, she shifted shape so quickly that Zoe's mind could not comprehend it. She became a bobcat, springing away into the underbrush.

Zoe came to consciousness on her bed, weeping.

"Oh, God," she sobbed. "What's happening to me? I'm so afraid."

PART II.
The Road of Trials

No passage without blood.
No growth without pain from demons.
No change without injury or wound.

Mircea Eliade
Personal communication
with Robert Moore, 1984

The truth is, in order to heal, we need to tell our stories and have them witnessed . . . The story itself becomes a vessel that holds us up, that sustains, that allows us to order our jumbled experiences into meaning.

Sue Monk Kidd
The Dance of the Dissident Daughter
New York, Harper One, 1996. p 201

CHAPTER 11.
Surprises

Father's Day. And Kathy's fifth birthday. The birthday, Zoe knew how to celebrate. She would go with David and Kathy to Bucky's Circus and have presents and cake.

Father's Day was more difficult. It was Zoe's first Father's Day since her father's death.

She decided to phone her mother, who hadn't spoken with her, except briefly, for several weeks. Zoe didn't look forward to the call, but she felt a stirring of sympathy. Her mother had lost her husband of forty years, the man she had, perhaps, loved.

Zoe phoned before time for church, so Mrs. Thomas would be able to tell her church friends that her daughter had been thoughtful enough to call.

"Oh, I'm all right, Zoe," her mother said, a tremble in her voice. "A little sad today, but someone is coming in a few minutes to give me a ride to church. And I'm looking forward to my cruise."

"Your cruise?"

"Yes, I'm going on a Caribbean cruise. Didn't I mention it to you?"

"No. But hooray for you, Mother. That's wonderful."

"Your dear father couldn't bear the idea of being 'trapped on a cruise ship,' as he said, even for a week. He could never just sit and relax. Always had to be busy, busy, busy."

"I know. Anyway, the cruise sounds exciting. I'm so glad you're doing it."

"Well, my friend has come to the door. Thank you so much for calling, dear."

When her mother hung up, Zoe felt, once again, as if she did not know her mother. Elizabeth Thomas seemed not to be the person Zoe expected her to be.

And her father? She had always thought of him as her loving teacher, a saintly man who was devoted to her. Not the emotionally distant, punishing, neglectful, or absent father some of her friends suffered. He never spanked her, nor had she given him cause to. He took time with her, devoted himself extravagantly to her education. He always made it clear that she was the most important person in his life.

But now, she wasn't so sure about any of it. She had *thought* having such a father had been her good fortune. But something troubling was happening to her image of him.

Late morning, Zoe heard a thumping on her front door and opened it to find a dancing Kathy, scarcely able to contain her excitement. This would be the happy part of Father's Day.

"Are you ready? It's birthday time. My daddy already gave me a *beautiful* lavender bike. I wish you could see it, but I had to leave it at my mom's house."

Her golden hair was caught up in two ponytails that bounced as she danced about. She wore pink tights, a skirt with little Pink Panthers everywhere, and a short-sleeved blouse with pink sparkles across the shoulders.

"Hello, Kathy," Zoe said. "Happy birthday. Yes, I'm ready. Would you like to come in while I get my things?"

"Yes." Kathy skipped in. She stopped in the middle of the first floor, looking around. "It's different from my daddy's house. You have lots of things."

"You're right, Kathy. I have lots of things. Come on upstairs with me."

Kathy danced over to the steps and scrambled up, ahead of Zoe. When they reached the second level, she ran immediately to the dining room table, on which were two packages, one especially large, wrapped in brightly colored paper, with a huge green bow; and a second, smaller one, also brightly wrapped. Kathy didn't touch the packages, but Zoe could see she was intensely curious about them.

"Oh, presents," Kathy said.

"The big one is for you."

"Oh, goody. When may I open it?"

"Can you wait until we're all together? I imagine your daddy would enjoy being there to see. The other one is for him."

"A present for my daddy? What is it?"

"Oh Kathy, let's let it be a surprise for both of you."

"Okay. I have a Father's Day present, too. I made it myself."

Her tone changed suddenly, from exuberant to sober. "It's to keep him from being lonely."

"Do you worry about your daddy being lonely?"

"Yes."

Zoe waited for a moment, wondering if Kathy would elaborate. She did not.

Zoe finally said, "I'm sure your present will mean a lot to him, especially because you want it to help him."

The little girl went to the window and looked out toward her daddy's house. Zoe could see a reflection of Kathy's wistful expression in the glass.

Zoe picked up her purse and the package for David and went to the kitchen to get the box with a small birthday cake. She called from the kitchen, "Kathy, would you like to carry your present?"

"Oh, yes," Kathy said, cheerful again, putting her hands on the sides of the box and lifting it carefully off the table. "It's big, but not very heavy."

Kathy cautiously stepped down the stairs, one by one, holding the package over her head so she could see her feet. Zoe shifted her purse and packages to free a hand, ready to catch hold of Kathy if she made a misstep, but she did not admonish Kathy to be careful.

Zoe's father had always warned Zoe about everything. *Zoe, watch your step. Don't fall. Hold tightly onto the railing.* He would have insisted on carrying the package for her, would have held her arm too tightly as she went down the steps.

Zoe sometimes wondered how she had learned to do anything for herself back then. But instead of making the child Zoe more careful, her father's constant warnings had made her reckless and militantly independent.

Kathy waited while Zoe opened the front door. She carried the big box across the passageway, calling, "Come *on*, Daddy. Let's go."

They all walked together to David's car. Kathy sat in the back seat, with the big package beside her and the smaller one on the floor. The box containing the birthday cake was at Zoe's feet.

Inside Bucky's Circus, a hundred small children swirled around the rooms in various stages of ecstasy or tragedy. There was a big dining room with long tables set up for half a dozen birthday parties, piled with hats and noisemakers and paper cups filled with nuts and brightly colored candies.

David located the birthday table set up for the three of them and a small pizza was served. Kathy received birthday presents from Bucky: a golden princess hat with a long lavender streamer trailing from it, and a wand with a silver star at the tip.

Huge balloons floated everywhere. At one end of the room was a stage filled with bigger-than-life animal characters, and the famous Bucky himself, a seven-foot purple clown with smiling cheeks and sad eyes. Bucky and the animals, by way of their inner humans, put on periodic theatrical performances, singing and dancing, wisecracking, and blinking their huge eyes.

The adults watched with glazed smiles while the children played happily underneath the stage, where a designer, in a moment of genius, had constructed crawl spaces and tunnels.

Another room of the sprawling converted warehouse was filled with dozens of child-sized rides: a Ferris wheel, a carousel, rocket ships, helicopters, and elephants.

In yet another room was a small castle with climbable ramparts, dungeons you could creep into, and a maze to get lost in. And there were the requisite swings and slides and teeter-totters in the castle yard.

David gave Kathy several coins, and she disappeared into the crowd. Conversation was impossible in the tumult, so Zoe and David smiled at one another and gestured a lot. After a few moments, Kathy reappeared, breathless and needing a pause, so David took photos of her looking adorable with her princess hat and wand.

The climax of the afternoon was the dive into the colored balls. Kathy had worked her way up to this event, filling herself to overflowing with happiness on the rides. Then she carefully removed the princess hat and handed it and the wand to David for safekeeping. Taking off her shoes, she stood poised for a moment at the carpeted edge of the tank, which was filled with hundreds of red, yellow, and blue Styrofoam balls, each perhaps five inches in diameter.

Kathy counted to three, took a deep breath, then flung herself with rapturous abandon into the tank. The balls splashed over her, like soft waves, and she disappeared into the bright colors, swimming among them, reemerging on the other side of the tank and clamoring up over the edge.

She turned, and, checking to see that David and Zoe were watching, waved. Then she flung herself in again, turning this way and that, like an otter. She climbed out and ran to them, grabbing Zoe's hand and pulling her eagerly, saying, "Come *on*, Zoe; you jump in, too."

"No, Kathy. No." Zoe laughed. "I'm a grown-up. This is for little people."

"You can do it, too. Daddy did it, didn't you Daddy? Come on, Zoe. They won't mind. Come *on*."

Zoe looked at David.

He gave her a gentle push. "Try it. I think they allow one jump per adult."

Zoe took off her shoes and stood at the edge of the tank. For a moment, she felt herself to be her five-year-old self, at the end of the pier at the lake. It was summer, at camp, and she was just learning to dive. She lifted her arms above her head, cupped her hands, holding her fingers together like the prow of a boat, curved her body forward, took a deep breath, and dived.

She sank down among the balls, and they covered her until she could see nothing but a blur of bright colors. There was a dusty odor, and the sounds of the room were muffled. She closed her eyes and floated happily in the pool of balls, not moving.

"Zoe, are you all right in there?"

Kathy gently brushed the balls away from Zoe's face, peering down at her anxiously.

Zoe struggled to sit up and moved unsteadily to the edge of the tank, where David reached down and, taking her hands, lifted her up and out almost effortlessly. She felt a strange, bubbling joy welling up in her and then she was awash with laughter, just at the edge of sobbing.

She got hold of herself and said, breathlessly, "That was great, Kathy. You're right. It was a lot of fun."

Kathy clapped her hands and brought Zoe's shoes to her, saying, "Now, let's open presents."

"Kathy," David said, "would you mind if we go somewhere quieter to open presents and have some supper? It would be nice to be able to talk with each other, and it's quite noisy here. Besides, all they have is pizza."

"Okay, Daddy," she said with good humor. She sat down on the carpet and put on her shoes, painstakingly tying the bows, the tip of her tongue protruding in her concentration. David, with an expression of consuming adoration, snapped another picture.

They found a rustic restaurant with dark wood walls and pretty stained-glass lamps. The hostess led them to a corner booth with curved leather seats. Kathy sat between Zoe and David, eyeing the big present. A cheerful waitress took their order and Zoe slipped her the box with the birthday cake and five pink candles.

Zoe moved the silverware and glasses away and placed the big package in front of Kathy, who stood up on her knees and eagerly pulled off the ribbon and bright paper. "Oh, goody!"

She reached into the pink tissue paper and pulled out a large stuffed green dragon. It had big golden eyes, a long red forked tongue, quilted satin wings, a soft white tummy, and a long, curling tail.

"Oh! Oh! I *love* it. I just *love* it." Kathy wrapped her arms around the dragon, which was almost as large as she was. Zoe and David caught the water glasses before the dragon's tail swept them away, and Kathy sat down again, still hugging the dragon tightly. She placed her cheek against the benign face of the creature. "I just *love* it."

She grew suddenly quiet, holding the dragon without moving, seeming to be deep in thought. Zoe looked at David. Neither spoke for a moment.

Then David said, "Well, Kathy, it seems Zoe knew just what you would like."

Kathy stirred from her reverie and looked into Zoe's face with an inexplicable expression. "Thank you, Zoe."

She petted Zoe's cheek tenderly. In that moment, Zoe surrendered her heart to Kathy, unquestioningly and forever.

"I'm so glad you like the dragon," Zoe said. "Something told me you might. I think it's about the best thing in the world to find just the right present for someone you care about."

They were all quiet for a moment. Then Zoe said, "Now, shall we give your daddy his presents?"

"Yes! Oh, goody! Me first."

Kathy gave the dragon a hug, then lovingly put it on the seat beside her and handed David a little package, which he had brought in from the car and just now placed unobtrusively on the table. Kathy had decorated the white wrapping paper with bright flowers and yellow suns with sunbeams streaming from them.

"I colored the paper with my crayons," she said proudly.

"It's beautiful, Kathy. I'll keep the paper always." David gently loosened the wrapping, careful not to tear it. Inside was a clay pancake with the impression of a hand, and the words, "For Daddy from Kathy."

"Kathy, is this the impression of your own hand?"

"Yes." She twinkled with delight. "I made it for you at church school."

"It's the best present I've ever had, Kathy. Thank you." He kissed her.

"Now, open Zoe's present, Daddy," she said.

Zoe handed him the package and he again carefully pulled off the ribbon and paper and opened the box. He took out two wolf hand puppets. They had benign, quizzical expressions on their tan and gray faces, and pink felt tongues that lolled out from the sides of their mouths.

David slipped his hand up into one and turned the soft wolf's muzzle to the sky, howling softly.

"How wonderful," he said. "Wherever did you ever find these? I've never seen anything like them. We wolves are not too popular with toy makers, it seems."

"Daddy, let me, let me." Kathy reached for the other puppet, slipping her hand into the sleeve, also making a howl.

"It took some doing," Zoe said.

David and Kathy held their wolves close together and howled again.

"Zoe, these are absolutely marvelous," he said.

Kathy bounced up and down on the seat, making her wolf smile and growl and catch things in its mouth. She made it lick Zoe's cheek and give her a flurry of kisses. They both made their wolves nuzzle and chew at one another and at Zoe, and they all laughed.

Dinner was served, so they put the dragon and wolves aside. David carefully wrapped the little clay handprint and put it into his pocket.

After dinner, all the waiters and waitresses gathered around the table and sang, "Happy . . . happy-happy birthday to you; happy . . . happy-happy birthday to you," clapping rhythmically, smiling at Kathy, and placing the birthday cake on the table.

Kathy closed her eyes, made a wish, and blew out the candles. The waitress brought plates, and Zoe cut a piece of cake for each of them. Kathy dove into the cake, getting fudge frosting on her cheeks and up her arms to her elbows. "Yum, yum, yum, yum, yum," she murmured. "Yum, yum, yum, yum, yum."

When she was satisfied, she carefully licked the chocolate off her fingers and forearms like a cat. She wiped fiercely at her face with the huge napkin until there was no trace of misplaced chocolate. Then she leaned back against the seat and closed her eyes, uttering a deep sigh, only partly in contentment.

David put his arm gently around Kathy and drew her against him. "Yes, it's getting toward time to go home, isn't it?"

Kathy kept her eyes closed. A resigned silence came over her.

David paid the check and put the wolves back into their box. Zoe carried it and the rest of the birthday cake, and Kathy held the dragon tightly.

In the car, Kathy sat in the back seat, saying nothing, leaning her head against the dragon's head. As they got closer to home, she began to sob softly.

By the time they arrived at the driveway of the large house with its sloping lawn and great, graceful trees, the child was shaken by sobs that tore up from deep within her.

David lifted her into his arms, struggling to contain his own tears.

"Kathy, Kathy," he murmured. "It's all right. We've had a big day. Everything feels overwhelming when we're tired. I'll call you tomorrow. I'm nearby. We'll be together again soon. It's all right. It's all right."

Kathy was inconsolable.

Zoe said, "Good night, Kathy. I had a happy day with you." But Kathy did not hear; grief absorbed her.

David carried her in one arm and the box with the cake in the other. Kathy clutched the dragon as they made their way to the front porch. They stood for a few minutes, waiting for the door to be opened. When it was, they disappeared into the house.

For half an hour, Zoe sat in the car, looking at the elegant homes. The lights behind picture windows glowed in the thickening dusk. Zoe saw people eating dinner by candlelight. It was seven o'clock. The evening grew cooler, so Zoe opened the window. The air was sweet with freshly mown grass and flowering bushes.

David re-emerged from the house, walking rapidly. He roughly opened the back door of the car, flinging the dragon and the cake box in and violently slamming the door. With trembling hands, he started the car. The tires squealed as he drove away. At the corner, he scarcely slowed down, his jaw muscles working tensely. He drove fast for several more blocks.

Zoe had weathered the painful aftermath of many a divorced man processing an encounter with his ex-wife. She knew to be calm and not to fan the flames, not to be afraid of the anger, or to take it on herself.

After a few minutes, he pulled into a small, wooded park, and the car skidded to a stop. He gripped the steering wheel and gasped, anger and tears choking him. He dropped his head forward onto the steering wheel, murmuring through clenched teeth, "I'll kill her. I'll kill her. I'll kill her."

After a moment, Zoe said quietly, "David, what happened?"

Wrathful tears spilled out over his fists. He pounded the steering wheel. The whole car shook. "The dragon. The dragon. Oh, God. I'll kill that woman."

"What about the dragon?"

"That . . . woman . . ." He spat the word out like a curse. "That . . . wretched . . . woman . . . wouldn't allow Kathy to keep the dragon." He pounded the steering wheel again and again.

"Why not?"

"She said it's a symbol of Satan. She said it represents evil and greed and treachery by wicked servants of Satan and that all such objects must be cast out of a Christian household. She threatened to burn it in the trash."

He was sobbing openly. "She snatched it out of Kathy's arms and tried to tear it apart. I shouted that it belonged to Kathy and that everything she said was lies. I shouted that there is no Satan, that Kathy is an innocent child, and that the dragon is a child's toy. A *birthday gift!*

"Christine screamed at me that Satan has me in his clutches and is poisoning Kathy through me. I shouted that *she's* poisoning Kathy with her crazy thinking.

"Poor Kathy. Poor little Kathy. All the while, she just huddled in the corner, shrinking from us. She was terrified of us. And I don't blame her.

"Zoe, I can't stand what's happening to that little girl. I don't know what I'm going to do."

Then the fierceness and rage went out of him. He fell against Zoe, who took him into her arms, also weeping.

"David, David," she said. She rocked him, holding him and comforting him as he had held and comforted Kathy earlier. "I'm so sorry. For you and for Kathy. I'm sorry it's so hard."

His body trembled and shook, heaving with great, choking sobs.

For a long time, Zoe held him.

At last, he sat up and reached across her, pulling a package of tissues from the glove compartment. He gave a handful to Zoe and took a handful for himself. They blew their noses and coughed and sighed.

"Thank you, Zoe. I don't know what I would have done if you hadn't been here." One last sob escaped from him, then he sat back, much as Kathy had done in the restaurant, closing his eyes, collecting himself.

"I'm glad I could help," Zoe said. "I'm just sorry it was my gift that caused such a scene."

"Dammit, Zoe. Kathy *loves* that dragon. It's a wonderful gift. It's not the dragon, it's Christine, with her crazy talk about Satan and evil and wickedness. She sees Satan everywhere. She sees Satan in me. What must Kathy think, hearing that Satan controls her father?

"What a terrible, cruel thing to say to a child. It's child abuse, just as if Christine had taken a belt and whipped Kathy until she was bloody."

He drew in a shuddering breath. "I don't know what to do. Should I try to get custody? But how? Oh, Zoe. Kathy's my child, and I feel helpless to protect her from her own mother."

He wept again, pounding the steering wheel.

He went on, his voice anguished. "Christine's final cruelty was to threaten to throw away the birthday cake. She called it 'filthy sugar' and accused me of trying to poison my daughter. My own child heard her mother accuse me of trying to *poison* her."

Shaking with new rage, he opened the car door and got out, leaving the door open and walking rapidly away. Zoe let him go, but she was prepared to follow if necessary. After a few minutes of pacing he came back to the car and got in, calmer.

"I'm sorry to have put you through this, Zoe. It was supposed to be a happy birthday celebration. I had no idea it would end like this."

Zoe kept her voice light, hoping to relieve the tension. "Well, David, things are evened up a bit. You've been through more than one crisis with me, so I'm glad I could return the favor."

She smiled. "Would you like me to drive?"

"No, I can drive. Thanks. My outburst is over." He shook out his arms and rubbed his shoulders. He coughed and sighed.

"I can endure all sorts of insults from Christine about *me*. But when she does it to Kathy, I just can't bear it."

Still keeping her voice light, Zoe said, "Children are amazingly resilient. They can withstand a great deal, especially if they know, as I'm sure Kathy knows about you, there's someone who truly and unconditionally loves them for who they are. I've seen you make that very clear to Kathy. Your love will be her protection, and she'll carry it inside her, even when you can't be there with her."

She gently patted David's arm. He caught her hand and held it tightly in his own still-trembling hands, giving her a long look of bleary, exhausted affection.

"Thank you, Zoe."

CHAPTER 12.
Thomas Family Values

These days, incest seemed to be proliferating. In the press, on the evening news, in twelve-step meetings, woman after woman came forward to tell her story of its trauma. They told of fathers who were surgeons or socialites or righteous ministers. Fathers who had turned their childhood, their adulthood, their marriage, their relationship with their own daughters, and their relationship with themselves into a web of phobias, nightmares, eating disorders, madness, perfectionism, and suicidal thoughts. And often, they told of stunning achievements.

Zoe looked at their pictures in the women's section of the Sunday paper. They were beauty queens. They were Olympic ice skaters. They were chess champions. They graduated Phi Beta Kappa from Ivy League colleges. They achieved, achieved, achieved. They were always, it seemed, making Daddy proud.

In photographs, they beamed under their crowns, in white strapless gowns, with ermine capes around their shoulders. Their smiles showed off perfect teeth. Their lovely, bare arms held long-stemmed roses or trophies.

But for each of them, there was a contrapuntal terror. It started as a whisper, but year by year it grew louder, until at last it drowned out the sound of the applause. It drowned out everything but its message: *Your life is a lie. You are a lie.* And sometimes, it said something else: *You must die.*

They were women like herself, Zoe realized.

You are a victim of incest, Zoe said to herself. Every time she heard the words, they shocked her. How could this be? There was never any answer. Everything in her life was called into question. Who *was* her father, really? Who was her mother? And what, exactly, had happened to her?

She thought about the women's stories. Their battles with anxiety and addiction. Their eating disorders and weight issues and suicide attempts. Their years of therapy, steadfast husbands, woman lovers. Sometimes, their abuser was dead. Sometimes, he was alive and had abused his grandchildren. Sometimes, the women had put him into prison for that. Sometimes, sisters shared stories after decades of silence. Mothers faced the truth. Or denied it.

What would her own mother say? Had her mother suspected it? Did she know? Had she taken sleeping pills to avoid being a wife? Did she say, *Better my daughter than me?*

Sometimes Zoe thought, *My childhood wasn't that bad. I didn't suffer what those women did.*

Sometimes she thought, *I'm making all this up. It never happened.*

One Saturday, life offered her a gift. Her cousin Suzanne, whom she had not seen in twenty years, phoned her from the airport.

"I'm on my way to England and thought I'd take a chance you're still in Chicago and listed in the phone book. I have a five-hour layover at O'Hare. Is there any chance you could come to the airport and have dinner with me? I know it's nervy of me to expect you even to know who I am after twenty years, but I decided to chance it."

"Suzanne!" Zoe said. "How could I forget my favorite cousin? I'm so glad to hear your voice. Of course, I'll come to the airport. I've thought about you so many times over the years. Where shall we meet?"

Zoe loved Suzanne. She had also been intimidated by her. Suzanne was three years older and seemed tougher, cannier, smarter, more accomplished, more talented, and just better at everything than Zoe.

They had spent a lot of time together in childhood, because their fathers were brothers, and their families regularly took shared vacations. The two cousins rode together in the back seat on driving trips to Niagara Falls and Mammoth Cave and Colonial Williamsburg.

But something unpleasant happened between the brothers and they never spoke to each other again. When Suzanne married, Zoe's family was not invited to the wedding. Zoe heard a few years later that Suzanne was divorced, but she never learned what happened between the brothers, or why her Christmas cards to Suzanne went unanswered.

Zoe's mind was full of these things as she drove to the airport and made her way to the Satellite Lounge. Suzanne was waiting outside. They could smell food and hear the clinking of dishes and silverware in the restaurant beyond.

"Let's have something to drink before dinner, if you have time," Suzanne said. They followed the hostess to a table in the bar area.

After they were settled, they looked searchingly at one another.

The bar was intentionally dark, the atmosphere created by a lighted screen behind the bottles of liquor, casting a gold and green and dark red luminousness through the bottles into the room. From time to time, flight boardings and departures were announced over a loudspeaker.

"Well. You're still beautiful," Suzanne said. "I resented you for that. My mother was always comparing me to you. Not to my advantage, I assure you."

"*Beautiful?*" Zoe laughed, embarrassed. "I'd have given everything for your brilliance, your confidence, your talent for everything. I worshipped you. I thought I was ugly."

"Goes to show you how mistaken people can be about themselves, sometimes."

Suzanne ordered a Coke, and Zoe did, too.

They talked about their divorces and gazed at one another. Suzanne had grown tall and angular. She had a strong chin; a large, aristocratic nose; fine cheekbones; and luminous brown eyes that were widely set. She wore no makeup. Her thick brown hair fell across her eyes. She kept sweeping it back with her hand and a toss of her head. Zoe found that distracting.

After a while, the waitress said a table was ready, and they followed her into the restaurant. Once they were seated, they studied the menu, holding it up to the table's small lamp. Both ordered bowls of chili and salads, and the waitress left them alone.

"Did you say that you're on your way to England?" Zoe said.

"Yes. I'll spend a few days in London on business. But the real purpose of my trip is to visit Wales. I'm doing some research on the family. We're Welsh, you know, at least on our fathers' side. That's the good news and the bad news."

"Oh, I know." Zoe chuckled. "When I was in high school, I discovered the poetry of Dylan Thomas, and I got excited about being Welsh, but my mother squelched that right away.

"'The Welsh are the lower class of the British Isles,' she said. Her ancestors came from England in 1612. I think she felt she'd married beneath her position by marrying my father."

"She probably did. My mother thought she put on airs. Mother said, 'Elizabeth Thomas considers herself *quite the lydie.*' She always pronounced it that way, and pretended to be sipping tea, her little finger in the air. How's your mother doing, by the way?"

"Well, my father died in February."

"I heard."

"She's doing better than I am. I always thought my mother was only marginally sane, but she's going off on a Caribbean cruise in a couple of weeks, all on her own. She's doing amazingly well. I didn't expect it. But then, there are a lot of things I didn't expect since my father's death."

Zoe paused to take a sip of the Coke, then hurried on, realizing that she didn't want Suzanne to ask what she meant. "But tell me about your trip to Wales."

"I'm writing a novel, and part of it is set in Wales, so I'm going to look around for a while and get a feeling for our ancestors and the world they came from and carried in their bones."

"What's the novel about?"

Suzanne was quiet for a moment before answering. "It's a kind of psychological mystery story." She took a deep breath. "My heroine has to come to terms with the realization that she was sexually abused as a child."

Zoe jerked back in her chair as if struck by a bullet. At last, she said softly, "Incest."

"Yes."

Neither woman spoke for a few minutes, while the waitress brought their chili and salads.

"Suzanne," Zoe said hesitantly, "of course, I'm wondering if your book is based on your own experience. But before you say anything, I want to tell you something about me."

She again hesitated, then went on. "I'm not sure why I'm telling you this, when we've just met again after so long. But I think I'm a victim of incest."

"Well. That makes sense."

"What, Suzanne? *What* makes sense?"

"Now *I* have something to tell *you*. My brother abused me from the time I was three until I was fifteen. That's when he moved to the West Coast to begin his medical practice. He lived at home while he was going to college and medical school and even during his residency. As you know, he's eleven years older."

"Oh, Suzanne!"

"Several years ago, when I was first doing recovery work and I told my mother about the abuse, she refused to believe me. She reminded me that my brother is a doctor, by which she meant that *he's* respectable and respected, and therefore more trustworthy than I am."

Suzanne tossed her hair back.

"But that's in the past, Zoe. When I called you, and you said you'd come to meet me, I didn't expect to say anything about the incest. But now that it's come out, I feel a kind of relief."

"Oh, Suzanne, so do I. Your mother didn't believe you?"

"I wasn't surprised by her reaction. I was hurt, and then infuriated, but not surprised. She dotes on my brother. I've always been a disappointment to her. Besides, she can't accept that I'm a lesbian."

"A—"

"Lesbian. She insisted that I keep all of it from my father. Family secrets." Her voice was bitter.

"We seem to have a lot of them." Zoe's voice was also bitter.

"And I may as well get it all out now that I've started. I'm also an alcoholic. I've been in AA for years."

She brushed her hair back. "Zoe, I don't mean to equate being a lesbian with being an alcoholic. Although both have given me the best things I've ever had in my life."

"Oh, Suzanne, I understand what you mean. I'm an alcoholic too. I also go to AA."

Suzanne smiled. "How could it be otherwise?"

She sighed and ordered another Coke for them both.

After a few moments of silence, Zoe spoke first. "I envied you your glamorous brother. He was so handsome, so brilliant. I didn't know him very well because he was so much older. But whenever I saw you together, he seemed to adore you. To treat you as if you were special."

"He treated me as if I was special, all right. But he was nice to me only in public. In private, he was a monster. My therapist thinks he's a psychopath. He was the only babysitter I ever had. My parents were very social. They left me with him night after night."

Her hair fell over her face again, and she didn't brush it away. Her eyes were hidden. "The minute they left the house, the ordeal would begin. He'd start by turning off all the lights. I'd try to hide, but he stalked me until he caught me. He'd creep around in the dark, making terrifying noises and whispering that he was going to kill me."

She looked directly at Zoe. "After hours of this, when I was almost catatonic with fear, he'd take me into the bedroom and strip us both naked and make me have oral sex with him. When I was nine, he began having intercourse with me. He did many sadistic things, Zoe. I was terrified throughout my entire childhood."

"My God." Zoe covered her face with her hands. It was too terrible to imagine.

"Zoe." Suzanne drew back suddenly, realizing how shaken Zoe was. "I didn't mean to tell you all this. I'm so sorry. I shouldn't be saying this, without preparing you for it. It's powerful stuff. I've been dealing with it now for years. But it's not fair for me to talk to you this way, after not having seen you in so long. After all, it's your family, too. This must be very painful for you to hear. Forgive me."

"No, Suzanne, please don't apologize. In a strange way, it's comforting--of course, it's terrible hearing how you suffered such dreadful things! But I've had such a hard time believing there could have been incest in my childhood that I've been telling myself I'm imagining it. We're *nice, middle-class people*. And it's only been since the death of my father that I've even begun to wonder if there might have been incest."

She turned her head away. "Just thinking that makes me feel so disloyal to him. But to talk with you about it is a relief."

"Yes. It's a relief to me, too, Zoe."

Suzanne took a long sip of her Coke and sighed, smiling ruefully. "That's probably why I blurted it out to you. Many times, I've wanted to write to you. But how do you do that after so many years of silence? I knew it would be unfair to you, unless somehow you were prepared for it. But I guess you *were* prepared for it, and I'm so sorry about that."

They had barely tasted the chili and salads. Zoe pushed the plates to one side and leaned forward.

"Suzanne, all this is very new to me. I went once to an incest survivors' meeting. And I have a therapist friend who's been helpful. But I've been gradually going crazy since my father's death. I'm really frightened. I feel out of control a lot of the time."

"You shouldn't do recovery work on your own, Zoe. Get lots of support. I don't know what I would have done without my therapist. And Charlie, my partner. Both women have literally saved my life."

She paused. "I attempted suicide several times."

"Oh, Suzanne." Zoe slowly absorbed this. Then she was flooded with gratitude. "Thank God you survived. And thank God you've come back into my life. I've missed you. I couldn't understand why our families broke off contact. No one would talk about it. Do you know what happened?"

"Oh, Zoe. *That,* I'd rather not say."

"Please, Suzanne. I want to know. What could be worse than what we've already said? Please. Tell me."

"It's worse."

"*What,* Suzanne? *What's* worse?"

Suzanne was silent again. She swept her hair back and took a deep breath. "It involved your father."

Now Zoe was silent. She, too, took a deep breath. At last, she said, "How?"

"Your father. And me, Zoe. Your father . . . molested me. My father found out about it. He told Uncle Percy that if he ever again had any contact with me, he'd be dead."

"My God." Zoe felt dizzy and slightly nauseated.

"I didn't want to tell you that, Zoe. I never intended to tell you."

After a pause, Zoe said, "Did my mother know about it?"

"Yes."

Zoe sat back and closed her eyes. When she opened them again, the two women regarded one another with sorrow. "Oh, Suzanne. Now I understand everything."

"Unfortunately, Zoe," Suzanne said after a pause, "not everything. There's one more thing that might help you understand what happened to you."

Zoe waited. After a long pause, Suzanne said, "One time I overheard my mother telling my dad about an incident that happened to you. Your dad was a clean freak. I'm sure you know that."

"I know." Zoe held her breath.

"He thought your mother didn't get you clean enough, and in the early years, he insisted on giving you your baths."

Zoe said, almost whispering, "I had forgotten completely about that. Then, the last time I was visiting my mother, I had a sudden memory about it, and I asked her about Daddy giving me baths when I was a child. I thought it was weird. But my mother didn't want to say much about it."

"It *was* weird. And even weirder, according to my mother, were the enemas. Your father apparently wanted you to be squeaky clean inside and out, and he gave you regular enemas."

She leaned toward Zoe and said, with controlled outrage, "One time, the nozzle went into the wrong place, and you bled profusely. The doctor had to be called."

Zoe thought she might vomit. She swallowed hard several times and breathed deeply. Suzanne waited, not moving. Zoe said nothing.

Suzanne went on. "The doctor put you back together, but that also put an end to the enemas. And the daddy-baths. It became another dark family secret. When my mother realized I'd overheard what she'd told my dad, she swore me to secrecy on pain of death."

Zoe sat silent for a long time.

Finally, she said, as if to herself, "That explains a lot. It explains why I was so traumatized when I started menstruating, why, that first time I bled, I thought I was dying. Why I locked myself in my room when my mother explained that menstruation is a natural part of being a woman and I would bleed every month while I was in my childbearing years, which to me seemed forever. It explains why I shouted that I didn't want to be a woman. Why I was so phobic about my body, why I hated my breasts, why I . . ."

After a pause, she said, "All of it, Suzanne. All of it." She was beyond tears.

Suzanne said, "Thomas family values, Zoe." Then she shook her head, as if to shake away memories.

"Zoe, can we not talk about this anymore? I'm wiped out. You are, too. I need to head for my plane in a few minutes, and I don't want us to end our time together with this ugliness."

She reached across the table and took Zoe's hands. "I love you, little cousin. I always have."

"I don't want to lose you again, Suzanne."

"I'm not going anywhere, Zoe."

She laughed suddenly, breaking the tension. "Well, I *am* going to London, and to Wales, and then back to my life in Palo Alto. But you know what I mean. I won't let the past keep us apart ever again, Zoe, I promise."

The waitress brought their checks and cleared the table.

Suzanne picked up both checks and said, "Let's call this a business expense." She handed money to the waitress and looked over at the people lining up behind the reception desk, waiting for a table to be free.

"Let them wait. We have just a few more minutes."

She turned back to Zoe and said, intensely, leaning forward, "Zoe, our lives are much larger and more beautiful than what happened to us in our sordid past."

The waitress came back with change and the receipt. "Thanks for dinner, boss," Suzanne said to the receipt as she tucked it into her purse.

In their last few minutes, after Suzanne gathered her suitcase and other things and they'd left the restaurant and were sitting on a bench in the corridor outside, Suzanne briefly told Zoe about her life in Palo Alto with Charlie, their two cats, their house and the garden with its avocado tree and hot tub, and finally, as if it were the least important thing in her life, about her position as a senior vice president of a pharmaceutical company. She was obviously very successful.

"Suzanne, I really admire what you've done, and are doing, with your life."

Suzanne brushed the admiration aside with a brief laugh and tossed her hair back. She pulled a page from a small notebook and wrote her home address, along with her phone number at work and her unlisted phone number at home. Handing the page to Zoe, she said, "Now, don't lose that, little cousin."

She embraced Zoe, promised to stay in touch, and headed for the international concourse.

Driving home, Zoe got a ticket for running a stop sign a block from her house.

CHAPTER 13.
Rehearsals

Anticipating the first rehearsal of Gudrun's play, Zoe was jittery all day. She went home from the office early and took a bath, did some relaxation and voice exercises she remembered from her theatre days, ate a quick supper, and drove to the spacious loft apartment in the DePaul neighborhood where Gudrun was staying with a friend during her seven weeks in Chicago.

The group was gathering. Musicians were tuning their instruments, setting up music stands and opening their scores, playing musical phrases, and breaking concentration occasionally to toss friendly insults at one another.

The actors laughed, teased, and reminisced. Everyone poured cups of coffee and picked up apples and grapes and bottles of water Gudrun had put out on the kitchen counter. Positive energy and eager expectation filled the room.

Zoe poured a cup of coffee and sat quietly on a tall stool at the counter. Gudrun was deep in conversation with one of the musicians. She turned her head briefly to acknowledge Zoe with a nod and a smile, then went back to her conversation.

After a few moments, Gudrun called everyone together and made introductions, mostly for the sake of Zoe and the musicians, since almost everyone else knew one another. The musicians included a cellist, an oboist, a flutist, and a percussionist with a large frame drum, a stand with a cymbal, and several small percussion instruments on a stool.

Gudrun, smiling, opened her arms. "I see here my dearest and most gifted Chicago friends. So much talent gathered here so we can pull together this play, which I call *Encounter with the Sacred: A Mythic Journey of Healing*. I've written it as the centerpiece of a scholarly conference at DePaul University with the very grand and challenging title of *Incest, Feminism, and the Sacred Feminine*."

Applause and cheers, whistles.

"With your help, we'll tell a story both ancient and modern. Though this is just a modest table-reading, I hope the play will touch our audience deeply and stir their thinking. My great genius composer friend Charlie Stark has written a sumptuous score that will carry the ideas into people's hearts more powerfully than my words ever could. Thank you, Charlie."

She blew him a kiss. Again, everyone applauded. Charlie tapped the music stand with his cello bow and smiled shyly. The percussionist offered a cymbal crash.

"And besides Charlie, we're fortunate to have Bill Bates on percussion, Julie Swan on flute, and Adam Albinson on oboe." They smiled back at her and waved.

"We're also fortunate to have the fabulous actors with whom years ago I shared such good times creating plays, when we were students dreaming of a life in the arts, before I went wrong and became a psychiatrist. And now, they are the critically acclaimed theatre company *l'Air du Temps.*"

Gudrun named them and each smiled and offered a thumbs up.

"And it's a special honor for me to have a colleague, Zoe Thomas, an actress trained at Northwestern, to be our Persephone, as well as Kay, the modern Persephone." Gudrun gestured to Zoe, and everyone turned toward her, smiling and clapping. "Thank you, Zoe, from the bottom of my heart."

Zoe gave a small wave and smiled bravely. But inside, she trembled.

"And Hecate? Where's my Hecate?" Gudrun looked around the room and spotted a regal woman with high cheekbones, a noble profile, and rich dark hair with streaks of grey at the temples.

"There! The great Shakespearean actress, Katherine Henderson." Katherine offered a brief smile and waved. Applause.

"And Hades—the mighty basso profundo and acclaimed Othello, Richard Steele!" An elegant man smiled and nodded. More applause.

Gudrun paused, eyes closed. The group sat expectantly.

"My thought is that we'll spend the first part of this evening on Act 1, to warm us up. We'll have a break, and when we come back, the gorgeous overture, and the prologue. I think that's the best use of our time while we're all together.

"Then on Thursday evening we'll have a small rehearsal back here at 7 p.m., for Act 2, the scenes with Kay, Margaret, Persephone, and Hades. That will involve only Katherine, Zoe, and Richard. Does that sound good?"

She looked around the room. Everyone nodded silently.

"So now, we begin. Chorus members?" She named six women.

"Are you ready?"

They stood, their scripts open. Gudrun read the stage directions, setting the mood.

The six chorus members read together:

> Cold. Cold.
> Never did we imagine our lives would come to this.

Gudrun let them finish the first stanza, then she stopped them. "Thank you. You did that beautifully. I understood every word. But hearing it now, I think it will work better if you say each line separately."

She assigned lines and they marked their scripts and began again. The rich intensity and grief they brought to each line, their trained voices rich and supple, thrilled Zoe. Something deep within her opened after being tightly closed for a long time.

"Beautiful!" Gudrun said. "Exactly what I hoped for. Powerful, my darlings. So now, Hecate." Gudrun read the stage directions and Katherine read, with a rich, contralto voice,

> Only I saw what happened.
> Only I know how she was taken,
> torn from her mother's golden world . . .

After a few more lines, Katherine paused and looked up expectantly to see if this was what Gudrun wanted. Gudrun nodded and gestured for her to continue.

When Katherine finished, Gudrun, clearly pleased, said, "Perfect. So now, chorus, as before, your lines, spoken individually."

As the rehearsal continued, the atmosphere in the room deepened with the actors' growing concentration. After the second run-through, Gudrun suggested a short break. While the others milled around and chatted, pouring fresh coffee and uncapping bottles of water, Gudrun took Zoe aside.

"So, Zoe, what do you think? Is this working?"

"It's magical, Gudrun. I'm *so* honored to be a part of it. I'd forgotten how much I love the energy of rehearsals. I'm having a wonderful time. I'm not even feeling terrified anymore. Just nervous."

"I'm glad, Zoe. And as you know, a little nervousness is a good thing. Pulls all our faculties together. We worry when we're not at least a bit nervous." She gave Zoe a quick hug and turned back to the group, clapping her hands. "Let's come together again, please."

She waited for the conversations to finish and said, "Prologue. Katherine as the Contralto Voice; Richard as the Boatman; Zoe as the Child's Voice. And now you have a treat in store. Musicians, the overture, please."

Charlie conducted with his cello bow. A phrase from the oboe was followed by the flute, then the cello, and finally, a soft throbbing of the drum.

Zoe recognized the sorrowful mood, like the opening phrases of Mahler's *Kindertotenlieder, Songs on the Death of Children*. She knew that beautiful song cycle well because as a young girl she had sung the songs with her mother, who was learning the piano accompaniment for a voice major at the conservatory, where Zoe's father taught. Her mother let Zoe sing Mahler's gorgeous songs while she practiced them at home.

Zoe felt tears stirring with the intensity of her memory, one of the few memories of her mother she treasured. Now, the rich harmonies of Charlie's music stirred an equally intense response.

The yearning melody of the oboe continued for a few moments. Underneath was the dark richness of the cello, and a pulsing energy of the great frame drum. They built suspense, with the flute breaking in from time to time, plaintive, fluttering, tremulous.

The music paused, as if holding its breath.

Gudrun said, "Out of profound darkness comes a voice."

Katherine spoke, her voice lush, every word exquisitely clear.

> Land birds grow silent.
> The sea smells dark and bitter.
> The Boatman comes
> to cast the child adrift.

After a few more lines, it was time for Zoe, who cried, in a child's voice, "Mother, Mother!"

Gudrun nodded.

Katherine delivered lines about the roiling, hissing sea, and Richard, about how the mother could not hear the child's cries. Then Zoe again, "*Mother! Mother!*"

Richard, his deep voice stirring a flutter of fear in Zoe, "Foolish child, when will you learn? Your mother sleeps."

Zoe felt her heart breaking as the yearning melody resumed, the cello sighing, the flute crying a wild frantic upward wail and dying away, and all gradually moving to a soft, aching resolution and a final thud of the drum.

A realization again flashed through Zoe's mind, as it had when she first read the play. *I was that child. That happened to me!*

Everyone was silent for a few moments. Then Gudrun spoke softly. "Musicians, gorgeous. Actors, perfect."

A burst of applause and laughter relieved the intensity.

They did another run-through of the Prologue, and Act 1. Everyone clearly loved being a part of this beautiful thing.

Gudrun stood and smiled. "I think we've done enough for our first rehearsal. Thank you for your excellent work. You're such pros. You intuitively know what I hope for. I don't need to direct. I can just enjoy. So, good night. I love you all. Safe home, darlings."

Scattered applause and a burst of conversation as people gathered their scripts, packed away musical instruments, and offered rides to one another. Gudrun moved among them, asking about their lives. She laughed, embraced, kidded, listened.

When she had seen the last of them out and closed the door, she returned to Zoe, who had waited, at Gudrun's request, sitting on her stool at the counter, both drained and energized.

Gudrun sat on the stool next to her and gave her a hug.

"Thank you, dear; I'm *so* glad we can share this."

"I am too, Gudrun. Thank you for taking the risk with me, without knowing what I could do."

"Zoe, I know all I need to know. You did a wonderful job."

Another warm embrace, and they said goodnight.

Driving home, Zoe felt a happiness she had not felt for months, maybe years. Her small contribution to the evening's rehearsal, with a few frightened, desperate words, had surprised her, had pleased her, even, with the strength and versatility of her voice, and her assurance as she spoke her lines.

Thursday evening, Zoe arrived at the loft just before 7 p.m. Gudrun greeted her warmly and went back to making coffee, as Zoe took her usual stool at the counter, not saying anything to break Gudrun's concentration.

A few moments later, the door buzzer sounded, and Gudrun pressed it to open the door downstairs in the entrance hall.

Katherine and Richard arrived together, deep in conversation. They piled their things on a chair, poured themselves coffee, and sat at the large dining table, opening their scripts.

Zoe had been working on her lines almost constantly. She felt the familiar and unwelcome sense of intimidation and inadequacy that had dogged her during her theatre years, but Katherine and Richard were so friendly and casual with her that she soon relaxed.

To Zoe's relief, they did not question her about her theatre background. Soon, all was business.

They began Act II, Scene I. As Gudrun read the stage directions, Zoe took some deep breaths, tensing and relaxing her shoulders. Then she delivered her lines.

"I'm sick and tired of being sick and tired, Margaret, as we say in AA." To her amazement, her voice sounded confident and steady. She didn't feel as confident as she sounded.

"I've been sober for five years, and I should feel better than I feel. My life is still a mess. You are my hundredth therapist. I'm having an affair with my thousandth married man."

Gudrun nodded approvingly. They worked their way through

the scene, the lines about girl-cooties and Kay's comment about loving women but not wanting to be one, Margaret's wry reminder to Kay that she *is* a woman, and Kay's outburst, "Oh. Say it isn't *so!*"

Zoe said the lines with such conviction she had the uncanny sense she wasn't acting but was *reliving* the experience.

Gudrun clapped her hands and exclaimed, "Oh, we've got a winner here! Brava! You're wonderful together. And the scene is cleverer than when I wrote the words. You're a great team."

"We are, aren't we, Zoe?" Katherine said, her gorgeous voice warm and affirming. Zoe was filled with happiness.

They rested, drinking coffee until Gudrun called them together for the second scene in Act II. Richard sat at the table across from Zoe, and Gudrun read the stage directions.

He spoke his lines in a voice that was rich, deep, and velvety. The thought flashed through Zoe's mind: *I'll bet he's an irresistible lover. He could seduce someone with his voice alone.*

They read through the scene, Zoe's confidence growing stronger with each line.

Richard's voice, and the nuanced and suggestive way he read the lines, thrilled Zoe.

The third scene went smoothly. Zoe relaxed into the experience. She was deeply stirred by the beauty of Kay's expressions of gratitude for the nine years of therapy, her reading of the poem, and Margaret's lines about the encounter with the sacred feminine.

Katherine seemed equally moved. When the rehearsal was finished, she chuckled and said, "Well, I'm quite a fine therapist, don't you agree?"

Zoe responded, in character, "A fine therapist. Thank you for nine amazing years, Margaret. I've encountered the Goddess."

It felt almost true.

Saturday, the whole group was together again in the loft apartment, milling about, chatting, teasing, having pre-rehearsal nerves.

Gudrun called them together and said, "I have exciting news. Katherine and Richard have envisioned greater things for us and have convinced me we can do more than a table-reading. Don't worry, it's nothing like a full staging. And the marvelous *l'Air du Temps* lighting and sound crews will give our production a professional finish."

She described the new plan. "Chorus, you'll be seated stage right and stage left on two-tiered risers, slightly above the main characters, who are at stage level. Each of the three soloists, centered between the risers, will have a chair and a music stand. You'll stand for your scenes, very much as you would in an oratorio. I'll serve as narrator, reading stage directions and setting the scene."

"Costumes are simple: black street clothes, as plain as possible, with colored scarves to suggest character.

"For Act III, I may add a spiral dance and some chanting. We'll try it out tonight and see if it works."

She looked from face to face, smiling, drawing them into her vision for the play.

"The only other items for the set are an arch, upstage center, with darkness behind it; the Wasteland Tree in Act I; and the Tree of Renewed Life in Act III. The *l'Air du Temps* scene shop has already created them.

"The Wasteland Tree is a large skeletal black wrought-iron coat-rack sort of thing with six jagged branches from which are suspended six *papier mâché* seedpods, each about twelve inches long. The Tree of Renewed Life is a similar wrought-iron stand, but it's graceful and painted green. Attached to its branches are large, brightly colored silk flowers and jeweled fruit.

"Overture and Prologue are in darkness, with only the Wasteland Tree spotlighted, downstage, left. How does it sound so far? Questions?"

They smiled and shook their heads.

"Good. So, let's go to work. We'll take it from the top, blocking the first two acts and working our way through Act III."

There was chaos for a few moments as they moved chairs and brought coat racks to represent the Wasteland Tree and the Tree of Renewed Life. Gudrun arranged the chorus members so their lines would be antiphonal.

This done, everyone grew quiet, and Gudrun said, "Musicians, may we have the overture, please?"

The lush music deepened the atmosphere, adding a feeling of sanctity. Zoe was filled with happiness.

"Beautiful," Gudrun said softly as they finished the overture. And then, louder, "Now, still in darkness, the Prologue."

Katherine, Zoe, and Richard stood and spoke their lines. When they were done, Gudrun whispered, "Gives me shivers! And now, Act I. Lights come up on a gray landscape, with the chorus of old women, voices deep, tragic, prophetic. Antiphonal, as we rehearsed."

They did this. "Beautiful," Gudrun said again, "And Hecate, please."

Katherine, her voice fierce and harsh with outrage, said,

> Only I saw what happened. Only I know how she
> was taken,
> torn from her mother's golden world . . .

They proceeded. The antiphonal voices of the chorus added to the intensity of the scene, and they finished, all together:

> Yes. Everything is wrong. And all of us, once
> beautiful and young ourselves, must suffer.

They blocked the first two acts, then took a break, during which they were mostly quiet. No teasing or laughter this time; the process absorbed everyone, and they repeated their lines softly to themselves. They stretched, sucked on lozenges, sipped water, poured more coffee.

Gudrun called everyone together again, and they blocked Act III, including a spiral dance and chanting. Gudrun decided they should move the risers and music stands back, and not use scripts for the final act, because of the dance, and the raised arms in the finale.

At last, Gudrun said, "Excellent, everyone. We have a winner!" There was a ripple of relief, but everyone was quiet, still under the spell of what they were creating together.

Gudrun said, "Next Tuesday, at 2 p.m., we'll run through everything from beginning to end here in the loft. We'll work late, so come rested. Thursday, we'll be in the performance space for the dress rehearsal, again beginning at 2 p.m.

"It will be another late night. We'll need to see how it works, managing the arch, the trees, the changing of scarves, Hecate's cane, the chanting, the raised arms, the spiral dance. I expect it will feel like a disaster. Dress rehearsals always do. Then, on Sunday, a perfect performance."

She applauded them. "And we will have given a great gift to everyone at the conference. I'm so grateful to each of you talented, generous friends."

CHAPTER 14.
Performance

The next day, Sunday, Zoe needed a break from the incredible intensity of the past weeks—the lunch with Anna, the incest survivors' group, her dinner with Suzanne, the rehearsals—so she sought respite in her garden, weeding, watering, savoring the beauty of the flowers.

And, she hoped, catching a glimpse of David.

As if in response to this thought, David opened his front door and wheeled his bike out. Zoe's heart leapt.

Seeing her, he rested the bike against the wall and came over.

Gudrun had said he'd be welcome at the play, but Zoe didn't want to embarrass herself in front of him in case she made a mess of it. Now, though, she was feeling so good about the rehearsals she decided to risk an invitation.

David remarked that they hadn't seen one another for a while, which gave her the opening.

"I'm in a play, David, after many years of intentionally *not* being in plays, and I've been busy with rehearsals. Gudrun seduced me into taking part in a play she's written for a conference at DePaul. Wait till you hear the subject of the conference: *Incest, Feminism, and the Sacred Feminine.*"

"Wow! Only Gudrun could pull *that* off!"

"The play is entitled, *Encounter with the Sacred: A Mythic Journey of Healing.* Does that stir your curiosity?"

David laughed. "It definitely does."

"You'd be welcome to attend. But the play is next Sunday afternoon. I know your weekends are for Kathy, so you don't have to come to please me. Kathy takes precedence, of course."

"Let me see what I can arrange." After a moment, he added, "I *want* to be there, Zoe, to discover this new dimension of you."

David's sincerity left her speechless.

Another pause, then he said, "I see your garden is more beautiful than ever. And the juniper smells delicious. I always come over and give it a sniff before I head out. That's what brought me over just now. Besides you, of course."

"David, you say such wonderful things." Her voice was warm.

It was his turn to be silent. With a sigh and a quick shake of his head, he said, "Well, I must be on my way. Riding north for most of the day. Thank you for inviting me to the play. I'll be there if at all possible. Let me know where to come, and what time."

Again, the smile, and he wheeled his bicycle out of the passageway.

The days leading up to the performance were challenging. Zoe had to juggle rehearsals with the Chief's demands. But she left at noon on

Tuesday for the run-through and on Thursday for the dress rehearsal. The latter, as Gudrun had predicted, was a disaster. Nothing went well. There were problems with the lighting and the scarves, and especially with the spiral dance and chanting that Gudrun had added to the final act.

Being at the office on Friday was almost a relief.

Sunday morning, performance day, Zoe was wide awake at 6 a.m. She kept asking herself, *Why did I let Gudrun talk me into this? I hate performing. That's why I quit the theatre. Why, why, why did I let myself be talked into this!*

Too tense to eat breakfast, she did her voice and relaxation exercises, read through the script one last time, then walked to DePaul, a few blocks from her townhouse, for the 11:30 call.

Backstage, everyone was busy. The actors were their usual merry selves, laughing quietly and having coffee and cigarettes as they put on makeup in front of large lighted mirrors. They brushed their hair, read their scripts, stretched.

Katherine came over to where Zoe sat and gave her a hug. "How's my client this morning?" she said, with her Lady Macbeth voice and sandpaper laugh.

"Oh, Margaret, I think I need an extra session."

"Nonsense. You're certifiably sane. I cured you, remember?"

"*This* is cured?"

"Sure is, darlin'. See you later."

Richard placed a cup of coffee on the shelf next to Zoe, gave her a light kiss on her cheek, and handed her the small gold Persephone crown. Zoe put it on.

"Beautiful, my queen," Richard said. "Now, have a bite of this delicious trifle. Take it into your lovely mouth. Just one small bite. Come, my queen, *eat.*"

He produced a glazed doughnut wrapped in a napkin. Zoe took the doughnut from him, laughing, thanked him and, to be polite, took a small bite.

"Oh, Richard. I'm wondering how I ever let Gudrun talk me into this."

"Zoe, no one can resist Gudrun. Impossible. Everyone here is hopelessly in love with her. But not to worry. You'll be great. You're a fine actress, I can see that. You might think about joining us at *l'Air du Temps.*"

"Oh!" Zoe was so overwhelmed by Richard's invitation, she almost wept. "Oh, *thank you,* Richard." Pleasure and anxiety flooded through her. "What an amazing offer! But no. *No.* I'm an indentured servant. My owner wouldn't allow that. But I'll remember your invitation forever. It'll comfort me in the night."

Richard laughed, patted her shoulder, and turned away, continuing his rounds, taking the crown with him for the prop person.

Zoe discreetly tucked the doughnut away. She had done her makeup at home, so she made her way to the stage, where the lighting people were stringing cords and adjusting spots and gels, and the sound people were placing speakers and tapping mics. All were totally absorbed in their work.

She sat in her chair, scarves draped across her lap, and placed her script on the music stand. Breathing deeply, she said a silent prayer to the Goddess of Foolhardy Undertakings, asking that she not make a fool of herself in front of David and that she not disappoint Gudrun or let down her fellow actors.

Then a calm came over her. Her lines were clear in her mind. The words seemed to belong to her, to express her own life.

At last, it was time. The actors and musicians gathered in a circle, holding hands. Gudrun said, "May this performance bring the greatest possible good to all concerned." After a moment of silence, Gudrun said, "The circle is cast."

The doors were opened, and the audience flooded in and took their seats.

Zoe briefly wondered if David was somewhere among them.

With the first notes of music, the magic began. Everyone in the cast was inspired and felt the perfect unfolding of the ancient story they were telling together.

After Act II, there was a brief intermission, during which the risers and chairs and music stands were moved back. For a few moments, many in the audience stood and spoke in soft voices with one another. Others sat quietly, absorbed in thought. Then, the lights were lowered, and everyone settled again into their seats.

On the darkened stage, the actors and musicians filed quietly in and took their places.

The musical interlude that opened Act III began with a soft pulsing of the frame drum. Then the oboe added a lively melody, like an English country dance.

The lights came up. The two chorus members who represented the Maiden aspect of the Triple Goddess chanted in soprano voices, "Call me the Maiden; I am the springtime; I am life blossoming."

They moved in a formal, rhythmic dance, spiraling into the center and spiraling out again.

The two representing the Mother aspect joined in the dance, spiraling in and then out, while chanting "Call me the Mother; I am the nurturer; I am the cherisher."

Then the two representing the Crone joined the dance, chanting, their voices in harmony, "Call me the Crone; I see things hidden; I govern endings, eternal beginnings."

After a few moments, the chanting stopped, but the spiral dance continued, and the pulsing of the great drum began, like a heartbeat. It continued while Zoe, as Persephone, stepped out from the darkness behind the arch, with Hecate entering behind her.

Music, dancers, and drumbeat stopped, and Hecate, brilliant in a center-stage spotlight, lifted off Persephone's purple scarf and replaced it with a golden one, telling how Persephone, beloved of life, now stepped again into the light, and the waiting earth blossomed.

But she warned that no one returns from the Realm of Shadows unchanged. Then, with joyous voices, one woman at a time, the chorus members chanted, antiphonally,

> No one returns from the Realm of Shadows
>   unchanged.
> But she, Beloved of Life, returns with wisdom for
>   us all:
> Deep knowing, compassion, healing love.
> She knows the terrible cost of suffering,
> Knows the awful descent into darkness.
> She guides us—ourselves once wounded,

wandering, lost—
Now healed and joyous, again into the light!

They chanted the last line together, as the drumbeat began again and the other instruments joined, repeating the intricate fugue of the spiral dance, and with the joined voices growing in volume and intensity, the music swelled into a rich, triumphant crescendo.

With their arms raised, the chorus, Hecate, and Persephone chanted together,

> Again, into the light! Yes!
> Again, again, again, again,
> Again, into the light! Yes!
> Again, again, again, again,
> Again, into the light!

Abruptly, the voices and music stopped, with a final reverberating beat of the drum. The lights went down.

For several moments, there was a breathless silence. Then the audience burst into applause, shouts, and whistles. "Bravo! Bravo! Bravo!"

As the lights came up again, Zoe saw David standing in the back row, applauding wildly.

Gudrun moved to the front of the stage. Someone ran in from the wings and placed a bouquet of red, purple, and gold blossoms in her arms. She turned and lifted the bouquet up for her actors and musicians, handed it to Charlie, then gestured toward the cast in acknowledgment. Together, they took hands and bowed deeply.

The risers and chairs were quickly returned to the stage for the actors, and Gudrun motioned for everyone to be seated. A tall stool was brought for her, and she turned to the audience and sat on the stool, waiting while they settled and the applause quieted.

"Dear audience," she said, "this conference has been ambitious. Each of our presenters whose papers you heard yesterday, and whose ideas and insights you shared during this morning's panel presentation, is an accomplished scholar who has thought long and diligently about the psychological and cultural aspects of incest. They have considered incest from many perspectives—in history, in myth and symbolism, in the social sciences and the arts, in psychotherapeutic theory and practice, and in religion and feminism. And what they have offered has been illuminating.

"But what I wish to speak about for a few moments now, to draw together all we have experienced this weekend, is the idea that when one suffering woman makes her way to the consulting room of a woman therapist, hoping to relieve the profound wounding of trauma, her act is more than personal."

Gudrun stood and moved the stool back and to one side, seeming to find it confining. As she continued, she paced slowly across the stage. "The suffering woman doesn't know what to expect, but her wounding is so pervasive that at last, she must begin the heroic and daunting journey of recovery and transformation known in mythology as the Road of Trials. And although no one has taken *her* individual journey before, this journey of transformation is as old as humankind."

Gudrun paused, deep in thought.

"To remind you of the ancient story that provides the framework and context for our play, Persephone is the young daughter of Demeter, the powerful Goddess of Grain and of the fields where grain is planted and harvested. By a secret arrangement between Zeus, Persephone's father, and his brother, Hades, it is agreed that Hades will claim Persephone as his queen, so she might rule over the Underworld.

"Ignorant of her dark destiny, Persephone is playing with her friends in a field, the realm of her mother, when she notices a flower more beautiful than the others. As she reaches for the flower, the earth gapes open and Hades comes forth, seizes Persephone, and carries her down to the Dark Realm. With this act of violence, he possesses her."

Gudrun turned to face the audience with a look of outrage. "Persephone's abductor is a wealthy and darkly powerful man, for in the Roman version of the myth, Hades is called Pluto, which refers to the enormous wealth and riches of the Underworld. But to be Queen of the Underworld is a perverse privilege, for it takes Persephone away from her life in the world of light."

The audience was hushed, giving Gudrun their rapt attention. Taking a breath, and speaking with new intensity, Gudrun continued, "If we look at this story from a psychological perspective, we see family dysfunction involving incest, in which a person of power, a father or other family member, makes a young girl special with a violent act, or with subtle enmeshment, separating her from her mother and her friends and her rightful life. She is caught in the perverse and terrible specialness of incest."

A shudder seemed to pass through the audience at those words, *the perverse and terrible specialness of incest.*

"In the legend, for this curse to be reversed and for the abducted girl to be returned to the light, her mother, Demeter, in her aspect as the great Mother Goddess, must intervene in the men's dark plot."

Gudrun began pacing again. When she reached one side of the stage, she stopped and turned back, shifting to a new perspective. "And so, dear audience, let us leave mythic time and come into the present, and the consulting room of the therapist we spoke of earlier and the wounded woman seeking relief from her troubled life. Perhaps the woman has a father she idealizes and forms an alliance with against a mother she disparages, all the while suffering from shame, low self-esteem, guilt, and self-loathing prompted by incest's dark secrecy.

"Perhaps the early trauma has become buried in protective forgetfulness and has gone into her unconscious, but as an adult, she engages in telltale behaviors: perhaps compulsive, failed relationships with married men, or male therapists, or bosses and other men of power. Also, perhaps, affairs with women. She is likely to be troubled by an eating disorder or depression, workaholism or other addictions.

"All signal to the therapist the trauma of incest, which, even if closed away from consciousness in the deep darkness of the psyche, impacts many aspects of the woman's life: her body, her spirit, her relationships, her work, her choices, her very sense of self."

Gudrun leaned toward the audience. They seemed to lean forward in response.

"When the suffering woman makes the appointment with

a woman therapist, she doesn't imagine she has entered upon a *spiritual* journey to encounter the Goddess. By this, we mean that the Goddess is a *metaphor* for the sacred feminine, the inviolate feminine self.

"In the protection and sanctuary of the consulting room, the therapist, during her time with the client, will become a symbolic expression of Demeter, the Mother Goddess, who will search for and at last rescue her abducted daughter and bring her back to the world of light.

"And the client must undergo a transformation of consciousness to experience and take into herself the cherishing love and fierce valuing by the Mother Goddess, so that her broken connection to her own feminine self can be restored."

Gudrun looked from person to person in the audience, drawing each one into the drama of the tale she was unfolding. "And the wise therapist knows that this radical transformation of consciousness cannot happen in ordinary time. The consulting room must become a secure vessel, a place of heightened power— of sacred time and space.

"The therapist also knows she herself must have the shamanic ability to shape-shift—to become, for a time, a manifestation of the Mother Goddess. This encounter will require all the skill the therapist has attained in order to create white magic, evoking an experience in the client strong enough to counteract and reverse the powerful curse of the father's black magic and the toxic specialness of incest."

Feeling her audience's attention now completely captured by her words, Gudrun took a moment to move the stool back to center, where she half sat on it and half stood, one foot on the floor for support.

"But no one returns from the Dark Realm unchanged," Gudrun continued. "Our journeyer is no longer the innocent girl who was happily picking flowers with her friends in her mother's field. The fraught and dangerous ordeal on the Road of Trials, with its necessary transformation of consciousness—which is, in fact, the healing process—has changed her. And although she has become free from the Underworld, she now has *shadows behind her eyes*."

Gudrun paused for dramatic effect, echoing that phrase from the play. "For, as the legend tells us, Persephone ate those six seeds of the pomegranate at the insistence of Hades. She partook of food in the Underworld, and what that means, symbolically, for our modern Persephone, is that she now carries some of that darkness of the ordeal, of the Underworld, within her."

Gudrun wanted to be clear. Not sure she was succeeding, she asked, "But what, exactly, *is* this necessary transformation, this enlargement of consciousness?" She paused, almost as if she expected someone in the audience to volunteer an answer, but she quickly went on. "The suffering, which the woman had experienced as encompassing and enclosing, has been relieved. The transformation of consciousness is the larger perspective with which she can now see her life. She no longer defines herself only in terms of incest, or of the outward behaviors that mark its damaging effect on her life. She sees new possibilities, experiences new ways of thinking, is able to make more life-enhancing choices.

"And perhaps her greatest realization is that those dark places of wounding and terror and loss, which all human life is heir to, are also, in some mysterious way, the deep sources of life-energy that fuel courage, profound wisdom, and empathy. And with empathy, she can open her heart in compassion to the suffering of another.

"This healing experience, this transformation, could be described as a *rebirth,* or *resurrection,* of the free and authentic self that arises from the depths of the psyche. And the woman's healing will be experienced in her outer life as the freedom to choose on her own behalf. She'll have the freedom to love and be loved truly and deeply. She'll have the freedom to do the soul work that calls forth her unique gifts and talents and creative yearnings, work that has the greatest meaning for her. And she'll have the freedom to believe that her life belongs to herself and not to the past, with its traumas and abuses and deep wounds. She'll live *authentically,* realizing and claiming her sovereignty."

Gudrun smiled and again looked from person to person.

"Our journeyer returns to the light sadder but wiser—wise with lessons learned on the journey itself. She now knows healing is possible and how it can be achieved, and because she has gained the ability to travel between the worlds of dark and light, she becomes a Guide of Souls, who can, with her compassionate understanding and empathy, point other lost and abducted sufferers toward the path out of the darkness and the binding enmeshment of trauma.

"She would not have that agency without the transformation of consciousness that her encounter with the Goddess has made possible. In the containment of the therapist's consulting room, she has become a Wounded Healer, and not of incest only, but of all the traumas and wounds that take us down into darkness, away from our true, luminous, authentic lives."

Gudrun clapped her hands in delight. The audience breathed a collective sigh, and a few people spontaneously joined her in brief applause. Realizing she had been talking for a long time already and must let her audience go on with their lives, Gudrun pressed on toward the epiphany.

"And so, dear audience, the woman, by traveling the metaphoric Road of Trials that is the healing process, experiences herself in a radically new way. No longer the shamed, traumatized person who first came into the therapist's consulting room, she now shines with the inner radiance of a person who has realized the sacred feminine within herself, who now claims her sovereignty and has direct knowing of the true magnitude of her own life, and of Life itself, for that *magnitude* of the human spirit is inherent within each of us."

Still half-seated on the stool, Gudrun shifted to sit fully on it. With this small movement, she gave the audience time to absorb what she had said. Now she moved her presentation toward its climax.

"One last thought I'd like to lift up for you is that, in a sense, the whole mythic story we have experienced today is a story of *initiation*, which occurs when an old, outgrown self dies and a new, more evolved and conscious and fully realized self comes into being. Persephone suffers the trauma of being taken down into the darkness of wounding and suffering, a trauma that happens to her and is beyond her control. And before she can be released to return to the world of light, she is induced to eat those six seeds of the pomegranate, the consequence of which is that her eventual freedom from the Dark Realm comes with a price: She will never be entirely free of the experience of the trauma, with its suffering and its wounds, and she will be able to return to the world of light *for only a part of the year."*

Gudrun now stood and again paced for a moment, graceful and thoughtful, while the audience considered her words.

"The difficult journey that brings healing will at last allow her to claim her life as her own. Yet she now lives in both worlds; as our story tells us, she returns to the world of light with shadows behind her eyes. And isn't that true of the human condition, dear audience? To be human, and to be fully conscious and awake in our lives is to know the inevitable sorrow, suffering, and loss that are an inescapable part of being alive in this world.

"And yet, to be fully alive and aware of the richness of existence also means to feel life's most beautiful emotions, to be enthusiastic—which is, literally, to be filled with sacred energy—and to be joyous, creative, ever open to possibility, and to experience the erotic energy that allows us to savor the senses without shame. In the profoundest expression of passion, to be compassionate, empathic, and acquainted with grief. And in experiencing the fullness of the self, to know the connectedness of things, to feel oneself to be a part of the wholeness and movement of the vast universe and, yes, to feel love for the world and all its creatures.

"That, dear audience, is what becomes possible when we are able to travel between the realms of darkness and light, to be conscious of both the sorrow and the rapture of life. That is the promise for each of us, the promise of the healing journey each of us must take, whatever our own personal journey of wounding and healing has been so that we can become fully human and whole and fully alive."

Gudrun opened her arms as if in a great, inclusive embrace

and exclaimed with conviction, "Perhaps the greatest reward of the enlargement of consciousness, with its gifts of wisdom and openness to beauty and experiencing the capacity for compassion, is that this powerful realization will radiate out from our individual journeyer to touch others close to her, even to her community and, ultimately, to the greater world.

"For, you see, the healing transformation must happen one person at a time, and without one individual's transformation of consciousness, *society's* transformation of consciousness will not be possible. And our courageous journeyer discovers that where she had once thought to be alone in the isolation of shame and dark secrecy, she is now, in her renewed and fully realized humanity, with all the world."

Gudrun stepped forward, toward the audience, her palms turned outward in blessing. "*That* is the hopeful message of our conference and of our small, but earnest, play.

"And with that message of hope, we thank each of you for sharing the journey with us this weekend, and we wish you a beautiful rest of the day."

The applause was subdued but deeply appreciative, as everyone stood and slowly made their way out of the theatre, smiling and speaking softly with one another.

David waited by the door, and Zoe went to him. He embraced her, murmuring, "It was beautiful, Zoe. *You* were beautiful."

He let her go but kept holding her hand. "How do you feel?"

"David, it was magical. All of it. And oh, Gudrun's speech! I didn't anticipate that she would add such an amazing illumination of all that had gone before in the conference and the play. I don't think any of us anticipated that."

"It *was* amazing!"

The theatre was almost empty.

David added, "So now, do you want to go home? Or would you like to stop for something to eat?"

"I'd love some food. I've eaten nothing all day, except for one bite of a glazed doughnut backstage. Not exactly nourishing. Hades made me eat it."

"That's Hades for you."

They decided on a Mexican restaurant in the neighborhood. Seated under an umbrella at a table in the back garden patio, in the afternoon warmth, Zoe leaned back and closed her eyes.

"This is the first time I've felt happiness like this for a very long time."

Tears came. "Here I go again. Even when I talk about being happy, I cry! Oh, David. I'm certifiable." She brushed away the tears. "But you're used to me by now, and you haven't fled yet. Thank you for handling my peculiarities—at least the ones I've let you see. I've got a million of them."

"Zoe. Zoe!" David reached across the table and took her hand.

He has the world's gentlest touch, Zoe thought.

"The tears are all right," he said, kindly. "And maybe you can let yourself be happy to be part of the beautiful play."

"I *am*, David. And the pleasure of being on stage again, after so long—it was all really a wonderful experience, despite my tears."

The waiter brought chips and salsa and took their order.

The conversation shifted to talk about Kathy, the intriguing neighborhood David was discovering, his renovation projects.

And each privately savored the delight of being together.

The chicken enchiladas and shrimp fajitas arrived, and for the rest of the time, Zoe didn't mention the play again, and neither did David.

But he had so often experienced her tears and emotional vulnerability that he promised himself he'd watch over her as much as she'd allow.

CHAPTER 15.
Farewell Dinner

Monday morning, back at the office, still reeling from the intensity of the play, Zoe faced the final arrangements for the International Congress in Amsterdam the third week in September.

Gudrun would go back to Denmark on Thursday, and her few remaining days in town were packed with plans. Everyone wanted time with her, but the last evening she saved so she could have dinner with Zoe.

On Wednesday evening, Gudrun arrived at Zoe's house in a cab, which delivered them to a brownstone mansion a few blocks west of Michigan Avenue.

No sign indicated that it was a restaurant. The only evidence of something special, besides the grandeur of the building, was a small blue and white porcelain Royal Copenhagen plaque to the left of the mahogany front door, showing the street address. It was a private Danish club so exclusive Zoe had never heard of it, though she had walked past the building and noted its unusual porcelain address plaque many times.

They climbed the broad front staircase and rang the bell. A

beautiful blond woman opened the door and said, "Good evening, Dr. Skjerne, Ms. Thomas."

Inside, everything was muted elegance. The young woman stepped behind a desk and wrote something in a large ledger. Beside the desk was a wrought-iron stand with a bouquet of white roses and vivid blue clematis blossoms in an enormous blue-and-white Royal Copenhagen vase. The hostess had Royal Copenhagen blue eyes.

At the entrance to the dining room, the *maître d'* greeted them and, bowing briefly, showed them to a table away from the entrance, near a small parquet dance floor where a harpist, spotlighted and golden, played soft music, adding to the sumptuous atmosphere of the room.

The tables were placed far apart from one another. Half a dozen diners, mostly couples, talked quietly.

After Gudrun and Zoe were seated and the waiter, Christian, whom Gudrun greeted warmly, had brought wine for Gudrun and sparkling water for Zoe, Gudrun opened her purse and drew out a small package wrapped in golden paper, handing it to Zoe with a smile. It was a leather-bound copy of the script, signed *For Zoe, my wonderful Kay, with gratitude and love.*

Zoe was overwhelmed. She thanked Gudrun tearfully. But the tears were not only for the gift. She was already experiencing Gudrun's departure as a keen loss and told her so.

"Yes, Zoe. I'll miss you, too, my dear friend. I'm grateful for my time with you, for all you contributed to our play, and that you and David came to see my paintings. But, Zoe, we'll soon see one another again in Amsterdam. And perhaps you can spend some time with me in Copenhagen after the Congress. It's not far from Amsterdam."

"I'd love to, Gudrun. That sounds wonderful. Thank you."

Gudrun sighed. "Alas, I really must get back. I've had several phone calls from my daughter, who tells me my clients are leaving many messages on my answering machine. I suspect they're firing up their psyches for my return."

"We all need you, Gudrun." Tears stirred again, but Zoe brushed them away and shook her head. "You've come into my life at a challenging time, and everything about you seems to resonate with something significant happening to me."

Gudrun tilted her head with an unspoken question and waited for Zoe to continue.

"Of course, the play, but also your paintings, Gudrun. I was overwhelmed by them. It's as if you'd revealed my deepest self, there on the canvases."

"You mentioned the paintings when we had lunch after the exhibit." Gudrun smiled and paused. "And I promised myself I wouldn't leave Chicago without having a better idea of what you meant. That's why I've saved this time for us."

"Thank you, Gudrun. I'm truly grateful for your concern. But you should be able to enjoy your last evening in Chicago without worrying about me."

It occurred to Zoe that life-changing conversations kept happening to her in restaurants these days. But this restaurant was so beautiful, with its subdued elegance and peace, no clattering dishes, no loud voices. Discreet waiters took orders and served food and refreshed coffee and wine unobtrusively, leaving the diners to intimate conversations.

"Zoe, I *want* to know more about what is happening in your life. You've said a number of things suggesting that you're going through a difficult time. Perhaps I can help. And we'll have some time tomorrow. My plane doesn't leave until evening, and in the morning, we can talk about a plan, once we've had a good night's sleep and I've thought about what you've told me, *if* you're willing to tell me."

"I'm willing to tell you. But Gudrun, my life is so . . . disgusting these days." Zoe imitated Kay. "Incest cooties! Yuck! Get them off me!"

Gudrun laughed loudly, then remembered where she was and quieted her voice.

"Oh, Zoe," she gasped, "You truly *are* Kay!"

Then she was serious. "We can do all of it, Zoe, hear about your life and your response to my paintings and all the while enjoy our dinner on this last evening in my beloved Chicago. That's why I chose this very special restaurant. Here, we can linger over after-dinner coffee and chocolate mints and talk to our hearts' content, and no one will make us feel we should leave."

She sat back and sighed with contentment.

They both ordered *steak au poivre* and watched as Christian wheeled a cart to their table and quickly created a masterpiece in a gleaming copper pan over a candle flame, adding the filets to sizzling butter, briefly grinding peppercorns onto them from an enormous peppermill, flaming the whole thing with a dramatic blaze of cognac, and gently placing the filets onto large, warm plates.

He rapidly stirred cream into the juices in the pan and, with a flourish, poured sauce over the filets, wiping away any errant drops with his napkin and setting the plates carefully before his appreciative audience of two, then he deftly spooned tiny potatoes and mushrooms around the filets.

The whole performance lasted only moments. He poured more

wine for Gudrun and sparkling water for Zoe, and with a smile and a courtly bow, assured that they needed nothing more, he put out the candle flame with the back of a large spoon, wheeled the tray silently away, and left them to their pleasure.

When they had finished the meal and delighted in strawberries dipped in dark chocolate, and were sipping coffee out of fragile cups, Zoe thanked Gudrun and said how perfect it all had been.

They sat silent for a few moments, happily sated.

Then Gudrun said, "Now, my dear Zoe, please tell me more about your response to my paintings."

Taking a deep breath, Zoe mentioned what was most important about the exhibit. "Gudrun, the large painting in the back room. That's Persephone and Hades, isn't it?"

Gudrun nodded.

"For some reason, that painting upset me so much I had a panic attack and fled from the gallery.

"I didn't want to mention that earlier. It was such a beautiful event, and David and I felt so honored to be included. But now I can tell you. I was profoundly shaken by that particular painting and, considering the play and all that it revealed, and what you said afterward, and the troubling things that have been happening since the death of my father, I think I understand why."

"The painting has great personal significance for me, too, Zoe." Gudrun took a sip of wine.

The harpist finished for the evening and put a leather cover over the harp. Gudrun and Zoe, along with the few other diners, acknowledged her with quiet applause. She nodded to them and smiled briefly. They watched as she gathered her music and purse and left.

Then Gudrun said, "Zoe, I expect you've realized that my great interest in the trauma of incest is not just a professional matter. Understanding how trauma is passed on from generation to generation, and how it can be stopped, has both professional and personal significance to me. Zoe, we therapists tend to be Wounded Healers. We hope to heal in others what needs to be healed in ourselves. My interest comes out of my own dark childhood, my own woundedness from incest. So does my art."

Giving Zoe time to absorb this, she signaled Christian, requesting more coffee, more strawberries, and more mints. He smiled and removed the cups half-filled with cold coffee and returned moments later, balancing a tray with fresh cups and a plate with chocolate-covered strawberries and a mound of mints. He disappeared again and after a moment returned with a huge silver carafe from which he poured steaming coffee.

"Ah, Christian!" Gudrun purred. "You truly are a prince!" He smiled again, bowed, and moved quietly away, graceful as a dancer.

Zoe said, "The play shed light into my own dark childhood, Gudrun. Especially what you said afterward. When you described the 'suffering woman' and what took her to the consulting room of the woman therapist, you told my life story exactly."

After a pause, she added, "And those words, 'the perverse and terrible specialness of incest'—like everyone else, I shuddered to hear them."

Gudrun said, her voice kind, and concerned, "Yes, Zoe. This doesn't surprise me."

Zoe hurried on. "But it's all new to me. There's so much I don't understand, don't even remember.

"And Gudrun," Zoe felt anger stirring, and bitterness, "I must tell you that I really don't have the time to take that 'healing journey' you've described, or to achieve the 'transformation and enlargement of consciousness' that you consider so important. I don't have either the time or the inclination for *any* of that."

She sat back and closed her eyes, shaking her head and sighing a heartrending sigh.

Then, realizing she had perhaps sounded rude, she softened what she had said with some experiences she appreciated.

"My friend Anna has been a help. More than a year ago, she told me about her own struggle with incest. And a couple of weeks ago, when I told her what I've been going through lately, she took me to a meeting of her incest survivors' support group."

Gudrun said, "A support group can be very helpful."

Zoe added, the antagonism gone from her voice, "And something else occurred recently that is so weirdly coincidental I can hardly believe it happened. My first cousin Suzanne reappeared after twenty years of silence, and over dinner during her layover at O'Hare, she solved some family mysteries for me."

Zoe told Gudrun about Suzanne's revelations.

"How hard it must have been to hear that," Gudrun said.

"I was devastated. But I'm so glad to have Suzanne back in my life. It was such a loss, not hearing from her all those years. Now I understand why."

"Suzanne's given you important validation, Zoe. That will help you greatly in your recovery work."

Zoe's anger flared again. "*Recovery work?* Dammit, Gudrun, I don't have *time* for recovery work. I've got to hold myself together for the Congress."

She spat out her words bitterly. She was close to tears.

"And I can't do nine years of analysis the way Kay did. Or go on the Road of Trials or encounter the Goddess or integrate the sacred feminine into my psyche or become a Wounded Healer and save society one life at a time. I have enough trouble just getting from day to day without going mad."

She concluded her outburst with a sob. "And worst of all, tomorrow you're leaving for Denmark."

Gudrun leaned forward and took Zoe's hand, her voice gently insistent. "Zoe, I won't abandon you, I promise. I'll phone you in the morning at your office and perhaps you can slip away for a little while and meet me downstairs in the coffee shop.

"Meanwhile, I'll be thinking about how I can give you the most support until we see one another in Amsterdam."

She paused to take a sip of coffee, then she pressed on.

"Zoe, each journey of healing is unique. It does not need to be done the way Kay did it, or as I described it in my remarks afterward. Your own life will show you how your healing must take place. I cannot say how that should happen, or when.

"And despite what I said about the great battle between white and black magic, though that needs to happen, it will happen in its own time, not in ours. All you and I need to do for now is to trust the unfolding of your unique healing journey in its own way."

Gudrun paused, then added, with a smile, "And, dear Zoe, it seems already to be underway, with or without your permission, or mine. So be of good cheer. It's all unfolding to perfection."

"Perfection, Gudrun? I don't think so."

Zoe looked regretfully around the dining room. They were almost the last ones, and she said, "Dammit, Gudrun. I've behaved badly. Incest has ruined our beautiful evening like it ruins everything else. And now, I've got to go to the restroom."

Gudrun's voice was filled with love. "Zoe, your feelings are totally normal and understandable, and nothing is ruined. Your life can be set right. Many of us have faced what you're facing and have regained our lives. All will be well, dear. But now, go to the restroom. It's over there, by the exit light."

While Zoe was gone, Gudrun settled the bill and waited by the entrance with Zoe's script and then guided her out of the building and down the front steps.

A cab was waiting, and Gudrun gave the driver Zoe's address. When they arrived, Gudrun asked the driver to wait while they walked together to the front door, Gudrun's arm around Zoe's shoulders in comforting protectiveness.

She saw Zoe into the lighted house, kissed her, and handed her the package with the script.

Zoe said, "Thank you for this beautiful copy of the script, and for the beautiful play, and for the beautiful dinner, and for your beautiful kindness and understanding and forgiving nature when I behave badly. And thank you for your friendship and wisdom and—for everything. Thank you. Thank you."

When they had finished their farewells, Gudrun pulled Zoe's front door closed and got into the waiting cab, leaning forward from the back seat to give the driver the address of the loft building.

CHAPTER 16.
Gudrun's Plan

"So, Zoe, I've given thought to how I might support you from Denmark, while your life here is so challenging."

Gudrun and Zoe were sitting in a small coffee shop on the mezzanine of the John Hancock Center. It was after the morning rush, and they had the place to themselves.

"I've come up with something that might be helpful for now, a way for you to continue your inner work, which must be attended to, but will help you contain and focus it while you go on with your outer requirements.

"It's only a suggestion, of course, and I offer it to you as a friend and colleague, not as your therapist."

Gudrun looked appraisingly at Zoe and added, "I'll also give you the name of a therapist friend, a woman I think you'll like, who is experienced in working with incest survivors. I took the liberty of phoning her this morning and mentioning your situation. She'll welcome a call from you when you're ready."

Gudrun placed her own business card on the table before Zoe; on the back she had written the therapist's name and phone number.

Silently, Zoe said, *Oh, Gudrun, please don't ask me to see another damned therapist.* But not wanting to be rude once again, she took the card and put it quickly into her purse.

"I realize you can't consider therapy now, with the Congress looming. I've given you her name and number in case you need some support later. But meanwhile, I have another way you and I could do some long-distance work together."

Zoe took a sip of coffee, slowly put the cup down, and looked expectantly at Gudrun.

"Perhaps you could think of my suggestion as an artwork," Gudrun said. "As if we're fellow artists working on a collaboration, as we did with the play. The idea I had is that you would write to me—"

Zoe burst in, with a laugh, "*That,* I can do!" She experienced a flood of relief.

"But it would not be the usual letter, Zoe. You would write as if you were speaking directly to me, almost as if we were sitting with one another here.

"But it would also be like a journal entry. Something on paper, which you could respond to and work with more deeply later. You would do some writing each day, if possible, and you'd try to concentrate all your concerns about the incest only while you're writing. Other times, you'd put away thoughts of incest. That will help you contain them and keep them from overwhelming you but will not push them completely out of your consciousness, which you must not do. Then, from time to time, you'll send copies of the pages to me. I'll respond with further suggestions. Would you care to try that?"

"Oh, yes. Gladly." Zoe began to feel hopeful.

"Good. It's a technique I sometimes use with my clients when we can't meet in my consulting room. It works remarkably well.

"I'd like you to reconstruct your life with your father and mother, without interpretation or judgment, as factually as possible, noting everything you can remember of your relationship with each of them, during each year of your life. Take one year at a time, and record as many specific events as you can tie to it."

Gudrun continued, "It would be helpful if you could find pictures from that time and write whatever associations they produce. Mention any dreams you remember, as well as uncanny experiences, body memories, spiritual beliefs and questionings, enlargement of faith or loss of it, hopes and doubts you had about yourself—"

"I'll have difficulty with that, Gudrun. I seem to have lost whole years of my childhood." Zoe shook her head. "Second grade? Third, fourth, fifth grade? Complete blanks."

"Once you begin," Gudrun said, her voice reassuring, "I think you'll find that memories come back to you. You might try to recreate actual conversations you had with your father and mother. If you can't remember them exactly, put in what you think might have been said. Don't worry about making things up. You cannot make a mistake in this. Whatever you write will be instructive."

Gudrun shifted and leaned forward. "And there's one other procedural thing. I'd like you to write about yourself in the third person, as if you were speaking about someone else. You may use your own name, if you wish, but you will speak of Zoe from the outside. You'll watch her go through her childhood. You'll watch her grow up."

Gudrun took a sip of her coffee and quickly put the paper cup down, pushing it away with a look of disgust.

"You'll be like Ingmar Bergman. Do you know the work of that great Swedish filmmaker and neighbor of the Danes?"

"My favorite films in the world are *Wild Strawberries* and *The Magician.*"

"Wonderful. Then perhaps you know that Bergman filmed situations from his own life when he was undergoing personal challenges and feeling deeply troubled and was engaged in introspection, which seemed to happen a lot. Good fortune for us because it resulted in some very great films."

"Yes," Zoe said. She felt a surge of happiness, remembering the darkly powerful and intriguing films.

"What's of special interest to us, Zoe, is that Bergman described his way of working as seeing into everything as if he were God, as you will do, writing about Zoe from a larger, more objective perspective.

"Also, he referred to *Wild Strawberries* as a 'journey film,' in which a character goes on a journey back into the past to confront a deep problem within himself and, as a result, achieves a reintegration of personality."

Gudrun smiled and briefly touched Zoe's hand, a reassuring gesture.

"Zoe, I'm not asking you to become Ingmar Bergman. But like him, you are taking a journey into the past, occasioned by the death of your father and all it has stirred in your psyche. I feel certain this journey will bring you a reintegration of personality, as it did for Bergman."

Zoe suddenly felt overwhelmed. "I wonder if I can do what you suggest."

"Well, try it, Zoe. I think you'll find the process illuminating.

But if you don't, that's perfectly all right. There are other things we can try. You might paint or sketch or create images in some other medium, images with which to work later. I've done that myself. It's what stirred many of my paintings. But I've done the writing, also. It's been helpful."

Having offered Zoe this plan, Gudrun said, "Now, my dear Zoe, I must be on my way. I hope you're feeling encouraged and supported by our plan."

"I feel *very* supported and a *little* encouraged, Gudrun. A million thanks."

"Good." With a kiss and a jasmine-scented embrace, Gudrun said goodbye.

Zoe's eyes filled with tears. "You're a wonderful friend. Have a safe trip home."

She sat down again at the table after Gudrun left and ordered another cup of coffee.

CHAPTER 17.
Letters

Saturday, July 29, 1972
Chicago, Illinois

Dear Gudrun:

This is how the story of Zoe begins. Somehow, around the age of five or six, Zoe lost her mother. Her mother did not die physically, but she died in another way, and Zoe's happy life in the garden ended.

Her mother was in the garden. Her mother *was* the garden.

Zoe's mother planted purple violets beside the back porch steps, and by the end of summer, the leaves grew huge, overwhelming everything else. Her mother had brought the violets from the woods at the end of Spring Street, near the railroad tracks and the trestle, because Zoe's early childhood with her mother included not only the garden behind her house but also the woods, where together they gathered wildflowers and beautiful weeds.

And it included fields, and country roads along which they gathered sweet, tiny wild strawberries. The fields were marked off by ditches, reflecting the sky in their shallow water, with cattails and rushes and milkweed stalks on which red-winged blackbirds lighted briefly and whistled.

In autumn, wild apple trees in the fields were filled with rounds of vivid red, so beautiful at a distance, but up close, almost always imperfect. The fruit had been stung by wasps or had fallen to the ground and had been infested by worms. Later, after the milkweed pods had burst open and sent their tiny white dancers waltzing into the world, the fallen apples exuded the most delicious fragrance.

Zoe's mother knew everything about gardens and woods and fields. She taught Zoe the Latin names of flowers and revealed the mysteries of the earth and the turning seasons.

In early spring, she showed Zoe where the first blossoms were hidden under the snow, on the hillside above an icy river. She would lead Zoe to the very spot where new life was stirring in secret, under the snow, and she lifted the icy crust and the odorous layer of damp, matted leaves to reveal the pale buds of hepaticas on their fragile, translucent stems.

When the snow was gone, her mother's garden in the small back yard would burst forth with crocuses and then hyacinths and jonquils; later, Easter lilies, pansies, lilies of the valley, and lilacs.

Throughout the summer, there was continual blossoming of nasturtiums, asters, zinnias, petunias, bachelor's buttons.

Later, there were chrysanthemums and Japanese lanterns, which her mother took into the house as a Thanksgiving bouquet.

Zoe remembered this garden, and the woods and fields, with yearning, but also with a sense of loss, because somehow, when she was six, her mother faded away.

At night, when Zoe felt afraid and called for her mother, her father came.

So, Gudrun. That's all I can write for now.

With love,

Zoe

Saturday, August 5, 1972
Copenhagen, Denmark

Dear Zoe:

How good that you've made this beginning. I congratulate you.

I'm interested that you've started Zoe's story with her mother's garden, and the visits with her mother to the woods and fields. I cannot help thinking of Persephone, abducted from the field, her mother's realm, where she had been playing happily and innocently.

Zoe seemed happy in her mother's garden and being with her mother in the woods and the fields, gathering blossoms and beautiful weeds and wild strawberries.

In her first six years, she seems to have known her mother's nurturance. That is important to remember.

Could you now perhaps speak of the marital context into which Zoe was born? Who were Zoe's parents before they were her mother and father? What kinds of families did they come from? You need not say more than you know. You need not try to explain or interpret.

But whatever information you have about these two individuals, and the circumstances that brought them together in a marriage, would be helpful.

Once again, I congratulate you on your fine beginning.

I send a warm embrace.

Gudrun

CHAPTER 18.
A Dark Turn

Monday, August 7, 1972
Chicago, Illinois

Dear Gudrun:

I wonder if I should go on with this. The night after I mailed the first letter, I had a nightmare from which I awakened sick with dread.

I dreamed I was a young child, maybe five years old. I felt myself to be inside a child's small body, and I was playing among the violets by the steps to the back porch. The violets were in full bloom. They were on long stems and had large, bright leaves and vivid blue and purple blossoms.

I was down among them, feeling joyous and safe. I wanted to pick a bouquet to take to my mother.

As I pushed the leaves aside, I noticed a dark opening under the steps. I leaned down to see what the opening was and felt a stinging on the inside of my hand. When I turned my hand over to look, a huge black spider clung to my palm. The spider was almost the size of my hand. I screamed and scrambled frantically backwards and fell onto the grass, feeling dizzy with pain and terror.

My hand throbbed and began to swell.

As I watched, the garden wilted and turned to blighted weeds. I got up to run away, and when I looked again at my throbbing wound, I saw that the place where the spider had stung me had become a tiny vagina, ripped wide, pulsing with pain. Blood began flowing out of it. Soon, there was blood all over my skirt and even flowing down between my legs.

My screaming woke me up.

I've had to summon my courage even to write this for you here. I've been afraid to go to sleep ever since.

Help!

Zoe

The phone rang early the following Saturday morning. Zoe anxiously answered. Phone calls early on weekends were never good news.

"Zoe, I've just now received your letter about the dream. Are you all right?"

"Oh, Gudrun." Zoe had just finished breakfast and was about to go to her garden and absorb its gentle beauty and comfort. "How wonderful of you to call. Yes, I'm all right now. It was rough for a few days after the dream. I just kept feeling terrified. I had difficulty making myself believe it hadn't really happened. I kept looking at the palm of my hand, expecting to see that appalling wound."

"Zoe, I'm concerned. I think I underestimated your need for

support just now. I want you to see the therapist right away. Please phone her today and set up an appointment as soon as you can arrange it. Tell her, please, that I've requested that you do so.

"If you get her answering machine, leave that message and I'm sure she'll get back to you right away. I've let her know how special you are to me, though that would not matter; she'll offer you her best expertise in any case.

"And I want you to stay in close touch with your friend Anna and the incest survivors' group. And with me. I'll offer you all the support I can from here, but you must use your resources close at hand."

"Gudrun, your concern is frightening."

"I don't mean to frighten you. But I *am* concerned. And I *do* mean for you to take this seriously. This is an important time for you. Not one to be ignored."

"I don't have time for this. It's interfering with my life. I have the Congress to run."

"Zoe, this *is* your life. You *must* attend to it. The Congress will go on; everything is in place."

"Not without my full attention for the next few weeks. The Congress begins in a month. I'll just have to wait until it's over to go crazy."

"Zoe! You're *not* going to go crazy. You're going to reclaim your life."

"My life?" Zoe laughed bitterly. "My life is my career. My life is the Congress."

"No. Your life is not those things. Your life is something else, of infinitely greater value."

"I don't know what you're talking about." Zoe's voice was bitter. "I have no life, outside of my work.

"And Gudrun, sometimes, as I'm going along, suddenly I don't feel real to myself. I have a sensation that I'm not connected to anything. It's as if I've slipped out of my body and lost my connection to the world. I repeat my name to myself, and I can't make it seem like my name. I can't understand who I am."

"Many people have described what you're describing, Zoe. It goes with the incest."

"I thought I was just crazy."

"It's called *dissociation*. With recovery, dissociation goes away. That's part of what I mean about reclaiming your life. But only part."

"*Damn* my father. *Damn* him."

Zoe realized she was gripping the phone so tightly her hand and wrist ached. "Whatever happened took place years ago. Why is this happening to me now? Why?"

"Because it was time. It's not unusual for the death of the perpetrator to create a crisis for the victim of incest. When the lid of the casket closes, Pandora's box opens. But it is a crisis of *healing*, Zoe. It's a chance for rebirth."

"*Rebirth!* Dammit, Gudrun!" Zoe was shouting into the phone now. "That's what they said about AA. How many rebirths must I endure?" She sobbed.

Gudrun's voice was calm, firm, reassuring. "For Persephone, and perhaps for all of us, it happens again and again. After the dark time in the Underworld, there is a return to the light. Spring always comes after the darkness of winter. That's one meaning of the Persephone myth. Rebirth, in nature, and in the psyche."

"I don't want to do this, Gudrun. Not now."

Gudrun was emphatic. "Your life chooses the time, Zoe. Not you. But this is a gift, an opportunity. This is not a bad thing."

"Why does it feel so awful?"

"Life is a glorious adventure, except that it hurts."

"Am I going to get through this, Gudrun?"

"Of course." Gudrun's laugh was warm and kind.

"I need to be able to do my work. I want to do it, Gudrun. I know in the greater scheme of things, what I do in my job isn't all that important, but it is to me."

"I understand, Zoe. That's why I'm urging you to surround yourself with support, to see the therapist. These are powerful forces coming up from your unconscious. They don't care whether you have a Congress, or a schedule, or even a life. They must be dealt with."

"*Damn* my father," Zoe said again.

"You're going to take your life back from him, Zoe, to claim your life as your own." Gudrun's voice was insistent. "You have a right to the fullness of your life. To know joy. To know the rapture of being alive. Those are yours to have. And you *will* have them, dear.

"But now, you must call the therapist. Call her today. I've told her to expect your call. Please, Zoe. Do it."

"I'll try to reach her."

"Good. And for now, put aside the writing. It's a powerful tool, at the proper time. I think this is not the proper time. And stay in touch with me, dear."

After the call ended, Zoe sat with her eyes closed for a long time, not moving.

Then she went to the garden and watered her flowers.

But she did not call the therapist.

After Gudrun's phone call, Zoe did not allow herself to think about incest. She did not think about anything but the Congress.

She worked until nine every night, sometimes until midnight. She went to the office at seven in the morning. She ate lunch at her desk or went to a noontime AA meeting, but at the meeting she said nothing about herself.

Day after day, she grew more exhausted, more numb. That had always worked for her before when she was avoiding feelings.

She saw neither friend nor therapist. She didn't talk to David. She didn't even talk to the Chief, who had gone away for two weeks to the Eastern Shore with Mrs. Chief and, uncharacteristically, didn't phone in, correctly assuming Zoe would take care of everything.

CHAPTER 19.
Cataclysmic Encounter

In early September, Zoe's mother arrived unexpectedly for a visit, not considering that Zoe was tremendously busy preparing for the Congress.

"I'll be leaving for my cruise in two weeks," she said. "I thought I should visit you. We never know which visit might be the last."

Zoe did not respond to this provocative statement. Anyway, her mother was here now. Zoe met her at the airport, and they stopped for dinner at a quiet Italian restaurant a few blocks from home.

When they had ordered, her mother said, "I miss the companionship of a man. I don't fancy rooming with two old maids on the cruise, but that's all I could afford."

This was a veiled reference to her father's "meager professor's salary," which her mother had always considered a disappointment.

Elizabeth Thomas chatted about buying the first slacks she'd ever owned. She'd always worn sensible dresses with matching jackets, as ladies of her generation did, so for her to consider wearing something as casual as slacks was a surprise, one of many, these days.

And she looked wonderful. Her pale blue eyes sparkled and were full of life, and her silvery hair was perfectly coiffed. She seemed to be getting younger.

As they had after-dinner coffee and her mother was finishing a second daiquiri—yet another surprise, considering her mother's Methodist upbringing—Zoe said, "Mother, guess who I saw recently. Your long-lost niece, Suzanne."

"Really?" Mrs. Thomas's eyes stopped sparkling. She carefully put down her daiquiri glass.

"Yes. For the first time in twenty years. She phoned me from O'Hare. She was on a layover on her way to London. It was good to see her, Mother."

"Well, well." Mrs. Thomas's voice was icy.

"I've wondered why she never answered my Christmas cards. I faithfully wrote to her every Christmas, all those years, and she never responded. Now, I understand why."

Zoe's mother stiffened. "Well, dear. She's not a reliable source. She's an alcoholic."

"Mother, for God's sake. That has nothing to do with it. I'm an alcoholic, too."

"No, you're not, dear."

"Dammit, Mother. It infuriates me when you say that. I'm an alcoholic. *Why* can't you face it? There's nothing to be ashamed of. It's just a fact of my life."

They'd had this discussion many times. Mrs. Thomas never changed her position on the subject.

"You've always been overly dramatic, Zoe. I don't know where you got such a ridiculous notion. Our family doesn't drink. We're Methodists."

Zoe stifled a laugh. Her mother was drinking her second daiquiri. But Elizabeth Thomas went on, pointing out that Zoe managed a successful career with a famous psychiatrist and handled her many responsibilities exceptionally well (uncharacteristic praise) finishing firmly, "You're *not* an alcoholic."

Zoe responded, with exaggerated patience, "I'm a high-bottom drunk, Mother. And I'm grateful to be in recovery. I'm one of the lucky ones. I didn't have to lose everything."

Then she almost shouted, "But I *am* a fucking alcoholic!"

"Zoe, please. Ladies don't use that kind of language. And lower your voice."

Zoe said, loudly, "I'm not a lady, Mother. You should know that."

Mrs. Thomas looked around to see if people had heard. The few couples at tables nearby went on with their conversations.

Zoe pressed on, her voice now low and taunting. "Don't you want to know what Suzanne told me? Aren't you even curious?"

"Not in the slightest," Mrs. Thomas said, dismissively. "Your cousin is a liar. That's why we have had nothing to do with her or her family all these years. I have no interest in the filth she spews forth."

Zoe continued her taunting. "How do you know it's filth? How do you know she spewed forth anything?"

Her tone became almost defiant. "She's a wonderful person. I've missed her. I'm glad she's back in my life."

Zoe's mother sat back and scowled. "That makes me very sad, Zoe. I hoped we were through with that disgusting part of your father's family forever. I prefer that you not see her again or have any further contact with her."

"Why, Mother?" Zoe leaned forward and looked intently into her face. "*Why?*"

"I don't owe you any explanations."

Mrs. Thomas looked away and paused, seeming to decide something. She looked back at Zoe, and her voice became unequivocal. "I *demand* that you not see Suzanne ever again. I *demand* that you not mention her or her family to me ever again. And now, I *demand* that we end this conversation. I'm going to the ladies' room, and I shall wait for you outside the restaurant so we can go home."

With enormous dignity, she picked up her patent leather purse and her gloves and made her way, as regal as the Queen Mother, out of the dining room. Zoe paid the bill and went to get the car.

At home, the atmosphere was strained; they said only what was necessary. Zoe carried her mother's suitcase upstairs and put it onto the luggage rack at the foot of the bed in the guest bedroom. She curtly showed her mother where she could find fresh towels and washcloths, and she turned down the covers on the bed.

Mrs. Thomas followed Zoe downstairs again and watched, silent and tense, as Zoe set up the coffeemaker and showed her how to turn it on in the morning if she woke early.

"I know you like your morning coffee, Mother. I'll be leaving early for the office. I won't take time for breakfast; I have too much to do before I leave for the Congress."

She hoped her mother would get her meaning, that this visit was an imposition. "Fix yourself some breakfast if you wish."

"Thank you. Coffee is all I need in the morning."

Without further discussion, they went back upstairs, said a tense goodnight, and closed the doors to their bedrooms.

Each morning, Zoe looked in on her mother before she left for the office. Her mother, still in bed but always quite awake, got up and put on her lacy pink robe and her pink slippers, walked Zoe to the front door, gave her a perfunctory kiss, and said goodbye.

When Zoe was gone and Mrs. Thomas was alone in the townhouse, she had a cup of coffee and got dressed. She spent the day reading, or taking a walk, or shopping at Marshall Field's, where perhaps she would meet Zoe for a ladies' lunch at the Walnut Room. Sometimes, she had supper waiting when Zoe came home.

Through it all, there was only casual conversation. No more talk of alcoholism. Family secrets remained secret.

Zoe was glad, in a way. The Chief had returned from the Eastern Shore, irritable after too much time with Mrs. Chief. Zoe had all she could do to manage the Chief's anxiety, her own, and preparations for the Congress.

At home in the evenings, Zoe and her mother circled cautiously around one another. Zoe desperately needed to finish the conversation they had begun at the restaurant, but they both seemed reluctant to do so, as if realizing that it would be terrible.

On Friday, her mother's next to the last night, it happened. And it *was* terrible.

They had finished dinner and were still sitting at the dining room table. Zoe had served a special dessert of strawberry tarts, a small attempt to make amends for having been an ungracious hostess all week. She left the dinner dishes on the table, took a deep breath, and began, with a pounding heart and hands visibly trembling.

"Mother, my inner world is in shambles. I can't go on pretending that it's not. I must talk to you about it. I don't mean to confront or blame you. This is not about you. It's about me, and my struggle to understand what happened to me in the past, because it's still affecting my life in negative ways."

Mrs. Thomas said nothing. Tense and alert, she simply put down her coffee cup and looked at Zoe.

"Mother," Zoe said, "ever since Daddy's death, terrible things have been happening to me, but they were *not* caused by anything Suzanne told me." Zoe was adamant. "My meeting with Suzanne was recent, and what she said helped me understand what's happening to me, but this is *not* because of my conversation with her. This started right after Daddy's death."

Mrs. Thomas still said nothing.

After a long pause, Zoe continued. "In fact, the things that are happening to me are not, for the most part, external events. But within me, it's been chaos. I've been having nightmares, Mother. Shadowy, vague scraps of memories of dark things from my childhood."

"Zoe, you had a happy childhood," Mrs. Thomas said firmly. She had told Zoe this a thousand times. It was a fiction she seemed to take pride in.

Zoe became breathless; her voice rose.

"No, Mother. It only *seemed* happy to people on the outside. Inside, there was fear, shame, and secrets, secrets that were hidden even from me. But the truth is coming out now. I didn't want it to, but it is demanding to be known."

"Zoe, you're talking nonsense. You had a happy childhood. You were loved and gently raised. You were privileged. You had cultural benefits other children did not have."

"I don't dispute the cultural benefits. But Mother—"

"Your father, despite his meager professor's salary, spread the world's cultural riches before you, taking us traveling to see beautiful, historic places, taking us to Europe—"

"I *know*, Mother. That's not what I'm talking about."

"And you spent every summer in northern Michigan studying music, dance, and drama. Most children never have that privilege, and your father made that possible for you, summer after summer."

"*Mother*! I'm not talking about my *cultural benefits*."

Zoe's voice became louder. "I'm talking about the other part of my childhood. The nightmares, the nights when—"

"All children have nightmares." The louder Zoe's voice became, the more softly her mother spoke.

"Not like mine, Mother!" Zoe was shouting now. "Mine had Daddy in them. Daddy *made* the nightmares, Mother."

"Zoe, I forbid you to continue with this!"

Mrs. Thomas was now shouting too. "Your father was a fine man and now he's dead." She choked back a sob. "He's dead, and your duty as his daughter is to revere his memory."

"Mother! We can't go on pretending any more. We can't go on living with the pretense. A monster has gotten loose and now it must be dealt with."

"I forbid you to say these things."

"Oh, Mother," Zoe cried. Her voice was shrill, her throat tight with tears. "You can't forbid anything anymore. I wish you could. But this time, it won't go away, whatever either of us says."

"It, it, it. What is this *it*? No, I don't want to hear."

Mrs. Thomas lifted her hands and covered her ears.

"Suzanne put lies into your head. I *told* you, Zoe. Suzanne is a liar. You can't believe anything she says."

"Suzanne only confirmed what I already suspected, Mother," Zoe shouted. "*I am a victim of incest.*"

"No, Zoe! *No.*"

There was silence.

They sat, stunned.

After a long moment, Zoe went on, her voice guttural as she spat out the words. "Daddy abused me, Mother, while you slept. He abused me when he gave me baths. He abused me with enemas. And all the while you were closed away in your bedroom. You slept through the whole terrible thing."

"No! None of this is true, Zoe!"

Mrs. Thomas stood, and with her sudden movement she caught the edge of a dinner plate with her sleeve and sent it skittering across the table, jangling the silverware and overturning a water glass.

She ran to the stairs and started to climb. Zoe ran after her and caught her roughly by the arm, turning her around. They faced one another.

"You *lie*, Zoe."

"Mother, the only lie is what I said about not blaming you, not holding you accountable. I *accuse* you of not protecting me. I *accuse* you of not coming when I called for you in the night. I was frightened, Mother. I had night terrors and I called for you. You never came, Mother. You never came!"

She sobbed. "*Daddy* came. He told me to be quiet. He told me you weren't well. He said you needed your sleep. He told me not to disturb you. He got into bed with me. He did . . ."

"What? What did he do?"

"I don't know," Zoe sobbed. "But the baths, the enemas . . ."

"You don't know? *You don't know?* Baths and enemas aren't—I won't even say that filthy word! You accuse him, as if things any devoted parent would do were terrible things. How dare you, Zoe! You're defiling your father's good name, making filthy accusations. You're crazy, Zoe. A crazy alcoholic."

Zoe laughed hysterically. "Good! Good! At least now you admit I'm an alcoholic."

"You're crazy, Zoe," Mrs. Thomas shouted again.

"Yes, I *am* crazy," Zoe shouted back. "Crazy with pain. But I'm not a liar, Mother."

"You *are* lying. You have no evidence!"

"My *life* is my evidence."

"What's wrong with your life, Zoe?"

"It's all fucked up."

"Zoe, *stop this filth!*"

Mrs. Thomas raised her hand as if to strike Zoe, then tried to put it over Zoe's mouth. "Stop this hysteria. And stop shouting. Do you want your neighbors to hear?"

"I don't give a shit about the neighbors, Mother. Let them hear. I don't want to pretend any more. I'll shout it out the windows. I'll shout it into the passageway."

Zoe started toward the stairs to the first floor.

Her mother ran after her, clawing at her blouse, tearing the silk with her fingernails.

Zoe struggled free and stumbled on, reaching the front door, and trying unsuccessfully to open it. The bolt stuck for a moment, and Zoe kicked at the door furiously. Finally, she got the door open and threw her weight against the storm door, almost shattering it.

"Incest!" she screamed into the passageway. "Incest!"

"Zoe, what is it? What's happened?"

It was David, standing in the passageway just outside his front door, about to unlock it as he returned home. He rushed toward her, reaching out protectively.

Zoe's mother appeared in the doorway, wringing her hands. When she saw David, she quickly stepped back into the house and closed the door, which locked automatically.

"Zoe, what is it?" David said again, holding her.

With David's arms around her, Zoe's hysteria drained away. She gasped with emotion. For a few minutes, she let him hold her. Then she laughed wildly, with sobs intermixed.

David let her go and looked intently at her. Unsure how to respond, he waited until her sobbing laughter died away.

"Oh, David," Zoe said bitterly, struggling to become calm, "my mother and I were just having a chat. Come. You *must* meet her."

She tried to open the locked door and pounded the knocker furiously. After a moment, Mrs. Thomas figured out how to unlock the door and opened it, the picture of composure.

Zoe and David went in.

"Mother," Zoe said with exaggerated politeness, "I'd like you to meet one of the neighbors we were just speaking about."

Her mother forced a smile. There was no evidence of the frenzy of emotion just moments before.

Zoe said, "This is David Wolf. He lives across the passageway from me. David, this is my mother, Elizabeth Thomas. She's visiting from Ohio. We were just talking about the neighbors."

David and Mrs. Thomas shook hands.

"May I offer you some coffee, David?" Zoe's words were now calm, but her voice sounded almost threatening.

"Well, I . . ." He looked confused, probably because Zoe seemed demented.

"Yes," Zoe's voice took on a hysterical edge. She began speaking too rapidly. "You *must* have some coffee, David. I won't take no for an answer. Mother and I were just enjoying a little postprandial chat. Come upstairs, both of you, and let's sit for a few minutes and enjoy some light-hearted banter. My mother is the queen of light-hearted banter, David. She's won prizes in competitions and everything."

"Zoe, please," Mrs. Thomas said.

She followed Zoe upstairs, going ahead of David, and watched nervously as Zoe began clearing the table, clattering the dishes and glasses, carrying them roughly into the kitchen, where she flung them into the sink.

Zoe stumbled back into the dining room to mop up the spilled water with a dish towel. Then she went back into the kitchen, where she violently poured water into the coffeemaker and dumped coffee, unmeasured, into the filter. She started the coffee brewing, and a rich fragrance filled the room. The pleasurable odor contrasted with the tension.

"Perhaps your neighbor would rather come back some other time," Mrs. Thomas said anxiously.

"Nonsense, Mother. David wants some coffee. Don't you, David? And I'm sure he wants to get to know you." Zoe went on slamming things around in the kitchen.

"Zoe," David said, his voice kind, "why don't you and your mother sit, and I'll pour the coffee? Mrs. Thomas, my kitchen is the mirror image of your daughter's. Everything is in about the same place."

He took Zoe's hand and led her from the kitchen to the dining room. The two women sat silently on either side of the table. They did not look at each other.

After a few minutes, David brought the coffeepot and three mugs from the kitchen and poured coffee for each of them. He sensed something cataclysmic had taken place, and maybe was still taking place. The tension in the room was enormous.

He wanted to help.

"I've just come from a day with my little daughter, Kathy," David said after a moment, to Zoe's mother. "We've been to the zoo. Have you been to the zoo in Lincoln Park, Mrs. Thomas? It's only a few blocks from here."

"No, I don't think so." She was doing her best to appear collected.

"Well, you might enjoy it. They have some timber wolves there that are quite wonderful. I feel a special fondness for wolves because Wolf is my last name. Kathy and I feel as if we're visiting our family when we go to see them."

He laughed lightly and glanced at Zoe to see how she was doing. "Kathy's just five."

Zoe sat, sipping her coffee quietly. She seemed to have stepped back somewhat from the edge of hysteria.

"Perhaps I shall visit the zoo, sometime," Mrs. Thomas said, standing up. "But now, if you'll excuse me, I have some things to do upstairs. It was nice to meet you."

She extended her hand to David, who had risen politely.

"It was nice to meet you, Mrs. Thomas," he said, shaking her hand. "I hope you'll enjoy your visit."

She went up the stairs and closed the bedroom door. Once she was gone, David looked questioningly at Zoe.

"We were just reminiscing about the family," Zoe said.

"Was that reminiscing, there in the passageway?"

"Our version of it."

"I see."

He gently took Zoe's hand. "Is there anything I can do? Would you like me to stay? Get you more coffee? Just tell me how I can help."

"David, I didn't know there were people as wonderful as you."

"There aren't. I'm a wolf. Remember? I'd howl for you, but that probably wouldn't be the best thing just now."

They sat for a few moments saying nothing.

Zoe's mother appeared at the head of the stairs.

"Zoe," she said, "I'm afraid my plans have changed. I need to return home immediately. I have phoned the airport and there's a plane at eight. I have a reservation. That will give me just time to pack and get to the airport. Will you drive me, or shall I phone for a taxi?"

David looked at Zoe. She said nothing.

After a minute, he said, "If it will help, I'll be glad to drive you to the airport, Mrs. Thomas."

"Thank you. I'll be ready right away." She went back into the bedroom.

"Do what you want, Mother," Zoe said to the closed door.

"If you prefer to stay here, Zoe, that's all right. I'll get your mother there safely."

"I'll come. I wouldn't think of leaving you alone with a madwoman.

Although she seems to be dangerous only to me. I'm also a madwoman, David. That's heredity for you."

"Did something terrible happen?"

"Oh, just nostalgia."

"Right."

As they drove to the airport, David talked about his renovation project, which they passed on the way. Zoe and her mother were quiet.

David let Mrs. Thomas off at the curb, as she insisted, and handed her suitcase to the redcap.

Zoe did not embrace her mother, nor did her mother seem to want it. They said a strained, formal goodbye, and she was gone.

CHAPTER 20.
Aftermath

Riding home with David from the airport after her mother's abrupt departure, Zoe said very little. David distracted her with a story about the last time he'd come to the airport, and she allowed herself to be distracted.

But after they'd parked and had gotten to her front door, she turned to him and said, quietly, "David, I'm afraid to go in there and be alone. It's full of haunts."

He laughed warmly, put his arm around her shoulders, and guided her to his own front door. Unlocking it, he led her upstairs to the living room, where she sank into a large, lush, tan leather chair.

David disappeared into the kitchen and, while Zoe waited, grateful simply to sit and be quiet, he brewed aromatic coffee, topped it with foamed milk, and brought two gleaming, ceramic mugs, one of which he placed on the small table next to her, carefully turning the handle toward her.

She inhaled the fragrance of the coffee and commented on the beauty of the magenta and forest green and cobalt blue glaze of the mugs, thinking how much she liked this man, who took such care as he served coffee in an artwork.

"They are beautiful, aren't they?" he said as he pulled a chair out from the dining table and sat down, placing his own mug with the same care.

"I've become friends with the artist who made them. I've been collecting her work for years. It's an annual event for me, selecting a few new pieces at the Old Town Art Fair, where she has a booth each year. Even after Christine and I moved up north a few years ago, I'd make a pilgrimage back to the art fair just to see Sarah Jo and discover what wonderful new things she'd done in her kiln."

Taking a sip of coffee, he added, with a trace of bitterness, "When Christine asked me to leave, I insisted on bringing several mugs and bowls and plates with me. I was willing to leave most of my other things behind, but not these. Besides, Christine thinks they're crude. She prefers Limoges."

Zoe couldn't think of a response.

After an uncomfortable pause, she managed, "Well, *I* think the mugs are beautiful. And the coffee is delicious. Thank you."

David smiled and raised his eyebrows.

She felt she should say something about what had happened, but she wasn't ready to talk about it.

After another pause, she asked, "How is it going with Christine?"

David shook his head. "She's still insisting on a divorce. At the same time, she's furious with me for abandoning her and Kathy. She claims that once again, I've let them down.

"She points out numerous occasions when I wasn't there for her. She sees my leaving the law firm as one of the many ways I didn't keep my part of the bargain. She accuses me of being selfish and irresponsible and maliciously self-destructive.

"The way she describes me, I sound truly scurrilous. I wonder, sometimes, if she's right."

"Scurrilous?" Zoe laughed, delighted by the quaint word, and relieved to be talking about something besides her own problems.

"Impossible. If you were scurrilous, I'd have seen it by now."

"I hope you're right. I really don't want to be scurrilous."

"You're kind and perceptive. You always know exactly the right thing to say."

Another pause, and a sigh. She added, "Furthermore, you keep saving my life. Somehow, when I most need protection or comfort, you show up. Today, for example."

"I'm glad you find me useful."

"David, if saving my life is useful, you're useful."

He leaned forward and, taking a long match from an enamel box, he lit the large beeswax candle in the center of the table. The candlelight and the coffee fragrance surrounded them with comfort.

"I'm glad I can be useful to you, Zoe," he said again. His voice was soft and warm, like the candlelight.

Zoe was silent for a long moment.

Then, taking a deep breath, she said, "And since no good deed goes unpunished, would you like to hear about my crazy life?"

"If you want to tell me, of course."

She took another sip of coffee. "The situation with my mother is only a small part of it, David. Just the latest nasty chapter. And I should warn you: It's not pretty. But at least, it's not boring." She laughed cynically.

He smiled. "I've been wondering what could create a creature as intriguing as you."

"Intriguing? I'm intriguing?"

"Among other things." He said this with affection.

She took a sip of coffee from the beautiful mug. "I like being intriguing."

Another pause, another deep breath. "David, you're probably wondering why I was shouting in the passageway about incest. What that was all about . . . what that was all about was that I had just confronted my mother with the fact that I think my father abused me sexually when I was a child."

"My God," he said softly.

"And my mother did what she has always done with anything she doesn't want to hear. She denied it and accused me of lying."

"She wasn't concerned for you?"

"No."

"How is that possible?"

"I don't know. Maybe if she had ever been concerned for me, the incest wouldn't have happened. Parents are supposed to protect their children from danger. My father *was* the danger, and she didn't protect me from him. I'm trying to understand how that could be, but it's painful."

"I can imagine . . ."

He paused. "No, I can't. Not really. My parents weren't perfect, but . . ."

This was new territory for David, and he proceeded cautiously, not wanting to say something, out of ignorance, that would be hurtful.

He wanted only to be supportive and a good friend.

After a moment, she went on, hesitantly, "This all started coming up when my father died. I *adored* my father." She shook her head.

"I've never been close to my mother. It was always Daddy and me."
She shuddered.

"But since his death, the dark side of our relationship has forced
itself into my consciousness. And now, my cousin Suzanne has come
back into my life after a silence of twenty years. A silence I didn't
understand until now."

She told David about the meeting with Suzanne at O'Hare.

"Amazing," he said softly, doing his best not to seem shocked.

"And you happened to be at your front door just after I tried to
tell my mother what Suzanne had said. I was tired of the pretense
and was going to shout the family secrets to the world. Or at least,
into the passageway."

Then she added, ruefully, "I guess my mother is right. I *am*
overly dramatic."

David smiled but said nothing. She sighed and looked anxiously
at him.

"Should I go on with this, or is it too disgusting to hear?"

She shifted her position in the chair and leaned into its soft
leather. The incident with her mother felt too ugly to talk about.

"Zoe," he said earnestly, "as I said before, if you have the courage
to face these things and talk about them, of course I'll listen."

"Thank you." She shook her head. "You saw how my mother
responded. She left town."

"It must have been a shock for her," David ventured.

Zoe shifted again in the chair.

"You're a kind person, David, thinking of her shock. But
Suzanne said my mother knew about the incest and dealt with
it by not dealing with it. Instead, she broke off all contact with

Suzanne's family, which is also my father's family, and *my* family. I didn't understand why there was a sudden change. Our families had always been so close."

Zoe laughed bitterly. "I've always resented that my mother wouldn't face up to things. Not that I did much better. When the world got too much for me, I turned to alcohol."

"I didn't know you then, Zoe, but now, I know you to be a courageous and straightforward person."

"I *am* much better these days. At least, I thought I was. Mostly because I gave up drinking and went to AA."

Her mood seemed to lighten for a moment, but only briefly.

She sighed and looked remorseful. "AA is, as they say, a program of honesty. Unfortunately, honesty has never been my strong suit, but I'm beginning to understand why. There were certain facts of my early life that were just too terrible to face.

"It comes to me now that I learned to lie to survive. But I used to think it was just that I was *incapable* of being honest. I thought I was rotten to the core. A liar and an ingrate. Cold and unfeeling.

"That's why when my mother accuses me of those same things now, it hits me so hard."

She shuddered. "David, it's so complicated."

She took several sips of coffee, finishing it and gently placing the mug back on the table.

"Would you like more coffee?" David sensed that she needed a break.

"Yes, please."

"Again, with steamed milk?"

"Yes, please. It's so comforting."

David carried both of their mugs to the kitchen. There were sounds of water being turned on and off, the fragrance of fresh coffee, the hissing of steam as he foamed the milk.

His intuition was right; she was grateful for a few moments to reflect on what she was telling him. Part of her didn't want him to know these sordid things, but the greater part of her trusted him to accept what she said without judging her. She sensed his essential kindness, his compassionate heart.

He returned with her mug and a bottle of wine. He placed the coffee mug on her table and asked, "Would you mind if I have some wine?"

"Of course not."

"Thank you." He screwed the opener into the cork and pulled it out of the bottle with a *thunk*. He brought a wineglass from the credenza under the window, set it carefully on the table, poured a small amount of red wine into it, and sat down again, lifting the goblet and smiling at her, an honoring gesture.

She lifted her coffee mug toward him and nodded in response. Both drank and were silent.

After a few moments, Zoe slowly continued. "I had a lot of fears and night terrors when I was a child, especially around the time I was six and started first grade. Thinking back to that time now, I remember that night after night I was terrified that a poisonous snake was crawling down the wall toward the bed, or that the roof was on fire, or that there were spiders in my bed. I was terrified, and I called for my mommy.

"David, it was exactly like the prologue of Gudrun's play: I called for my mother, and she didn't come. My daddy always came.

He told me not to wake my mother, that she needed her rest because she wasn't well."

She considered this, frowning. It was always her father who interpreted the situation for her. Zoe couldn't recall that her mother had ever told her not to call for her at night, or that her mother had ever told her she needed her rest because she wasn't well. It was always *the world as seen through the eyes of her father.*

David sat quietly, letting her take her time.

"Then my father got into bed with me. But what happened after that is a blank. That's what makes me wonder if I'm just making things up about incest. Maybe *nothing* happened. Maybe that's why it's a blank.

"'*You have no proof,*' my mother said. I told her what Suzanne said about Daddy giving me baths and enemas, about the accident with the enema nozzle. My mother shouted that Suzanne is a liar."

Zoe shifted in her chair again and shook her head. "My mother accused me of falsely accusing Daddy, of ruining his good name.

"And I accused her of not protecting me, of not coming when I called. I needed my mommy, but she never came."

David said, almost in a whisper, "The thought of something like that happening to Kathy—"

"Yes, David, I know. I know. Since I've gotten to know Kathy, I'm beginning to remember what it was like when I was her age."

Zoe was silent for a long time, conflicted about whether to end the story here. She already felt stirrings of the old self-loathing, disgust, and shame.

She stood and walked to the window, the one that had been open that Sunday morning when she first heard the Brahms symphony floating down into her garden. It now seemed so long ago.

Needing a break from her story, she began to explore the second floor. She had rarely visited Ted's house when he lived here and certainly not since his departure for San Francisco on a business assignment a few months earlier.

Ted was a bachelor, and Zoe had long admired his excellent taste: the lush soft leather sofa and chairs, all matching, all expensive, downstairs, as well as matching ones here on the second floor, and the glass and chrome dining table above which was suspended a stunning chrome and crystal chandelier, the orderly, well-stocked bookshelves, and the top-of-the-line sound system gleaming in a corner.

And she now realized she was grateful that Ted had inadvertently brought David into her life.

It was obvious to Zoe that David was living in Ted's house respectfully, without disturbing its order. There seemed to be almost nothing of David's belongings anywhere that she could see, except for the treasured mugs and, on the slim tan-and-white French enamel credenza under the window, two ceramic plates and two bowls, all with the same beautiful glaze as the mugs, and a second fragile-looking long-stemmed wineglass.

As Zoe moved about, she spoke about how much she liked Ted, and David walked with her, reminiscing about how he and Ted had become friends at college, how their lives had diverged and then had come back together, and how now Ted had generously offered David sanctuary in his vacant house.

While they toured the second floor, Zoe decided she would entrust David with more of her story. They sat down again, and she continued. It seemed as if new awarenesses were coming to her as she spoke.

"I've started to remember other things. It wasn't just my father, David. When I was eight or nine, there was another professor, a family friend and colleague of my father's, who made me his sexual plaything whenever our families were together, which was often, for family picnics in the park and New Year's Eve celebrations. He had six young children and a nice wife, but that didn't seem to matter. He'd get me alone and put me on his lap and fondle me."

She sighed and looked questioningly at David.

"Does it seem strange for me to say I forgot about these things? Well, they weren't exactly *forgotten*. I just put them away somewhere in the back of my mind. I didn't think about them anymore, as if they had happened to someone else in some other lifetime."

David said, "A lot of life seems strange to me these days, Zoe."

She went on. "I think it was just that I had no language for what was happening. Oh, I knew what he was doing was weird, but I just . . . accepted it as the way life is, the way grown men behave."

She sighed again and said, as if the thought had come to her for the first time, "I think maybe I also blamed myself. I clearly remember being puzzled about why this grown man with daughters about my age was doing these things to me.

"But David, what made it so confusing was that, in a strange way, I think I was flattered; I rather liked having this colleague of my father so focused on me. The specialness of it. But I also felt guilt and shame. That's why, when Gudrun spoke about *the perverse and terrible specialness of incest,* it was so powerful."

"Zoe," David said quietly, "you were so young and alone with it, and it was so . . ." He shook his head.

She pressed on. "That's what made it so confusing. I knew

it wasn't right, but I didn't try to stop it, and I didn't want my parents to know. I lived a double life. Most of the time, I was a perfectly well-behaved young daughter. But at other times, I was her evil twin.

"And the most amazing thing of all, David, is that I didn't even realize, until recently, especially since Gudrun's play, that what I was experiencing was *abuse*."

Her voice was full of disbelief.

David stood and paced for a few moments. "It's hard to hear these things, Zoe, thinking of you experiencing what no child should have to experience."

"Would you rather not hear any more?" Zoe again felt a stirring of shame and regret, anticipating his judgment.

"No—that's not what I meant. It's just that what you're saying stirs strong feelings in me, that's all."

"Well, I appreciate your being willing to listen." Zoe felt relief. He wasn't judging her.

"The fight with my mother, her refusing to believe me, discounting what I told her, saying I've always been overly dramatic, accusing me of making everything up—it's shaken me, because I worry that she's right."

Tears flooded her cheeks. Her nose ran. She searched unsuccessfully in her purse for a tissue, wiped her nose with her sleeve, like a child, and said, with exasperation, "Do you have some Kleenex? I never have any Kleenex when I need it."

David brought a box of tissues and put it on the table next to her.

"Thank you." She wiped her tears and blew her nose. "I can't seem to cry without my nose running."

"The human condition, Zoe," he said with a gentle laugh.

"Anyway," Zoe continued, "talking to you about these things helps so much as I try to make sense of it all. What I can see now is that the early relationship with my father made me vulnerable to that relationship with his professor friend, and it absolutely shaped how I felt about my mother, which had a profound impact on how I felt about myself.

"Because from about the age of six, I thought of my mother as a nuisance. I *disdained* her—that was the word Gudrun used when she described the characteristics of the woman traumatized by incest. Honestly, David, hearing Gudrun describing the typical incest patient, I could be a poster child for incest victims!"

She laughed grimly.

"I *disdained* my mother. Sometimes, I even hated her. But then I felt guilty about the disdain, the hate. All my friends *loved* their mothers. Everybody loved their mothers but me. I concluded that I must be incapable of tenderness or natural feelings and therefore I must be a monster."

"A monster, Zoe? A young girl, so innocent and vulnerable, so hurt by circumstances over which you had no control, a *monster?* And there was no one to tell you it wasn't true. How terrible."

He went to her chair and sat on the arm, gently embracing her. She leaned into his embrace.

After a moment, she looked up into his face and asked anxiously, "Are you sure you can stand to hear more, David? Because believe it or not, it gets worse, really awful."

"I can handle it, but if it gets worse, I'll need more wine." He said this lightly and smiled, hoping she would hear his humor and would not think of it as disapproval.

He stood and refilled his glass. When he sat again at the table, she continued.

"When I was older, in high school, there was a disgusting and humiliating encounter with another professor, my father's mentor, who was in his eighties and getting senile when my parents and I visited him after his retirement.

"He invited me to see his rose garden and when we were out of sight of the house, he grabbed me and kissed me. I remember his rank breath, the sharp whiskers on his shrunken cheeks, and the way he pawed at my breasts."

She shuddered and shook her head. "When I pushed him away, he claimed to have fathered me. He said, nastily, that my father had been unable to make my mother pregnant and that he had done the job.

"I knew that wasn't true. But it was another thing I couldn't tell my parents. I felt defiled, and I wondered why these things kept happening to me. Again, I blamed myself."

David sat back and closed his eyes for a moment. Then he said, quietly, "Sometimes, I'm ashamed of being a man, when I hear about some of the things that men do. Such ugly things. I think that's why I prefer to think of myself as a wolf."

"I know, David. It's hard for me to think of you as a man."

David laughed. "Thank you, I think."

She laughed too, and then went on.

"In college, I had another affair with a professor—I certainly specialized in professors, didn't I. Somehow, he found ways to be alone with me in his apartment. What he did with his wife at those times, I don't know, but he cooked elaborate feasts for me with lots of May wine. He played Mahler full blast on the record player as we made love.

"We were both quite drunk by the time we went to the bedroom. But he was very adoring and worshipful, and it was exotic, if not erotic, to have him quoting Faust and suggesting that he saw me as *das Ewig-Weibliche*, the Eternal Feminine. Pretty heady stuff for a college sophomore in bed with her revered professor."

She was quiet for a moment. With a deep breath, she added, "And I was also more experienced sexually by this time because I had a full-time lover."

Zoe took another breath. "A woman."

David's eyebrows went up, but he said nothing.

"Yes," Zoe continued. "As soon as I moved away from home for the first time and was at college, I fell in love with my roommate. I initiated it. She didn't date during that first quarter of freshman year, and night after night, she lay on her dorm-room bunk, brooding.

"I was trying to be a normal co-ed, so I went out on dates, but I always came back early, weeping with outrage and disgust because the boys were so crude and stupid and immature and seemed to want nothing but booze and sex. I couldn't bear for them to touch me." She shuddered.

"Ah, yes," David said with a sigh. "College boys."

"She would hold me and comfort me, and one night, it occurred to me to kiss her on the neck, and an erotic world opened to us unlike anything I had ever known before.

"She dazzled me. She had thick, gorgeous blond hair and wide-set blue eyes with a glint of madness in them. She played the piano brilliantly. I was a singer in those days, and she played for me to sing German *Lieder*."

Memories flooded back. "Erica. I thought her name was so beautiful; it reminded me of *Eroica,* a Beethoven symphony I love. She was breathtakingly intelligent, a true intellectual. She could discuss Kant and Nietzsche and the nature of tragedy. She could recite long passages of *The Wasteland* and explain James Joyce. She knew about botany and was interested in science, which was a mystery to me. She planned to become a doctor."

The memories became more intense. "We became heavy drinkers together and made love right under the noses of our other roommates." Zoe laughed without mirth.

"We were in a suite with two connecting triple dorm rooms, and we caused a scandal. Lesbianism wasn't yet fashionable . . ." She paused to appreciate her own irony.

This part of the story didn't stir feelings of shame; she almost enjoyed talking about it. "At least, not with our parents and the housemother and the dean of women. They all did their best to break up our 'special' friendship, as they called it, without success.

"After we graduated, we clandestinely lived together for a while. My affair with the professor continued for a while, too. My erotic life was quite full."

"I can imagine," David said quietly.

"Eventually, she left me for another woman, and I closed the door on that part of my life. Too much obsession and pain.

"After that, I had a series of affairs with married men, just like that 'suffering woman' in the psychiatrist's consulting room Gudrun spoke of. I knew better how to manage those. Married men come with built-in boundaries.

"With Erica, there were no boundaries. I lost myself completely. I was absorbed into her powerful personality. My poor, wispy little ego disappeared moments after I met her and only years later has it begun to re-emerge. Or maybe it hasn't re-emerged yet."

"I'm pretty sure it has re-emerged, Zoe," David said with affection.

She smiled at him but shook her head. "Maybe. But looking back now, I see that I turned to Erica for safety, believing, from my unfortunate experience, that men were not trustworthy. It seems to me now that the problem was that, because I had been sexualized by the incest, the only way I knew how to be close to anyone was through sex, even with a woman. Does that make sense?"

She didn't wait for him to answer. "Oh, I have no regrets about my relationship with Erica. Many things about it were beautiful. We shared music and art and literature. And the eroticism was truly intense.

"But she teased me rather savagely and treated me as her intellectual inferior, which I suppose I was. I agreed with her that *she* was the genius, and I accepted her occasional scorn as my due."

"It's hard to imagine you believing you weren't brilliant, when you clearly are."

"If I'm so smart, how come my life is such a mess?" She laughed bitterly. "Oh, David, of course, I've already answered that question. But as I'm telling you these things, I'm understanding that what happened to me didn't happen because I'm a monster."

"Good."

Zoe laughed again, but this time with genuine amusement.

"David, you always say just the right thing. And now, please excuse me for a few minutes."

She stood and went upstairs to the bathroom.

She was exhausted, and she sat on the closed toilet seat for a long time and wept quietly. When her tears subsided, she stood and peered at herself in the mirror. "I look terrible," she murmured, and splashed cool water on her face. She repaired her mascara and sat back down and waited, hoping the cool water would make her eyes less red and her eyelids less puffy. It didn't.

Back downstairs, she found that David had brought out a cutting board with half a dozen cheeses, some grapes and apple slices, and a basket with crackers.

Zoe ate hungrily, glad not to be talking about herself. But after a few moments, she asked, "So, what do you think of all this, David? Have I totally shocked you?"

He took a deep breath and smiled. "Not exactly, Zoe." He paused. "But I'm sure if I'd met you when we were younger, when all of that was going on in your life, I wouldn't have known what to make of you. I was quite naive. But I would probably have fallen in love with you."

Zoe was both embarrassed and warmed by his comment.

"Well, I was definitely—what was your word? *Intriguing.* As our travel guide during the summer my parents took me to Europe put it: 'Here comes trouble.'

"He ended up getting me pregnant."

"Pregnant!"

"I had an abortion once I got back to the States. Illegal, of course, and dangerous. I almost died of complications. Afterward, I felt so depressed and so dead inside that I went into therapy, and after a year or two, I seemed to be back on an even keel.

"I married a nice Republican man, to the relief of my mother. My whole group therapy group, complete with therapist, came to the wedding. Unfortunately, my new husband was an alcoholic."

"My God, Zoe." David could not contain his shock. "Your life sounds like a pulp novel!"

But he said this with a laugh, hoping to soften the impact of his words.

To David's relief, Zoe also laughed.

"Yes, it does, doesn't it? Kinky sex. Forbidden men. Forbidden women. Dire consequences. Scandal. Alcohol. Never a dull moment."

Relieved to have at last said it all, she stopped to savor the grapes and apple slices. "Delicious, David. The most marvelous grapes and apple slices I've ever tasted!"

"I'm glad, Zoe."

She began again. "What Gudrun said after the play was so powerful for me, David, like her paintings, which, as you know, stirred such a strong response in me at the gallery."

She paused again to eat some cheese. Her mood seemed to be lightening.

"And Gudrun not only described my problems exactly, but she also described the healing process. Alas, although I'm now seeing my problem more clearly, I *really* don't have time to do the healing she described, those nine years of Jungian analysis, the journey on the Road of Trials, the transformation of consciousness. Nor do I have the inclination to take that journey. Not now, not in my life as I am living it.

"Besides, I'm already working on my life in AA. I regularly go to meetings. I work a good program."

Then she laughed again. "Speaking of AA, you can imagine what I thought life would be like after I stopped drinking! I didn't want to do the hard work of healing then, either, though, thank goodness, when I first started going to meetings, they didn't detail the AA Road of Trials that lay ahead of me.

"In those days, I couldn't imagine life without champagne and high drama, or a party, or even breakfast without wine."

"*Breakfast?* Did you go to work?"

"Of course."

"How did you manage a career?"

"With brilliance, charm, and sex with the boss."

"Amazing."

They both laughed again, and the atmosphere lightened.

"In reality, David, life since AA has been rather good. I was enjoying living without the rollercoaster ride and every day being the Fourth of July, and I was even gingerly exploring the possibility of a spiritual life."

She paused to take another slice of apple and cheese.

"Then my father died, and all this incest stuff started coming up, and it's thrown everything into chaos again. But hearing about the lives of other incest victims, and what Suzanne told me, and what the people said in the incest survivors' meeting I attended, it seems that all our lives sound strangely alike, even though superficially they may differ.

"The bad news is that it's always a story of shame and suffering. The good news, Gudrun assures me, is that knowing the truth of what happened is the beginning of healing."

"I hope so, Zoe. And I have a feeling Gudrun will help you take that journey in a way that is right for you."

"Thank you, David. I hope you're right. What gives *me* a glimmer of hope is what I learned from Gudrun's play, how Kay and her mythic twin, Persephone, were at last able to step out of the darkness of the past and return to the light. And, of course, what Gudrun said about the healing process in her brilliant elucidation after the play."

She sighed, and added, her voice anxious, "But David, what if, in my case, it's all *just a myth*? Certainly, I'm not willing to spend nine more years of my life in therapy."

Then her tone lightened. "But Gudrun assures me that somehow it may be possible, with her help, to get through this difficult time and beyond it.

"Maybe there will be no more nightmares, no more dark secrets, no more married men, no more fainting spells and waking up in tears, no more self-loathing, no more . . ."

Zoe sat back and closed her eyes.

When she awakened almost an hour later, David was still sitting at the table, but the wineglass was gone, and the beautiful coffee mug had replaced it.

He smiled at her. "Welcome back."

"Oh, David! I'm so *embarrassed*. You were being such a gracious host, and I fell asleep. How rude!"

David laughed. But then he became serious.

"You look like a little girl when you sleep. I've been sitting here watching you, with your innocent expression, and imagining you as a little girl, like Kathy, so intelligent and eager to please. So beautiful. I've been thinking of how you had to grow up so fast, and how wrong it was that you could not have a childhood.

"I thought of you jumping into the brightly colored balls at Bucky's Circus on Kathy's birthday, and how much fun Kathy and I had with you. And how she loved you right away."

Tears came to Zoe's eyes, but she said nothing.

After a moment and a deep breath, David continued, his voice full of emotion.

"I think of all that you've been through, and yet you are still innocent, still a pure spirit. Even though terrible things were done to you, they did not touch the essence of you, which to me is beautiful and good and generous and kind. That's the person I know.

"Oh, Zoe, I have nothing to offer you right now except friendship, but I want you to know that, sitting here, watching you sleep, I've realized that I love you."

Zoe was flooded with sweet wonder.

Men had spoken to her of love many times and had meant many complicated and contradictory things, but their words had never touched her heart the way David's simple statement stirred in her such pure, boundless rapture.

She said softly, also with emotion, "Oh, David, your friendship is what I need more than anything else in the world. Whatever I'm going through, I'm afraid I have a long way to go before I reach the other side. But you, dear David, have been such a good friend the whole time I've known you. You are a blessing, an unearned gift, gratefully received."

She stood and went to him. She kissed him softly on the forehead and caressed his cheek and looked lovingly into his eyes.

"Thank you, David. Thank you. And now, I must go home."

He stood and took her hand in his. His touch was warm and gentle. Together, they went down the stairs and, still holding her hand, David walked her to her door. She unlocked it and turned back to him.

"David, my dear friend, thank you for your love, for your friendship, for every beautiful thing that you are."

"Goodnight, Zoe."

With a brief embrace, he saw her into the house and went back across the passageway.

CHAPTER 21.
Confrontation, Congress, Crisis

At the office, Zoe sensed a shift in her feelings toward the Chief. They had always been complicated, like the relationship.

He was twenty years older than Zoe. He had been married to the same woman for many years, and although he spoke of Mrs. Lehrer more as if she were an exasperating teenage daughter than a wife, Zoe had no doubt that he would be married to her for many years hence. Their two adult children were graduates of the best Ivy League colleges, and both were in stellar careers. Yet the Chief also spoke of them with the lofty disdain he sometimes used when he spoke to Zoe.

Zoe now found this attitude infuriating.

The last straw came when the Chief made belittling remarks about Gudrun.

Zoe was in her office, and she knew the Chief was preparing for his drive home, because the pungent odor of pipe smoke suddenly flowed into the room. She heard him talking with a colleague on the phone. She heard his chair creak as he leaned back and balanced himself, the toe of his shoe against the desk, the pipe clamped between his teeth. He laughed a low, cynical laugh, and said, "Yes, Wonder

Woman was in town, doing her artsy-fartsy things and causing me no end of aggravation."

Zoe realized he meant Gudrun.

A rage swelled in her throat. That brilliant woman, spoken of in such an insulting tone, with such scornful words?

Zoe felt as if the Chief had struck her. She'd rarely felt such rage. She jumped up from her chair and began pacing the office, clenching and unclenching her fists.

Hearing the Chief speak scornfully of Gudrun was more enraging than any scornful thing he had ever said to Zoe.

What could she do with these overwhelming feelings? Zoe thought of David pounding the steering wheel and sobbing, and she understood his helpless fury.

The Chief chatted on, but Zoe could not listen. He laughed again. The smoke from his pipe nauseated her. She kept pacing and pounding her fist into the piles of papers on her desk and striking the back of the chair.

The Chief squeaked his chair again and hung up the phone. There was silence, and then the sound of a flushing toilet in his private bathroom. Finally, he appeared in the doorway, with his pipe in one hand and his briefcase in the other. He had a jaunty smile on his face. When he saw her raging, he stopped in surprise.

"How dare you speak of Gudrun that way?" she spat at him. "In that tone of voice? How *dare* you?"

He laughed. "Oh, come on, Zoe. I have enough troubles with my wife and Gudrun. Don't *you* turn on me, too."

For a moment, Zoe was speechless. Then she erupted. "Gudrun is *brilliant*. A brilliant therapist, a brilliant artist, a brilliant person.

She is *not* 'Wonder Woman,' the way you meant it, to diminish her. She *is* a *wonder*. A great woman. You are puny, puny, puny beside her."

He frowned. "Come *on*, Zoe. Calm down. Don't get insulting."

"*You're* the one who's insulting. You've insulted Gudrun."

"Nonsense." He moved toward the door, as if finished with the conversation.

"I won't tolerate it. I won't tolerate your speaking that way about her."

He turned back toward her and said, with an edge of anger, "And I won't tolerate your speaking this way to me. Don't push me too far, Zoe. I've been very patient with you.

"Your work is not good. You have the ability, but your work is not good these days. You speak of not tolerating what I said in a conversation with a colleague that did not include you and is none of your business. But *I* must tolerate a lot from *you* these days. You've been acting neurotic. I don't need you as a client. Another boss with less understanding of neurosis would have fired you long ago.

"As for Gudrun, I don't know why you've suddenly become so protective of her, but in my opinion, she's neurotic, too. I wonder how she can help her patients, when she is obviously more interested in being artsy and doing those ridiculous paintings than in being a scientist.

"I'm extremely annoyed with you, Zoe, so you had better watch your step with me. Both of you."

He shifted his pipe to the hand that was holding the briefcase and strode out, slamming the door behind him.

Zoe stood with her fists still clenched, staring after the Chief, the sound of the slamming door echoing in her ears.

Then it swept over her. Shame. She was overwhelmed with shame, and she turned against herself. She struck at her breast with her fist. Pain radiated from the epicenter. She struck herself again, this time so hard she saw stars. With the third blow, she began to vomit. She staggered forward and fell to her knees, hanging her head over the wastebasket. She coughed and gagged. Bitter bile and bits of food poured out of her mouth, and searing fluid dripped from her nostrils.

All the while, she struck herself with her fists, making inhuman shrieking sounds, raining blows onto her torso, her thighs, her belly, clawing at her clothes, hearing the fabric tear.

When she could no longer bring up anything from her gut, she fell to the floor, sobbing, her fists and forearms flaming with pain, her throat raw from her sobs and the bitterness of the bile.

With one last surge of effort, she flung her head sideways, and it struck the leg of the desk. In a pinwheel of agony and shooting points of light, Zoe lost consciousness.

Hours later, Zoe woke suddenly on the floor beside her desk. Outside the window, it was dark, and she heard the cleaning woman next door in the Chief's office. She painfully stood and picked up the vomit-filled wastebasket, wondering what to do with it. She pushed it back under her desk.

Then she grabbed her purse and hobbled out the side door and down the hall to the public restroom. She noticed a lump on the side of her forehead and tried unsuccessfully to comb her hair over it and to pull herself together. Then, still wobbly, she took the bus home, grateful that she was the only passenger at so late an hour.

During the days following the argument, the Chief and Zoe finished their work for the Congress, scarcely speaking to one another, avoiding eye contact or any interaction except what was necessary.

Zoe's days were consumed with preparations. No time for her inner life. During the day at the office, the Chief's usual clients came and went, as Zoe filled trunks with materials for the Congress and arranged for their shipment.

At home later, exhausted from the pressures of the day, she gathered clothes and personal items that would make her appear professional during the day and elegant at the evening banquets and other entertainments.

A few days before Zoe left, she met briefly with David to give him the key to her townhouse. He offered to water her plants and take in her mail. She gave him a detailed itinerary, in case of emergency. He doubted there would be any reason for him to disturb her at the Congress or during her visit to Copenhagen for a week with Gudrun afterward.

The night before Zoe's flight, when her luggage was carefully packed with all but the last-minute things she would need in the morning, she went to bed early. The next day she would go to the office to phone Amsterdam to be sure the trunks with the meeting materials had arrived safely at the hotel and to do some other last-minute things, grateful to have the office to herself.

The Chief would leave from home and meet her at the airport later.

They had an all-night flight.

Mid-afternoon, Zoe met the Chief near the KLM counter. He was cheerful and a little anxious, his unlit pipe clamped in his teeth. They checked their luggage through and went to the airline lounge, where he made phone calls, and she sat quietly, grateful to rest after the rush and stress of the past weeks.

With his phone calls completed, the Chief relaxed. He smiled at Zoe and, to her amazement, he kissed her hand. Then he said, with intimacy in his voice, "I'm glad we'll have some time together at the Congress. I'm very fond of you, you know."

Zoe looked surprised. "No, I didn't know, Chief. You've been a beast to me for months."

But she had been thinking about her behavior during their argument. She had learned in AA to make amends for behavior she was ashamed of. It was not good to carry around resentments and regrets, because they are a danger to sobriety, so she added, "Chief, I apologize for the argument the other day. I was out of line."

She was still angry about his comments about Gudrun, but she realized he was right when he pointed out that she had overheard a conversation she was not a part of and was none of her business.

And she had to admit, at least to herself, that she had overreacted. She seemed to overreact to everything these days.

Also, she was certain Gudrun would not have allowed the Chief's comments to upset her. Gudrun would have brushed the whole incident aside with amusement.

"Yes, you were out of line, Zoe," the Chief said. "But I've taken into account that you were stressed. I forgive you."

Zoe considered continuing the discussion, then thought better of it. She could not afford another argument, especially now. She said, simply, "Thank you."

But he continued, "I know you're hypersensitive these days. I've done my best to be patient with you, to bear in mind that you've been under pressure with the Congress coming up.

"And, of course, the death of your father. But you've handled that quite well, I think, and you've been a good support to your mother. I admire that, Zoe.

"I may point out the times when you don't use that impressive brain of yours, and you must admit that you sometimes don't think. But I have a lot of admiration for you. Your intelligence. Your ability to deal with people. You are very astute."

Zoe couldn't resist saying, sarcastically, "If I'm so astute, why didn't I notice your positive assessment of my competence? I missed that entirely."

He didn't take the bait. "Come on, now." He was cajoling. "You know I wouldn't turn everything over to you if I didn't trust you to make it all happen perfectly. I depend on you for many things, Zoe. I don't know what I'd do without you."

He took her hand again and, smiling, patted it affectionately.

Their flight was announced.

Seated next to Zoe in first class, the Chief had two martinis, some Dom Perignon with dinner, and a Courvoisier afterward with dessert, while Zoe sipped her soda and lime and picked at her food.

After coffee and brandy, the Chief fell asleep with his head on Zoe's shoulder.

But Zoe sat awake. Now, in the humming peace of the plane, flying over the dark ocean, she allowed herself to think about her life.

She thought about the bitter argument with her mother, and paradoxically, how her mother seemed to be thriving in widowhood, and now, she was going on a cruise.

She thought about the Chief, about *their* bitter argument, and how, also paradoxically, he was now sleeping with his head on her shoulder.

She thought about Suzanne and her dreadful disclosures, but also, about the joy she felt at having Suzanne back in her life.

She thought about Gudrun's beautiful play and her generosity in including Zoe, and how much she had loved being in a play again.

She thought about David, his friendship, his loving kindness, his enchanting little Kathy.

Yes, there was so much ugliness. And, as David had said, so much beauty.

And she thought about the Congress ahead, the huge effort she had given to it, despite these many stresses in her personal life, and how important it was to her that it would go smoothly.

She prayed that nothing would happen to spoil it.

Once they arrived at Schiphol Airport in Amsterdam at eight in the morning, the Chief was all business. There was no suggestion of the affection he had expressed just hours earlier.

The limousine that was a regular part of his life carried them slowly and silently through the busy Amsterdam streets and turned in at the narrow cobblestone lane that led to the elegant conference hotel.

In the marble lobby, Zoe and the Chief were welcomed as old friends by the beautiful manager. After arranging a meeting with her for later, they were shown to their rooms.

Zoe's was in the front of the hotel, on the top floor, a room with a cathedral ceiling and French doors that opened onto a tiny balcony from which she could look out over rooftops, the canal, the many houseboats moored along the wall of the canal, the myriad bicycles and toy cars the Dutch fancied, and the miniature, perfect trees.

The Chief's room was somewhere else in the hotel.

By eleven, Zoe had unpacked, taken a bath to wash away the weariness of flying all night, and had redone her face and hair. Now she was sitting in a small conference room with the Chief, having rich, dark Dutch coffee.

The manager checked with them briefly, assuring them that everything was in order. They went over lists and last-minute arrangements with her, and then they had an early lunch in the dining room, surrounded by flowers and sunlight pouring down through the skylight.

While they were having lunch, Gudrun arrived, a little breathless, as always. She was welcomed and invited to join them. She had a chocolate dessert and an espresso as they talked.

Everything was ready. The participants were beginning to arrive. In the afternoon, Zoe went with the manager to the conference rooms to meet with the audiovisual people and the staff. She checked seating arrangements, opened the trunks, and set up the meeting, which would begin the next morning.

Forty psychiatrists from various parts of the world would present scholarly papers, which Zoe would later make into a book. She had organized many such meetings during her years with the Chief. The Congresses followed a format Zoe and the Chief had developed long since, and everything always went smoothly.

Here in Amsterdam, Zoe was not an incest victim. There was only the outer world, which she could manage, shape, organize. The Chief opened and closed the sessions and sat next to her during the presentations, whispering suggestions and comments as various papers were presented.

Gudrun, as the scientific director, introduced the speakers and moderated the discussions.

As the week went on, Zoe felt herself wearing down. Her intense concentration and need to be "on," from the moment she awakened at six until she fell asleep exhausted at midnight, took its toll. Each morning, her eyes were more irritated.

By Friday noon, when the final session concluded, she had visibly aged. There was a farewell luncheon and then the participants went on their way. Zoe spent Friday afternoon packing up the trunks and settling accounts with the hotel.

Dinner that last night in Amsterdam was in a quiet upstairs restaurant several blocks from the hotel. The Chief had Zoe on one arm and Gudrun on the other as they walked along the narrow streets, crossing two canals. The twinkling lights that lined the arched bridges had come on in the dusk and made reflections in the dark water.

The trio entered the crowded first floor bar of the restaurant. Everyone looked like descendants of people who had modeled for Vermeer or Vincent van Gogh. The Chief followed Gudrun and Zoe as they climbed the narrow staircase, single file, and stepped into the candlelit dining room, where the walls were lined with books and dark paintings. The *maître d'* greeted them warmly and led them to a table that looked out over the canal.

Zoe let Gudrun and the Chief do most of the talking. She sat silently as they discussed the Congress, their colleagues, their plans. They were vivacious and laughed a lot. The Chief showed no evidence that he felt disdain for Gudrun. He was, in fact, quite charming and flattering to her, even flirtatious, Zoe thought. And the two of them seemed to have boundless energy.

But Zoe felt herself sinking into depression.

After dinner, they walked together slowly back to the hotel, through the cool night. The Chief and Gudrun had enjoyed a bottle of wine with dinner, and cognac afterward, and the alcohol made them even more lively and good-humored.

Back at the hotel, Zoe and the Chief walked Gudrun to her room and said good night.

Then, instead of going toward Zoe's room, at the front of the hotel, the Chief took Zoe's arm and drew her down the hallway toward his room. He led her around a corner and down a flight of steps, along another hallway, and up another flight of steps. The hotel, created from once-private homes, had many levels. Then they were standing by the back elevators, which would take them to the Chief's suite in a newer part of the hotel.

Walking with the Chief through the silent corridors, Zoe said nothing, but her mind was in turmoil. She didn't want to go with him. She was exhausted and just wanted to go to bed alone in her beautiful room.

She didn't want to have sex, but she couldn't imagine not doing it; there was too much history between them. How could she explain, after sleeping with him on so many other occasions, that now she did not want to?

As he opened the door and waited for her to go in, she thought, *Oh, well. I'll just go through with it. It's too complicated to say no.* She went into the room, walked to the large picture window, and stood, looking out over the lighted trees in the enclosed courtyard below.

Meanwhile, the Chief was in the bathroom, changing out of his suit and into the fine white terrycloth bathrobe the maid had laid out for him, turning water on and off, gargling, brushing his teeth, flushing, and clinking the crystal water glass against the marble sink as he took his vitamins.

Zoe had witnessed this ritual many times.

He emerged with the robe tied around his portly tummy. Barefoot, he padded to the bar and poured himself a drink from the complimentary bottle of Courvoisier. He offered Zoe some.

She declined, thinking that it was one of the many ironies of their relationship that, though she was willing to have sex with him, she was not willing to share such a personal thing about her life as being a member of AA.

It must have been obvious to him, after all this time, that she didn't drink alcohol, but he never commented on it and continued to offer her drinks in these situations. She always declined. He never asked why.

He lit his pipe and sat down on the couch across from Zoe. He patted his knees and said, "Come here, Zoe, and give me a kiss."

Panic flooded through her at the thought of being close to him, of having to kiss him. The feeling was so intense that it took her breath away.

Stalling for time, she said, "Let's just sit and talk for a moment, Chief."

She sat in a chair across the room from him. "It feels good to relax. I'm very tired."

"Well then," he said, "I'll have my pipe and cognac."

She was silent for a few minutes. She felt defeated.

The Chief got up and went to the bar. He drank the cognac and poured some more. After he had fussed with his pipe for a few minutes, he said, "Good Congress, Zoe. Good job. I admire the way you handled everything. You're a remarkable woman, you know."

"Thank you, Chief."

"Yes. Remarkable. Now, come and give me a kiss." His voice was insistent.

He sat back down on the couch and set his cognac glass and his pipe on the coffee table.

Zoe's panic increased, but she rose from the chair and crossed to him. He again patted his knees and Zoe sat on them, thinking how absurd it was to sit on his lap as if she were a child.

He chuckled and put his arms around her. Zoe put her arms around his shoulders and touched his hair.

The panic changed to something more complicated, a kind of erotic despair.

The Chief reached under her blouse, unhooked her bra, and began sucking her breasts, making slurping noises and murmuring to himself. She felt herself separating from her body and floating up to the ceiling, looking down on the scene, thinking how horrifying and ridiculous it all was.

After a while, the Chief slid his body off the couch, holding Zoe, and rolling with her onto the floor with a grunt, so they were partly under the coffee table. It had a glass top, and Zoe could see above her the bottom of the cognac glass and the big crystal ash tray with his pipe resting in it.

The Chief pushed the coffee table away with his foot and pulled off Zoe's clothes, so she was lying naked on the soft blue carpet, surrounded by furniture legs and shoes.

Suddenly, music flooded into the room. Mahler. The Chief looked odd to Zoe, larger than he had been, and older. He had a huge head and small, gray eyes; there was gray hair all over his barrel chest, which was marked by a long, pale scar.

He began singing to her, and the sound became very loud, building toward a deafening climax. The swelling, throbbing orchestra and the angel chorus were loud, too, and now he was singing in a gasping, hoarse voice, in rhythm with his thrusts. *Ewig, ewig, zieht uns hinan, das Ewig-Weibliche zieht uns hinan,* he sang, over and over again, thrusting and thrusting. *Ewig, ewig, zieht uns hinan, das Ewig-Weibliche zieht uns hinan, das Ewig-Weibliche, das Ewig-Weibliche, das Ewig-Weibliche.*

And then the music became space, with sounds like twinkling stars and vast distances.

And then, he was no longer a man, but an enormous spider. He plunged his stinger into Zoe, again and again, filling her with venom and clutching at her with many black, hairy legs.

With a mighty effort, Zoe pushed the huge spider off her body and rolled away. But there were spiders everywhere, so many Zoe could no longer see the blue carpet. They were all over the glass coffee table and the chairs and the bed.

Zoe screamed and screamed, and then she felt the venom overtaking her.

There was a loud buzzing in her head and a bitter, metallic taste in her mouth, and she felt herself sinking into whirling darkness.

CHAPTER 22.
Into the Realm of the Goddess

"Walther, I assure you we have modern medicine in Denmark. Don't worry. I'll see that Zoe gets the care she needs."

They were at the airport, near the ticket counter. Zoe sat, mute and passive, not thinking about what Gudrun and the Chief were saying. She didn't care. Nothing made sense to her.

The night before, the Chief had needed to switch gears from lothario to psychiatrist as rapidly as Zoe had gone from administrative director having an assignation with the boss to psychiatric patient. He had quieted her with tranquilizers from his travel pharmacy and had gotten them both dressed.

He led her back to her room, where he phoned Gudrun and asked her to come, saying Zoe had suffered a breakdown and required her help. He needed Gudrun to deal with the situation, he said, because he was to meet his wife in Paris the next day.

It was obvious to Gudrun what had happened, but she gave Walther no indication of that, nor did she ask for more than a cursory explanation. Both chose to leave the details unspoken, and both were entirely professional in demeanor.

In Zoe's room, Gudrun packed Zoe's things while Zoe rested numbly on the unopened bed and Walther called for a porter to move everything to Gudrun's room for the rest of the night.

Zoe already had plans to go with Gudrun to Copenhagen for a week after the Congress, so once the Chief had accompanied the two women to Gudrun's room, he went on with his business, seemingly unshaken.

In the morning, they all went together to the airport. The Chief was his professional best, but he was clearly anxious. With last night's crisis handled, and in the light of morning, he seemed to feel he should say something more about the situation.

"She's always been emotional," he ventured, "but I would not have considered her a candidate for this kind of a breakdown. I didn't see it coming, I'm afraid."

"It seems she's been dealing with a personal crisis," Gudrun said.

"Something to do with her father's death, I assume."

"Something to do with it."

"I thought she was handling that quite well. But then, she rarely discusses her personal life."

"Well, Walther, they're announcing our plane. Don't worry. She'll be fine. She just needs some time away from outer pressures, so she can concentrate on dealing with the inner ones."

Relieved to have Gudrun dealing with the situation, the Chief offered help. "I could arrange for her to see someone in Chicago. Perhaps she could come into the office on a part-time basis."

"No, Walther. Thank you for the suggestion, but we must go. I'll phone you from Copenhagen. I know you'll be concerned about her progress. I'm sure she'll be fine. Goodbye."

He didn't look at Zoe. Gudrun shook his hand and turned away. With her arm protectively around Zoe's shoulders, Gudrun guided her to the bus that took them out across the tarmac to the plane. Each had a small carry-on bag.

Once inside the plane, Zoe sank into the seat as Gudrun put their bags into an overhead compartment and fastened both of their seat belts. Zoe immediately fell asleep.

The rest of the trip was a blur. Zoe was vaguely aware of following Gudrun off the plane and waiting blankly as a customs official looked through their luggage. She was aware of getting into a taxi and riding through city streets. The taxi jerked and swerved, and the driver smelled of sweat.

When the ride was over, Gudrun and Zoe went into a white house with lots of plants and light. When Gudrun showed her to the bedroom, Zoe fell onto the bed and murmured a few words of gratitude as Gudrun, like a mommy, gently pulled the covers over her and gave her a kiss.

Again, Zoe slept.

For several days, Zoe had dream after dream. Sometimes, she awakened in terror. Gudrun would find her hiding in the closet or backed into a corner of the bedroom. At other times, Zoe wept, and Gudrun held her and reassured her until the wrenching sobs subsided. Sometimes, Zoe spoke about the strange spirits and ordeals she had encountered in her nightmares.

Listening intently, Gudrun became acquainted with the

denizens of Zoe's unconscious, who, despite their remarkable dimensions and capabilities, seemed very human.

Trusting Zoe's inner process, Gudrun waited for it to indicate what it required of them both.

One morning, almost a week after arriving in Copenhagen, Zoe awakened, got up slowly, and made her way cautiously out of the bedroom to the interior balcony that ran the width of the upstairs and afforded a view of the kitchen below. The floor to ceiling windows of the kitchen looked out onto a small walled garden, adding to the bright, spacious feeling of the house.

Zoe heard voices. Looking down, she saw Gudrun and a young woman with silver-blond hair. A purple streak ran through her hair from a side part, across her forehead and down the side of her face to her shoulder. The purple complemented her dark blue eyes. She wore no makeup and appeared to be about thirty years old. Both women looked up from their coffee and smiled at Zoe.

"Good morning," Gudrun said. "Have you slept yourself out?"

"I feel as if I've slept for a hundred years."

"You have, dear. Come on down and have some breakfast. You remember Inge?"

Zoe nodded and smiled, recalling that Inge was Gudrun's daughter, who lived with her mother. Inge had been helping to care for Zoe, who had not until now left the upstairs.

Inge had been a reassuring presence when Zoe was especially restless at night, and she sometimes took Zoe breakfast trays in the mornings, doing it all with her mother's same calm competence.

Inge was accustomed to her mother's sheltering "wounded birds," as she referred to them.

Now, Zoe came carefully down the spiral staircase from the balcony and sat unsteadily at the table, feeling dizzy.

"Hi, Zoe. Glad to see you're feeling better." Inge's voice was rich and husky; her manner was cool but kind.

"Thanks for breakfast, Mom. It was great." Inge spoke English with no trace of an accent. She cleared her breakfast dishes from the table, washed them in the sink, and rinsed her coffee cup.

"I'm on my way. See you two later." She took a bicycle from the front hallway and went out.

Gudrun said, "And you've traveled a journey of a hundred miles, Zoe. How are you feeling?"

"Exhausted. But it doesn't seem right to be exhausted since I've slept so long."

"You've been very busy, dear. Only your conscious mind has been sleeping. Would you like some coffee?" Gudrun got up and went to pour coffee.

"Yes, I think so. Thank you."

Gudrun handed Zoe the coffee mug and sat across from her. Zoe breathed in the coffee's fragrance and tentatively took a sip. "The coffee tastes really good, Gudrun. Maybe it will clear my head. I do vaguely remember being on the plane. And something about a taxi ride. The driver smelled terrible."

"He did, didn't he?" Gudrun laughed. "It's funny what gets through. You were pretty doped up."

"Oh, dear. I hope I didn't embarrass you."

Gudrun patted Zoe's hand. "You were gentle as a lamb. Behaved perfectly. No one paid any attention. Everyone was completely self-absorbed. Even, or I should say especially, Walther."

"Oh dear. Walther . . ."

Gudrun laughed again. "Zoe, years ago I was studying hypnosis, and it amused me very much to think that I was learning how to put people *into* trance. What I should have been learning was how to get people *out* of trance. Walther, for all his competence as a therapist, is a good example. He seems remarkably oblivious to the subtext of his own personal life. But then, I've always considered his gifts to be more administrative than shamanic."

Zoe searched her memory. As she gathered pieces, walking back to the hotel with Gudrun and the Chief after their dinner, going with the Chief to his room rather than hers, being on the floor with him naked, looking up at the bottoms of things, and then, the spiders, she felt sick. "Oh, Gudrun. It's beginning to come back to me. Oh, dear."

"You've had quite an adventure." Her voice was gentle and light, with no trace of judgment.

Zoe said, grimly, "When were you called in on the case?"

"Walther phoned me from your room around midnight and asked me to come. He said you were having a crisis. He was very concerned about you.

"You were tearful but very withdrawn. Something upsetting had obviously recently occurred because you'd seemed all right at dinner just a few hours before."

Gudrun patted Zoe's hand again and stood up. "Would you like a croissant and some strawberry jam? And I need some more coffee. How about you?"

In the sunny kitchen, with its white counters, golden wood, plants, and delicious fragrances, Gudrun washed the breakfast dishes as she waited for the coffee to brew.

"I noticed that you were very quiet at dinner, but it was understandable that you'd feel utterly exhausted and let down after so many months of hard work. The Congress was a great success, much of that because of you.

"But I know something of what you've been going through in your personal life, especially with the writing I suggested, which I had hoped would give some containment for the stresses associated with the death of your father."

Gudrun smiled at Zoe and shook her head. "I knew you weren't likely to see the therapist when I suggested it, because you were driving yourself to keep going for the Congress. That's a lot for anyone to deal with. And, Zoe, I think it's amazing you could keep everything together so the Congress could succeed as it did. It's a testament to your essential sanity, despite the tremendous pressures of your inner life. And a let-down now that the Congress is over is to be expected."

Tears came to Zoe's eyes.

Gudrun went on. "But Zoe, even someone with your abilities can't go on forever attending to outer requirements without attending to inner ones."

The coffeemaker steamed and coughed. Gudrun refilled their cups and brought a plate with croissants and a crystal container of strawberry jam. Zoe broke off a small piece of a croissant, put a bit of jam on it, took a bite, and put it down.

Gudrun sat down across from Zoe and sipped her coffee. "Obviously, something had happened between you and Walther. He didn't explain, and I didn't ask. Anyway, I don't need to know about that, Zoe. I'm sure it isn't the real cause of what you're going through, so explanations from Walther were unnecessary. I expect I understood more about what was going on at that moment than he did."

"I'm afraid I acted really crazy."

"Not when I got to your room, and the minute you got settled into my room, you slept quietly for the rest of the night. Walther went with us to the airport. I could see that he was torn between giving up control and not wanting to deal with whatever you were going through, so I sent him on to Paris to meet up with his wife.

"I felt certain what you needed was a safe place and as much protection as I could provide while you struggled with your inner demons, and time, once the struggle was over, to rest. And finally, you needed to understand what had happened so that you could go on with your life."

"*Am* I going to be able to go on with my life, Gudrun?"

"I'm certain you will. You'll come to trust your life, as I do, to carry you where you need to go, and to unfold as it needs to unfold."

"How can I trust my life, Gudrun? The cosmic chair has been pulled out so many times, just as I was going to sit down."

Gudrun laughed, delighted by the image.

"You'll see, Zoe," she said. "You'll see."

CHAPTER 23.
Triple Goddess

In the sanctuary of Gudrun's warm, embracing home, Zoe was content to rest during the day, while Gudrun saw clients at her office, a few blocks away. Zoe and Gudrun would have breakfast together, occasionally with Inge.

Zoe discovered that Inge also had a daughter, Justine, a serious, quiet child of six, who joined them sometimes and regarded Zoe with large grey-green eyes but was too shy to say much, though she was able to speak English. Justine was very well-behaved and seemed older than her years. Zoe was drawn to her, but like the child, she was shy, and she mainly acknowledged Justine by making eye contact and smiling.

For the most part, Zoe was content to let the others talk. Out of politeness, Gudrun and Inge spoke English, and only when Zoe appeared lost in her own thoughts did they speak to one another in Danish. Zoe didn't mind. She was relieved to be free of feeling she should participate in the conversation.

Zoe was, however, gradually learning the history of this all-female household. The story was the stuff of legend. Gudrun, she discovered, was the only child of Danish aristocrats. Her father had been a notable scientist and diplomat and her mother a famous painter.

Gudrun had suffered incest with her father and, as a young woman, in an act of rebellion and tremendous courage, had fled to America, to make her life away from the control of her powerful family and go to college and medical school in Chicago. She had planned to remain in America.

In medical school, she fell in love with a brilliant young doctor, and Inge was their child. Then, the doctor committed suicide. This tragedy had a tremendous impact on Gudrun's relationship with Inge, and the two developed an especially intense closeness.

After earning her bachelor's and medical degrees from the University of Illinois, Gudrun did graduate work in psychiatry at the University of Chicago, earning an advanced degree in Freudian analysis.

Inge spent her early years in a private school in Chicago's Hyde Park neighborhood, which explained her perfect English.

Meanwhile, Gudrun earned two additional degrees, one as an Adlerian therapist before finding her home as a Jungian psychoanalyst. She became involved in the women's spirituality community, and she studied painting, her first love since childhood, at the School of the Art Institute of Chicago.

She also spent all the time she could spare with a group of actors in a theatre company, designing sets for their productions. With them, and doing her painting, she was happily an artist, and she began to question how she should spend her future—as a scientist, like her father, or as an artist, like her mother.

But Gudrun and Inge were summoned back to Denmark by

another tragedy, the death of Gudrun's parents in an automobile accident. Gudrun inherited a vast fortune, including a castle on a remote island off the north coast of Denmark, but she established her life with Inge, and her psychiatric practice, in Copenhagen.

Inge, brilliant and fiercely independent, became a physicist. Also, determined from the time she was a young girl to be a single mom, she gave birth to Justine, whose father had no part of their life. Inge chose not to disclose his identity.

Zoe found Gudrun's exotic history to be daunting, yet Gudrun, despite her wealth and brilliance and artistic abilities, was earthy and unassuming and lived quite simply. She was devoted to her practice, her daughter, and her granddaughter. And now she was devoted to Zoe, whom she graciously welcomed into her family. Zoe was overwhelmed by this generosity.

Inge and Justine were rarely around during the day. They had their own apartment in a separate wing of the house, which Zoe discovered was much larger than it first had seemed. On rare occasions, they joined Gudrun and Zoe for breakfast or supper, but mostly, they lived their own lives and Zoe did not see them.

Each morning, Gudrun had breakfast with Zoe before she went to her office to see clients. During the day, Zoe often just sat and looked out the bedroom window into the walled garden with its trees, which were changing color.

Somehow, it had become October, long past the week she had planned to spend with Gudrun. She couldn't account for the lost time; weeks had simply disappeared, but Zoe did not question this.

Gudrun came home mid-day and made lunch for the two of

them, a quiche or a salad or a fruit concoction. After lunch, Gudrun gave Zoe a hug and went back to her office.

There was a large book about Carl Jung on the coffee table in the living room, and Zoe spent much time looking through it and savoring the many illustrations. The pages were full of images: artworks, masks, sand paintings. There were references to plays, books, and films, as well as to shamanic rituals and West African Vodun. There were photographs of cathedrals and castles, earthworks and pyramids, and hundreds of mythic and symbolic creations by people from all parts of the world, during all periods of history.

Zoe could not concentrate enough to read the text, but she savored the images, which whispered their secrets and mysteries to her. The images, which were beautiful and elaborate, simple or ugly or terrifying, commonplace or bizarre, ephemeral as dreams or enduring as stones, seemed to resonate with the images of the inner world stirring in her own dreams at night.

Zoe found these images in the book oddly comforting; they somehow made her feel less alone, less crazy. Often, when Gudrun came home for the day at around four, Zoe would be peacefully asleep on the sofa with the book open on her lap.

As Gudrun made dinner, she would put a record on the turntable, string quartets or classical piano music, and Zoe felt a deep contentment at the richness of life. Not life in the outer world, from which she felt so alienated, but life lived at the center of being. This was where Gudrun seemed to live, and where Zoe, in Gudrun's presence, seemed also to live.

Zoe could not have said what her own center was. She simply felt herself to be resting in it. Or perhaps it was Gudrun's center, and

Zoe had magically been transported into it, and here she could rest, without desire or fear.

It felt to Zoe like a sacred place.

CHAPTER 24.
Painting

For many days, Zoe was content with this simple routine. One Monday morning after breakfast, however, she realized she was beginning to feel restless. Gudrun realized it too, and she led Zoe into her studio, which was a large sunny room upstairs at the front of the house, facing north, beyond the bedrooms.

Leaning against the walls were dozens of finished canvases. Near the large windows was Gudrun's easel with a blank canvas resting on it, and her well-used palette, along with dozens of jumbled paint tubes in baskets. Countless brushes were stored in pitchers on shelves around the room, which smelled of oil paint and turpentine.

Zoe looked around in wonder, wanting to explore, but Gudrun called her attention back. "Look, Zoe, a present for you."

On a drawing board at the center of the room was a package. Zoe hesitantly removed the paper and discovered a box of Winsor watercolor paints and sable brushes. Already laid out on the drawing board were several sheets of thick watercolor paper.

Seeing Zoe's surprise and delight, Gudrun smiled triumphantly. "Have you ever painted?"

"A long time ago. Not for many years."

"I thought you might like to paint some of the dream images you've spoken to me about. It's not an assignment, but I've found it very helpful in doing my own inner work. I sense you're ready to take some action, and perhaps during the day when you're here alone, you would find it interesting to try painting."

Zoe said, "I stopped painting because I could never decide why I should paint this object as opposed to that one. I didn't seem to have any inner direction, so finally I just gave it up."

Gudrun laughed. "I know about that myself, Zoe. My mother, who was a prolific painter, seemed to find everything interesting to paint, but like you, I didn't see the point of painting just anything until I became a Jungian analyst and began painting my inner images."

She looked appraisingly at Zoe. "But I don't want to put pressure on you to paint if it doesn't feel right to you. If you're willing to try, I suggest that you not be concerned with objects outside of yourself. Just let yourself paint what comes from within you, with your eyes half-closed, looking inward for the image and then letting it take shape on the paper."

"I don't know if I can . . ."

"Well, dear, the paints will be here for you if you decide to try. Let me show you."

She squeezed some blue from one of the little tubes into a dish and, after filling a coffee mug with water, she dipped a big brush into the water and into the pigment and brushed it lightly across the paper. Then, dipping the brush into the water again, she drew the paint out into a pale wash.

"You work with lots of water and just a little paint. See?"

She then squeezed out a dab of purple and blended it into the blue. Zoe had an impression of sky and a feeling of great expansiveness. Also, a sense of place and possibility:

"It's amazing, Gudrun. With just a few strokes of the brush, you've made something beautiful and real. Something that moves me and invites me in."

"Would you like to try?"

She handed the brush to Zoe, who did her best to repeat Gudrun's actions. Her streak of color was heavier on the paper, but she drew it out to a pale wash. Happiness flooded through her.

"Oh, Gudrun. I think I'm going to enjoy this. Thank you."

Gudrun smiled. "Have fun, dear." She patted Zoe's cheek and left her in the sunny studio.

For a long time, Zoe sat, looking at the two dozen small tubes of paint, picking them up, turning them in her hand, reading their names: alizarin crimson, chrome yellow, rose madder, French ultramarine, Indian red, Chinese white, cobalt blue—the names of friends from long ago. In her early life, she had shown an aptitude for painting and had even studied figure painting at the School of the Art Institute for a while after college, but as with so many other expressions of her inner being, her career crowded it out.

She squeezed out several colors and brushed them in pale washes across the page, trying to discover the behavior of the paint.

As she worked, something suggested itself to her, out of the strokes of pigment on the paper. It was only the faintest suggestion of a form, but as she explored it, she saw that it was becoming a cottage.

She had not intended that. It seemed to take shape of its own accord. She felt that the cottage must have a three-section window to the left of the door and a single window to the right. Each panel of glass should have six small panes, and the glass should be tinted blue and lavender. Under the windows, there were flower boxes with primroses. She painted them in with the smallest brush.

At first, the cottage seemed simple, like a small forester's cottage. But it gradually took on a darker mood. After a while, she felt disquieted.

It seemed she had seen this cottage somewhere before; it was not just a chance image she made up, experimenting with the paints and brushes.

The realization intensified her unease, and she began to feel afraid. She had the uncanny sense that there was someone inside the cottage who might open the door and come out or would ask her to enter.

Then she thought she heard the front door of Gudrun's house open and close, and she was sure she heard heavy footsteps downstairs in the hallway.

Those were not Gudrun's footsteps. She heard a man's cough.

Whoever had come in was moving around now in the living room below her. She heard thumping, scraping of wood being piled into the grate, a fire being built. Then the sound of paper being crumpled and pushed under the grate. Then a match being scraped across the sandpaper side of a matchbox, followed by the smell of smoke as the fire flamed up, and the crackling and sizzling of damp wood.

Zoe held her breath and stood without moving by the open door of the studio. The paints and brushes lay forgotten.

She waited for something else to happen, but at last she realized there were no more sounds coming from downstairs. She no longer smelled smoke. She sensed that she was alone again.

Almost sick with anxiety, she crept down the spiral staircase and cautiously went into the living room and looked at the fireplace. There was no sign of a fire. The ashes were gray, and when Zoe held her hands closely over them, there was no warmth.

Moments later, Gudrun came home, ready to make lunch. Relieved, Zoe told her what had happened and showed her the painting. Looking at it again, Zoe had the same strong sense of unease.

Gudrun studied the painting and said, "Zoe, have you ever been hypnotized?"

"I've tried, but it never worked. I don't think I *can* be hypnotized. I resist letting go of control—although I seem to be out of control most of the time these days, so who knows?"

"It's not at all like being out of control. It's just allowing you to go to a deeper level of awareness, underneath your conscious mind where the ego thinks it runs things. In that deeper state, valuable truths and resources of wisdom exist that are not readily available to ordinary consciousness.

"I think you're ready for that information, Zoe. I think you will find it helpful. You've let me know quite a lot about your inner world these past weeks, and your dreams have suggested some things I'd like to explore with you in this way. Will you consider it?"

"Would it be an exorcism?" Zoe was only half joking.

Gudrun laughed heartily. "In a sense."

Then she took Zoe's cold hand in her two warm ones and said, seriously, "But you're not possessed by the devil, dearest. No, no, no. Nothing evil. But you do seem to have some interesting characters dwelling within you. I think one of them visited you today, when you created the painting of the cottage. Perhaps we can have a dialogue with that inner being, to find out who and what it is, and why your painting stirred it to build a fire here."

Gudrun motioned to Zoe to come with her into the kitchen while she made lunch.

"But we will have to do this when your conscious mind is not in charge. It thinks it's protecting you by keeping things from your awareness."

She created a bright, beautiful salad and served each of them a portion in blue-and-white porcelain bowls. Then she laid out a plate of croissants, and sat down across from Zoe, leaning toward her.

"Once, in that dangerous world of your childhood, you needed such protection. But you have resources you didn't have then, and now you need to know the truth with your conscious mind, so you can be free from the tyranny of the past."

The teapot whistled. Gudrun dropped a silver tea ball into the water and placed the teapot on the table so the tea could steep.

She smiled at Zoe. "I'm here to be certain no harm comes to you. There will be no more ordeals as terrible as what you've already been through. I'm certain of that. And you've survived them. You are here, and all is well. Don't you think so?"

"If you'd asked me that an hour ago, I would have said no. I was sure a man was building a fire in the fireplace. I was sure I heard him cough. I was sure I smelled smoke.

"Oh, Gudrun. I've never believed in ghosts. Now, look at me."

Gudrun laughed. "As my countryman, Hamlet, said, 'There are more things in heaven and earth, Horatio, than are dreamt of in your philosophy.'

"The conscious mind is a very small part of a person, Zoe. It likes to think it's running things, but it's only a participant in a far greater process. Of course, you know this, but I'm going to help you experience that greater part of yourself, and it will give you your life in a way that you haven't dreamt of in your philosophy."

Zoe sighed. "Maybe I believe you a little, Gudrun. I do feel a shift taking place in me. But I also feel mentally challenged. Maybe all this sleeping is giving me brain damage. And now, it seems that I'm haunted."

"We're all haunted, Zoe. Most of us just don't realize it. The part that haunts us is our shadow side, as we Jungians call it. It's the part we close away from the light of consciousness because we're ashamed of it or because we think it won't be accepted by others. Perhaps we've been punished by someone because of it.

"And what is wonderful, Zoe, is that the shadow side also contains great energies of creativity and healing and life-potentials *if* we are able to become aware of them and harness their transformative power."

Gudrun paused as she poured the tea into two cups and brought honey and slices of lemon, then she continued, her voice intense.

"Zoe, we don't make a conscious choice to push things down out of our awareness. But something happens to energies when they have been rejected or denied and thrust down into the darkness. Sometimes, they become angry. Sometimes they become dangerous. The great myths tell us that a god that is not propitiated becomes a rageful demon. It then makes its demands, sometimes urgently and violently. We no longer have any choice but to recognize its existence. It confronts us on the path and engages us in battle. And it does not care if we die in the process."

Gudrun was quiet for a moment, buttering a croissant and taking a bite. "I don't mean to suggest that you are dealing with *rageful* spirits. I do think you've been doing battle with *impatient* spirits wanting your attention, and probably you've been experiencing that ever since your father died.

"Together, Zoe, we will lessen their impatience by acknowledging them and engaging them in dialogue. Then, perhaps, they will no longer be so troubled and so troublesome. We will put them to rest. It's my experience that they ask only that we not deny them and that we know who they truly are, that we see what they want us to see and understand what they want us to understand. I feel certain that they mean to help us live with greater understanding of what our deep, inner life is asking of us."

She went around to Zoe's side of the table and sat next to her, embracing her, and saying, with conviction, "Jung considered this shadow aspect of our psyche to be 'pure gold.' He wanted us to mine our psyche for this gold. And, dear Zoe, that's what we're going to do."

Zoe leaned against Gudrun and sighed.

"Don't worry," Gudrun said. "Over the years, I've come to know these shadow beings very well. I meet them daily in my consulting room. I've studied their behavior. And Zoe, I feel affection and compassion for them. Some are quite sad when you come to know them. And sometimes they are funny, endearing, ridiculous, and noble. Oftentimes, they have great wisdom; they may even reveal the secrets of the universe. And all of them, in their way, reveal important truths about our own life."

Gudrun gently removed her arm from around Zoe's shoulders and stood. Together, they spent a few moments clearing away the luncheon dishes and putting the kitchen again into beautiful order.

Then Gudrun said, "Now, dear, I must get back to the office."

At the door as she was leaving, Gudrun turned back to Zoe and said, cheerfully, "So, a grand adventure awaits us."

"Oh, good. An adventure." Zoe's voice was grim.

Gudrun smiled. "Trust life, Zoe." And she was gone.

CHAPTER 25.
The Spider King

The following Sunday morning, Gudrun and Zoe were in Gudrun's office. The consulting room was peaceful, filled with artworks, flowers, and a fireplace, where Gudrun had lit a fire. Beside the desk, on a tall stand, was the large bronze head of a magnificent horse.

Zoe was resting on a leather couch and Gudrun sat in a chair behind and to her left.

"I think you'll find this is not a strange experience," Gudrun said. "We are simply going to allow you to relax into a deeper level of awareness and bypass the guard-gate of your conscious mind. We're going to crawl under the gate because on the other side lies a treasure: the truth.

"I'll record our session so we can review it later and learn from it, be guided by it. But you will also be able to remember what happened."

Gudrun was quiet for a moment.

"These are important steps in the process of integrating your inner life and your conscious outer life, so as to help you experience a feeling of wholeness. That is the healing process, Zoe. Your inner and outer lives become harmonious with one another, so you no longer have unpleasant surprises coming up out of the darkness."

"I want to believe you, Gudrun."

"Good. Now, do you have questions before we begin?"

"No."

"All right, then. I'd like you to lie back on the couch and make yourself comfortable."

Gudrun asked Zoe to flex and relax each part of her body, working up slowly from her feet to the crown of her head, and then to concentrate on her breathing and focus her eyes on a spot high above her head until she could keep her eyes open no longer.

Gudrun then counted backwards from ten, as Zoe went more and more deeply into the center of herself. Gudrun finished counting, "...three...two...one...and you are standing before the cottage you have shown in your painting. Do you see the cottage, Zoe?"

After a moment Zoe murmured, "Yes."

"Can you describe it to me? What do you see?"

"A small cottage with a thatched roof. There are window boxes with primroses in them."

Gudrun waited a few moments to see if Zoe would continue. When Zoe seemed lost in thought, Gudrun prompted her. "What stirs in you as you stand here, outside this cottage?"

"I must go in, but I'm afraid."

"Why must you go in, Zoe? Why are you afraid?"

"*He* is there. He's calling me. But not with his voice . . . with something else. Need. I know he needs me. I must go in, now."

"You can choose not to go in, Zoe. You can stay out here with me."

"No, I must go in. I must."

"I'll go in with you, Zoe."

"I'm afraid . . ."

"It's all right, Zoe. I'll be with you."

Gudrun waited. Zoe was quiet for a long time. She seemed to be gathering courage.

"I'm ready, now. I'm stepping onto the front step . . . I'm opening the front door . . . Oh . . ." Zoe began to tremble and whimper.

Gudrun said, "I'm here with you, Zoe."

"I'm going into the cottage." Zoe's voice became childlike, very different from her regular voice.

There was a long pause. Gudrun watched Zoe's entire physical being change. She could almost believe Zoe's body became smaller, more delicate, vulnerable.

Then, with a shudder, Zoe drew herself up and, in a gruff voice, she said, "Ah, Zoe. Where have you been? I've been waiting for you."

"Who are you?" Gudrun asked softly.

"You don't recognize the Spider King?" the gruff voice continued. "Ach . . . it is sorrowful to be the Spider King. Sorrowful and lonely. I am here in this cottage with my books and my regrets. My only comfort is this child."

Zoe reached her hand out, and Gudrun saw that it was the Spider King's hand, beckoning the child to come closer to him. In the young girl's voice, Zoe said, "Poor Spider King."

Tears came from her closed eyes and rolled down her cheeks.

"How can a young girl comfort a king?" Gudrun asked the Spider King, her voice neutral.

"She feels my sorrow," he responded through Zoe. "She is beauty and life. I am dead, except for her. Come, sit on my lap, Zoe, and give me a kiss. Yes, darling. Oh, thank you."

Zoe's Spider King seemed to receive her on his lap and to lean forward and receive her kiss. "Poor Spider King," Zoe's young girl voice said again.

The Spider King sighed, and then said to Gudrun, "You see, I was wounded here." He gestured toward his groin. "In my pain, I came to this place to be with my books. Until this child came into my life, like dawn light. Like the pale buds of early spring. Like the streams beginning to flow again after the winter. Like young animals, taking their first steps, eyes newly opened to the world. She was innocent and full of promise. She was everything I was not."

"Yes, she was those things. But what of her life? What of her promise? Were those not hers to fulfill?"

"I thought she had come to comfort me, to heal me. With her innocence, she sanctified my corrupted soul. With her promise, she gave me new life."

"No," Gudrun said. "You took her innocence. You took her life."

"Did I?" He began to sob. "I meant only to love her. I wanted only to give her something of value in return for the beauty she had given me. I gave her everything I possessed—music, poetry, great teachings of the world. I opened her spirit to the transcendent mystery."

"She was a young girl. She had her own life to live. You took that from her. You were selfish, blind to her needs."

"I had nothing else to give her."

"She belonged to life, not to you. She belonged to herself."

"I was so lonely. I had nothing else." The Spider King was sobbing raucously, now. Through Zoe, he hunched over, his face in his hands.

"You had your own life. Didn't you realize that?"

The Spider King said nothing.

After a pause, Gudrun said, "You wounded her with your love. It became not love but imprisonment."

He sobbed.

Gudrun's voice was steady but intense. "You seduced her with beauty, entrapped her spirit with *beauty*! That was perverse."

"I didn't know I was doing that." His voice was anguished.

Gudrun said, "Zoe, it's time for us to leave. Tell the Spider King goodbye."

Zoe gradually stopped sobbing as the Spider King and became, again, the young girl.

"Goodbye, Spider King," she whispered, her voice tremulous.

"Tell the Spider King you are going out of the cottage now to live your own life. Sorry as you are that he is suffering, you cannot heal his wound or relieve his suffering. He will need to do that for himself. You must leave him because you have your own life to live. Please tell him that, Zoe."

Zoe spoke in her trembling, young girl's voice. "I must leave you, Spider King. I'm sorry for your suffering."

She sobbed for a long time, heartrending sobbing. "I can't suffer for you anymore. I can't make you well." Her whole frame shook with her grief. "I can't live your life for you. I can't. I tried to. But I must live my own life now."

She sobbed and sobbed, the tears spilling down over her cheeks and onto her breast.

Gudrun said, firmly, "Now, Zoe, it's time for us to leave."

"Goodbye, Spider King. I must leave now."

"Zoe, we are now walking together out of the cottage." Gudrun's voice was steady.

Zoe, her eyes closed, shook with sobs.

Again, she said, "Goodbye, Spider King. Goodbye."

Zoe seemed to draw all her strength into herself.

Gudrun saw that she was experiencing a transformation so powerful that it was manifested in her body. The fragile girl disappeared as Zoe stepped through the doorway of the cottage and became, once again, an adult woman.

The adult woman, too, was grief stricken. But she did not weep with a child's heartbroken sobbing. Rather, hers was the grief of a person who, knowing life's sorrow and loss, lets grief flow through her like a river, and does not try to hold it back. And flowing through, the river follows its course to the sea, and she is not drowned or swept away by its whirling currents.

Gradually, Zoe's weeping quieted. She fell over on her side and lay on the couch, exhausted.

After a few moments, Gudrun said, "Good, Zoe. Good. Now, it's time to come back from your journey. As I count backwards from ten, I want you, slowly, and as you are ready, to come up to full consciousness and be back in the room with me."

Gudrun counted slowly. "When you come fully awake, you will feel refreshed and will have a great sense of relief, after the good work you have done, and you will remember all that has happened.

"And now you are going to be fully awake and will open your eyes when I say *one.*"

Zoe opened her eyes. Gudrun smiled at her.

Zoe sat up a little shakily and wiped away her tears with her hands. Gudrun handed her a tissue. Zoe blew her nose and sighed. "Well."

Gudrun chuckled. "Yes. That was quite a journey. You did good work, Zoe."

She sat back and looked appraisingly at Zoe for a few moments. "How do you feel?"

"Exhausted. But also, as if a great weight has been lifted from me. It was nothing like I'd expected. Amazing."

"Yes, dear. A simple but powerful process."

"Not what I expected. I remember everything . . ."

"Not the usual idea of hypnosis."

Zoe blew her nose again.

"We can talk later about what happened with the Spider King and begin to make sense of it and learn from it. But for now, you've done enough. It's time to rest. Would you like to have some tea? I have a few things to do for about half an hour, and then we can go home and have lunch. But for now, why don't you rest here on the couch?"

Zoe leaned back and closed her eyes, and in a few minutes, Gudrun came back with a cup of lemon-flavored tea with honey, which soothed Zoe's throat and gave her a sense of deep comfort.

She dozed until Gudrun gently awakened her and they went home.

The next afternoon, Zoe and Gudrun were again in the consulting room, after Gudrun had finished seeing clients.

Dusk came early to Copenhagen in October, and in the darkening afternoon, in the firelight's warmth, Gudrun played back the recording of the Spider King session for Zoe to hear.

Zoe listened with amazement as her everyday voice changed to the young girl's voice, and then to the gruff man's voice. It was eerie. There were clearly four voices on the tape: hers, Gudrun's, the young Zoe's, and the Spider King's.

Zoe could see, almost as if she were actually there, the cottage where she had been with the Spider King. She clearly saw him in her mind's eye, his small gray eyes, big beak of a nose, thinning gray hair, his barrel chest and his gold-and-black sweater with the leather patches at the elbows.

She saw the hundreds of books, the fireplace, the rough-hewn dining table with its candles and its wooden chairs. She was sure she had been there, but how could that be?

She asked Gudrun.

"Remember, Zoe, there are more things in heaven and earth," Gudrun said. "But let's not ask how. It isn't very useful to analyze and explain. We need to behold and attend to our inner knowing. If we can savor our inner experience as it comes to us by way of imagery, without judgment and analysis, we can simply live our way into new understandings, new ways of seeing things. For now, the important thing is, what can we learn from the Spider King? What is he showing us?"

"I felt so sad for him," said Zoe. "But why is he called the 'Spider King'? And who is he?"

"The unconscious communicates through metaphors, Zoe. If it could put its process into words, it might say, *Let me tell you what I want you to know with a story. Once upon a time there was a sad and wounded king called the Spider King who fell in love with a beautiful young girl and wanted to lay the riches of his kingdom at her feet.*"

"Oh, Gudrun! I feel frustrated sometimes, needing to have you guide me through my weird inner landscape."

Gudrun said, "Learning to understand and relate to our inner images is a skill, Zoe; one that can be easily learned. Anyway," she continued, "that's how the deep psyche communicates with us. Maybe it's bored and needs to amuse itself. I would guess when you're tens of thousands of years old, you get to entertaining yourself by creating strange stories and curious images, finding intriguing ways of expressing things."

Zoe sighed.

"I'm teasing a little bit, Zoe, but not really. That seems to be how the psyche functions. The unconscious expresses itself in metaphors. Even the concept of the unconscious is a metaphor. We call our discipline *depth psychology* and even the term *depth* is a metaphor, as if something lies *under* the conscious mind. But we are trying to describe something that is vast; mere words cannot describe it. And yet we try."

"All right, Gudrun," Zoe said, laughing. "I'll stop asking why."

"Good." But then Gudrun went on, not wanting to dismiss Zoe's question without a thoughtful answer.

"What we do know, Zoe, is that the energies of the deep psyche come to us as revelations, interior phenomena that we call images, images of many kinds. Sometimes as single words or lines of poetry. Sometimes as phrases of music and songs. Sometimes as pictures seen with the inner eye, sensations in the body, mathematical formulas, odors. And sometimes even as dream characters who speak to us in dialogue about the requirements and necessities of our lives. The variety of images is endless."

She smiled and leaned forward, her voice kind, reassuring. "And Zoe, I've learned that these dreams and images have a profound intentionality, and they invariably benefit our life. They tell us the truth, if we attend to them and trust them and treat them as sacred revelations. What we are doing here, Zoe, in our time together, is giving them our attention, entering into dialogue with them, inviting them to become our teachers."

"That's your magic, Gudrun."

"Yes, it *is* a kind of magic, Zoe, this healing process we're engaged in. We must be able to summon and engage with and harness the powerful energies of the psyche on behalf of our conscious life."

After a pause, Gudrun added, "Zoe, as we listened to the recording of the session with the Spider King, you heard him say he wanted to love that young Zoe, but he was himself wounded. His need was so great he was blind to her need.

"But Zoe, he was not a monster, though his actions were sometimes monstrous. He offered young Zoe what he could. You heard him enumerate his gifts to Zoe: music, poetry, great teachings of the world."

Gudrun paused, deep in thought.

"That's very like my father, Gudrun," Zoe said quietly.

"Yes, Zoe. And those are magnificent gifts. But the Spider King, who is perhaps the shadow aspect of your father, asked too much of young Zoe in return. She sacrificed her own life in the exchange. Of course, being so young, she could not realize she was making so great a sacrifice.

"As you heard, the young Zoe was, even in her childishness, compassionate and loving. She did her best to be kind and helpful. Children do that. When they have the misfortune to be born into a world ruled over by a wounded king, or a world that is in some other way disordered, they do whatever they can to set things right. Not realizing the terrible cost, they give their life to such an effort, as young Zoe gave her life to bring relief and comfort to the Spider King. And, alas, he accepted her sacrifice."

Zoe was quiet for a few moments. "That seems to be true of me and my father—my father, the Spider King."

"Yes, Zoe," Gudrun said.

Then, after another pause, she added, "So, Zoe, you've done the most healing thing already. You've said goodbye to the Spider King and have left him there in the cottage with his books.

"But to speak about the process for a moment, we've gone back together, using the white magic of hypnosis and imagery, to an earlier time of your life, as we can do in this amazing inner world of ours."

With a gesture to describe what she meant, she said, "It's as if we stretched a rubber band back to include what happened earlier and now we have drawn that same rubber band forward to include the present, to include resources and understandings you've gained by living and growing wiser, so that you can now make more life-enhancing choices, so that you can claim for yourself the life that is rightfully yours, leaving behind the Spider King, who once laid claim to that life."

Zoe sighed a tremulous sigh. "I think I'll need time to process this and make sense of it all."

"You'll have that time, Zoe, here in the sanctuary of my consulting room, and the loving safety of my home."

"I'm profoundly grateful for that, Gudrun, and for you."

CHAPTER 26.
Cat

A few nights after the Spider King session, Zoe had a vivid dream.

She was in the cottage she had pictured. She felt herself to be a young girl.

She heard another girl's voice outside. "Zoe, Zoe, come out. Zoe, come out."

Alone in the cottage, Zoe looked out the window. It was morning; the sun was high in the sky. She opened the front door and stepped out onto the stone doorstep.

A blond girl, a little taller than she was, also barefoot and dressed in shorts, said, "Come on, Zoe. Come with me." And the girl ran across the grass in front of the cottage.

Zoe recognized her friend, Cat.

Zoe ran after her, trying to catch up, but Cat was swift-footed, and Zoe could never quite reach her side as they ran along a sandy road through the woods.

Cat laughed and looked back at Zoe, her golden hair blowing across her face. She called out, "Come on, come on, Zoe. Run faster. You're such a lazy girl. Run faster."

Zoe fell farther behind. She had a cramp in her side and was having trouble catching her breath. The muscles in her calves burned.

As Cat ran farther and farther ahead, the road in front of Zoe shifted under her feet. Suddenly, it tore apart right ahead of her. She looked down into a deep, gaping hole.

"Cat!" Zoe screamed.

The girl turned back and saw the hole in the road.

"Leap across, Zoe. Leap across."

"I can't. I can't."

"Leap across, Zoe. You *must*. Come on, Zoe. You can do it. Don't be afraid."

"I can't! I can't!" Zoe felt the road collapsing under her, and she screamed again.

"Leap, Zoe, leap!"

Zoe was about to leap when her own screaming woke her up.

At breakfast, Zoe told Gudrun the dream about Cat.

"Well," Gudrun said. "Your unconscious is working overtime. It wants you to know everything so you can be whole. Perhaps tomorrow, at my office, we can learn what Cat can teach us. I'm certain it will be something wonderful."

Gudrun's voice was full of delight.

Zoe said, "Gudrun, why are you so cheerful?"

"This is the grand part of the adventure, Zoe. The romp out of the Realm of Shadows back to the everyday world you left so long ago to travel the Road of Trials. Oh, there are still monsters along the path, but they no longer have the power to harm you. Nothing can keep you from your return now, Zoe. You will bring back your healing boon. You will triumph." She laughed and clapped her hands.

As Gudrun cleared the breakfast dishes, Zoe helped her, saying, "I won't ask you how you know this, Gudrun."

"It's an ancient story, dear."

She gathered her things and, hugging Zoe, left for her office.

The next day, in the consulting room, Gudrun guided Zoe again through the induction process with relaxing and counting.

As Zoe's eyelids fluttered and closed, and her breathing slowed, Gudrun said, "You are in the cottage, now, Zoe, and it's morning. Can you tell me what you see?"

Zoe replied in the young girl's voice, "Sunlight is coming through the window."

"Someone outside the cottage is calling you. Do you hear it?"

Zoe listened intently. "Yes. Cat is calling me."

"Who is Cat, Zoe?"

"My friend. I love her, but she makes fun of me. Sometimes she gets mad at me."

"Why does she do that?"

"I don't know."

"Let's go outside and ask her."

Gudrun waited as Zoe, in her inner process, went out of the cottage. Then Gudrun asked Zoe what she was seeing.

"Cat's standing there, waiting for me. Hello, Cat."

Zoe's voice became jocular, and lower in pitch, like a cello. "Hi, kiddo."

As herself, Zoe said, "This is my friend Gudrun, Cat. She wants to talk to you."

"Oh, yeah?" Cat sounded dubious.

"She wants to know why you get so mad at me."

"Why should I tell her?"

"Oh, Cat. She's a friend."

"How would you know? You're such a numbskull. Your judgment isn't worth shit, kiddo, when it comes to who your friends are. You *know* what I mean."

"I *never* know what you mean, Cat. You talk in riddles."

Gudrun leaned forward, joining the conversation. "Cat, could you explain to me why you get angry at Zoe?"

Cat was exasperated. "I already said. Her judgment is terrible. She has no sense. She got herself entangled with that pervert, the Spider King. I warned her that was dangerous. I told her one of these days he would kill her and then I couldn't save her. I can do a lot, but once she's dead, there's nothing I can do."

"I see," said Gudrun. "You seem to know a lot, Cat."

"Yes, I'm smart. I'm resourceful. I'm devoted. I'm tough. She's lucky to have me, the little dummy."

Zoe became indignant. "You always call me a dummy, Cat."

"Aren't you? Why do you let that creep do weird stuff to you? You don't like it. And then, you get in over your head. You know. The rape. The fire. Justice-Bringer."

Zoe said nothing.

Gudrun asked, "What about the rape, and what about the fire, Cat? What is Justice-Bringer? What happened?"

"Ritual rape," Cat said. "The son-of-a-bitch." A sob caught in her throat.

"Candles. Hocus-pocus. He got her drunk, painted her face, made her get naked while he dressed up in that hideous dead animal skin and knelt before her and called her the Goddess and said he was going to plow her field as the god, as the fucking *male principle*.

"And then he raped her with an ivory gizmo. Pushed it right up into her little body. The son-of-a-bitch. He did that to my darling." Cat's voice was filled with rage and pain.

"I hate him. I shot him in the heart with an arrow. Justice-Bringer is my bow. He wounded her so badly I took her to the old woman. I couldn't think of anything else to do. I was so afraid she would die." Cat sobbed.

"What old woman, Cat?"

"The Dark Mother."

Cat struggled to regain her composure. After a moment, she said, "All of this is hers. The Spider King is her consort. She's the center of everything. Very powerful. I shouldn't be speaking of her. Don't ask me anything more. I'll be in trouble."

Gudrun said, "We don't want to make trouble for you, Cat."

"Thanks, lady. I've got my hands full with this one. Right, kiddo?"

Zoe said nothing. Gudrun said, "Cat, thank you for watching over Zoe."

"Well, it isn't easy. But I love the little lamebrain, despite it all."

"Zoe needs you, Cat. You're a good friend to her, probably the most important one in her life. I hope you'll stay around."

"Oh, sure. I always stand ready to serve. She knows that. Don't you, kiddo? You know I love you."

"I guess so," Zoe said. "Sometimes it doesn't seem that way. You're always making fun of me. You insult my intelligence."

Cat exploded with amusement. "Could there be any doubt that you're lacking something in the mental department, kiddo? Look at the facts. But it doesn't make me love you any less. In fact, it makes me feel important. It's exciting, galloping in at the last minute and saving the princess from the evil king. Or the toad. Or whatever. But I wouldn't mind a little peace and quiet for a while, kiddo. Really."

Gudrun's voice was firm. "You'll have that peace and quiet now, Cat. We're going to make sure of that."

"You think so? Sometimes I think she's terminally gullible."

"That's going to be different now."

"So, will I be out of a job?"

Gudrun laughed gently. "A friend like you is never out of a job, Cat. Zoe is going to need you more than ever. She needs you to tell her the truth. She needs you to show her how and when to feel anger, how to maintain her boundaries. She needs your energy, your spunk, your courage, your resourcefulness. She needs your ability to say *no* when necessary and to call a spade a spade."

"I *am* pretty amazing."

"Cat, you're the best thing that ever happened to Zoe."

"I'm glad someone finally noticed."

Gudrun said, "Zoe, is there anything you'd like to say to Cat before we go back?"

"Oh, Cat, I love you. Don't ever leave me."

"I won't, kiddo. You can count on it."

Gudrun gradually took Zoe back to consciousness and sat smiling triumphantly as Zoe opened her eyes.

"Perhaps you begin to see, Zoe, what resources lie within you."

"But that's you, Gudrun, *your* resourcefulness, and I am allowed to share in it."

"No, Zoe. Don't give away your power. What you are experiencing is your own inner resourcefulness. We could call it *direct knowing* of the wisdom waiting in your depths. I have simply created the environment in which you can realize those resources and gain access to their power, their life-energy.

"For most of us, most of the time, the world is too loud and complicated and distracting for us to listen to our inner voices, hear the wise teachings of our bodies, deepen our awareness of the subtle and eloquent messages of our dreams. But here, during this healing time, this return from your Road of Trials, you can open your consciousness to your own inner realm, where everything you need for wisdom and wholeness resides. It is there within you, and it always has been within you, waiting to be known."

Zoe needed a pause, so she stood up and walked over to Gudrun's desk, beside which the magnificent horse's head rested on its stand. She touched it briefly, drawn to its beauty.

Gudrun smiled and said, "That sculpture arose from the powerful inner resources of one of my clients. It symbolizes for her the strength she discovered in herself as we worked together. A powerful, noble horse is the image that came to her, and because she had been trained as a sculptor, she could shape her image into that splendid artwork.

"And, Zoe, you have that same powerful resource of imagery and creativity and strength within you too, though the outer form in which you represent it symbolically will be different, shaped by your own creative sensibilities. Perhaps for you, that image of inner strength has come to you as Cat, with her courage and spunk, toughness and protectiveness, ability to know the truth, and her own special ability to handle great challenges.

"The important thing is for you to realize that power within yourself, as you have done here in our work together, and then for you to integrate those images and realizations into your conscious life so they're available as you face whatever new challenges your life holds."

Zoe returned to the couch, sat down again, leaned back, and sighed.

"I feel as if I've been living in a wasteland, Gudrun. I didn't realize that, and I only know it now because of how changed I feel with you. It's as if the life that happened before I came to Copenhagen was lived by someone else, a sad, suffering stranger, who lived in black and white and gray. Now, that stranger is gone, and in her place is a new person. Still a stranger, but one who can see in color. The paintings you helped me to make seem to me to be my introduction to the world of color."

Gudrun became excited, her voice intense. "Yes, Zoe. You've expressed it beautifully! Our best creative acts always create us as we create them. Making art from the images arising from our depths is affirming, clarifying, empowering.

"And, Zoe, our creativity makes us whole. The horse's head you've admired represents my client's experience of healing. With it, she returned to her work as a sculptor, which had been stalled for years, paralyzed by her inner suffering."

Zoe leaned forward, also excited. "How wonderful! How beautiful, the way you've described this amazing process! And Gudrun, putting the brush to paper and watching the colors flow out into shapes was so—*thrilling* is the best word for it. It felt almost erotic."

Gudrun laughed with delight. "Yes! That's the perfect description of your *elan vital,* Zoe. Your life force, the erotic, thrilling creative urge within each of us, expressing itself to our consciousness. As you and I work more together, you'll come to know that *elan vital* well. It powers our existence."

Gudrun closed her eyes for a moment, savoring this thought.

"Dylan Thomas called it *the force that through the green fuse drives the flower.*

"Evoking that force is at the heart of my work, Zoe. I help people evoke their *elan vital,* and then I teach them what is required to behave properly toward that sacred energy, to regulate and focus its tremendous power once they have come into its presence. For the *elan vital* is truly sacred, Zoe.

"But the wise ones also tell us that behaving with proper respect in the presence of the sacred requires ritual. What we have been doing here together is ritual, Zoe. It evokes the sacred energy and transforms it into healing power."

Then Gudrun added, her voice passionate, her eyes glowing with intensity, "But Zoe, the authentic life arising from our depths wants so much more for us than the healing of our woundedness. It wants us to realize the vast resources of creativity waiting in our depths to be expressed in the creative works of our outer lives.

"And it wants us to move toward an experience of wholeness and the magnitude that is our true nature, and to know we are one with the beauties of our beloved green earth, and the white moon radiant among the stars, and the mysteries of the deep waters.

"It wants us to have an experience and direct knowing of the meaning of our individual life, and the transcendent meaning of Life itself, and of our rightful place in the great web of the universe.

"And ultimately, Zoe, it wants us to know *holiness*, to know the sacredness of our own life and of all life."

Zoe closed her eyes, which were flooded with tears of love.

"You are a very evolved person, Gudrun."

"*Evolving*, dear—as you are. As we all are."

CHAPTER 27.
What Does Rilke Have to Do with Anything?

Zoe and Gudrun were sitting at breakfast. An awareness had come to Zoe.

"Gudrun, the other day, you said the imagery of the deep psyche sometimes comes through lines of poetry. That reminds me of an experience I had recently. I came to consciousness after one of my fainting spells with a line of poetry clearly resonating in my mind. I remember it exactly: *Sein Blick is vom Vorübergehn der Stäbe.*"

"Rilke," Gudrun said.

"Yes. The first line of Rilke's poem, *Der Panther.* Erica, my college roommate, was crazy in love with Rilke's poetry. That poem became a favorite of mine as well as hers."

Zoe uttered a deep sigh, remembering. "I never tired of hearing Erica recite it in German! It always stirred me deeply. It felt so profound and heartbreaking.

"But after the fainting spell, I've been wondering, *What does Rilke have to do with anything?*"

"Well, Zoe, what you're saying is very interesting to me. I feel like a cat that has just noticed a cricket, or a mouse, and immediately focuses on it totally and gathers its muscles to pounce and then to play with it for a while before dispatching it."

Zoe smiled at the image.

"So," Gudrun said, laughing her melodic laugh, "let's pounce on this line of poetry and play with it for a while. Let's test the theory that such images have meaningful messages for us, if only we give them our full attention.

"That was a very specific line of poetry, which we can consider to be an image, so let's stay close to it. Besides Erica's love of the poem, what stirred *you* about it? What made it so *profound and heartbreaking* to you? Because that line of poetry is *your* image, after all; it came up to you from *your* depths at a very specific moment in your life. So, let's *see* what Rilke has to do with anything."

Giving it thought, Zoe said, "In the poem, Rilke describes a panther he saw in the zoo of the botanical garden in Paris. Rilke lived in Paris for a while in his early life, and he served as the secretary to Auguste Rodin, the great sculptor, whose theory of artistic methods profoundly influenced the way Rilke used imagery in his poetry."

Zoe searched for the right words. "Influenced by Rodin, Rilke didn't want, in his poetry, to describe something from the outside, as an observer, but somehow to express the essence, the essential truth, of an object.

"And that's what I experienced in that poem, Gudrun. In some mysterious way. I *became* the panther, which had been taken from its rightful place in nature and imprisoned in a cage at the zoo.

"I could feel, as if from deep within myself, the spirit of the magnificent animal; I could *feel* the movement of his powerful, soft strides, which Rilke described as being like a ritual dance around a center, in which the panther's mighty will stood paralyzed, because it could no longer choose to do what it was meant to do. It was no longer free."

Zoe suddenly wept for the panther, and for herself. Gudrun handed her a tissue but said nothing.

"And the panther had been imprisoned for so long, says Rilke, that all it saw, at last, were the bars of the cage, and *behind the bars, no world.* Those words always made me tremble, Gudrun. *Behind the bars, no world.*

"So terrible, the idea of seeing only one's prison, and to have forgotten that there is a world beyond where it is possible to be free." Zoe wiped away her tears. "Rilke shows both the beauty and the tragedy of the panther."

"Yes, Zoe," Gudrun said quietly.

Zoe was also quiet for a few moments, as memories flooded through her mind and stirred her heart.

"It was such a dark and radiant time with Erica. I fell in love with her, Gudrun. We became lovers and were together for three more years after we graduated. But our relationship caused such a scandal!"

Zoe laughed bitterly. "My parents conspired with the housemother and dean of women to send me to the campus psychiatrist. I sat silently in her office week after week and refused to participate. Incidentally, when I said I never had a woman therapist, I'd forgotten the campus psychiatrist was a woman. But I can't say I did therapy with her.

"Anyway, it seemed that everyone treated my relationship with Erica either as a psychiatric disorder or as a sin, and I was terribly shamed by their horror and disgust. My father said to me, 'There are institutions for people like you.'"

Zoe's eyes again filled with tears. "I don't think anything ever hurt me as much as hearing my adored father say that to me, as if I was so evil and dangerous that I needed to be locked up in a prison cell, or a madhouse. His voice was filled with such rage and cruel conviction that I knew—I *knew*, Gudrun—he would have burned me at the stake for what I had done, had it been allowed."

Gudrun murmured, "How painful that must have been."

"Yes. It was a terrible time for me. And Erica, being Erica, laughed it all off! She refused to be shamed. But I felt cast out of the protection of my father's love, out of society. Besides, I was accustomed to having my secret life stay secret. It had never before become a public scandal."

Zoe again laughed bitterly, remembering. Then she continued, her voice intense.

"But Gudrun, along with the scandal and shaming, our relationship included much beauty, immersed as we were in the glorious music of Mahler and Schumann, Mozart and Beethoven, the writing of T.S. Eliot and James Joyce, the ideas of Nietzsche and Kant. We shared a treasure-trove of art and ideas and so much more that brought me rapture in the midst of pain."

Her voice was passionate. "And Rilke! Rilke's poems, which were so like my relationship with Erica, with all its beauty, as well as the darkness."

After a pause, Zoe said, her voice almost reverent, "And there was something else, Gudrun. The powerful intensity of Erica's kisses, her soft woman's mouth, her breasts and belly against mine. I remember gazing into Erica's eyes and feeling myself also to be beautiful in that moment, as if my own woman's essence was being reflected back to me.

"The intimacy with Erica always felt, somehow, sacred, despite what society was saying about it, though I would not, *could* not, have used that word *sacred* back then, when I was an atheist.

"But I had the powerful conviction that being with Erica completed something essential in me, a conviction so strong it overcame all the pain." Zoe paused and sighed a deep sigh.

"But finally, Erica went on without me, Gudrun—like Cat, in the dream, urging me to leap over the terrible opening in the road and I couldn't leap across. Like Cat, Erica went on without me." Zoe wept.

Gudrun, her voice gentle, said, "It seems, Zoe, that the feeling of completion you experienced with Erica was your reconnection with your essential feminine self, a connection you had lost. But it could not be truly lost, Zoe, for like the soul, it is inviolate and immutable. But the circumstances of trauma had broken your sense of connection to that sacred feminine part of you. What was *intended,* by your deepest and most profound self, your *soul,* was to reunite you with that forgotten, sacred feminine essence, however it could be achieved."

Gudrun paused, giving Zoe time to absorb this.

"Alas," she continued, "that *spiritual* yearning for the sacred feminine, which would have been so healing for you, was misunderstood at the time. It was *diagnosed* in worldly terms, called sinful and profane by your father and pathological by the housemother and the dean of women, and by society, and perhaps even by the campus psychiatrist, though I hope she would have known better, if she had been given a chance."

Zoe sat back and closed her eyes, which were flooded with

tears. She was filled with memories of Erica, of love and loss and now, love again.

After a few moments of silence, Gudrun said, taking a breath and standing, "Yes. And now, dear Zoe, let me make us some comforting tea as we rest for a few moments, after all the intensity. But I'm not quite ready to say goodbye to our friend Rilke."

They savored the tea as Gudrun returned to Rilke. "Zoe, does that particular Rilke poem suggest anything to you about your life *now,* anything about what your life is asking of you at this time?"

Zoe thought for a moment. "Well, maybe, because of his intense focus on me, my father took me prisoner in the relationship, and like the panther, I have been pacing ever since in a ritual dance of compulsive behavior. It now seems to me that I've been Rilke's panther all along."

Zoe shook her head in exasperation. "But Gudrun, I'm depressed by the thought that I'm *still in the cage,* despite all your help. To tell you the truth, even now, it feels as if my will still stands paralyzed."

Zoe's voice became intense, urgent. "And yet I know I must get free. I *must.* I think that's what that poem is telling me. But I feel so hopeless about it all."

Gudrun reached across the table and took Zoe's hand in both of hers. "Dear Zoe. I feel certain that now you will free that beautiful inner panther from its cage so it can live the life it is meant to live. I think that is already happening. And look, Zoe!"

Gudrun smiled happily, letting go of Zoe's hand and leaning back with a contented sigh. "You've just now proven the theory about our imagery being purposive and offering us important truths.

"You've answered the question that came to you after the fainting spell. *What does Rilke have to do with anything?*"

"Yes." Zoe also leaned back and sighed, but with the suggestion of a frown. "I now know. *Everything.*"

CHAPTER 28.
The Dark Mother

Several days later, Zoe did another painting. In the sunny quiet of Gudrun's studio, she sat before the blank paper for a long time, waiting for something to stir within her.

After a while, she was moved to wet the paper and lay in some blocks of gray and beige. Then she felt that the center of the page needed to be gold and circular. The shapes suggested that she was looking into a broad, rectangular room. As she worked, the room seemed to be filled with colored light, like the jeweled light that shines through stained glass. She therefore painted two stained-glass windows in the back wall of the room, ruby and emerald and cobalt blue.

The walls seemed to be very thick, and the windows were in deep recesses.

As she painted, Zoe felt herself being drawn into the room. With all her senses responding, she became aware that a fire burned in a fireplace. Despite the fire, the room was cool. The floor was composed of richly patterned, colorful marble. In the foreground, she painted a large table. She knew it was heavy and ornately carved, though she couldn't show that with her paint.

Suddenly, she understood what was to be in the center: a very particular old woman. Her face, shoulders, and arms were angular and bony. Her hands were gnarled, with swollen knuckles and twisted fingers. The old woman's skin was yellowish, and there were dark circles under her eyes. She had yellow-gray hair braided and twisted around her head like a crown of serpents. She was dressed in a long, black gown, and she wore a circular copper breastplate.

Zoe felt she knew this old woman, who was sitting on a throne on a dais and held a cane of carved wood. Zoe despaired of adequately painting the old woman, but in her mind, she saw that the old woman sat with her back to the fireplace and flames seemed to emanate from her, conveying power and magic.

Zoe had been working quickly, only suggesting what she wanted to paint more clearly later.

Once she had completed the figure of the old woman, Zoe sat for a long time, wondering at the strength of her inner conviction about how the picture should be. Her conscious mind had not decided what to paint. And she was equally aware of feeling she had been in the room, in the old woman's presence, of *knowing* her.

Zoe must have slipped into a deeper level of awareness, or perhaps she dozed and had a brief dream, because she noticed her heart beating with a loud, steady, echoing thump. But she realized that the thumping was not her heartbeat. It was the old woman, striking her cane on the marble floor. Startled, Zoe came to full consciousness, the sound of the thumping ringing in her ears.

Gudrun found her sitting, still looking at the painting, when she returned later.

The next day in her consulting room, when she had finished seeing clients, Gudrun guided Zoe through the relaxation, induction, and counting. It was becoming easier for Zoe to enter this twilight realm of awareness.

Gudrun asked, quietly, "Are you ready to take me with you into the room you showed in your painting, Zoe?"

"Yes," Zoe murmured.

Gudrun waited to see if Zoe would say anything more. When she did not, Gudrun prompted her. "Where are we now?"

Again, a pause; Zoe was clearly engaged in an inner process. Gudrun waited another few moments, then again prompted her. "Zoe, where are we now?"

"In the great house. We're just outside the chapel."

"Is the chapel the room you painted?"

"Yes."

"How do you go into the room?"

A pause. Then, "I'm summoned."

"How does the summons come?"

"It just comes. I feel I am called."

"Then what do you do?"

"I go in." Zoe's body seemed to grow smaller. "I'm dressed in soft leather. The leather smells good."

Her voice became lighter, the younger Zoe's voice. "I'm going into the chapel."

Zoe was quiet and deep in concentration. She seemed to be experiencing something, but she said nothing. After a few minutes,

Gudrun asked, "What do you see now, Zoe?"

"The Dark Mother."

"What do you do?"

Again, a pause. Then, "I kneel before her."

"Do you speak to her, Zoe?"

Zoe shook her head emphatically. "She speaks, I listen."

"What does she say?"

"She gives me instructions. I'm afraid of her."

"Why?"

Zoe struggled to find an answer. "She asks me to do difficult things."

"Zoe, will you ask her if I might speak with her?"

Zoe was quiet again, deep in concentration. "She'll speak with you," Zoe's young voice said at last.

Gudrun said, "Thank you. How shall I address her?"

"I don't know."

"I'll speak to her now, Zoe."

"All right," Zoe murmured.

"Thank you for meeting with us," Gudrun said. "Is there a way you prefer that I address you?"

Zoe answered in the voice of the old woman. "Suit yourself. I have many names. All of them wrong."

Through Zoe, the old woman sighed, then continued. "Wherever you find a crossroads, I'm there somewhere. Not always apparent, but there, hidden in plain sight. Most of them don't notice." She cackled. "Too busy trying to figure out which way to go. If they'd ask me, I'd tell 'em. But they don't think to ask. Poor little things. Stumbling around in the dark. Zigging when they should be zagging. Making themselves and everyone else miserable."

She sighed again and shook her head.

"What about Zoe?"

"She asked for help. Clever child. Wait. Maybe *she* didn't ask."

After a pause, the Old Woman's voice continued. "No. She didn't ask. Someone else asked on her behalf. The other one. Yes. It was the other one. Hard to tell 'em apart. But never mind. I sent this one off on a journey. Lots of ordeals. Lessons, you know."

"Did she satisfy your requirements?"

"Not *my* requirements. *The* requirements. If they had not been satisfied, she would have perished. But she did well."

The old woman was silent.

After a moment, Gudrun said, "Is anything more required of her?"

"She must retrieve her heart. I cannot return her heart to her. That she must do for herself. She obviously cannot live her life when her heart is elsewhere."

The old woman seemed to be finished speaking. Then she added, as an afterthought, but with conviction, "And she must bring home the child. The child is precious to me."

Then another long pause, as Gudrun waited for her to explain. When the old woman said nothing more, Gudrun asked, "How is she to do that?"

"Questions! Questions! You try my patience."

"I'm sorry. I'm trying to understand."

The old woman repeated slowly, with exaggerated clarity. "*First,* she must retrieve her heart, *then* she must return home with the child."

She sighed. "I'm tired, now. Leave me. I have no more to say."

"Of course. Thank you for meeting with us."

Zoe, her eyes still closed, leaned forward and rested her forehead on her knees, the picture of closure. For a long time, she didn't stir.

Gudrun waited in silence until she sensed that Zoe was ready to return. Then, very softly, Gudrun said, "Zoe, I'd like you to come slowly back."

As Gudrun finished counting, Zoe opened her eyes with an expression of wonder.

"Good, Zoe," Gudrun said, her smile warm. "Good."

As before, Gudrun let Zoe rest while she did some work, then they headed home for the day.

The next morning, when they had finished breakfast, Zoe said, "Am I crazy, Gudrun? These voices in me, these people—the Spider King, Cat, the Dark Mother. Do I have a multiple personality, like the woman in *The Three Faces of Eve*?"

Gudrun laughed. "Oh, Zoe. Not in any pathological sense. Not in a way that makes you different from supposedly 'normal' people, if there are any such creatures. What has happened to you is described in myths and fairy tales as old as spoken language. An ordinary person, on an ordinary day, is going along doing ordinary things, and suddenly kicks a certain stone or sees a gold ring in the grass or, like Persephone, sees an especially beautiful flower and reaches out for it. In that moment, the person moves out of ordinary time and into another dimension."

Zoe said, with a sense of discovery, "Gudrun, I think that's what happened to me when I went into the basement of my childhood home, just after my father died, and I was thinking about having to clear out the house to sell it. I went into my father's office and sat at his desk, and while I was sitting there, a spider bit me. Did I tell you that?"

Gudrun smiled and nodded, waiting for Zoe to continue.

"Looking back, I think that was the beginning of the nightmare. That's when the earth started collapsing under my feet."

"How very human the adventure has been for you, and how like the ancient stories. A small creature, or a wizened old woman or man, or some other odd being or animal appears at the interface of the two worlds, the ordinary world and the other, extraordinary one.

"This creature is the guardian of the threshold and is the one who mediates the journey from ordinary time to sacred time. Sacred time can be many things, Zoe. It is not necessarily peaceful and beautiful. The sacred can also be terrifying.

"And for you, Zoe, perhaps the threshold guardian is the spider. Does that sound right?"

Zoe was excited. "Yes. Yes! Whenever I've been about to faint, it's because there is a spider near me, in the washbowl, on my pillow. Yes. Oh, Gudrun. That's amazing. The spider, a threshold guardian!"

"And it's interesting that the first one who came to us from your other world was the Spider King. What do you associate with spiders, the way spiders behave?"

"Spiders . . ." Zoe shuddered. "I think of poison. Paralysis. The way the spider spins a web and then waits for a small creature to fly into it. How the spider paralyzes the victim with its venom and wraps it in silk until it is time to devour it."

"In psychological terms," Gudrun said, "we think of *enmeshment*—the way a parent enmeshes a child in the web of the family drama. A parent might capture the child in a psychological web, bind it, and feed on it emotionally.

"Of course, in the world of nature, the spider in its web is beautiful and perfect; living and behaving in accord with its inherent purpose. But in symbolic, psychological terms, it suggests compulsive behavior, a ritualized and rigid perfectionism that does not allow for freedom or spontaneity in the family, and especially does not allow the child ever to leave home emotionally. Does any of this sound familiar, Zoe?"

"Yes, yes."

Again, Zoe was excited by this new realization. "My father. All ritual and routine. Daddy *was* compulsive. He never *sat* in a chair; he perched on the edge. He was restless, always fixing, polishing, straightening, taking notes. He kept lists and gave me detailed instructions about everything.

"And I'm beginning to realize, thanks to you, that my own behavior in my relationships, especially with men, has also been compulsive for many years."

"These are important awarenesses to have, Zoe. A good morning's work."

Gudrun stood and said, "Alas, I must get to the office."

With Zoe's help, she cleared the breakfast dishes. Then she walked Zoe to the stairs, where she embraced her and said, "Perhaps you can do some painting until I come home for lunch."

Zoe spent the morning in Gudrun's studio, but not painting, simply appreciating the beauty and magic of the paintings resting against one another along the walls, eloquently revealing Gudrun's interior landscape.

Zoe realized that with Gudrun's help, she was discovering her own interior landscape.

CHAPTER 29.
One Last Necessary Task

The next morning, Gudrun said, "Zoe, there's one more thing we must do. The Dark Mother told us what it is. You must ask your father to give your heart back. You must reclaim your heart so you can live your life fully, and can offer love freely, as you choose. If you cannot love freely, you'll keep repeating the same tired drama in your relationships."

"There has been a depressing sameness." Zoe uttered a shuddering sigh. "Oh, Gudrun. I want to be free."

Later that dark fall afternoon, after Gudrun had finished seeing clients, Zoe sat on the consulting room couch, feeling anxious. With Gudrun's induction, Zoe easily relaxed into the process.

This time, however, she would not become young Zoe but would be her present self.

In the silence after the counting, Gudrun waited while Zoe's breathing slowed. Then she asked Zoe to describe what she was seeing.

"I'm in my daddy's office at the music school."

She paused, seeming to experience the office. "There are bookshelves and file cabinets holding music scores, books, piles of papers. On the cabinets are musical instruments in open cases, and his own silver trumpet, which he played so beautifully. On the wall are signed photographs of revered teachers, students who have become famous, composer friends. And the odor. Always an odor about him. Unpleasant."

Gudrun could see from the way Zoe flared her nostrils that she smelled the odor.

"Is your daddy here, Zoe?"

"Yes. He's seated at his desk. He has a notebook open to a fresh page, and a pen. He plans to take notes."

"Please greet him, Zoe, and tell him you appreciate his willingness to meet with us. And please introduce us."

Zoe did, and after a long pause, Gudrun said, "What does he do, Zoe?"

After several more moments of silence, Zoe said, "He stands."

Zoe's voice became his voice, resonant and musical, almost as if he were singing. "Hello, Dr. Skjerne."

In deep concentration, Zoe seemed to be moving about in her inner world. Though outwardly, she did not change position, her face and body responded subtly.

"Daddy," she said, as her grown self, "thank you for all the beautiful things you brought into my life. The music, the travels when I was young, the trip to Europe when I graduated from college. Thank you for all those summers at music camp. Thank you for the Christmas Eve brass choir concerts where the music came down around us from the bell tower, the notes mingling with sparkling snowflakes. Thank you for my wonderful education, for so many expressions of the greatness of the human spirit.

"And Daddy, thank you for believing I was worthy of that richness and for wanting to share it all with me."

Zoe's voice became her father's voice. "I wanted the best for you. You were a gifted child. I was proud of you, Zoe."

"I know, Daddy. For that, I am grateful."

She sat silent for a long time, her body beginning to tense. Her breathing quickened.

Gudrun again prompted her, "Zoe. What more do you want to say to him?"

"Daddy, I . . ." She stopped. Her hands trembled.

"It's all right, Zoe," Gudrun said. "Take your time."

"Daddy, you died—" Zoe sobbed for a moment. "You died without giving my heart back to me."

Zoe's father's voice said, "What do you mean?"

"When you died, you took my heart with you. Daddy, you took my heart when I was a child, and you kept it always for yourself."

Another pause. Then, his voice grew firm, pedantic, a teacher schooling a pupil. "Zoe, you had your life. You had college, a marriage, a career, achievements. You made your mother and me proud."

"But Daddy, those things you were proud of brought me no satisfaction or happiness. I felt only shame and unworthiness."

"Zoe, you were so good, so beautiful, always doing your best to please. I loved that about you."

"Oh, Daddy. You loved me *too much*. Or in the wrong way sometimes. But I haven't come to accuse you or talk about the past. I need this one final thing from you. I need you to return my heart."

"How can I do that, Zoe? I don't understand."

"I don't either, Daddy." She paused, then said, "Gudrun, how do we do this?"

Gudrun said, "It's simple, Professor Thomas. Gently take Zoe's heart from your chest, where you've kept it close to your own all these years. Place it tenderly in Zoe's hands, so she can return it to its rightful place, in her own body. Will you do that?"

After a long pause, and a sigh, he said, "If that will make things right."

"Yes, Professor Thomas. It will make things right. Zoe, hold out your hands to receive your daddy's gift."

Zoe held out her trembling hands with a look of reverence. Gudrun could see her receiving the heart in her cupped hands, lifting it, a treasured thing, to her chest, seeming to take it into her body.

She leaned back, her tears flowing freely.

For a few moments, there was silence, except for the weeping.

Then Gudrun said, quietly, "Thank you, Professor Thomas. You have done a loving thing."

Zoe said, "Thank you, Daddy."

After a moment, his voice responded with emotion, "I only wanted to love you, Zoe."

"I know, Daddy." There was another long silence.

"Zoe, I think we're ready to go back. We've achieved what we came to do. Goodbye, Professor Thomas. Thank you. Zoe, tell your father goodbye."

"Goodbye, Daddy."

With a sob, Zoe fell forward on the couch, her face in her hands.

After another few minutes, Gudrun said, "Now, Zoe, it's time to come back to full consciousness. As before, you'll awaken refreshed and relieved, and you'll remember all that has happened here."

As Gudrun counted down, Zoe came fully awake and said, "Gudrun. I thought it was going to be so difficult. There were no accusations. There was no anger or ugliness. No need for open-heart surgery. No ghoulish opening of caskets."

"You left that darkness on the Road of Trials, Zoe; that time is past. Your heart is yours now. It's in its rightful place.

"Dr. Jung tells us our unresolved past becomes our destiny without conscious integration of our traumas. You've achieved that conscious integration here, during the courageous work you've been doing. And now, with this simple, symbolic process you've just undergone, your heart now belongs to you; and you're free to move into your future fully alive and whole."

Zoe was filled with wonder at the power, and yet the simplicity, of what had just happened.

"I'm so grateful, Gudrun. Thank you."

PART III.
The Return: Master Of Two Worlds

If we knew the whole story, we would have compassion.

Elizabeth Thomas Templeton

There are levels of reality within us that are much greater than our analytical minds can know. Nonetheless, we can make them accessible to our awareness so that they become channels by which we reconnect ourselves to the great sources of life. Evoking the depths of ourselves is a way to the renewal of our humanity.

Ira Progoff
The Symbolic and the Real
New York, McGraw-Hill, 1963, p xiv

CHAPTER 30.
Clarity

Several days after the encounter with her father in Gudrun's consulting room, Zoe appeared at breakfast and said, "Gudrun, I'm feeling clear. It's silent in my head, as if an electric fan, which had been running with a hum for so long that I didn't notice it, had suddenly stopped. I'm stunned by the silence."

"Good morning, dear," Gudrun said. "Come, have some coffee and breakfast."

Smiling, she studied Zoe intently for a few moments. "Yes, I sense a difference this morning. You seem quite serene."

She poured coffee for Zoe and herself and placed a plate of fruit and croissants on the table and they took their places across from one another. For a few moments, they savored the fragrance of the coffee, the deliciousness of the fruit and croissants, and the contentment of the sunny kitchen.

Then Zoe said, "Gudrun, I should go home. I've been thinking about how long I've been here. I was planning to be here for a week, but you took me in and have cared for me for many weeks. I can't imagine how to repay you.

"I haven't even thought about the Chief. What has he been doing without me? Did he fire me?"

"No, no, Zoe." Gudrun laughed. "Several graduate students have been helping him. He grumbles, but he's been managing. Of course, he hopes you'll come back as soon as possible."

"And what about David? He must be wondering what became of me. All my plants must be dead. My poor garden."

"I spoke with David when you first came. I told him only that I asked you to stay and do some work with me here in Copenhagen. He was watering your plants and taking in your mail. He said he'd arranged that with you."

"Did he wonder why I didn't phone him myself?"

"If he did, he didn't mention it. He simply accepted what I said and asked me to give you his greetings, and Kathy's."

"Isn't that odd that I haven't thought of my life in Chicago for all these weeks? What's happened to me?"

"You've been in the crucible, Zoe. In the crucible, all distinctions break down; there's no linear time, no outer world. The old order dissolves and the new order begins to form within you.

"What I told David is true. You've stayed on to do work with me, Zoe."

"How long has it been?"

"Today is November first."

"That means I've been here more than a month! I must go home. I must pay bills. I can't just live with you for the rest of my life, though sometimes I think I'd like to. I've disrupted your family, but you've been incredibly generous.

"This is a sanctuary of peace and holiness, with three generations of women—the Triple Goddess, Gudrun! Maiden, Mother, and Crone, though you are a Crone only in your wisdom, you are hardly an old woman with a cane.

"And here, I've witnessed feminine strength, integrity, and honor in the sanctity of your home and the sanctuary of your consulting room. And miracle of miracles," Zoe laughed with amazement, "I've begun to take that sense of feminine integrity and strength into myself, somehow. I feel it in me."

Gudrun poured more coffee for them. "As I hoped when I brought you here after the Congress, you have experienced this protected time as a vessel of transformation, Zoe. That's what any good consulting room is, with its containment and sanctuary, with the proper understanding and mastery of ritual, and the powerful energies it calls up from our depths, and especially, the way those energies can be harnessed in the service of life. I think that has happened here."

"Gudrun, yes! In you I've encountered the Goddess. In the play, you told us by way of Margaret that an encounter with the Goddess needs to happen, and you described the whole healing process so clearly and beautifully during your amazing speech to the audience after the play."

"And now, Zoe, once again," Gudrun said, smiling, "with this part of your deep inner work completed, I again become simply your friend and colleague Gudrun, with Inge and Justine also simply your friends."

She leaned across the table and took Zoe's hands in her own. "We've been glad to have you here with us, dear. And when you're ready to go back, everything can be straightened out there. You'll see."

"I think I'm ready now, Gudrun. Today, my head is clear for the first time in so long. I'm sure it's time."

The next day, Zoe phoned Chicago. "David, it's Zoe. Remember me?"

"Zoe. How good to hear your voice! Are you still in Copenhagen with Gudrun?"

"Yes, but I'm coming home."

Hearing David's voice gave Zoe a sense of connection to her life, a sense of being real. It was a feeling she hadn't had for a long time.

"How has the work been going? Gudrun said you stayed on to do some work with her."

"The first part of the project is finished, David. It's a large project, but I think I can do the next part at home. But I wonder what I'll find. I didn't plan to be gone this long."

"Don't worry. Everything's all right here. You haven't gotten any pink slips from Ma Bell or the electric company. I've been watching. And Kathy keeps asking me when you're coming home."

"How is she? How are you?"

"We're managing."

"I suppose the garden doesn't need water, since it's November. Do I have any plants left?"

"Oh, yes. When the flowers seemed to finish blossoming for the season, Kathy insisted we bring cuttings of the coleus plants here so they can grow new roots and we can plant them in your garden again in the spring. She tends them faithfully."

He paused and took a breath. "She misses you, Zoe. So do I. I'm glad you'll be home soon. Would you like to have us come to the airport to meet you?"

"I'd like that very much. It will be so good to see you both."

"When will you arrive?"

"Sunday, November 5th, 1:30 p.m., at O'Hare."

"We'll be there. We miss you," he said again.

Zoe felt a stirring of tears.

Then he said, "Can we celebrate Thanksgiving together?"

"Yes, David."

"Good. Hurry home, Zoe."

At the Copenhagen airport, with her farewell embrace, Gudrun handed Zoe a small package and an envelope. "For you to open once you're on the way, dear Zoe."

"Oh, Gudrun, how can I ever thank you for all your kindness? And now, this."

"Seeing you smiling, happy, and free is all the thanks I need. Safe home, darling."

When the plane was airborne, Zoe opened the gift. She unfolded the tissue paper to discover a small golden spider, rendered in exquisite detail. It was radiant in the galley light shining down from above her seat.

There was also a copy of the children's book, *Charlotte's Web*. Gudrun had asked Zoe earlier if she knew the book. Zoe did not. In the story, Gudrun explained, Charlotte is a beneficent spider and the heroine of a tale of love, courage, setting things right, growing up, and growing wise.

In the card, Gudrun wrote,

My dear Zoe:

Joseph Campbell, describing the Hero's Journey, this journey you have taken these past months, wrote that *where we had thought to find an abomination, we shall find a god.* Perhaps the monstrous image of the dreaded spider, which you experienced as an abomination, and masculine, poisonous, and deadly, enmeshing its victims in silken bonds before devouring them, can now be transformed.

Perhaps you can now experience the spider in its positive, feminine aspect, as the ancient, pre-patriarchal Creatrix, an aspect of the great Mother Goddess weaving the world into being, connecting all that exists in one great web of relatedness, a magnificent integrated whole.

Like you, dear Zoe, as all parts of yourself are accepted and integrated and experienced as a perfect, cohesive, beautiful self, so you can return home free to love as you choose, and to live a truly authentic, creative, and fulfilling life.

And I hope *Charlotte's Web* will help young Zoe not to be afraid of spiders.

With all my love,
Gudrun

CHAPTER 31.
Wounded Healer:
Bringing the Lost Child Home

The plane touched down on the runway, bounced, and taxied for a long time before coming to a stop. Everyone waited, standing numbly in the aisles until the doors were opened and they could file out slowly, feeding into buses to be taken to the international terminal. David and Kathy would be waiting outside the restricted area.

Zoe's excitement mounted as she stood in line to have her passport stamped, and then waited for her luggage to come along the belt, and then waited again for the customs officer to make his inspection.

Finally, she pushed her luggage cart along the corridor and through the automatic doors, past the dozens of expectant people waiting with smiles and signs.

How will I ever find them in this crowd? Zoe thought. Then she saw David, standing back a little. He noticed her too and came forward. They embraced for a long time.

"Welcome home," David said. "It's good to see you. We've missed you."

"Thank you, David." Zoe let herself savor the embrace. She felt strength and tension in his arms. "It feels as if I've been away for a lifetime."

When she looked at him next, she realized he wasn't smiling.

"Where's Kathy?" Zoe suddenly felt anxiety, remembering the tension in David's embrace.

"I don't know." David's voice broke.

Zoe's anxiety increased, and the exhaustion of the intensity of her life since she'd last seen David, and her fatigue from the long flight, changed to hypervigilance.

"Why, David? What's happened?"

"Kathy's run away, Zoe. I went to pick her up at Christine's house at noon, so she could come with me. But when we went to get her, she wasn't in her room.

"Christine wasn't forthcoming about what had happened earlier in the day, but I've deduced this much: Kathy showed her excitement about coming to the airport, and that enraged Christine. There was an argument, and Christine punished Kathy by telling her she couldn't come with me. Christine admitted that Kathy had sobbed wildly and even kicked at her.

"Then, suddenly, Kathy became very quiet, got a stony expression on her face, went into her room, and closed the door. Christine, being Christine, left her there to 'think about her bad behavior' until I arrived. She planned to make Kathy explain to me why she couldn't come and then apologize in front of both of us."

They had begun walking, almost running, toward the parking garage.

David continued, a little breathlessly, "That's Christine's idea of justice. Anyway, Kathy was gone. Her Barbie suitcase was also gone, and some of her clothes, and her piggy bank. She must have gone down the back stairs and out through the garden. The back door was unlocked.

"We searched the house and went around the neighborhood calling her and checking with the neighbors. No one had seen her. How long she'd been gone, Christine didn't know.

"Zoe, that woman is a devil. She's always seeing Satan everywhere around her, but if there is a devil, it's surely in her." His voice was hoarse with rage.

"David, we must find Kathy."

"I left Christine to call the police and keep searching while I came here to get you. I couldn't leave you waiting at the airport, Zoe. Besides, I wanted—*I needed*—to see you again. I've missed you. And Christine, *damn her*, was looking for an excuse to forbid Kathy to come with me. She's furious that Kathy likes you. If something happens to Kathy, I'll kill Christine. I'll kill her."

"We'll find her, David. Kathy's very smart. She's resourceful."

Zoe sounded more confident than she felt. She was filled with dread.

They loaded Zoe's luggage into the trunk and waited interminably for car after car to creep up to the exit booth to pay. When they were finally through, they headed north.

Once they reached Highland Park, Zoe waited in the car while David went into the house to see if there was any news. A few minutes later, he came out, shaking with rage, and got into the car.

"No sign of Kathy. The police are looking. Christine has called everywhere she thought Kathy might go. No one's seen her."

"Let's try to think like Kathy. What would make sense to her?

It sounds as if, when she got so quiet, she was formulating a plan. What plan would she make? If she took her clothes, she must have decided not to go back home for a while. Could she be planning to get to your house?"

"That's thirty miles, Zoe."

"She's made the trip with you many times. Do you think she decided to walk it? We could drive along the route you usually take. She couldn't have gotten very far."

Still too shaken to strategize well, he was grateful for Zoe's suggestion. He started the car and squealed away from the curb. By the next block, he was calmer. They drove slowly along streets overarched with elm trees, past houses set far back on lawns. No one walked on these lawns. It seemed that leaves didn't even fall on them. No one sat in the gardens. No one used the tennis courts. The swimming pools had been drained and covered. The neighborhood was terribly empty.

David looked at his watch. "It's almost three o'clock. She's been gone for at least three hours, maybe more. How far could she have gotten?"

Stopping frequently to get out of the car and call for Kathy, they went as far as the intersection where they would turn south onto the main highway toward Chicago. David pulled into the gas station at the corner and stopped, leaning his head back and closing his eyes.

"I can't bear the thought of her walking along the highway," he said. "What if someone picked her up? She knows about not getting into a car with a stranger, but what if she ..."

Zoe said, "Maybe we should check with the police."

They found the police station where Christine had made her

report. The officer on duty seemed concerned and sympathetic but had nothing to offer. He assured them he was doing all he could. "She's probably at a friend's house," he offered. "Forgot to tell her mom."

David said, "Kathy was upset. She didn't forget. She ran away."

"I'll check with Thompson." The officer spoke into a walkie-talkie and waited, drumming his fingers on the desk. It crackled a garbled response, and he said, "10-4," and shook his head. "No dice." Then, seeing their disappointment, he added, kindly, "But she'll be back. Most of them come back. Have you talked to your wife?"

"My wife?" David's voice was bitter. He started to say something, then stopped. He said only, "I should check. May I use your phone?"

He made the call, and when he hung up, he shook his head and said to the officer, "Thanks for trying," and stalked out. Zoe followed. They got into the car and began driving again.

"David," Zoe said. "What about Bucky's Circus? Could she have gone there?"

David looked suddenly hopeful. "It's possible. I'm surprised I didn't think of that. It's a happy place for her."

It was suppertime at Bucky's Circus. The place was a madhouse. The children were overheated, overstimulated, overtired. They raced around, long since bored with Bucky and the rides, too hyped to have fun. Parents, numb and out of patience, were trying to capture and hold them long enough to induce them to eat a bite of pizza and get ready to go home.

Bucky and his troupe of critters were singing "I say *happy*, you say *birthday!* Happy birthday, happy birthday!" They clapped at a sobbing child while his friends blew on party horns. He hit at the children to make them stop.

David went to find the manager. Zoe stood in the center of the swirling room and slowly looked around. The sea of children roiled. She closed her eyes for a moment. Among the squeals and crying and screaming, she made herself quiet.

Kathy's here, something told her. She opened her eyes. There, by the colored balls, was the Barbie suitcase. Zoe pushed her way through the children.

"Kathy," she shouted. "Kathy!"

"Zoe! Zoe!" It was Kathy's voice. She scrambled up out of the pool of colored balls and ran to Zoe, flinging herself so forcefully into Zoe's arms that Zoe lost her balance and went down on her knees, holding the child tightly.

"Zoe, Zoe, Zoe," Kathy wept.

Zoe wept, too, and held her. "Kathy, oh Kathy. We were so worried. Let's find your daddy right away and show him that you're safe."

But then David was there, embracing them both tightly, his body shaking. For a long time, the three of them stayed like that as the manager stood by, smiling awkwardly, and the wild children raced around them.

David stood up with Kathy in his arms. Zoe picked up the suitcase.

"But how did you get in here, Kathy?" David asked.

"I asked a parent waiting at the door to help me," she said proudly. "I said you were inside and that I went out to the car to get my suitcase and needed to get back inside. I cried a little, and the parent felt sorry for me and let me go in with her kids. I had money from my piggybank, but I didn't need it."

"Clever child," the manager commented, smiling.

"Too much for her own good sometimes, I guess," David smiled back, shaking his head. "And may I use the phone in your office? I need to let her mother know we've found Kathy and she's all right."

But Kathy became distraught. "No, Daddy. Please don't tell her you've found me. Please, Daddy. Please. Don't."

She struggled in his arms and clenched her hands into fists, beating them against his chest. "Please don't tell her where I am. Please, Daddy. Please."

"Kathy, your mother is very worried. We must tell her you're all right."

"No, Daddy, no. Please." Her voice became shrill. "Please don't call her. Please!" She tugged frantically at his shirt.

David looked at Zoe. His expression said, *What is the wisest thing to do?*

"You can call Christine from home," Zoe suggested quietly. "We'll be home in forty minutes. Christine will worry, but we know Kathy is safe."

"You're right, Zoe. Let's go home."

They thanked the manager, who had been waiting nearby in case they needed something more from him, and they went to the parking lot. Kathy crawled into the front seat between David and Zoe. She clung to David, her head under his arm and her arms around his waist. She was calmer, holding him tightly, no longer sobbing.

David stroked her hair and moved the seat back so she could hold him more fully. After a few minutes, he turned on the ignition. Kathy let go of him and leaned against Zoe, who put her arm around the child. They drove toward Chicago, riding in silence.

Kathy fell asleep. David and Zoe continued their silence, not wanting to wake her.

They parked in front of the house. Kathy woke up and looked anxiously out the window. When she saw that they were at David's house, she said, softly, "Oh, yay." She jumped out of the car and got her suitcase and ran ahead while David carried Zoe's suitcases and Zoe found her house key at the bottom of her purse.

"I'll help Zoe," Kathy said. She was lively and eager, with no more tears or anxiety. They all went into Zoe's house, which smelled musty. Zoe turned on the light just inside the door. "My electricity is still connected. What a relief."

She went up to the second floor, David and Kathy following.

"Shall I take your suitcases up to the bedroom?" David asked.

"Yes, David. Thank you."

There were piles of mail on the counter, neatly stacked. "I sorted your mail for you," Kathy said.

"Good girl. You did a wonderful job."

"Somebody sent you a present." Kathy pointed to a package with no return address. Zoe recognized her mother's handwriting.

"You and your daddy are the only present that I care about just now, Kathy." To David, who had come back down from the bedroom, Zoe said, "If you can spare some milk, I'll make us cocoa."

"Yes, yes. Cocoa. Yummy." Kathy skipped around the table. Zoe noticed the chill and turned the dial on the thermostat; there was a dull thump from below as the heat came on, emitting a dusty odor.

David went across the passageway to his house. When he came back a few moments later, he handed her a carton of milk and said softly, "While you're making the cocoa, I'll call Christine. I'll be back in a few minutes."

Upstairs again, Zoe put the carton of milk in the kitchen, and, stalling for time while David made his call, she said, "Kathy, come upstairs with me while I check the bedroom."

Kathy happily scrambled up the stairs ahead of her. In the bedroom, everything was dusty. Zoe opened her big suitcase.

"I'll help you unpack," Kathy said.

"That can wait until later. I just wanted to see if the bedroom is still here."

"Did you think it would fly away?"

"I don't know what I thought, Kathy." Zoe laughed. "It seems as if I've been away a very long time."

"It *was* a long time. Forty-four days. I counted." Kathy said this with satisfaction.

"It's wonderful to have a friend who notices those things, Kathy. Thank you."

"We're friends, aren't we?"

"Yes, Kathy."

"Are we going to have cocoa soon?"

"Let's go back downstairs right now and heat the milk."

Zoe and Kathy had finished their first cup of cocoa and Zoe was telling Kathy about the Wedgwood teapot and cups they were drinking from, and how she had brought them long ago from England, when David knocked at the door again. Zoe let him in, and they went upstairs together.

He was pale and his hands shook as he took a seat at the table. Kathy crawled onto his lap while Zoe made a cup of cocoa for him.

"You'll be staying with me at my house tonight, Kathy," he said at last, stroking her hair. Kathy heaved a long, happy sigh and closed her eyes, leaning her head against his chest.

Later, at David's house, Kathy was asleep in the cheerful guest bedroom, her arms wrapped tightly around the birthday dragon he'd rescued when Christine tried to throw it into the trash.

Downstairs on the first floor, Zoe sat with David on the lush leather couch in front of the fire. "Christine was outraged that I brought Kathy here," he said. "She seemed to be furious that we had found her. She wanted to know if you were with me. I didn't lie to her. But when I said yes, she went into a frenzy. It's bad, Zoe. She frightens me. I'm afraid for Kathy."

Zoe also felt a stirring of fear, hearing about Christine's hostility toward her. Despite her long experience with men going through divorces, and despite the fact that Zoe was not implicated in this divorce, the situation felt personal, as if Christine had attacked her. In a sense, she had.

But Zoe put a clamp on her feelings. She didn't want to further complicate things by adding her own feelings into the mix, so she said, sounding more magnanimous than she felt, "Christine has been under a lot of strain today. She no doubt feels defensive because Kathy ran away."

"She didn't seem to care that Kathy's all right. She just went into a tirade, accusing me of terrible things."

"Maybe she'll be more reasonable after she's gotten some rest. How did you leave it with her?"

"She demanded that I bring Kathy back tomorrow morning by seven so Kathy can have breakfast with her and get ready for kindergarten. That means getting Kathy up before it's light. I don't want to do that, Zoe. It's inhumane. I don't know what to do."

"You're tired, too, David." Zoe did her best to keep her voice reassuring. "It's almost ten o'clock. I can scarcely believe I arrived at O'Hare just this afternoon. So much has happened since then. Why not see how you and Kathy feel in the morning?"

David slid down so he could rest his head against the back of the sofa. He closed his eyes. "I'm so sorry we welcomed you home with this. I had something else in mind. I've missed you, Zoe." He sat up and turned toward her. "Kathy did, too. She was counting the days."

"She told me." After a pause, Zoe added, "I took a very long and difficult journey in those forty-four days. Sometimes, I didn't think I'd get back. But here I am, by some miracle, and Gudrun's incredible kindness and wisdom. She's the most generous person I've ever known. I think without Gudrun, I would not have gotten back."

David watched her intently, expecting her to explain. She said, "I'll tell you about it, but not tonight. There's too much. And we have time."

"Yes." He smiled and closed his eyes, murmuring, as if to himself, "We have time." His voice felt to Zoe like a caress.

"Thank you for coming to meet my plane in the midst of your own crisis." She touched his hand, and he closed his warm hand gently around hers.

"I was being selfish, Zoe. I needed you. I needed your wisdom. You understand Kathy. You knew where to find her."

Zoe smiled sadly. "Probably because there's a Kathy inside of me, David. Gudrun helped me find her. In a sense, that's what I was doing in Copenhagen. With Gudrun's help, I've been able to bring my own Kathy home."

"Zoe," David said quietly, his eyes shining in the firelight. "I love you."

She closed her eyes, taking this in. It pulsed through her body.

"Oh, David. Dear David." There was much she wanted to say to him in response, but it felt so much greater than words. All she could think of was to lean over and softly kiss his hand, as it clasped hers.

Then, for a long time, they sat silently in front of the fire, holding hands, leaning against one another.

Back in her house, utterly exhausted and emotionally drained, Zoe picked up the package from her mother and sat at the table without moving. It had a UK postmark and a customs label. With trembling hands, she pulled the wrapping off.

Inside was a small metal card box, which Zoe recognized. It was filled with her mother's recipes, copied neatly onto index cards in beautiful, careful handwriting. And a dozen pages of sheet music, the songs she had taught Zoe to sing as a young girl.

Clipped to the first page was an envelope marked, simply, *Zoe*. Scarcely breathing, Zoe opened the note, which was written on elegant cream-colored stationery with the embossed initials, ETT. The two Ts puzzled Zoe for a moment, but after reading the note, she understood.

Sunday, October 22, 1972

Dear Zoe:

I am writing to you from London, and the Mayfair apartment my husband owns here. Yes, I have remarried, a widower I met on the cruise. Charles Templeton is a fine man, a retired art importer. We were seated at the same table for meals, and it soon became apparent we have a great deal in common.

Shortly after we got back from the cruise, we were married and together returned to the States briefly to close the house. With Charles's great help, I put everything into storage. In the rush, I had time only to select the recipes and the sheet music to send you, thinking they might have some meaning for you.

Charles and I are very happy. He wants to "show me the world" before we settle into a home together, and in a week, we will leave for the Far East on an extended honeymoon. He is very good to me and for me. I love him and, of course, I am pleased to be "shown the world."

Though this may seem sudden, he has offered me a chance for happiness, and I have taken it.

Once we have a permanent address, I shall let you know.

Mother

For the second time during this momentous day, Zoe was overwhelmed by inexplicable emotions.

CHAPTER 32.
No One Returns from the Realm of Shadows Unchanged

On Monday morning, Zoe returned to the office.

"Well, Zoe. You're back. Look in your office. See? I've saved all your work for you." The Chief's voice was jaunty.

"Hello, Walther. Yes, I'm back."

She realized she had called him Walther, not the Chief. Did he notice? He seemed not to, but to Zoe, calling him Walther signaled a change in their relationship, a new distance. Was this an indication of how she had been changed by the ordeal of the past months?

He stood and went to Zoe. He shook her hand and said, rather formally, "Well. I hope you're feeling better."

"I'm fine, now. It's good to be back in Chicago."

The phone rang. The Chief turned away to answer it, spoke briefly and hung up. "I've been my own secretary while you were away."

He'd never *had* a secretary. Zoe's title was administrative director, but she singlehandedly managed his scheduling and correspondence and all the other office business.

"Gudrun said you've had graduate students helping out."

"Not much help, Zoe. Got everything hopelessly confused. I had to undo what they did and redo everything myself after they left."

"Poor Walther."

"Glad you're back, Zoe. I suppose I missed you."

"I suppose you did."

Then, rather gruffly, as if not sure what else to say, "Well, go sort out the mail. I'll take you to dinner as a reward."

Though she said nothing, she thought, *Dinner as a "reward"? A reward for what? Not acting crazy now that I'm back in the office?* And then, *This is going to be difficult*, as she went into her office and closed the door—another change, the closed door. She was going to need to say no about dinner. She wanted to be with David, not with Walther, on her first full night back from her long journey.

On her desk was a mountain of mail. Letters with notes clipped to them in a variety of graduate-student scrawls, with questions, comments, reports of action taken.

I've never said no to him before, Zoe thought, *except in a rage. Afterward, I wiped up the floor with myself, apologizing.*

After sorting halfway through the mail, Zoe went into the Chief's office. Taking a deep breath, she said, "Walther, I have dinner plans tonight. However, we could do a welcome-home lunch later this week if you wish."

He looked surprised. "A lunch? A welcome-home lunch? Yes, I suppose we could do that."

"Good. Let me know when."

"How about tomorrow? We could go to the club."

"That would be very nice, Walther."

"I'll even make the arrangements. I've gotten good at making my own arrangements since you've been gone."

"That makes it perfect."

The moment of crisis Zoe anticipated had passed without drama. She had a sudden image of the Chief as a dog, rolling over in surrender with its paws in the air, and in her relief, she stifled a surge of giddy laughter.

He had accepted her alternate plan without argument. Had he changed, or had Zoe's own behavior created the tensions that seemed to be a constant in their previous relationship? It struck her that, in fact, his nature was rather . . . what? Simple. Maybe it was she who had complicated things for them.

Oh, brave new world, she thought, as she went back to her office to finish reading through the mail.

Mid-afternoon, Zoe phoned David. "I didn't see any lights or signs of activity in your house this morning when I left for work around seven thirty," she said, "so I didn't disturb you. Then when I called around eleven thirty, there was no answer."

"We had already left by then," he said. "I let Kathy sleep until she was ready to wake up on her own, at about eight. I phoned Christine at seven and told her what I was doing. Christine was outraged, of course, but I promised to have Kathy back right after lunch. I delivered her to the door promptly at one o'clock."

Zoe asked how Christine had received this news.

He laughed humorlessly. "It's so strange, Zoe. I told Christine that if there were any reprisals, or if Christine was anything but civil and welcoming, I would take Kathy back with me, and I would take drastic action. I'm not sure what I meant by 'drastic action,' but I was serious. Christine shouted that I was threatening her, and I assured her that I was indeed threatening her.

"Then, suddenly, she became almost friendly. It's totally baffling. When I'm polite to Christine, she walks all over me. When I talk tough, she becomes conciliatory. It's hard for me to remember the woman I thought I loved. The one I married."

"Did Kathy say anything about why she ran away?"

"When I asked her if she wanted to talk about it, she shook her head and closed her eyes tightly. She was emphatic. I felt I should respect that, at least for now, but I'm very concerned about what went on, what goes on, in that household behind closed doors."

"Oh, David. I'm so sorry you and Kathy have all this pain."

Zoe didn't add that she shared that pain, that gradually she was being drawn into the complexities of their life, and that it mattered very much to her personally that David could resolve the conflicts with Christine.

There was a pause. Then, as if he had heard her unspoken thoughts, David said, hesitantly, "Zoe, last night, I sat up for a long time after you left, thinking about you. And Kathy. And me . . ."

Zoe closed her eyes and waited, sensing that he was about to say what her heart deeply yearned for, though she had not allowed herself to realize it. In this moment, she felt her life was about to become something utterly new and wondrous.

This awareness flooded through her like a wave sweeping up a beach and then, having fulfilled its process, drawing back down again into itself. In that fleeting, flooding moment, Zoe felt gratitude for all she had suffered on the Road of Trials, accepting that it had been necessary to release her from the entrapment of the past and had made her ready for this moment of promise and possibility.

"Zoe," he went on, "I'm almost afraid to say this. Especially without being able to see your face. But I thought about how you and Kathy and I already seem . . . like a family." He was searching for the right words. "I know that's crazy. You and I are friends, only friends, in the conventional sense. We've never been intimate—well, in some ways we've been *very* intimate, but we've never . . . made love."

Then his words came quickly, breathlessly. "Zoe, I shouldn't be saying this to you over the phone. There you are at your office, in that other world, so far away from me." He hurried on. "I planned to do this differently. I don't even really know a lot about you—I mean, about your personal life, what your plans are, or your commitments. You've told me some personal things . . . and I have such . . . I respect you so . . . I *honor* you for your courage, your intelligence, and your understanding of Kathy and me. The love you've shown us—"

She stopped him, her voice also intense. "David. You're right. You shouldn't be telling me this over the phone. I want you to tell me in person. Will you wait until I come home? I can be home in twenty minutes. Shall I come now?"

"Yes. Please come, Zoe."

"Twenty minutes, David. I'll be at your door."

Zoe hung up the phone, quickly gathered her coat and purse and opened the door to the Chief's office. "Walther," she said, "I'm afraid this is going to be a short first day back. I need to leave. I'll be here first thing in the morning. And I look forward to our lunch tomorrow at the club. Bye, now."

The Chief, smoking his pipe at his desk, looked startled. "Well. Well, all right, Zoe. Yes, I suppose so. Get some rest." And he went back to his reading.

David opened the door to Zoe. Opened his arms. Opened himself. Together, they leaned against the door to push it softly closed, then they leaned into one another, an embrace so complete and soft and strong that Zoe felt her boundaries dissolve. She sensed that David felt it, too.

They began to waltz, slowly, into the room. Then, shedding garments and moving together, as their lips and tongues shaped greetings and blessings, their waltz slowed to an intense rhumba as they moved together around the arm of the sofa and softly, gracefully, cradled each other's fall, so that everything flowed gently and with infinite tenderness.

They plunged into the deep, soft leather of the sofa and surrendered themselves to the emergent, utterly new existence that was the two of them together, that was coming into being in this merging and drawing away to merge again, this wilderness, this new country they went into together, exploring, discovering, getting lost together. And they came home to a place neither had been before, here, in this breathless moment.

Zoe's heart was at last hers to give, and now she gave it utterly to David, whispering the offering to him again and again, with reverence and rapture.

Hours later, surfeited and amazed, laughing and playful, they built a fire and lounged, languid, looking sometimes into the flames and sometimes into one another, their faces relaxed and clear, their eyes wide and full of wonder, all through the afternoon and evening.

Thus, they wove their lives together with such devotion and understanding, now, of how such weaving must be done, that the fabric they made in that enterprise retained its beauty, the rich textures their integrity, long after the colors had blended into one another, as colors must do when a fabric is part of daily living through the years.

CHAPTER 33.
Endings and Beginnings

Thursday, November 23, 1972

Dear Gudrun:

It is Thanksgiving morning. From the window where I write this, I can see treetops, branches mostly bare, not moving. A few golden leaves, and rare crimson ones, still hold fast to the branches after yesterday's blustery rain.

Oh, Gudrun, there's so much to tell you. I know, now, that I love David, and my heart is at last mine to offer to him freely and utterly. And to Kathy, of course. I have no idea how we will work out the complications of our lives, but I know that whatever happens, we are a family.

When I returned home from Copenhagen, a letter from my mother was waiting for me, telling me she had met a widower on the Caribbean cruise she went on while we were in Amsterdam for the Congress, and she has married him. She wrote from London but said she and Charles Templeton, her new husband, will be traveling in the Far East for their honeymoon and will not have a permanent address for a while. Of course, I wish her well.

In the package with her letter, my mother included some sheet music, those beautiful songs I sang as a young girl when she rehearsed them at home so she could accompany voice majors at the conservatory.

This morning, looking through the music, I came upon *Gitanjali,* songs the composer, John Alden Carpenter, wrote for poems by Rabindranath Tagore, and one of the songs especially brought tears of remembrance.

> When I bring to you colour'd toys, my child,
> I understand why there is such a play of colours on
>   clouds,
> on water, and why flowers are painted in tints—
> when I give colour'd toys to you, my child.
>
> When I sing to make you dance,
> I truly know why there is music in leaves,
> And why waves send their chorus of voices to the
> heart of the listening earth—
> When I sing to make you dance.
>
> When I bring sweet things to your greedy hands,
> I know why there is honey in the cup of the flower,
> And why fruits are secretly filled with sweet
>   juice—
> When I bring sweet things to your greedy hands.

Gudrun, my mother offered that music, that poetry, that beauty. as a gift, and I now remember there was a time when my life with her was filled with color, music, beauty, and sweetness, like the loving words of the song, a time when it seemed that my mother intended those words for me.

Oh, Gudrun! *That* was the mother my father took from me!

Also included in the package with my mother's letter and the music was a small box with her recipes. Opening the box opened another treasury of memories that had been closed away for many years, memories of standing happily next to her in the kitchen as she rolled out cookie dough, sprinkling flour onto waxed paper, lifting and turning the dough until it was ready, and then together we made cornucopias, Christmas trees, and wreaths, and I sprinkled green and red sugars and pressed little silver balls into them.

Many such memories were stirred in me.

Oh, Gudrun, how could I have forgotten those happy times with her, times of sharing beauty and goodness in a house filled with love and delicious fragrances and her beautiful songs and, yes, her nurturance?

Of course, I now know the answer, that though there *were* sweet times with my mother in my childhood, they became obscured by the darkness of shame and terrible family secrets. But I also know, now, that the darkness is not the whole story.

And Gudrun, a curious thing happened. I found, tucked among the pages of music, one of my mother's poems, which she recited for me before I realized that it, and so many other poems she recited when I was growing up, she herself had written.

Finding the poem, I wondered: *Did she put it there on purpose?*

> One perfect rose I cannot place
> Within a slender crystal vase
> And revel in its beauty there
> Conventional and chastely fair,
> When I can have a mass of blooms,
> Great bowls of flowers in all my rooms—
> Fresh purple asters by the door,
> And marigolds that flame and burn
> Like torches in a copper urn.
> And in a vase of Sicily's
> Gold sunshine, dark anemones,
> Nasturtiums in a silver vase.
> Between red candles, Queen Anne's Lace,
> And in that basket, blazing sheaves
> Of scarlet oak and maple leaves.
> Lest I should lose one glowing part,
> I gather beauty to my heart.

That was my Demeter mother, before my father took her from me and at the same time took me from her.

Last Saturday, at the farmer's market, I discovered great golden chrysanthemums and *blazing sheaves of scarlet maple leaves.* and I brought home bouquets of them and placed them in copper bowls, *gathering beauty to my heart* in honor of my mother.

And so, Gudrun, today, on this day of thanksgiving, I feel gratitude for the life I am living, the one that is fully connected to the past and that moves in its own amazing way into the future.

I feel gratitude for David and for Kathy, who in a few hours will come into this fragrant house to celebrate our first Thanksgiving as a family in our wondrous new life.

I feel gratitude that Walther seems more benign and human than before. He took me to lunch at the club to welcome me home. Sitting there with him, at the very table where you and I had lunch last summer as my journey was only beginning, I was able to see him simply as Walther, an exasperating, charming, brilliant, flawed, and vulnerable human being. And because I am different, and free of my own dark complexities, our relationship is different, and free to become what it should be: collegial and kind.

Especially, I feel gratitude for you, my wise and generous friend, dear shapeshifter, and evoker of white magic, for your gift of healing, without which all these other gratitudes would not be possible.

Zoe

CHAPTER 34.
Farewell, Too Soon

London, Wednesday, May 2, 1973

Dear Zoe:

Please allow me to introduce myself. I am Charles Templeton, your mother's second husband. It is my sad duty to inform you of your mother's death on Tuesday, May 1, 1973.

Elizabeth and I were married only a little over half a year. Upon returning from our trip to the Far East following our wedding, she was found to have advanced pancreatic cancer, which, as perhaps you know, is a dire diagnosis. The course of her illness was rapid. She died here in London, where we had planned to make a permanent home, and where we had hoped expert medical care could save her. Alas, it was not to be.

Our too-brief time together was happy. It was my great pleasure to introduce her to some beautiful places in the world I had come to know during my years as an importer of fine art. She was a delightful traveling companion, and with her lively intellect, she savored the cultural riches of places it was my privilege to share with her.

Of her past life, she said almost nothing. To be honest, the happiness of our travels left little time for either of us to reminisce. I want you to know, though, that in her last weeks and months, she spoke often of you, always with love and admiration for your fine career, your beauty, and your many talents.

I regret I was not able to meet you while she was alive. She was insistent, however, that you should not be informed of her illness. She felt she must give her full attention to her own ordeal. As you can imagine, the diagnosis was devastating to her.

Because of the severity of the diagnosis, we felt she should have some psychological support. We were fortunate to be referred to a highly respected psychoanalyst, Dr. Helen Lieb, an associate of Dr. Jung who practices here in London. Your mother met with Dr. Lieb several times a week during the months she felt well enough to do so, and though I was not privy to their work together, I know Dr. Lieb brought your mother great comfort, and helped her accept the fate she was facing.

As Elizabeth grew weaker, she spent a good deal of her waning energy writing a letter to you, which I have enclosed. She asked that I not send it to you until after her death, and of course I have honored her request. Writing the letter seemed to bring your mother relief and resolution, and, she hoped, the reconnection with you for which she yearned.

Characteristically, Elizabeth did not discuss the contents of the letter, but in her last days, it was the focus of her attention, and she gave it profound thought. I truly hope what she has written will bring you comfort, as it did your mother.

With deepest sympathy,
Charles Templeton

The envelope was sealed and marked "For Zoe." The handwriting had a slight tremble but otherwise, it was her mother's same graceful script.

Zoe sat, gently holding the unopened envelope, her eyes closed.

She was stunned by the news that her mother was dead. Stunned, and numb.

She could not open the envelope now. That would take preparation. What kind of preparation, she didn't know. She knew only that now was too soon.

Though Zoe had no idea what the letter would say, she realized that it was of monumental significance.

Zoe placed the unopened letter in an enamel box she had found years earlier in a drawer in her family home. The lovely box had seemed so neglected, shut away in the drawer, that Zoe had asked her mother if she could have it. Her mother gave the little box to Zoe, saying it had been a gift from her closest friend, who had inherited it from her Danish ancestors.

The enamel box was very old, very beautiful, and very valuable. Zoe, thinking of Gudrun, her own close Danish friend, felt certain the treasured box was the perfect place to keep the letter safe until she could consult with Gudrun about when and under what circumstances she should open it.

CHAPTER 35.
Reconciliation

Sunday, May 13, 1973. Mother's Day. With Gudrun's encouragement, Zoe had chosen Mother's Day to open her mother's letter.

Zoe sat in her reading chair, looking out at the spring treetops. St. Michael's was filling the morning air with the music of its resonant bells, calling the faithful to worship.

Perhaps, Zoe imagined, it was on Mother's Day that Demeter had won Persephone's freedom from the Realm of Shadows and Persephone had stepped, transformed, once again into the light, into the joy of her mother's embrace.

On this Mother's Day, perhaps another mother and daughter would at last be reunited, this time by way of a letter. At least, that was Zoe's hope. She and her mother had parted so bitterly.

Now, reverent, trembling, and a little breathless, Zoe took the letter out of the enamel box. "Well, Mother, we are together again," she said softly.

My dear Zoe:

How shall I begin? I have found great joy in my life with

Charles. Our marriage was precipitous, our courtship lasted mere weeks, but he offered me love and happiness and I gratefully accepted.

Then, while we were visiting Kuala Lumpur, Malaysia, I became ill. We returned to London, where I received the news that I had advanced pancreatic cancer, and the prognosis was mere months to live. I was stricken with grief and bitterness. It seemed too cruel. I could not accept that God had snatched happiness from me in so brutal a manner, after giving me only a brief taste.

Through Charles's connections, we were put in touch with Dr. Helen Lieb, a psychoanalyst practicing in London, and a former colleague of the late Dr. Carl Jung. Dr. Lieb is a woman of great understanding, kindness, and wisdom. I went to her consulting room four times a week for four months. Gradually, with her help, I was able to accept my fate. When I became too weak to visit her, she came to me.

Of greatest anguish to me, Zoe, was the abrupt and bitter way you and I parted that last time. As my time has grown shorter, I have desperately needed to come to terms with what you told me, and with the terrible argument that resulted.

Dr. Lieb brought me some self-forgiveness by telling me that often mothers who have themselves been the victims of incest do not recognize the signs that it is happening to their daughters.

Yes, Zoe, I have had to face the truth that I, too, experienced the trauma of incest in my childhood. Dr.

Lieb thought it unnecessary to go into detail about my own experience, so I will take that dark story to my grave. But she and I both felt it important to tell you this much, hoping that perhaps someday you can find it in your heart to forgive me for fleeing from the truth and denying it to you so vehemently.

It was a terrible shock to hear it from you, at a time when I was newly grieving the death of your father, and it tore open a wounded place in me that I had kept closed away for many years. But Zoe, what you told me about your suffering should not have been met with denial and outrage. Please forgive me for that.

Dr. Lieb also told me that it is not uncommon for a woman who has experienced incest in her early life to marry a man who is himself a perpetrator. My having that information has helped me feel less alone and more of a person also in need of understanding and compassion.

I cannot tell you how you should address these issues in your own life. I can only pray that you will find a wise psychiatrist, and Dr. Lieb feels it should be a woman, who can guide you safely through the dark and fearful interior landscape that must be traveled for incest recovery to become possible.

And Zoe, I regret the unkind things I said about Suzanne. I am certain she told you the truth. That ugly family tragedy was the most devastating part of my life with your father.

As for your father, I realize there was much suffering

in his life, though he never spoke of it. Perhaps it was buried in his unconscious, as mine was, and whatever he did came out of his own woundedness.

But Zoe, there was much that was gentle, idealistic, intelligent, and good in your father. Though our marriage was troubled, and I failed him in some important ways, as he did me, together we brought a beautiful, gifted daughter into the world. I can see you with clear eyes now, and I am in admiration of you, of your intelligence and the way you have expressed your many gifts.

I admire your courage in facing hard truths about our troubled family dynamic, and it is a profound sorrow for me that I will not live long enough for us to know one another as we are now, in the light of this greater understanding.

It is also a profound sorrow that I could not see you or be in touch with you during this last part of my life as, with Dr. Lieb's help, I have experienced such healing of my spirit and have known such happiness, too briefly, with a loving and wise husband.

I hope someday you will meet Charles. I am sure you will appreciate one another.

Alas, after my diagnosis, I was so overwhelmed by circumstances and my impending death that I needed to give that my full attention. I am grateful that Charles understood and was supportive of me in that decision.

And so, Zoe, as my life comes to an end, I wonder what, of lasting meaning, I can leave as your inheritance.

I love you, my beloved daughter, and I hope you will discover, through this strange and unexpected unfolding of our lives, that love is stronger than death. And though I have loved you imperfectly in life, once my life is complete, perhaps at last my love for you can be perfect.

We can never know another person's whole story, or even our own. So much is a mystery. But of this I am certain: If we knew the whole story, we would have compassion.

With everlasting love,
Mother

In a flood of tears, Zoe carefully folded the letter and put it lovingly back into the beautiful little enamel box. Now, at last, Zoe understood the goodness and the tragedy, the darkness and radiance, of her mother's life.

And she grieved the many years she had seen her mother through the eyes of her father, when now, seen through the eyes of love and reconciliation, her mother was so beautiful.

Reverently, she whispered, *Thank you, dear mother, for giving me this blessing as I step into the light of my wondrous new life.*

Yes, you are correct. We can never know anyone's whole story, even our own, but in this moment, my heart is filled with compassion for you, as well as for Daddy and for myself, each of us having traveled a Road of Trials through this sorrowing and beautiful world.

EPILOGUE

Much had changed in the year since Zoe returned from Copenhagen after the Congress and her time with Gudrun in Amsterdam. And much had not changed.

Zoe's neighbor, Ted, had settled in San Francisco and sold the townhouse to David. This simplified living arrangements for David and Zoe.

David's law school buddy, Joel Stein, a brilliant divorce lawyer and a personal friend of both David and Christine who genuinely loved Kathy, had by an act of legal magic negotiated with Christine's lawyer to allow Kathy, who was now six, to attend the excellent Waldorf school on the north side of Chicago.

This achievement was almost inconceivable, considering that the school was not Christian but was based on the teachings of a German philosopher, Rudolf Steiner. The educational approach was intended to develop pupils' intellectual, artistic, and practical skills in an integrated and holistic manner.

David had attended a Waldorf school, too, and he felt it would support and encourage Kathy's rich imagination and creativity, giving her the freedom to move at her own pace intellectually and socially.

For Kathy to attend the Waldorf school meant she would not

be totally immersed in Christine's Evangelical world and mindset. The school had significant social status, and several of its talented graduates were achieving remarkable careers in the arts. This sweetened the situation for Christine, who, despite her Evangelical convictions, was not above appreciating social status and the worldly achievements of other people's children.

The Waldorf School came at considerable cost to David, not only because he paid Kathy's tuition and pledged additional financial support to the school, but also because Christine required that he deliver Kathy there each day.

This meant waking at 5:00 a.m., driving from his townhouse in Chicago against rush-hour traffic to pick up Kathy in Highland Park and then take her back to Chicago in rush-hour traffic by 8:00 a.m. At the end of each school day, he collected Kathy and returned her to Christine, something his schedule would never have allowed if he were still at the law firm.

The great benefit for David was seeing Kathy almost every day. He loved hearing her talk excitedly about what she was learning, friends she was discovering, and the lovely Swedish teacher she adored, who adored her as well.

Brilliant little Kathy settled happily into her new life and seemed to accept that she had a difficult mother. Kathy still loved and had compassion for her mother, who struggled constantly with bitterness and resentments, blaming David and Zoe for her unhappiness. But when Kathy was with her Chicago family, there was never critical talk of Christine. Kathy kept her counsel about what happened in the two households, able to hold them separate in her mind.

Without complaint, Kathy went to church four times a week,

doing her best to be a well-behaved Christian girl, because she knew it mattered so much to her mother. But she had her own clear values and beliefs, among them the choice to be a vegetarian, because, as she said, she wouldn't eat anything with eyes.

Zoe continued working with Walther, who accepted David as an established part of her life, and grew to like and respect him, though always referring to him as "your friend," without giving David a name. And Walther let Zoe know that David's leaving a prestigious law firm to form his own building-rehab company suggested a certain concerning instability.

Kathy knew Walther and called him "Uncle Chief," which delighted him. Like everyone else, he found her irresistible, and he stopped his work to pay attention to her when she visited Zoe at the office. Kathy was full of questions about the art objects he had collected on travels, his pretty majolica demitasse coffee set, and his gleaming, very expensive espresso maker. He sometimes made cups of espresso for Kathy and added lots of sweet foam that she happily lapped up, leaving the coffee in the cup.

Walther's attitude toward Zoe was improving. He seemed to value her more now that he realized she had a life outside the office. One day he said, "I'm glad you have David. Now I won't need to worry about who will take care of you if something were to happen to me."

Zoe found this greatly amusing, but she said, simply, "Thank you, Walther. I'm glad, too." But she could hardly wait to tell David, so they could have a hearty laugh.

Otherwise, Zoe's work for the IADP flowed along without drama. She edited the proceedings of the Amsterdam Congress, and then she had a respite before beginning work on the next

Congress. It would be held in London the following year, and Zoe looked forward to meeting Charles Templeton then.

The stream of clients also flowed along, and the women continued to say adoring things about the wonderful Doctor Lehrer as they chatted with Zoe before their sessions.

Zoe and Gudrun talked regularly, not only as colleagues but as close friends.

She was doing healing work with the therapist Gudrun referred her to, she received continuing support and encouragement from Anna and Suzanne, and she faithfully attended AA meetings.

Most of all, she savored her sweet, uncomplicated relationship with David, her beloved. Zoe and David shared the belief that their previous lives had been a long journey toward their inevitable meeting, and that their deep connection had no need for civil or religious certification. Though years later, they were married by a justice of the peace, they knew theirs had always been a true marriage.

Zoe never for an instant had wanted to bear children. For years, her refrain was, *what woman in her right mind would want a daughter who would grow up hating her?* Meaning, of course, a daughter like herself. But she was now a daughter gratefully reunited with her mother.

Zoe had easily developed a nurturing, deeply loving way of being with Kathy; they were, as Kathy had recognized early in their relationship, friends.

Unlike Zoe, Kathy had a father who asked nothing of her other than that her life unfold fully expressive of her abundant abilities. Kathy was free to flower as her true, exuberant sovereign self.

Zoe was grateful to share in that beautiful blossoming.

Acknowledgments

My publisher, Andrew Durkin's brilliant, scholarly book, *Decomposition: A Music Manifesto* (New York: Pantheon Books, 2014), is a long meditation on how the making of art, not only music but art in all its forms, is essentially a collaborative process. And that is surely true of *The Realm of Persephone*. It is a collaboration between Andrew and me, for though the story and images and language are all mine, the careful crafting of it as a finished work of literature and its beautiful design are his.

My collaborators are also Meinrad Craighead, who early on offered me encouragement and an appreciation of the sacred feminine, which is the theme of all her magnificent work, and whose "Mother and Daughter" is so perfect for the cover, and Meinrad's friend and guardian angel, Amy Dosser, who made it possible for that gorgeous image to bless this book.

And, Andrew says, the collaborators of an artwork include all those who influenced the artist's character and evolution and understanding of how the world works. And so my collaborators are also C.G. Jung, Joseph Campbell, Ira Progoff, and Robert Moore, for their insights, teachings and writings on depth psychology and myth; and how the imagery of the deep psyche shapes our inner and outer lives; and how we grow toward wholeness and are able to live the lives we are meant to live and, ultimately, claim our sovereignty—as is Marie-Louise von Franz, with her writings on the psychological meaning of myths and fairy tales; and as are Marion Woodman and all the other brilliant authors who have shared their insights on conscious femininity and the relevance of the Demeter-Persephone myth to "father's daughters," and how incest and other forms of trauma can be healed.

Other collaborators are my dear friend Jenny Koll, who sent me the beautiful book of poems, *Hermit Thrush* (Portland: Inkwater Press, 2016), by her sister Amy Minato, which inspired my own writing and ultimately led me to Andrew Durkin. And my beloved husband and dear companion on the path, Fred Hodges, who witnessed the evolution of the story from the very first words to completion of the first draft, as I read to him the pages I had gathered in early morning writings and we celebrated the day's harvest over lunch at Fiesta Mexicana in Chicago—and then the unfolding tale that years later we read aloud to one another in its entirety, sitting by the fire in our home-away-from-home, Walnut Cottage, at Heath Farm, near Chipping Norton in the lovely Cotswolds of England.

Yet other collaborators are my treasured, trusted friends Pat Cornett, Judy Creasy, Jean Feraca, Sue Moore, and Barbara Vazsonyi, who read early drafts and cheered me on, and also my brother of the spirit, David Hodges and Jessi Mahan, who reviewed certain chapters for their authenticity, and my sister-celebrants of the Wheel of the Year, Bonnie Reagan Walker, Mary Ann Johnson, and Christine Boos, who shared with me the rich realm of women's spirituality, and Dr. Margaret Shanahan, in whose consulting room

I encountered the Goddess. I have profound gratitude for all they have contributed to this collaboration.

And especially important among the collaborators are my loyal and ever-encouraging friends who have for so long eagerly anticipated the book's completion.

And I am grateful for you, dear reader, also truly a collaborator, to whom I have told this tale.

A Note on the Type

This book's body text is set in the award-winning serif font, Bely. Created by the French designer Roxane Gataud in 2014, Bely is an elegant, subtle variation of the popular Garamond font. It is notable for a remarkable balance of legibility and beauty.

The headings are set in Trattatello, created by the American designer James Griershaber in 2005. This gorgeous, classic lettering has a handwritten, calligraphic feel that suggests an underlying complexity.